COPPER ROAD

COPPER ROAD

MARION DEEDS

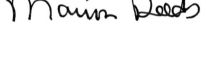

For Ed—

Marion Deeds

FALSTAFF
BOOKS
WWW.FALSTAFFBOOKS.COM

This book is dedicated to three women. Author Marta Randall has been a mentor, a teacher, a friend, and a beacon of inspiration for forty years. Every day, Sharon Fleming teaches me something about compassion, perseverance, humor, and the value of a good martini. Carol Pace, my neighbor across the street, is the best fan and supporter a newly published writer could have. I'm blessed to have the three of you in my life.

I

IN WHITE BLUFFS

1

Martes, 17 Uno, Year 331

The sisuree had gone cold in her cup, but Aideen Langtree gulped it down anyway. She finished the article of a waterspout sighting in the grand canal the previous night and folded the White Bluffs newssheet to give to Dolores. Her housekeeper liked to keep up on local news too.

She also subscribed to the _Crescent Noticias_, the daily newssheet printed in the capital, even though it arrived a day late. Another caravan had been robbed by mestengos on the south stretch of the Copper Road two days before, but the _Noticias_ made no mention of it.

Dolores tapped on the frame of the open sala manyana's door. "Yorita, there is a messenger."

"Come," Aideen said, stifling a clutch of fear in her throat. Had something happened to her brother? Dolores entered, a short man in a messenger's vest following. She felt an instant of relief; he wore the city plaid. He was not a fast messenger bringing bad news from the east.

His bow was brief, little more than a nod. "Yorita Langtree," he said, "there's been an accident with your father."

The relief fled, driven out by cold fear. "Where? Up at the cages?" She came around the table. "Dolores, my boots please."

The messenger shook his head. "He is not at the cages, yorita, but at the office."

"The office? Why?" On Martes, Father went to inspect the fire elemental cages. He didn't go to the office.

The messenger rubbed his clasped hands. "That is where he is, yorita."

"What has happened? Is he—" She choked on the word.

"He was alive when I left."

Dolores carried in her boots and stood so Aideen could rest one hand on the housekeeper's shoulder as she pulled them on. *Alive when I left.* "Dolores, the stablemaster," she said.

"I have a sprite cart, yorita," the messenger said.

Aideen tried to stay calm as she strode out the door and down the steps, the messenger following. She gripped the sides of the cart as he engaged the copper plate with a clunk. The plate connected with the quartz cylinder that held a dozen sprites. The glowing creatures whirled, streaming light, and the cart jolted forward.

They made good time, especially once they reached the floor of the valley and rolled along the wide boulevard next to the canal at a brisk pace.

Why had Father gone to the offices without telling her? Why had he gone at all? He was a man of routine, and it was his day to inspect the cages.

The cart juddered to a stop in front of the two-story building, the proud loomin letters proclaiming LANGTREE COMPANY, and in smaller painted letters, Langtree and Silvestro Enterprises. She fumbled in her purse for a coin, but the messenger shook his head. With a word of thanks, she jumped out, nearly falling as her foot caught in her skirt, and ran up the steps.

People crowded the lobby, huddled in knots of three and four, murmuring. The murmurs died when she entered. A man shifted his way through the crowd—Edmund, her father's secretary. "This way, yorita," he said, touching her arm.

4

"Edmund? Is he well? Is he...alive?"

"Alive, yorita, and awake after a fashion, but he cannot speak. He fell from his window."

"What? From his window?"

Edmund rolled his shoulders helplessly. "They found him on the street. We think he stood to open the window and lost his balance."

He directed her toward an empty meeting room where a thicker clot of people waited. Edmund pushed at the shoulders of the people blocking the door. "Let us through! Yorita Aideen is here!" The people gave way, and she stepped in to see her father lying on the floor, unmoving.

"Thank Dios you are here, Aideen." Peter Olafson, Father's doctor, glanced up from where he knelt near her father's head. She joined him. Someone had made a nest of jackets and even a few blankets to cushion her father's body. His left wrist was splinted and wrapped in a linen bandage. She reached across her father's body and took his right hand. "Father? Father, it's Aideen."

"Oh," he said. He stared past her, into the corner, his eyes glazed. "Oh, oh, oh." Half his face was slack as if melted.

"That's all he's said." Olafson sat back on his heels.

She stood up. "We must take him back to the house. Edmund? Send for a boat and have a cart ready at the landing."

"I've sent for them, yorita." Aideen felt a weight leave her shoulders at the sound of that familiar voice. Paloma Quinn, the company's accountant, stood in the doorway at the back of the knot of bodies.

"Paloma, thank the Mother you're here." She scanned the room. "Can someone tell me why my father was in the office today? Did he have an appointment? Is there a chance someone attacked him? A sneak thief or a mestengo?"

A fair-haired man in a fine, shiny green suit spoke up before anyone else could. "The papers on his desk in his office are tossed about as if he were in a rage, and the window is broken. No stranger has been seen in the office today to my knowledge."

"You are...?"

"Darwin Oakley, from the Copper Coalition."

5

She saw the pin on his jacket lapel now: A circle of loomin and one of copper, overlapping. "Did you have an appointment with him, Yor Oakley?"

"Yes."

She said, "Edmund? Did you see any strangers this morning?"

"None, yorita." Edmund glanced sideways at the Copper Coalition man. "Your father had no appointments. It was his day at the cages."

Yor Oakley shrugged. "We planned to meet, yorita," he said.

"The boat is here," someone called from outside. Aideen stepped aside as Olafson and the Copper Coalition man gathered up the edges of the blankets and lifted her father.

Paloma had moved through the crowd and now stood at her side. "Yorita, a moment of your time," she said. In her simple gray skirt and jacket, her hair sleeked back in two thick braids, the woman radiated efficiency like a charm.

"What is it, Paloma?"

"I know you wish to be with your father, but I wonder if you could stay for a bit and speak to the senior staff."

Aideen was ready to say she must go, but something in the accountant's gaze stopped her. "What is it you need of me?"

"Edmund is upset, and the staff is in…disarray. You are a Langtree. They would listen to you. It would calm them."

The invisible Langtree, she thought. This was not the moment for bitterness. The staff would be worried, but she needed to be with her father. "Shouldn't Jefe Silvestro speak? He's a partner."

Paloma blinked, and Aideen thought she recognized the woman's attempt to be diplomatic. "People here know you; they see you regularly. They would be…comforted, by some words from you."

"Very well. Tell them I'll meet them in the downstairs meeting room in half an hour. And…" She spoke on impulse. "Now I want to see my father's office."

When she returned from the chaos of her father's working space, Edmund followed her into the meeting room. He stood, his hands folded, the knuckles white, as she sat down in the chair Father used.

"Edmund, have we sent a note up to the cages? They will be expecting my father."

"No, I...no, yorita."

"Say he has had an accident, he is being treated immediately, and we hope for the best."

"Yes, I... Do you wish to see it, yorita, before I send it?"

She *did* wish to see it. She wished to write it herself, but Edmund was rubbing his thumbs together, faster and faster, and she knew he needed to feel she had confidence in him. "No. I know you will say just the right thing."

He sketched a bow and hurried out.

She drew a breath and sat up straight as the senior staff filed in.

H e had a brain tempest," Yor Olafson said. They stood just outside her father's room. Aideen had drawn open the curtains and left the window slightly open. Her father slept with open windows and always had his office window opened unless it was snowing. It was one reason she did not believe he had fallen. Another reason was the glass clicking like sand under her shoes when she had visited his office with Paloma.

They had gotten Father safely into bed, and Olafson had brewed a cup of saintswort. They propped him up and poured it into his mouth one drop at a time, so it wouldn't go down his windpipe.

"What should we expect?" Aideen said.

"Well, he could recover," Olafson said. "Some do."

Aideen knew many more did not, withering away instead.

"Prayer is always good," the doctor said, touching the cross at his throat. Like Dolores, he was a dioso. Aideen nodded. There was never a reason to say no to a prayer. "And, Aideen, I think you should prepare. Even if everything goes well, he may not regain full use of the right side of his body."

She nodded. "Are there other doctors you would consult with? Coin is not an obstacle."

"I have a colleague in the capital. I will send a letter to her. She has more experience with brain tempests and other injuries of the brain. For now, let him rest and keep him warm. We will talk about some exercises, so his muscles don't deteriorate. And broth is about the only food he can take." He reached for his coat.

"Yor Olafson, did you see my father's office?"

He paused, one hand extended. "I did not. Why?"

"Papers and chairs were tossed up against the walls," she said. "And there was glass on the floor."

He picked up his coat. "Yes?"

"Inside the office, not out on the street below."

"There was glass on the street, I was told."

She inclined her head. "Some, but it might have come from chips caught in his jacket."

"What are you thinking, Aideen?"

"There was a waterspout seen last night on the canal. Those can happen when an air elemental flies close over water."

"You think an air elemental attacked your father?"

She hesitated. She didn't want to be labeled foolish, not now. But the air elementals were strange. You could anticipate, to some extent, an earth elemental's behavior, provided you could track it, and fire elementals were easy to predict. It was what made them easy to capture. "I merely point out facts."

"I see. I think it's possible, certainly. But unlikely. As for a human attacker, his window faces the canal. A climber on the wall, even before dawn, would have been noticed, by sprite-takers and lamp-tenders if no one else."

"That's true," she said. Paloma had told her much more, but for now, she would keep those thoughts to herself. "I'll focus my attention on Father's health," she said, "and the company."

He picked up the coat, finally. "Good. And...Aideen, if you have a way to reach Trevian, a message to him would be good."

"Yes." She'd rehearsed a note on the way back to the house. *Father gravely ill. The company needs you. Father needs you.* Mentally, she'd struck that out. *I need you.* The truth was, she didn't know the words to bring her brother back home.

After she checked on Father, she changed into trousers, boots, and a jacket. Dolores sent for her trail caballo. Keeping up routine would help with morale, and today had been Father's day to inspect the cages with Moises Lopez. Father inspected early in the morning, not past noon, but it couldn't be helped.

Her caballo made his way up the familiar trail with no fuss. The city and the neighborhoods dropped away. She waved to a couple of farmers who were out working. The trail climbed more steeply closer to the mountains. They'd placed the cages close to the vents leading to the emberbeds. Transporting fire elementals was difficult and risky, and so was releasing them. The shorter the distance, the safer.

She glanced around, breathing in the spring air, enjoying, for a moment, the bright green day. Through the brush and the tall grass growing above the bowl of the valley, copper glinted. In some places, where they could, Father ordered the cords buried, to protect them from animals, storms, and snowfall.

As an exercise, she tried to envision the expansion, with copper cord running all the way down mountain to the Sheeplands, but she lacked Father's imagination. Instead, she thought about the conversation she had with Paloma Quinn before she had left the company building.

"My office is close to your father's," Paloma had said, as they stood in the center of the devastated room. "He had no appointments, but I heard him shouting. I couldn't make out the words, yorita, but from the pauses and the rhythm, I thought he was arguing with someone."

"The Copper Coalition man?"

"When I made my way downstairs, he was already there."

Aideen considered this. "Did you hear glass breaking?"

Paloma shook her head. "I only heard a scream from the street and then shouting."

"Very strange," Aideen said. "Forgive me, Paloma, but I must ask. You heard my father shouting, but you didn't think to check on him?"

"I did not." Paloma's gaze shifted, then came back to Aideen's face. "Shouting from your father's office is not anything new. He argues frequently with Jefe Silvestro. They roar at each other like osos over a carcass. And he threw the new Copper Coalition man out of his office a sennight ago. It's another reason I question his so-called appointment today."

"I see." Aideen smoothed her skirt. "Do you think my father went turvy and threw himself out his window?"

"I do not." There was no surprise or indignation in Paloma's voice. Clearly, she had expected the question and thought about the answer.

"If someone were in the office, how did they leave without being seen?"

Paloma shrugged. "None of us ran to the office. We went down to the street."

"So anyone could have walked out later and left during the confusion."

"Or stayed," Paloma said, which gave Aideen a whole new set of questions.

Her caballo tossed its head and snorted, and from the clearing ahead, a couple of tethered mounts whickered in answer. Beyond the hitching post and the water trough rose the mouth of the cave which held the cages. A thick bundle of copper cords ran out along one side. Aideen tipped back her head. The rock face above the entrance curved forward, looming over the opening. She dismounted and tethered her animal. Lopez hurried out. The skin between his eyebrows was wrinkled. "Yorita," he said. "Your father, is he—"

She squeezed his outstretched hand. "He is resting, and we're hopeful," she said, cursing herself for her thoughtlessness. After Edmund's note, Lopez probably assumed the worst when he saw her. "Since the inspection was set for today, I thought we should go forward."

He blinked. "Of course, yorita," he said.

She followed him into the tunnel. The air grew ten degrees

warmer. At a wave from Lopez, a worker went running, and by the time they reached the first pylon, strung with copper cables as thick as her arm, a group of team leaders clustered, waiting. "I hope you'll say a few words," Lopez said.

This was part of her purpose, to try to offer comfort. She said many of the same words she'd used at the office: Her father was being cared for, he was resting, and prayers were appreciated. The crew murmured words of thanks and one member of Mother congregation pressed a prayer bead into Aideen's hand. She thanked the woman and slipped it into her pocket.

Lopez led her farther down, into the tunnels where the cages waited. As she ducked under a strand of braided copper, she said, "Are you ready to bring in a sibling group?" A sibling group was Father's latest idea: To use a cluster of jovenes rather than the single creature, mimicking the way they lived on their own in an attempt to make the energy flow more stable.

"Not yet, yorita. The cage isn't ready."

"But Jefe Silvestro has a contract with a fabricker. We've made two payments already."

"I don't know the reason, yorita, but the cages aren't ready, and the replacement cages haven't been provided either."

She walked past a large square of clouded quartz and loomin. This was the oldest cage. It should be in a display of the history of the Langtree Company. At its center, a coil of purple and blue ebbed and swelled, like a banked blackrock fire. The copper cords that connected to the fine copper mesh on top of the cage now lay disconnected in a roll on the floor. Workers had pushed a corridor of quartz up against the wall of the cage. The long transparent trail ran down to a hole drilled into the emberbed. Lopez gestured for her to move back as two experts came to the wall of the cage and unfastened the fittings on each side.

"That's an old one." Aideen pointed her chin at the swelling coil of purple. "It looks weak."

"We're releasing it today. We kept it far longer than we usually do, because I thought we'd have the jovenes. But we brought in another adult this morning instead. It's a sennight late; I worry we've drained this flame."

"It will survive, won't it?"

Lopez shrugged. "I hope so."

The elemental shifted from a coil to a pyramid. The two workers slid the cage wall sideways, opening the space into the corridor. The flame flickered, and orange lights danced at its core. It flickered out of view, and it took Aideen a moment to track it as it shimmered into her vision far down the corridor. It vanished again. Fire elementals didn't move like animals. They moved like fire, and it was frightening how far they could move, and how fast.

"It's in," a worker called from the end of the corridor. Everyone in the cavern relaxed. Aideen felt her own tension flow away.

These delays were causing problems. A flame could starve to death if it was held too long. As Lopez led her through the cages, she noted a gap in the copper mesh on one cage, and a place where a scrap of the loomin framing had torn away. Lopez wrote down each problem, but on several he merely shook his head, and she knew he had already reported them.

The company wasn't failing, but it wasn't growing either, and she didn't understand these delays. There was no reason to defer basic repairs. When they went back to the surface and he poured her a cup of the brown, bitter tea the workers drank, she said, "And the cords running to the Sheeplands, how are they coming?"

He swallowed tea, looking at the ground. "You'll need to speak to Jefe Silvestro, yorita."

"Why? You're Father's second in command."

He was startled into smiling. "You're kind, yorita. I'm in charge of the cages and the generation of energy, but I'm not a partner."

She set down her cup. "The cord isn't getting strung," she said.

He shrugged. "There've been mestengo raids on the Company copper caravans."

Father had said nothing about these delays, which was no surprise. He expected her to keep the household budget and help with the company ledgers, yet he told her little. Aideen had learned the workings of the company herself, but he had left Trevian, his runaway son, as his heir. She was a useful object to her father like a chair or a pen, and nothing more.

"I'll talk to the partners," she said. "In the meantime, don't we know a quartz fabricker in Duermay?"

He sighed, and she read relief in the set of his shoulders. "The Alatriste Company. We've used them before with good success."

"I'll have Father's secretary write to them."

He escorted her out and thanked her again. She mounted, letting her caballo have his head as he trotted down the trail. She did stop for a moment to look down at White Bluffs, nestled in the valley as if cupped by two giant hands. At the edge of the horizon, the green sky glowed with a hint of lavender, and sunlight glinted off the waterfall, the Endless Steps, carved up the cliffside running up alongside it, and below them both the canal. Beyond the buildings to the west, a stand of blue-thorn trees smudged the feet of the cliffs.

Every plan Father had made was blocked by circumstance, and now he'd fallen out his window.

⸻

There is a letter by fast messenger for you, yorita." Dolores met her at the door holding out the square of paper. "I sent the messenger to the kitchen and told her to wait, in case there is a reply. She came from Lily Bend."

Aideen snatched the paper.

Aideen:

First things first; I am well and I am not turvy. A warning. If our Uncle Oshane comes to the house or the office, do NOT receive him. He has become very dangerous and he carries dangerous charms. DO NOT let him in—take great care, you and our father, to watch the skies carefully. He has tethered an air elemental. I fear our uncle has followed the path of Grandfather, dwelling in madness, but his turvy turn is deadly. I know he has taken lives. He imprisoned me. He was recently burned by flames that he also imprisoned.

I hope you will believe I am still sane. I travel to the capital with a woman named Eyrin Dosmanos. She is not our cousin, although she springs from the same family line. We have uncovered something that puts our world at risk— our world, Aideen, not just the Crescent. We must close a frontera.

Please heed my warning.

Trevian

Close a frontera? Frontera were naturally occurring—rare, it was true, but not bound by human whim. What was he thinking? It was her brother's writing, though. She wheeled and went into the kitchen where a young rider sat eating cold lamb.

Seeing Aideen, the rider pushed back her chair, just as the kitchen chica set a cup of ale in front of her.

Aideen said, "No, keep your seat, and finish your bite." The rider swallowed and washed the morsel down with a swallow of ale.

Aideen held out the letter. "Did my brother hand you this himself?"

"Yes, yorita."

"And you know him?"

"I've seen him in Lily Bend and delivered another message for him once."

"How did he seem?"

"Tired. He limped and favored one shoulder, and he said he had a knife cut from a fight. But he was in his wits. There were three people with him."

"Three?"

A nod. "A woman and man old enough to be my Ma and Da, and a woman perhaps your age, yorita. They had strange accents. I thought they might be from down mountain or even Pais Lewelyn, but they said they were out-of-worlders. The young woman too. And they weren't laughing when they said it. They'd just come back from Merrylake Landing, they said. He, your brother, said they were stopping in the field of Ancient where he prospects, and then headed to the capital. Is there a message in return, yorita?"

"Yes." Why was Trevian singling out their uncle? Uncle Oshane sent letters but only to Trevian—through Aideen, always the way station. And now he was putting the Crescent at risk? The entire *world*? "Yes. Do you need a mount?"

"I'll get one from the station, yorita. If you'll take mine there when she's rested, I'd count it a favor."

"We will take care of it," Dolores said. "Hilda, make up a packet of provisions for the messenger, for the road."

"My thanks, Jefa," the messenger said to the housekeeper. She knew the right methods of address, probably from delivering messages to many boss and jefe houses across the Crescent.

This messenger would ride all the way to the capital. The fast messengers traded mounts in a relay and rode at a fast pace, but the rider would still need food and water for the journey.

Aideen could distract herself no longer. She needed to write to her brother.

2

Veyernes, 19 Uno, Year 331

Two days later, she went to visit Father's first partner.

She dressed even more formally than she would have for the office, in a straight ankle-length skirt of dark red, her dress boots, and a white blouse whose bodice was stiff with white embroidery. A short jacket in matching red, with wide lapels, completed her attire.

All her life, Jefe Silvestro had been Don Leo to her, an honorific used by someone who was almost blood family. Two years ago, that had changed when Trevian had broken a marriage pledge and abandoned Don Leo's daughter in a dying little town upmountain to go off copper-hunting.

Privately, Aideen didn't mourn the change from "Don" to Jefe. Leo Silvestro's sudden roaring rages, often about nothing, had frightened her ever since she was little. It was the loss of her friend Ilsanja she grieved over. When Trevian abandoned Ilsanja and made her the juicy meat of a nine-day scandal, he had also destroyed the friendship Aideen cherished more than anything else in her life. No more afternoons drinking sisuree and sharing gossip about the boss families and those who aspired to be bosses; no more detailed talk of Ilsanja's hobby raising trail caballos, a hobby that Aideen had heard now made a profit. No more watching her friend choose fabrics and colors that hurt the eyes and transform them into high fashion. Three sennights ago, Aideen had attended Ilsanja's nameday celebration with Father. Ilsanja's hand had been cool, and the smile she gave Aideen was one Aideen had seen many times, bestowed on others. Politeness. There was no friendship there any longer.

The previous day had flown like a fever-dream. Dolores had created a schedule for the chicas to help care for Father. Aideen had talked again to Yor Olafson and reviewed the household accounts. And she'd spent a long time with Paloma.

She tapped on the Silvestros' door, monitoring her breathing to keep it deep and even. She wondered if he would keep her waiting, but the housekeeper opened the door and ushered her in. "Good noon, Yorita Langtree."

"Thank you, Helen."

"The Jefe will see you in a few minutes. You may wait outside his study. Do you wish sisuree? Water?"

"No thank you."

The housekeeper showed her into the dark familiar anteroom. Ilsanja's mother had been a westerner from Shevastin, and most of the house's furnishings had been her bride-gift. The gleaming wooden chairs, tables, desks, and wall decorations were a source of pride still. Aideen sat down in one of the chairs, its arms carved with snarling oso heads. Across the room hung a carving of a sinuous fish creature, done in a beautiful reddish wood Aideen hadn't seen anywhere else.

Ilsanja's mother Shandren had been a charmcaster. Gold, not copper, spoke to her, and her charms were powerful. She had done work for the Crescent Council itself. The charm Don Leo brought to the partnership, used to strengthen the quartz cages enough to hold the flames, had come from Shandren, Ilsanja told her once. Ilsanja's odd name, with its throat-clearing J-sound, came from her mother's people in the west.

As with many charmcasters, the charms had eventually sickened Shandren with a wasting disease.

Aideen folded her hands. One foot was kicking. She stilled it. Breathe. Deep and even.

The intricately carved door opened, and Silvestro's secretary peered out. "Enter, yorita," he said. She stepped into Silvestro's study. Behind her, the secretary sat down at a small desk in the corner.

Ilsanja's father sat with his back to a broad window overlooking the stables and a corral. Beyond the outer curve of the fence, she could see over the rooftops of the town all the way to the white bluff with its cages and cords of copper.

"Be seated, Aideen," he said. His black beard, neatly trimmed, had more gray in it than she remembered. She sat down.

"How is Oswald?" he said.

"No change, but he is resting."

He gave a sharp nod. "My prayers," he said. The family were diosos, although Shandren had not followed their beliefs.

"Thank you," she said. "I visited the cages on Martes."

He tilted his head. "Why? With your father so ill, you weren't at home to care for him?"

"He was in good hands. I spoke to Yor Lopez, and I have some questions about the company. I thought you could help me."

"Let me put your fears at rest," he said. "The company is healthy, and Montez and I will manage until your father is well again."

"I didn't say I had fears. I have questions. We've lost two copper shipments due to mestengo raids, and the new cages are delayed. Those cages are the foundation of the expansion into Sheeplands. I spoke with Paloma Quinn. The project is months behind. It seems the company even returned some money to the Sheeplands Project Alliance because of the delays."

"We can't control the Copper Road," Silvestro said. "If the Crescent Council will not provide the protection our taxes pay for, there is little we can do."

"But what has delayed the cages? Why haven't we reached out to another fabricker?"

He clapped his hand down on the surface of the desk, not quite a slap, but close. "The cages are my responsibility, Aideen. You should be tending to your father."

"The company is our livelihood."

"I remind you that you are not your father's heir."

"True. My brother is, but he gave me his proxy."

"I know you help with the ledgers at times, and assist Quinn with the payroll, but it doesn't mean you know or understand this company. Your father and I started with almost nothing, and we've built up a company that provides light to an entire city. I tell you, don't let your worry for your father spill over into things about which you know nothing."

"I know some things. I know we've made payments to the fabrickers. They have not returned any of that coin."

"I am working with the fabrickers. They have been loyal contractors for ten years."

"I just seek to know the delay."

"Business has delays." He reached for a leather folder on his desk, pulled it toward him, and opened it.

Aideen waited, thinking he was going to read her something from it, but after several seconds, she realized he was dismissing her. She stood up. "Jefe Silvestro, I will remind *you*, I have my brother's proxy, and I must do whatever I can to protect the company while my father is—"

He slapped the desk hard, and his face flushed carrot-red. "Proxy! A note scribbled by your wastrel brother the night he abandoned my daughter and fled his responsibilities! Do you think that would stand before the City Council, Aideen? I'll have it set aside before you can draw a breath! Now tend your father and leave the company to those who know how to run it!"

She flushed, hot and cold at once. Her heart beat hard. "Since you cannot answer a single simple question, Jefe, I am not sure that is you," she said. Her hands might be shaking, but she was proud her voice did not. "Good day."

She pivoted on one heel. The secretary bolted to his feet. His face

19

was expressionless as he held the door for her. Plainly, it was not the first rude dismissal he had seen from this room. Aideen blinked rapidly, forcing away tears.

Helen waited for her by the door. "Yorita? Yorita Ilsanja asks you to meet her in the sala manyana."

She nearly said no. She felt stripped of a layer of skin, and she wanted to go away and think. She'd scrutinized the company books yesterday. There was more than just stolen copper and delays in deliveries. Three months ago, each of the partners had reduced their draws by ten percent. There had been no order to economize in her home. Father's income had not changed. There was some mystery at the heart of things, and her father's plunge from his window was wrapped up in its center like a sprite in a spiderweb. She did not need to face her sharp, bitter former friend right now.

Ilsanja might have answers though, or at least, information.

She sighed. "Of course," she said.

The sala manyana faced north. Gone were the dark tapestries and imposing furniture, except for a wooden table with a looping design inlaid in shell, and a set of chairs. The walls rippled with wall hangings shading from pale green to sand-colored, with a line of faintest pink, and the rugs were gold and green. There was a curious smell, earthy and sweet, in the air.

Ilsanja sat at the table. She wore loose trousers cuffed at the ankle, in soft black fabric, and a long tunic in shades of cobalt, turquoise, yellow, and black, figured with geometric designs. On anyone else, it would have been outlandish. On Ilsanja, it made Aideen, in formal attire, feel like a child's doll.

Various objects covered the table: a set of palm-sized drinking cups glazed river-water green, a cooking pot, steaming gently, a pitcher, a pair of ladles, and a shallow bowl piled with cubes of honeycomb.

"Come sit," Ilsanja said. Her glossy black hair, braided, formed a crown on her head.

Aideen sat across from her.

Some people said Ilsanja was too strange to be beautiful: her features too sharp, her eyes too oddly set. Some mocked her name, calling it bizarre. It did not take a brilliant person to recognize the envy behind those statements. Ilsanja's eyes, the endless black of her mother's, missed nothing. Her smile was a weapon, and her wit was like a knife, a knife she would wield against herself as well as others, as long as it led to a good laugh.

"How are you, Ilsanja?"

"Well. And Don Oswald?"

"There's no change, but he can swallow, so we can feed him, and he is resting." Aideen's hands hurt. She made herself unclench them.

"I will light a candle for him," Ilsanja said. "And your meeting with my father? How did it go?"

Aideen tipped her head. "Could you not hear it?"

Ilsanja smiled. "Only the end."

"It did not go well."

The other woman shrugged. "Well, I have no head for business as you know."

"Yes, I'm aware. How goes your hobby? The trail caballos? Bringing in coin, I hear."

Ilsanja smiled. "My stablemaster gets most of the credit, I think."

"I think not."

"Oh, enough, you flatterer. I haven't spoken to you in a long time, I wanted to visit." Ilsanja reached for the pitcher. It steamed slightly. "And I'd like you to try something."

It didn't smell like sisuree. Ilsanja had, for a time, experimented with different flavors of mead. Who knew what this concoction was? "Very well," Aideen said.

Ilsanja reached for one of the tiny cups. "It's a new beverage, a powder from the eastern continent. Kokolatal, they call it." She poured a dark brown syrup into the cup, a little less than halfway, and added a ladle of water from the steaming pot. It smelled acrid, a bit like the rare scent of woodsmoke. She stirred it vigorously and handed the cup to Aideen.

The bitter smell grew stronger, but it held within it a tempting scent, a bit like the air after a lightning strike or the wake of a flock of sprites. A second sniff brought nuttiness, moist earth, and sweetness. She lifted it to her lips and took a mouthful.

The bitterness spread through her mouth like blackrock ash, and her eyes stung. She choked, covering her mouth before she spewed liquid over her blouse. Her face had screwed up into a scowl, she knew, and she had no control over it. Gasping, choking, she set down the cup. While she struggled not to choke again, Ilsanja ladled warm water into another cup and handed it to her.

"Bitter?"

"You." Aideen flinched. She sipped the warm water, and sipped again. The bitterness faded, replaced now, cruelly, with the ghost of a haunting sweetness. "You did that on purpose."

Ilsanja moved her head, halfway between a nod and a shrug. "Perhaps."

"That's vile."

"Is it?"

Aideen paused. The aftertaste of sweetness almost made it worse. "Why did you do that? Is this some revenge?"

"A sip of bitterness," Ilsanja said, "for the friend of my heart who turned her face from me? Would I do that?"

"You certainly would. And I never turned my face from…"

"Aideen."

Finally, the taste was gone. Aideen set the second cup beside the first. "I knew you wouldn't want to see me after what my brother did. I tried to protect myself from your coldness, nothing more. You would have been right to turn from me."

"That should have been *my* choice, not yours to make for me."

Aideen wanted to argue, but the words died in her throat. "I see. I *do* see."

"Your brother broke his pledge and left me in Merrylake Landing as if he were a fast messenger and I was a caballo who'd pulled up lame. But, before he did, he saved me from Vallis Majeur, and most likely saved my life. He—"

"Your life? You believe that? I always thought Vallis planned for ransom."

"Possibly he did. The look in his partner's eyes, the one he killed, was very different. I knew I was in for something ugly, something I probably would not survive. Trevian rescued me." Ilsanja reached for her own cup and sipped. "Aideen, one of my few virtues is that I know the worth of things. I know my own worth. I would have survived a nine-day scandal, when most of the shame fell on Trevian anyway. I *have* survived it." She set down the cup again, and for the first time, shifted her gaze away from Aideen. "What I could not bear was my one friend crossing the street to avoid me."

"You have many friends. And, Ilsanja, I was ashamed."

Ilsanja did shrug then. "I have many who laugh at my wit and come to my nameday celebration, because my father is the second richest man in White Bluffs. I have, I *had*, one friend as I count friends."

Aideen felt closer to tears now than she had with Ilsanja's father bellowing at her. "I didn't know. You seemed, well, serene. And Father told me to keep my distance."

"When have you ever listened to your father when it was important?"

"Well," Aideen said, "I can't argue. Did you bring me here just to feed me poison? Should I try to make it home before the bitterness seizes my heart and I die?"

Ilsanja didn't smile, but it was a near thing and clearly took an effort to suppress. "Oh, you won't die. In fact, I'm drinking it now. The secret is honey. Will you try some?"

"Give you a second chance? Of course not."

Ilsanja laughed. "Coward! Here." She picked up the water cup, poured in more of the dreadful brown sludge, then, with tongs, added a cube of honeycomb. "Shall I try it first to reassure you?"

"No, because you have planned this revenge for a while, and I suspect you drank the vile stuff to develop a tolerance." Aideen reached for the cup.

"You give me too much credit."

Aideen sniffed cautiously. Smoky, still. She drew a tiny bit of the liquid into her mouth. With the sweetness of the honey, the flavors changed: smoky, yes, rich, nutty but something more, something warm, comforting. Another sip, and the flavors seemed to change, to swirl and meld. "It's…good."

"They drink it on the eastern continent, always with honey or with something they call cane syrup."

Aideen put down the cup. "Am I forgiven?"

"Perhaps. I have some questions for you. Your answers will help me decide if I can forgive you."

Aideen felt her heart begin to race. "Ask me anything."

"Why did you come to visit my father?"

"I have questions about the company. My father's fall seems strange, and there have been delays at the cages, with projects but also simply with maintenance. I came to ask him why, and instead he dismissed me."

Ilsanja nodded. She rubbed the back of her neck with one hand. After a moment she said, "Let's go see the caballos. I have a bloodline I'm very proud of." She rose and tugged on the bell cord. "Sera, bring water and oat cakes out to the stables," she said to the yellow-haired chica who entered.

Aideen followed her out. A cluster of caballos waited by the fence, whickering. Ilsanja stroked them, pointing out the strength of the haunches and the broad backs. The chica carried out a tray, and the two women sat on a rough bench with a small stone table nearby.

Ilsanja said, "Father has a favored fabricker, who has shaped cages for him for ten years or more. He gave them the contract for the larger cages and the replacements. Six months ago someone broke into their workshop and shattered the cages. Since then, they have had trouble procuring pure-enough quartz."

"A mestengo?"

"But why? No coin was stolen. There had been no threats made against the fabrickers. They had no rival for the contract."

"They do now," Aideen said, "as far as I'm concerned, because we've waited so long."

"I don't know a single fabricker who would wait six months on the chance of getting a rival's contract."

"Neither do I." Aideen went to the fence. She broke her oak cake into pieces, sharing it with a mare and her gangly colt w. approached the fence at once, hoping for a treat. "Your father could have told me this."

"Father's temper is his greatest weakness. His pride is his second greatest. You are aware the partnership has been strained."

Aideen nodded.

"My father seethed like a boiling pot over these discussions with your father. To have them with *you*..." She shrugged.

"The company is not thriving. There's the quartz. And copper caravans were raided. Does it seem as if the company has an adversary? One hidden in the shadows?"

"Any business can have a run of bad luck. It's too bad ours struck just as your father planned expansions."

"I suppose." The mare whuffed and lipped Aideen's open palm. She stroked the mount's face with her free hand.

"I have another question for you," Ilsanja said. "Have you had contact from Mark Majeur?"

"He'd hardly contact me."

"Or me, I would have thought." Ilsanja drew a crumpled paper from the pocket of her trousers. Aideen unfolded it.

"He seeks clemency? He wants Vallis's exile brand removed? Why? And why would he reach out to you? You of all people!"

"His boldness approaches madness."

"Did he send a letter to your father?"

"If he had, I think you would have heard my father's reaction from your house."

"How does he dare?" Aideen said. She folded the letter and handed it back. It crackled as Ilsanja shoved it back into her pocket.

"Well, he always dared much, and Vallis *is* his favorite."

Aideen shook her head. Vallis had received clemency already—exile instead of imprisonment. That his father would push to have the sentence commuted, the exile brand un-charmed, his son returned home to the Crescent, was beyond reasonable belief.

Ilsanja said, "Does Trevian know about your father?"

"I sent him a letter, begging him to come home, but I think he

down on the bench and poured herself water. "He
ιe capital to save the Crescent from some risk."

escent?" Ilsanja's lips quirked up at one corner.

dn't want to damage the fragile, newly repaired friend-
ιe needed someone to talk to. "He travels with a woman.

'1ι.   ᴊenger said she was an out-of-worlder."

Now Ilsanja stared. "Truly? Like from a wonder-tale?"

"Exactly."

"Did she come through a frontera, wreathed in light?"

"They all did, apparently. There were three of them, two of them older. They had some adventure, since Trevian had a wound from a fight. Frontera are part of the story, and he's traveling with the woman."

Ilsanja crossed her ankles. "That surprises you?"

"Well," Aideen hesitated. "When he turned away from you, I wondered if women just don't warm his blood."

Ilsanja laughed and shook her head. "I was never a woman to him, Aideen."

"Well, what were you then?"

"The collar of a harness he had no desire to wear."

Aideen blinked. Plainly, Ilsanja had given Trevian's betrayal a great deal of thought in the last two years.

As if her thoughts had followed a close track, Ilsanja said, "I have no quarrel with *what* your brother did. I've spoken to copper-hunters since then, and they tell me the impulse to seek out metals or charms is nearly impossible to contain. The insult lay in how he did it. He should have approached my father and paid the pledge-price, and let us announce the dissolution together."

"He feared Father," Aideen said. "He knew he'd never agree."

"If he had only spoken to me... I would have stood beside him. With both of us seeking dissolution, we would have prevailed."

"I love my brother, but he is not the brightest of men," Aideen said. "Speaking of my brother, he warned me urgently about my uncle."

"Uncle? One of your mother's people? I thought they—"

"No. Father's brother Oshane."

"Do I know that name?"

Aideen shrugged. "I haven't seen him since I was six, but Trevian says he has become a villain and taken lives. He says Oshane has a tethered air elemental at his command."

Ilsanja stared intently at her. "Do you think Trevian is ill? Has some poison cooked his wits?"

"I can't tell. He's going to the capital. I assume he means the Copper Coalition."

"Wouldn't he go to the Council if he fears the entire Crescent is at risk?"

"He's a copper-hunter. He'll go to those who know about charms."

"Stranger and stranger," Ilsanja said. "I hope this 'out-of-worlder' woman doesn't relieve him of his coin *and* his trust."

"I hope not." Aideen stood and smoothed her skirt. "Thank you. I'm glad—I'm glad we spoke. And—" She forced the words out in a rush before cowardice could stop her. "I am sorry I hurt you, Ilsanja. I never meant to. You are *my* only friend, and I never meant..."

"It's forgotten." Ilsanja rose. "Well, not *forgotten*, because I don't forget things, but it's set aside. Would you care for another cup of kokolatal?"

Once home, she checked on Father, to find him sleeping, and then sat in the sala, combing through the household accounts again. Six months ago, three months ago, today—there was no change, no reduction in their expenses. Which, since she kept the household ledgers, she had already known. The monthly statements from the Banco de Duloc revealed no secrets. Money went steadily into the accounts, and none was withdrawn beyond the regular expenses.

Paloma had confirmed the company accounts held the balances they should; Father was not lying and secretly taking a full draw; he wasn't embezzling.

The other partners were putting back one uno coin for every dessa they drew, and so was Father, but with no effect on their lives. Father had a steady trickle of income from the blackrock claim he owned and still worked, and the share of the sheep ranch that had been her mother's bride-gift to him. But the income from those sources hadn't changed either. Coin flowed into this house from some shadowy source.

She closed the ledgers, shook her head, and pushed back in the chair. Her father's keys lay on the table, and she picked up the ring, ready to take the ledgers back to his study and leave this riddle until after dinner. Instead, she shook the ring so the keys splayed out on her palm and stared down at them. The smallest key on the ring opened her father's strongbox.

Her father's strongbox. It sat in his study. She'd seen it once a sennight since her twelfth nameday, when Dolores had become the housekeeper and Father gave Aideen responsibility for the household accounts. Every Lunis she sat across from Father's desk and reviewed the accounts, while the square box, bound with charmed loomin and copper, sat on its black wooden stand, visible in the corner of her vision. Never once had he opened it in her presence.

She had never, never, dreamed of opening it. Even now, with the key in her hand, she still had doubts.

Was it the work of the charm? She didn't think so. This was no charm; this was the force of Father's will, making it clear she was not to know what was inside, convincing her so thoroughly that the box's existence flickered out of her memory, and while she searched for coin, she hadn't even thought to search there.

"Well, this changes," she said to herself, standing up, keys poking into her fingers as she clutched them. She headed for the stairs.

A clatter rang down the hall. "Help! Please!" Nila, the young chica tending to Father, cried. Aideen ran for the back of the house.

"Dimitri!" she yelled, calling for her father's valet. She reached the door. Nila clung to Father's arm, sobbing as she tried to pull him up. Father lay, his torso out of the bed, his legs aslant. He was growling. As Aideen stepped across the threshold, he arched like a hunting bow, his thrashing arm striking Nila in the face. Then he collapsed, limp, and slid farther off the bed.

Aideen leaped forward and caught his shoulders. "Dimitri!"

"Oh!" Father grunted. "Oh! Oh! Oh!"

"I couldn't hold him, yorita! He—he—"

"Hold his other shoulder." Aideen lifted, and Nila did the same.

Dimitri strode into the room. "What's happened? What did you *do,* you foolish girl?" He grabbed Father's legs and helped right him on the bed. Aideen made sure her father was safely placed. The mattress had shifted, and with Nila's help, she pushed it back into place. Father muttered over and over, the same syllable.

A wad of cloth squeezed out from under the mattress and plopped onto the floor. Aideen touched Father's neck, counting his pulse. "Nila, are you hurt? He struck you."

"I'm fine, yorita. I...I... He raised his good hand and he, he pointed to the window." The chica motioned to the window which was now closed. "I said, 'Do you want it closed, Jefe?' and he blinked."

"Jefe *always* has an open window," Dimitri said.

Aideen gritted her teeth. "Dimitri, send for Yor Olafson. Now, please."

For a moment, she thought he would challenge her, but it seemed he read something in her face, for he nodded and said, "Right away, yorita."

When he had left, Aideen said, "Then what happened, Nila?"

"I closed it, the window, and he lowered his arm. I was going to bathe him, so I checked the basin of water." She gestured to the spreading puddle of water Aideen hadn't noticed before. "Then he growled, and he, he bowed upward, like you saw. I reached for him, but he rolled and—" The girl lowered her head and wiped away tears.

Aideen put her hand on the girl's shoulder. "None of this was your fault. It is my father's sickness progressing. You couldn't have managed him yourself. And where was Dimitri during all this?"

Nila said, "He left to piss, nothing more. He is here most times, and he slept there last night." She pointed to the chair.

"Well, I think I will add an attendant. Father should not be alone. He might injure himself worse." She made herself smile. "I'm glad you

29

were here and so quick to catch him, Nila, before he fell onto the floor."

Nila nodded, still staring down. Aideen stepped back, and her foot came down on something soft. It was the wad of bedding, or something. She stooped to pick it up.

"I—yorita?"

"Yes?"

"Dimitri is right. The jefe—"

"Always has a window open," Aideen said. The wad was not cloth, but paper, several pages folded up into a square, wrinkled where the weight of the mattress had held them.

"But he did seem calmer."

She put her attention back on the nervous chica. "He fell out of a window. It's not strange he would want them closed now, even on the ground floor. You did right. Can you stay with him until I find another attendant? And the doctor should be here soon."

Nila jerked her head in a nod.

Yor Olafson arrived, Dimitri with him. Aideen waited in the hall while the doctor completed his examination. Olafson looked grave when he joined her.

"He had no further injuries, but your instinct to have a person with him at all times is a good one. That bowing upward of his body was a convulsion."

"What caused it?"

"Brain tempests often have this effect. It is like a flood. Imagine a rainstorm causing a river to flood. Before it overflows its banks, its tributaries swell and overflow theirs. That is happening in the brain."

"What can I do?"

"What you've done. My colleague will be here tomorrow. She may have more news for us."

Aideen held out her hand. "Thank you, yor. Will you return this evening and dine with me?"

"An honor," he said, nodding.

Dimitri leaned against the wall, his shoulders slumped. Once Aideen had escorted out the doctor, she came back to where he waited. He spoke quickly, in a way she would have taken as rude if she hadn't known of the valet's devotion to her father.

"Yorita, I only left for a moment. I never—"

"I know, Dimitri."

"I failed him."

"This is new territory for all of us." She'd been angry at how he'd treated Nila, but she saw now it had been his own guilt speaking. "I have an assignment for you," she said.

He bowed his head. "I understand if you no longer wish me to—"

She spoke over him. "I plan to hire attendants for Father, so he isn't alone, and so you and the others get the rest you need. I have the company and the household to attend to. I want you to interview and hire them."

His eyes widened. "Are you sure, yorita?"

"No one has been closer to Father than you. I know you will find people who are capable, and who give him comfort at the same time."

"I will, yorita."

"Dolores will send out the word. I want the position filled quickly, but I want quality first. We will make do with household staff if we need to."

"I'll speak to Dolores right now," he said and hurried past her.

She sat next to her father, to watch him until the next chica came on shift.

Yor Olafson preferred pork to lamb and Pais Lewelyn wine to mead, and the cook Susannah delivered a savory, satisfying meal. The doctor spoke of various things, Father's illness among them. He was blunt but hopeful about his healer friend from the capital. When Aideen was preparing for bed, hours later, the wad of paper made a murmuring as she unbuttoned her skirt, reminding her. Sitting at her writing desk, she reached out and pressed the glass bulb against the plate of copper on the wall. The horsehair filament inside flickered for a second, then bloomed into a steady warm glow.

31

Father's vision, Father's legacy. No need to chase sprites and transport them miles. Instead, copper lines carried the energy of the fire elementals to the copper plate, which heated the fibers inside until they glowed like blackrock. The horsehair was soaked in some solution of salts. Loomin transferred the charmed energy too, but the metal heated quickly and caused fires. Copper was the best.

People hadn't wanted the new light at first. Her father and Don Leo had told the story over and over again, usually at Midwinter or the Long Year festival, always after some shots of lick or the fourth or fifth cup of warm mead. People thought it wasn't safe. The Banco de Duloc refused to lend Father money, and the Copper Coalition told him he was a fool. Father did not try to convince or persuade. He ran wires to his house, and Don Leo's house, and later, at great cost, to the company offices. For six months, the company building glowed in the twilight like a comet. And then other boss families approached him, blackrock mine-owners, and eventually, the president of the Banco de Duloc said they would allow him to light some of their offices as an experiment. Father refused. There was no need to experiment, he said.

The workers, the chicas, the potters, the bakers, weavers, blackrock miners, canal boaters, and farmers, all began to grumble. Why did *they* have to be dependent on sprite-takers? And soon, the White Bluffs Council came to Father. Now the entire town, nearly, got its light this way. The Banco had been lit the last and paid the most for it, or at least, so said the rumors.

It was a bad idea to make an enemy of a banco, but Father was too powerful to fear enemies. Or so it had seemed.

She unfolded the papers and smoothed them out. They looked like standard ledger pages, with a running balance on the right side of the page. Each page had a different name at the top. There were seven pages.

Principle, Int Rate, Payments, Balance.

She caught her breath and closed her eyes when she saw the interest rate amounts. Opening them, she read the names and caught her breath again. She knew many of these families.

Some of the payments had been going on for years, and it was clear this was only the most recent page. Her father had lent money to some of the most powerful boss families. And there were names of people who lived beyond White Bluffs.

And the interest he was charging—Susannah's spiced pork and vegetables rose up in her throat and she swallowed hard.

He charged different people different interest rates, but they were all too high. Several were more than twenty percent; some approached thirty. Clearly, these were loans the families couldn't have gotten through a banco for some reason; her father was taking advantage of an indiscretion, helping pay off gaming debts, or funding a risky investment. The amounts, in several cases, were not huge, but the interest rates meant some would never be paid off.

Who would wish to see Father fall from a window? Here were seven.

She shuffled the pages. Halliday: a boss family, with a claim on a large vein of blackrock. Mary and Teresa Halliday had hung onto her at every nameday celebration, every concert, every social event until Trevian had abandoned Ilsanja and fled. Then they had snubbed her, as publicly and frequently as possible. She'd put it down to shallowness and hypocrisy, but now she wondered if hatred could be the cause. According to the running balance, Halliday was still paying.

Laying down Halliday's ledger sheet, she glanced at the next one.

Vallis Majeur's name rode at the top of the page.

She felt dizzy.

When Vallis Majeur had been exiled, he'd owed Father four cento and fifty. No payments had been made since then.

Vallis Majeur, her brother's friend, Ilsanja's abductor. He was like a plate richly glazed and burnished to a blinding luster, whose cracks showed only when you got close. He had a winning smile and a laugh that made everyone around him want to laugh too. His hair gleamed gold where it peeped from beneath his fine brown hat. On his prancing bay gelding, he drew all eyes when he rode each morning on the southern green. It was Ilsanja who commented that the girth on his saddle had been mended at least twice, as had his boots. And

Dolores had muttered something once when he'd come to the house to gather up Trevian. "He needn't strut so," she'd said, "with his three-year-old hat."

Ilsanja decided Vallis's father was holding back coin, trying to rein in his spirited son. Then the whispers about the gaming debts, and darker things, had started. Trevian and Ilsanja united in defense of their friend.

Aideen had admired Vallis the way she might a good piece of engineering. She knew he saved special glances for her, comments murmured in quiet moments for her ears alone, and gave her the brightest smiles. None of that was for *her*, but for the daughter of the richest man in White Bluffs. And he never thrilled her nerves as lovers did in the novels and stage plays. She was somewhat deficient in that area, she supposed.

Vallis owed coin not to shadowy moneylenders or games-masters, but to *Father*. Had this debt driven him to do what he had done?

She pulled her robe more closely around herself, gathered up the papers, and left her room. Once upstairs, she engaged the lamps on the staircase and the ones in Father's study. With more light, she pulled out a pencil and began figuring. Slowly, she separated the papers into two stacks. One contained four names. By any reasonable, human standard, those people had repaid the principle. Three, including Vallis, still owed on it.

She felt weak and shaky in spite of having the papers in order. Father had been committing usury. It was not a legal crime, just a social one. But it was cold and cruel. And Aideen didn't doubt it had led directly to Ilsanja's abduction at Vallis's hands.

Father let his two partners cut back their draws, setting aside their small luxuries, making economies, and let them think he was sharing in their austerity, while he changed nothing.

His keys were in the pocket of her robe. She knelt in front of the strongbox and unlocked it. The lid lifted smoothly, silently.

She set aside some folders to look at later. At the bottom were stacks of coin, including four disks of copper. She lifted one curiously. It was called a reale, and she had never touched one before. As wide across as a peach, three inches thick, it was impractical to carry. Bancos offered reali notes instead. In fact, there was a one-reale note at the bottom of the box; made from spider-silk paper; the charm embedded in it must be read by a charmed copper loupe. Only the Coalition, bancos and some privileged moneychangers could issue reali notes.

The most skilled workers at the cages, the ones who risked injury because they moved the flames, the highest-paid workers in town, made one reale a year. Her father had four. No, five, if she included the note. And he had two stacks of centos. A cento was half a year's rent for most people. No wonder a ten percent cut in his income from the company had meant nothing.

"Father," she whispered. She sat down on the floor, staring at the box. Nothing was as she had thought it was.

After a few minutes, she straightened up and scrubbed her face with her knuckles. There was no point in brooding. She put the ledger sheets in the box and locked it again, disengaged the lamps, and went downstairs to her room. Then, of course, she lay awake, staring at the ceiling, as sleep taunted her but stayed out of her reach. Her mind circled and paced, wondering what to do with Father, what the loans meant, and how he had fallen out of the window when all the broken glass was inside.

Resolutely, she shut her eyes. She imagined Ilsanja in her cobalt and turquoise tunic; her black eyes, her slanted smile. Soothed, she drifted into sleep.

3

Sabado, 20 Uno, Year 331

After breakfast, she went back to the study. Below the final balance figure on each of the loans where the principle showed, she put a zero. "Fully paid, Aideen Langtree for Oswald Langtree," she wrote, and the date. Except for Vallis's, she folded each sheet, sealed and addressed them, and carried them down to Dolores to be delivered that morning.

When Father recovered, he would be angry. She'd deal with his anger. He'd face a struggle to reinstate any payments, with her notation in the hands of the borrowers.

She had just handed Dolores the letters when the downstairs chica came in. "Yora Quinn is here to see you, yorita," she said.

"Yora Quinn? Show her into the sala. I'll follow shortly."

Paloma stood facing the door and spoke before Aideen could even wish her a good morning. "Yori—Aideen, I've come to tell you your uncle Oshane Langtree has arrived and will meet with the partners in one hour."

"What? When did he arrive? He didn't come to pay his respects—" Aideen made herself stop. "Would you care for sisuree? Is there time?

If the meeting is in one hour, why did they wait so long to send you?"

Paloma drew a deep breath.

"They didn't," she said.

"Oh," Aideen said, grasping it at the same moment.

Paloma stood straight, her hands at her sides as if she were delivering an account of a bad quarter for profits. She spoke rapidly. "No one sent me. They do not realize I heard Jefe Silvestro and Yor Oakley speaking."

"*Oakley?* What business does the Coalition have in this?"

"I wondered that also," Paloma said.

"You believe there was no plan to tell me."

"I do," Paloma said.

"I'll get my coat," said Aideen.

She could not leave quite so quickly. First, she checked on Father, who slept, while Dimitri sat by the bed. In her room, she stopped at her night table and unlocked the small box that held some jewels from her mother and her copy of the letter Trevian had sent two years before, awarding her his proxy. She folded it and slipped it into her skirt pocket.

Paloma had hired a sprite cart. It bumped and rattled along Canal Street. When they stopped at the company, Aideen said, "You go inside first. I'll wait a moment or two so we don't arrive together."

"They'll soon puzzle out who told you," Paloma said.

"Let them work for it."

Paloma climbed out. Aideen fished out a pair of unos and passed them to the driver. She waited a minute or two, then entered the offices. Several of the clerks in the lobby greeted her, and she returned their greetings, hoping she at least seemed calm. The upper story was quiet. Edmund must have seen her because he hurried out of Father's office. "Yorita, what are you doing here?"

"I've come to see Jefe Silvestro and Yor Montez. Are they both here, Edmund?" she said, trying to sound innocent.

"Yes, they are, yorita. I was, I was just sending you a note." He twitched slightly.

A note by messenger, which would not have arrived in time. She raised her eyebrows and merely said, "Well, good. I'll speak to both of them."

"I—I—I believe Yor Oakley is with them, and they," he gulped so hard she heard it, "they are expecting another, yorita. Oshane Langtree."

"Father's brother? Who Father has stated clearly would have no dealings with our company? Why would he come here?"

"I don't know, yorita."

Edmund had solved one problem for her at any rate. She strode up to the meeting room door and pushed it open without knocking. Oakley loomed over Montez, who had his arms folded, and from his other side, Jefe Silvestro leaned in. Both men stopped talking when she entered.

"Well met—" Oakley stopped, his face turning pink.

"What are you doing here, Aideen?" Silvestro said.

"I wanted to discuss company matters, but Edmund tells me you've approved a meeting, not only with a member of the Copper Coalition but with Oshane Langtree, who is not welcome in this building. As you both know."

"This is an extraordinary circumstance," Silvestro said, before Montez could speak.

"Not extraordinary enough to involve the Coalition in company business." Aideen spoke over her shoulder. "Edmund, a chair."

"Yes, yorita—"

"No chair!" Silvestro shouted.

Aideen's face grew hot. "Very well." She marched around the table and sat down in Father's seat. Her heartbeat nearly suffocated her, but she didn't look away from Silvestro's glare.

"What is your business here, Aideen? Surely Oswald needs tending."

"Father is well tended, and someone must protect the family's company."

Silvestro's upper lip curled into a snarl. "It's not your company."

"Review the charter, Jefe Silvestro," she said. "The Langtree family owns fifty-one percent of it."

"*Oswald* Langtree does. He is ill and you are not his heir."

"But I have his heir's proxy."

Montez coughed and leaned forward. "Aideen, there was no intent to sneak around you. Your uncle sent a note to each of us, early this morning. He offers to help."

"My father forbade him from this company fifteen years ago."

Montez shrugged. "Well, he's a Langtree."

"So you meet with a member of the family who has no knowledge of this company, who my father banned from it, while you send no word to the family member who has worked within it, and studied it, since she was a child."

Montez gave Jefe Silvestro a glance.

"If Langtree lineage is your standard," Aideen said, "why is Oakley here?"

Oakley said smoothly, before either other man could speak, "I only wish to offer help, yorita."

"Since when does the Coalition help? You seek to devalue our currency."

Oakley spread his hands. "That was the Crescent Council, not—"

"The *Crescent Noticias* printed the Copper Coalition's recommendation to the Council, word for word," she said. "'Currency must remain stable for a nation to thrive. The White Bluffs cinco coin is a leak in the cistern, which will lead to a flood of chaos. These tiny townships must be actively discouraged from stamping their own disks and calling it coinage. This practice leads to lawlessness, perhaps as bad as the days of the Interval.'"

All three men stared at her.

"Well, Elmaestro Tregannon," Oakley said, shrugging. "He's a prisoner of the old ways and not everyone agrees with him."

Behind them, Silvestro's secretary cleared his throat. "Jefe? Yor Langtree is here."

"Show him in," Silvestro said. "And bring a chair." He did not look at Aideen as he spoke, but Montez snorted softly.

The man who came through the door had a bandaged face and right hand. Beyond the edges of the bandage, the skin was pink, shiny, and sported yellowing blisters. He stood for a moment, scanning the room. His gaze stopped with her, and suddenly a smile blazed across his face, even as he winced. "It's Aideen? I haven't seen you since you were six!"

She nodded to him. "Oshane."

Behind him, the secretary stood holding a chair. Oshane stepped to one side. "I'm pleased to see you here, Niece, if surprised. How is my brother?"

"Resting and gaining strength."

"Good! I'm glad he grows well enough to let you leave his side. And my nephew?" As graceful as a dancer, he sat down on the chair. He did not offer his hand to any man across the table.

He looked at Aideen. "How *is* Trevian?"

She thought of Trevian's letter. "He's well."

"Good. Jefe Silvestro? And Yor Montez. Your names I know. Yor Oakley, didn't we meet once in Boskay?"

"I don't remember," Oakley said.

Oshane settled back in the chair. Those burns had to pain him, but he sat relaxed and at ease, like a boss preparing to listen to the two supplicants behind the table. "I came as soon as I heard my brother was ill. We argued, years ago, and I let my pride widen the gulf between us, but I am here to do what I can to protect my family."

"Do you know much of my father's business?" Aideen said. Silvestro glared at her, but she pretended not to see it. "We work daily with flames. How did you get injured, Uncle?"

"A joven flame. I was careless."

Aideen nodded as if she were pondering this statement.

Before she could speak again, Silvestro leaned forward. "You do not have experience with business, as I understand it. You prospect."

"I truly only wish to help. You two are the partners in my brother's business. I would of course be guided by your knowledge. I wish to keep the business steady until, well, until this situation runs its course."

"My father appointed an heir," Aideen said. "And it was not you, who has not been back to this town in fifteen years. Father's heir has given me his proxy, unless—" she turned her gaze to Silvestro "—unless you chose to act on your threat to challenge it."

Montez frowned. "No one ever..." He looked from Silvestro, whose face was as red as a southern plum, to Oakley, who gazed into the corner. "No one has suggested that, Aideen."

Montez owned the fewest number of shares. Father considered him the weakest of the partners in another sense. His charmed drill bits were no longer so necessary to the company, compared to the charmed loomin and quartz of the cages, or the ownership of the claim. He sounded bewildered. Possibly he was the only person in the room who knew less than she did of what was going on.

Silvestro muttered, "It is unusual and questionable. Young Langtree may not have been in his best wits when he wrote the letter."

Montez shook his head. "The proxy letter itself is clear. The language is straightforward, it does not ramble, it's—"

"Who knew what was in that boy's head?" Silvestro roared.

Aideen hoped her shaking fingers weren't noticeable. "I think everyone in this room, except my uncle, who was not *in* White Bluffs, can agree my brother's actions earlier that night were selfish and foolish. However, the letter is clear, and legally witnessed—"

"Who knows where the witness is now?" Silvestro said.

"Do we track witnesses to all legal statements? Every marriage document, must you know the whereabouts of each witness at every moment?"

Silvestro shook his head and waved his hands around, making Montez lean to one side. "Who even remembers what the letter says? We would have to send for it and review it. We don't have time."

"I brought my copy," Aideen said.

Silvestro made a sound like a growl. He flattened his hands on the table as if preparing to rise. Aideen forced herself to hold his gaze, as she might a marauding kiote she'd met at twilight. She would not be cowed by this man. She would *not* think of him as Ilsanja's father.

Oshane cleared his throat loudly. "This is easily solved," he said.

"Aideen, send for Trevian. Have him return home and state his preference in front of the partners. That's the task done."

"He left a clear letter of proxy so he would not have to return," Aideen said.

"Yes, but he could not have expected something so dire."

Montez said, "Well, what other circumstance would require a proxy letter except a dire one?"

Oshane spread his fingers, wincing slightly. "I mean only, well, choosing a sibling as a proxy is unusual. A husband or a wife, yes, they are the most common proxies, aren't they? Only in this case..." Aideen saw he had brought up the suggestion solely so he could remind Silvestro that Trevian had abandoned Ilsanja. Oshane *wanted* Trevian to return, as if his main purpose was to drag Trevian back into his orbit.

She shifted her attention to the three men on the other side of the table. Montez glanced from her to Oshane, growing more confused with each passing moment. Oakley and Silvestro would not look at each other. It was *Oakley* who had suggested challenging her proxy. She knew it as if the words were written in gold in front of her. This wasn't just a case of Silvestro's arrogance or anger. There was something deeper at work here, something threatening Father's company. Montez was not strong enough to stand before it. For a dizzying moment, she feared she was not either. Then she lifted her chin. They would not frighten her or silence her. She stood up.

"If you wish to challenge the proxy, I will see you before the town council this sennight," she said.

"No, no, no one's said that, Aideen. Calm down," Silvestro said. "We all wish the company to continue strong and safe."

"Yes, that's what we all want," Oshane said.

"Which would not mean bringing a stranger into the partnership, would it?"

Montez said, "It wouldn't." His eyes were wide, but his voice was steady. "We should see how the next few days go with Oswald."

Oshane stood up too. "I see I have brought discord when I meant to offer help," he said. "My apologies. I will be available if you choose to meet with me again."

"Where are you staying, Uncle?" Before he could think she extended an invitation, she added, "You know you are not welcome in Father's house." It sounded rude in her own ears and she didn't care.

He bowed slightly. "I would not imagine adding to your burdens, Aideen. Tending to my brother, running a household, must take all your time right now. No, I have a place to stay. As to how to reach me…"

Oakley said, "Give a message to me. I'll see Yor Langtree gets it."

"The Copper Coalition offices are in Sheeplands, aren't they?" Aideen said.

"I have a desk and a chair at the Banco de Duloc in town."

"Do you." Aideen nodded at Father's two partners, one of whom was so ready to give the company over to her uncle. "Good day," she said.

"I'll join you, Niece," Oshane said, and she couldn't find a way to refuse him. Oakley watched her with a level-eyed gaze as she left the room with her uncle.

"I'm sorry to have given distress," Oshane said. "Truly, Aideen, I wish only to help."

"There's nothing more to be done right now," she said, striding for the stairs.

He kept pace with her. "Do you believe he does not wish to see me?"

She nodded.

He put his hand over his heart. "That wounds me, even if I've earned it with my pride and my neglect. Even though Oswald is only three years younger than I am, I raised him, and his welfare has always been close to my heart."

"Raised him?" She started down the stairs, refusing to look at him.

"As good as. Surely you know, Niece, our father Fergal was addled-witted, far beyond turvy into true madness, most likely. To the extent there was food in our mouths, a warm place to sleep, and even the fact that Oswald learned his letters and his numbers was because of me."

"Well," she said, stepping down into the quiet lobby, "he grew up to become a strong and capable man."

"You see the problem with the proxy, don't you?"

Now she *did* look at him. "I see no problem with my brother's proxy."

The corners of Oshane's eyes crinkled with his smile, reminding her of the uncle who used to come at Midwinter, with songs and tales and toys. "You saw from a perfect seat the battle of wills between Oswald and Trevian. He made Trevian his heir to force him to return, to ignore the call for copper-hunting in his blood, and serve the business."

She knew that well, but she was surprised he did. Clearly, people in White Bluffs had been telling him tales, perhaps for a long time.

"Oswald took your skills for granted, like water in a stream. But seen from the outside, it's as if he distrusted you. Not that he *did* distrust you, only that it appeared so."

Did he know he had spoken in the past tense? She waited, sure there was more. Messengers trailed in and out, and the wedge of view left before the door swung shut framed a caballo tied to a post on Canal Street, a bay with a gleaming black mane and tail.

"If we could, well, *soothe* Jefe Silvestro, by agreeing to let me help, I would know to listen to you. You must know the daily workings of the company and Oswald's plans far better than either of them. Jefe Silvestro seems concerned only with his pride."

"I see, Uncle," she said.

He rolled his shoulders in a shrug. "Or, again, while I know he would balk at it, call Trevian back. A day in his life, to speak to his father's partners and set them straight? Surely he would return for you?"

Why was Trevian's return to White Bluffs so important to him? In that moment, she settled for silence.

Oshane lowered his voice. "Did I misunderstand before? *Do* you have contact with your brother?"

"I do, frequently," she said.

"What does he write of?"

"Oh, many things. Things of interest to a copper-hunter, usually, tales of prospectors, bits of Ancient he is intrigued by."

"Has he written of me?"

He would recognize a lie, she thought, holding his gaze.

"Yorita Langtree!" Montez called to her from the landing. She shifted her attention too quickly, she knew, but it was too late to repair the damage now.

"Yes, Yor?"

He hurried down the stairs. "Will you give me the pleasure of your company to your house? I brought my caballo-cart."

"You are kind, Yor Montez," she said.

Montez gave Oshane a nod. "Good day, Yor Langtree."

"Take care of those burns, Uncle," Aideen said. She stepped back to let Montez pass.

Oshane walked out with them but didn't speak again. Aideen stopped, pretending to check the cuff of her boot, to see if her uncle mounted the bay caballo, which he did. The animal's markings were familiar. She didn't know who owned it...but she knew someone who would.

Montez drove his own caballo-cart. With the fewest shares, he made the least profit, and she thought the ten percent reduction must have hurt him. He was comfortable and his children did well, but he was not a jefe. She wondered if it chafed him.

While she flailed around for something to say, he spoke. "You know, Jefe Silvestro bellows like a ram, but truly, the leader of the company has always been your father. Your father's wit and vision are what keep us growing and profitable."

She nodded.

"We are a little lost right now," he said.

She gave a brief laugh. "You don't have to explain Jefe Silvestro's behavior, yor. I've seen it often."

Montez nodded and was silent until they started up the hill toward the house. Then he said, "I assumed, wrongly I see now, that your uncle had reached out to you first and you were aware he had asked to meet with us."

"I know you would not have participated in such a discourtesy, Yor Montez. And this is part of the reason I distrust my uncle. He has not returned to White Bluffs for fifteen years, and when he arrives, he does not pay his respects to me or ask about Father's health. Instead, he proposes a meeting with Father's partners."

"Well, probably he knew he would not be welcome," Montez said.

"Welcome by my father, no. But wouldn't it have been right to greet me first?"

"Yes, it would."

"And why is Yor Oakley present at any meeting in the company? He was at the offices the day my father fell."

Montez chirruped to his caballo and adjusted the reins. "This I did not know."

She nodded without speaking.

After a few moments, Montez spoke again. "Oakley has been saying, to any jefe or jefa who will listen, how he wishes for a Coalition office in White Bluffs." Montez clucked to his caballo as the traffic eased. "He has talked openly of his support of the cinco coin. It might be simply because he sees White Bluffs growing into a town of influence, perhaps even capable of challenging Duloc someday, and he wishes to place his bet on the winning caballo. Why his interest in the Langtree Company? I don't know."

Aideen thought perhaps she did, if the expansion progressed and White Bluffs began providing energy to towns in Sheeplands. White Bluffs *would* become a power. And this, maybe, was the simple answer to her uncle's interest, too.

What if the Copper Coalition was behind the vandalized quartz and the stolen copper, as a way to slow the company's expansion?

She said, "Has Yor Oakley earned *your* trust?"

The caballo's hoofbeats marked out several seconds before Montez said, "No, yorita, he has not."

They were silent for the rest of the ride. When they reached the house, Aideen paused before she climbed down. "If Father is not asleep, would you like to visit him for a moment?"

The expression of eagerness on his face surprised her. "If it's no trouble, yorita, I would."

They tied up the caballo at the hitching post. Dolores met them inside, and when Montez was seated in the sala with a cup of sisuree, Aideen went down the hall to her father's room.

She heard Dimitri before she reached the door. "Jefe, please. Be calm. Jefe!" he said. She quickened her pace. Father was thrashing, grunting, his good hand flailing. The window was halfway open.

She ran in and closed it. "Why was this open?"

Father slumped back into the bed, panting.

"I only opened it five minutes ago," Dimitri said. "I don't understand. The jefe always wanted the window open."

She shut her eyes for a moment. "Dimitri, he fell from a window. An open window disturbs him now."

"I'm sorry, yorita. Perhaps I shouldn't be the one to sit with him…"

Father gripped Dimitri's wrist with his good hand. If it was coincidental, it was a powerful coincidence. Aideen said, "Just don't open the window again. He trusts you, you give him comfort, Dimitri, which is what he needs. Father, Yor Montez is here and I've told him he could see you." She didn't make it a question. From her father's agitation about the window, if he didn't want a visitor, he would react.

He sighed.

She brought Montez in. He stood for a minute at the side of the bed, biting his lower lip. "Jefe," he said. He pressed his hand gently on Father's shoulder. "I hope you are gathering strength. My family and I include you in our prayers."

Father grunted again and blinked twice. His head dropped to one side, facing Montez. There was no other reaction. Montez sat down next to the bed. Too late, she thought she should ask him not to mention Oshane, but he didn't. He spoke for a few moments about the cages and Lopez's latest report. Father's breathing deepened, and after a few minutes, he was asleep.

Dimitri sat on the other side of the bed, and Montez left quietly. When they were back at the entryway, he said, "Thank you, yorita. That meant a lot to me."

"I think it helped him, too, Yor Montez."

"Don't fear Jefe Silvestro's temper, yorita. It will blow past like a spring gale." He nodded and took his leave.

She stood, her hands clenched at her sides. She did fear it, not the rage, it meant little. She feared the actions of the men who goaded Silvestro's rage and drove it against her and Father.

In the sala, she sat down, thinking.

With Father ill, Silvestro was the most powerful man in the company. And then there was her uncle. Against them, she had a proxy letter written by her brother, admittedly under circumstances that put him in the wrong, and her knowledge of the workings of the company.

A moment later Dolores came in. "Ilsanja Silvestro is here to see you, yorita," she said. Her face and voice were neutral, carefully so.

"How does she seem?"

Dolores considered. "Polite, and intent upon seeing you."

Which told her little. "Show her in, and have refreshments brought, please, Dolores."

The housekeeper nodded. Ilsanja strode into the room. Her slim suit gleamed gray in one light and pale green in another, with a richly embroidered bodice and short puffed sleeves. She flung herself down into the chair across from Aideen and said, "Well, *you've* been busy this morning."

"I guess I'm no longer Donita Aideen at your house."

Ilsanja shrugged. "My father's rages are the worst when he knows in some part he is wrong. Thus, today's rage is the worst of the worst."

"How do you know what happened?"

Ilsanja waited until the downstairs chica brought a pot of sisuree and some tiny cakes. She said, "Petrie tells me what he can."

Petrie, Silvestro's secretary. Aideen said, "Why? For coin?"

Ilsanja leaned forward, picked up a cake, and bit into it. "Your Susannah is a miracle," she said. "I must bring her some kokolatal powder and see what she can do with it. No, not for coin. He bears a torch for me."

Aideen shook away the image of Silvestro's secretary standing on a lonely mountain peak, holding a blackrock lantern. "I have no idea what that means," she said.

"It's an expression from my mother's people. It means having feelings or regard for a person who does not return them."

"He loves you?"

"Of course not. He doesn't truly know me. He loves an image of me. He told me everything he knows about what happened today. Needless to say, since he wasn't in the room and no notes were taken, there are gaps in his version I'm sure you could fill."

"Or your father could." Aideen poured sisuree for both of them and sipped hers, to give herself time to think. Ilsanja's visit was strange. Their rekindled friendship was barely two days old. Had she come out of loyalty to her father, to probe Aideen's thinking?

"I would not ask my father," Ilsanja said, "and especially not when he's snorting and stamping around like a rutting ram. Here's what I know. Darwin Oakley was present. Oshane Langtree was expected, and then you appeared like the saint in a miracle play and cast everything into chaos."

"Not the most flattering description."

"I don't know what unfermented plan my father had, but you've stopped it for the moment. That's power, Aideen."

"My uncle wants to assume a role in the company in Father's place. I doubt the discussion ended simply because I objected."

"It's strange, Oshane Langtree appearing just after you've gotten Trevian's letter."

Aideen curled her hands around her warm cup. "And he's burned, badly, as Trevian said. The burns are fresh. How did he hear of Father's illness? How did he get here so quickly?"

"He's not staying here?"

"No." Aideen blinked, remembering the caballo. "Ilsanja, who owns a bay saddle mount with a black mane and tail?"

With a big sigh, Ilsanja dropped back deeper into the chair and crossed her ankles. "Several in town, I think, since Mark Majeur sold his stable. He bred a line with those markings, but after, well, after Vallis, he sold them. He's only kept two saddle mounts and the carriage caballos, grays."

"How do you know all this?"

"His stablemaster and mine meet every half-month or so, over mead. Why do you ask?"

"Oshane mounted that animal after he left the offices. I thought I had seen it before, but I don't have your eye."

"You think Oshane is staying with Majeur?" Ilsanja was silent and her energy seemed to coil inward. "My father would be interested to know that. I'll find out."

They were both silent for a moment.

Aideen said, "I still have Trevian's proxy. If it comes to a struggle before the town council, it should hold. And Oakley supports Oshane, which must work against him with the council."

Ilsanja swung her foot. "His support for your uncle may have some worth."

"Why? He's a Coalition man. The council hates the Coalition."

"The *Coalition*, yes, but they don't hate Oakley. He has slithered into the good graces of two council members. He says he supports the cinco."

It matched what Montez had told her. Aideen felt as if a rift had suddenly yawned open beneath her feet. Montez supported her, or said he did. Trevian's proxy letter was clear and legal, properly worded and properly witnessed. She had just assumed its legality meant the town council would honor it. "So, rightness, fairness, and good sense don't matter then." She couldn't stop her voice from shaking.

Ilsanja's spoke softly. "It still might. You're well regarded, and your uncle is a stranger." She straightened up in the chair. "There is something you're not saying. I can see it on your face."

"There's nothing."

"You're worried about something else."

She wanted to trust Ilsanja, but how far would Ilsanja's goodwill extend if she learned Father was the cause of her abduction? She could not risk it. "It's just despair," she said, trying to laugh.

Ilsanja's questioning expression fled, her eyes like black wells. "You want my help, but you still keep secrets. You say we are friends again, but you turn your face from me." Ilsanja's voice dropped to nearly a whisper. "Aideen, do not do to me what your brother did."

"I'm not. I... Besides, wouldn't it benefit your father to know whether Oshane is a confederate of Mark Majeur? This information doesn't only help me."

Ilsanja glared at her, but the corner of her mouth curled up. "So, you *do* negotiate. I'll see what I can learn about the caballo."

Dolores tapped on the door. "Pardon, yorita, but Yor Olafson is here with the healer from the capital."

Ilsanja stood up. "I'll be going, then. Prayers for your father, Aideen. Perhaps you'll have some time to consider what my help is worth to you."

Aideen sent notes to Paloma and Edmund, asking them to visit her. In case Jefe Silvestro or Oakley saw the one to Edmund, she kept it vague, asking that he bring Yor Lopez's most recent report. She frequently reviewed reports. If the message did fall into unfriendly hands, it should only look as if she were preparing an argument for why she should be the proxy partner.

Dolores came into the room, carrying a length of decorative chain. "If I may...yorita?"

"What is this?"

"It may be green foolishness, but this is a charm from Pais Lewelyn." Dolores held it up. The links gleamed pale gray, plata most likely, interspersed with a shimmering, milky stone Aideen hadn't seen before. "The gems are called moonstone. It's supposed to ward against air elementals. I thought—"

"You thought it would ease Father's fear if we strung it across the window."

The housekeeper nodded.

"Come," she said. "Let's try it."

Dimitri looked up when they entered. When he saw what they

51

were doing, he came to help fix the end of the chain to the sill. "Do you think it will make a difference?"

Aideen glanced at her father and said, "It protects against air elementals."

Dimitri shrugged. "If you say so, yorita."

An hour later the downstairs chica showed in Paloma. Aideen thought Edmund had refused to come, but he arrived fifteen minutes later.

"We didn't want to leave together," Paloma said.

She had them seated, offered refreshment, and answered their questions about Father. Edmund sat stiffly in his chair. "There's very little I can do for you, yorita. I work for the company."

"Can you share a report?"

"I, well, yes."

"Can you write a letter?"

"Of course I—" He stopped, frozen like a kiote scenting a trap. His gaze flicked from side to side. "I don't know. If you are setting yourself against the partners..."

"In what way, Edmund? I'm reviewing the operations of the company. I've done that at my father's side since I was small. Did you bring Lopez's report?"

Without speaking, he pulled out a sheaf of paper and handed it to her.

The engineer's report was clear and straightforward, but his wording in several places made her raise her eyebrows. "Have you both read this?"

They nodded.

Paloma said, "Yor Lopez has stopped bridling his frustration. They've delayed repairs for half a year now. He fears for the safety of the workers and the health of the flames. If the charmed copper peels away where it joins the loomin, or more quartz cracks—"

"He states he has surplus sheets of charmed quartz, but without new metal stripping he cannot replace the cracked sheets." Aideen flipped to the page where he had listed the projected costs. It was far less than the amount of coin in Father's strongbox.

"Paloma, I know all the partners reduced in their income. Is there anything in the partnership papers forbidding one from putting more personal money into the company?"

"Buying shares?" Edmund said.

"No. Covering an expense."

Paloma thought for a moment. "Nothing forbids it. It's uncommon with an established company, but it has been done."

"It creates gossip, I'm guessing," Aideen said, "if it's known."

"Yes."

Edmund said, "No one would see it as a *good* sign."

"And yet, in an unusual situation, such as the sudden illness of a partner, might it be noticed less? Or less remarked on?"

Paloma said, "I've never understood what gets remarked upon and what happens in total silence. Since you are at odds with one of the partners, it may draw more comment, not less."

"Yorita, is this wise?" Edmund said.

"Do you think I'm not capable of making a simple financial decision?"

His hands remained folded in his lap, but the knuckles were white. "Yorita Langtree, I have never doubted your abilities. I speak out of concern for the Jefe, and for you. We do not know how his—" He gulped. "How his illness will go. A financial action now that seems reasonable may leave you without coin later, when you need it most, if this, if..." His face flushed and he stopped speaking.

She hoped her surprise didn't show on her face. "I see. Edmund, thank you for your concern on Father's behalf. Father has another trickle or two of income, you know, and I am not afraid to economize. The household can survive this expense."

"Very well. I'm sure you know best, yorita."

She stopped herself from saying, "I don't know best, no one does." It wouldn't do to carve away the tiny bit of trust Edmund had in her. Instead, she said, "The maintenance of the company's key source of wealth and stability is of high importance right now. Paloma, how quickly can you draw up a record of me depositing coin to cover the cost of the repairs?"

"Do you have ink and paper?" Paloma said. "I can do it now."

Aiden pushed paper, ink, and a pen across the table to her. Paloma scooted her chair forward.

"Now, Edmund, there is another company of quartz fabrickers in Duermay, isn't there?"

He nodded.

"I'd like you to write a letter of introduction and we'll send Yor Lopez to meet them and inspect their product. We are not committing to a contract, merely exploring an alternative. Will you do that?"

Tension fell away from Edmund's torso and he gave a quick nod, oddly mirroring Paloma's. "That is what the Jefe would have done, yorita." He cleared his throat. "I thought you might ask, so I brought their address with me."

She smiled.

He reached out his hand and she gave him paper and a pen as well. She watched for a moment while they both wrote. "Edmund," she said, "Father is resting now, but later today, if it's possible, would you like to see him? He seemed cheered by a visit from Yor Montez. Say at six?"

"Yes, I'd like that. Thank you, yorita."

"Call me Aideen," she said.

Paloma accompanied her to deposit the money. The banco's lobby, accented in copper and gold, was quiet. In a corner, from behind a metal slab desk, Darwin Oakley watched her. The back of her neck crawled. Perhaps he would think she was withdrawing coin for household expenses or for Father's care.

As they walked out, she said quietly, "Is Oakley actually trusted by the town council?"

Paloma, as always, thought about the question before she answered. "I believe he is liked by some. Jefe Silvestro thinks so, at least. He believes Oakley brings good things for the company."

"Why?"

"Because he offers a voice in argument to Elmaestro Tregannon, who no one on the town council likes. Tregannon has taken steps to limit White Bluffs's influence. Oakley speaks of expanding it."

"He sings their song," Aideen said.

"He sings their song."

"Does he have the ability to do more than warble pleasing words?"

Paloma walked three steps before answering. "Likely not, but what matters is that they think he does."

Aideen studied her boot tips with each forward step. One of the company's partners wanted to displace her. Two members of the Council of White Bluffs would support him, and she knew a third member of the town council didn't like Father and never had.

It was more than possible she would lose the Langtree Company to Oshane, who Trevian said was a murderer.

Mere suspicion wouldn't help her, and what facts she had were of no help either. Even if Trevian could consent to return, which she doubted he would, he was not well-respected in White Bluffs. And she would not be the one to bring him into Oshane's grasp.

He has a tethered air elemental.

A broken window, a waterspout. A fall.

All of this and no proof of anything.

"You spoke, Aideen?"

"Your pardon. Thinking out loud. They will set aside Trevian's letter without a thought, all for a shining promise of future profit no more solid than morning mist."

"It isn't fair. Or good business," Paloma said. "It's a pity your mother left."

"Why?"

"A wife, at least, no one would question."

Paloma's statement was convoluted, but Aideen puzzled it out. The accountant didn't want to mention Ilsanja Silvestro, who would have been the wife of Father's heir, so she reached for the wife who had left without a word fifteen years before.

Paloma said, "They may see reason. Yor Montez supports you."

He did, but she couldn't help wondering how quickly his support would collapse under pressure from Jefe Silvestro. Another fact never stated aloud—her brother's scandal had brushed her. Both of Oswald Langtree's children were tainted by disgrace. As an unknown, Oshane might seem a *better* risk.

She was close to tears.

The canal rippled musically, as if mocking her. She had friends—Paloma, Yor Olafson, Yor Lopez and probably even Yor Montez—but they were friends without power. Oshane played the people around him as easily as he probably drew the notes from that flautine on his hip, luring out greed, anger, self-interest, all with a crinkle of his eyes and a charming smile.

Desperation built up in her like steam in a geyser. She couldn't heal her father, and she couldn't save their company. She had called herself the invisible Langtree for years, but now she was confronted with how true it was. She was worth nothing. A child but not an heir, a sister, not a wife. Good enough to keep things running: capable, reliable, and ultimately valueless.

Her vision blurred. Sunlight sparkled on the gentle ripples, flowing from one shape to another as she blinked her vision clear again.

"Aideen? Yorita?" Paloma gripped her arm.

She touched the other woman's fingers. "I'm well, Paloma."

There was one other person who might be considered a friend.

She said, "I'm crafting a plan, a desperate one. More desperate than throwing myself into the grand canal."

"*More* desperate?"

Aideen nodded. "Let's call a sprite cart," she said. "You must let Yor Lopez know his funds are available, and I must return to the house."

Isanja wore sturdy black trousers, clearly tailored for her, a plain long-sleeved blouse, and a smock jacket. Her hair was pulled back in one thick plait. "An intriguing summons, Aideen."

"You could have changed," Aideen said. "I would have waited that long. I would have waited as long as you needed."

"Ah. So I hold the power? I like the sound of that." Ilsanja plunked down on a chair and stretched out her legs, bringing with her the scent of caballo-sweat and manure. Aideen's heart dropped. Ilsanja was already taunting. She'd failed before she'd even started.

And yet—she was sure one reason Ilsanja hadn't stopped to change into visiting attire was so her father would not know she had gone out. She wanted him to think she was still working in her stables.

"Cakes? Ale or fruit?" Aideen said.

Ilsanja smiled. "Quit stalling. Are you prepared to tell me what had you so distressed this morning?"

"No. I have an idea and I wish to share it with you. It may benefit you."

"Let's hear this plan then."

"It's not a plan yet." Aideen kneaded her hands together. "I have decided to go to the capital."

"To seek out Trevian?"

Her heartbeat shook her chest and shoulders. "Yes."

"To persuade him to return? Do you think he will?"

"No. He will not. I wish you to come with me, Ilsanja."

Ilsanja's clear brow wrinkled. "Did you hit your head, Aideen? Perhaps you've forgotten how your brother and I left things, or how he left things with me."

"I haven't." Aideen gulped and blurted out her idea before she could freeze. "I wish you and he to marry, duly witnessed, and you to return with his partnership proxy for the company. Your father will not challenge it, and no one questions a husband or a wife as proxy. You will control fifty-one percent of the company."

The room got quiet.

"Oh." Ilsanja sat up, looking about as if just waking from a dream.

Aideen swallowed, her mouth dry.

"You surprise me," Ilsanja said.

Aideen rushed on before Ilsanja could interrupt, or worse, get up and leave. "It makes you Jefa Langtree, a title you wanted. The house would be yours to run as you saw fit. You would have the position, part of a boss couple. And—"

Ilsanja's face was carefully expressionless.

Aideen changed her direction. "I know how badly he hurt you, how he bruised your heart. I know just what I am asking of you."

"You don't, I think," Ilsanja said.

"I have no right to ask you to stick your hand once again into the hot coals, but we will lose this company if we do not do something. Oshane doesn't bring profit for you and your father either, Ilsanja, I am sure of it. He brings the entire company ruin, and ruin will wash over your family as well as mine."

"Aideen."

"And Trevian has this, this quest. The scent of copper pulls him, and he will not be back. You will not have to face him, I swear, and between you and your father, you will have control of the majority of the company."

"Aideen, stop." Ilsanja held up her hand. "Stop."

Aideen stopped. She was shaking.

Her friend stood up and went to the door. She peered out into the hallway, stepped back into the sala, and pulled the door shut. As calmly and gracefully as if she were finding her seat at a concert, she sat back down in the chair. "You do *not* know what you are asking," she said, "so I'm going to tell you."

Aideen nodded, tightening her folded hands until they hurt.

"I never loved your brother. He didn't thrill my nerves or set my heart dancing with sprite-lights. I *liked* him. We were friends. I thought he could be guided by me, he would value what I knew, and we would become a powerful boss family, just as you said. And I thought you would be at our side."

Aideen's heart swooped upward like a fish seeking a fly, for a moment. It fell again. Plainly, Vallis had been the man Ilsanja had loved. It explained her rage toward him, even now.

"Trevian never bruised my heart, Aideen. He never touched it. He battered my *pride*. I know my worth, and your brother tossed me aside as if I were a thing of no value."

"You are of great value," Aideen whispered.

"I am, it's true. Now, what you offer me, if it came to pass, *is* what I wanted from the first, but you cannot guarantee me Trevian will go along with this scheme. Subject my pride to the hammer of his indifference and have him turn his face from me again? This I will not bear."

"It will be me asking. Me demanding, forcing him to see his duty."

"You have no reason to think your brother understands duty."

"Ilsanja, don't you see? This frees him as well! It gives him a balm for his conscience. He balances the scales with you, and he does his duty to his family. He is free to continue this quest of his, with his new woman."

"And what if she wishes to be pledged to him?"

"I—" Aideen thought wildly, but no answers came to her. "She's an out-of-worlder, he says. Perhaps they don't have such things."

Ilsanja snorted.

"Well, that's a problem for the two of them to sort out. I do not know her; I do not care for her problems. I care about my family. Trevian needs to face some troubles, after all the trouble he's caused."

Ilsanja grinned, startling her. "I hear in those words the rehearsal of your talk with him," she said. "Well. The question is this: How do I trust you to persuade him, when you will not trust me?"

Aideen started to say, again, there was nothing, but she could not meet Ilsanja's gaze. "When you hear this, you will turn away from me and my family forever."

"It's a risk. I doubt it, myself, but anything is possible." Ilsanja's tone was light and detached, but from the edge of her vision, Aideen could see the tension in her friend's body.

To get Ilsanja to accompany her, she had to take this risk.

She drew a deep breath and met Ilsanja's gaze. "Vallis owed coin," she said.

"Gambling debts."

"Yes, and he borrowed from a private person to pay off those debts. The person holding his note charged him usurious interest." Her throat dried up. She swallowed. "It was Father."

"Where did you hear this rumor?"

"It's no rumor. I've seen the note. I think, I think Vallis planned your abduction to pay Father what he owed."

Ilsanja stared through her, as if at an object a league away. "That selfish monster," she said, conversationally.

Shame heated Aideen's chest and neck. "I know."

Ilsanja stood up and began to pace. "Usury is *vile*. And why would your father do that? He has coin enough."

"I think there can never be coin enough for Father."

With her back still to Aideen, Ilsanja said, "It's vulgar. I see why you didn't want to share it." She whirled and dropped back into the chair, one leg crossed over the other. "I am disappointed in your father to hear he did such a thing. But it was *Vallis* who treated me like a trinket he could sell for coin. It was *Vallis* who smiled at me and comforted me when I argued with Trevian, Vallis who brought me wine with a sleeping-potion in it. Vallis."

"But he wouldn't have, if—"

"Make no error. If it hadn't been your father who held his note, it would have been another. What your father did was bad, but Vallis takes the blame for what was done to me. All the blame." She looked at Aideen expectantly.

"What?" Aideen said.

"Is that all? I thought there was something terrible."

"That's all," Aideen said.

"Then how do we leave without attracting comment? Your father lies gravely ill. I can always ride west as if to visit my pasture lands, but you cannot so easily escape."

"I have thoughts on that, I... Wait. You're saying yes?"

"I thought you were the smart one, Aideen. I am saying yes."

L ike many plans, it was not as simple in fact. The burden of deceit fell on Dolores, who would tell anyone who called or sent messages that Aideen was secluded with her father. It was unfair, but Aideen could see no way around it. A deeper deceit poked at Aideen. Dolores believed her plan was to bring Trevian home.

"If...the worst happens, or word gets out I'm gone," she said, "then you must tell people I've gone to the capital to seek my brother and return with evidence of Yor Oshane Langtree's crimes."

Dolores frowned. "He has no right to what your father's built here, yorita. I'm sure Yor Trevian will see things plainly and make things right. Why do you go in secret though? And alone? It's not safe with mestengos in the hills."

Aideen said, "If I make it plain, I fear my uncle will move against Father in my absence. And I will be safe." She did not mention Ilsanja.

"I can send Julio with you," Dolores said. Julio was her oldest son and assisted the stablemaster.

"No, we need him here, Dolores, thank you."

"Your mother never trusted him either, yorita."

"Mother? Did she speak to you of him?" Dolores had been part of the Langtree household for as long as Aideen could remember, but she hadn't considered this. Dolores had talked to her mother, about everyday things, personal things. Aideen barely remembered the woman, but of course others did.

"She disliked and distrusted him," Dolores said. "He came to the house, now and then, in those days. You might remember. Usually for Midwinter. He was great with games for you, and songs for the chicas, but your mother watched him narrow-eyed and her smiles were tiny."

"I remember riding through the house on his back, like he was a caballo."

"Yes. And the songs on the flautine, and the smiles, all the while watching things with the eyes of a moneychanger, calculating value." Dolores shivered. "He has no right."

"He does not, and he will get nothing of Father's, Dolores, if I can help it."

"You're sure about Julio?"

"I am. Just bring around my trail caballo and help me pack. Quietly."

And now she waited, midway through the afternoon, at the trail just below the bluffs and the cages. The ground was damp from an early spring rain, and clouds massed on the eastern horizon.

Ilsanja had publicly started off heading west but should have doubled back beyond the town limits, taking a trail Aideen told her about, one she and Trevian had used years ago. If Ilsanja was truly coming, and not mocking her for her gullibility. If this was all not still an elaborate revenge.

But something in Ilsanja's expression, her voice, convinced Aideen the other woman was not taking vengeance, had not tricked her.

A shod hoof rang on rock, and Aideen's caballo nickered. Another mount answered from the shadows, and then those shadows solidified into a caballo and a rider. Ilsanja wore her trousers and long jacket, with a flat-crowned hat. Bulging saddlebags lay across the caballo's flanks. "I never knew that track was there," she said, riding up alongside.

"Trevian showed it to me when I was small. Well, he went out on his own—"

"To brood," Ilsanja said.

"Probably. And I followed. When he saw me, he didn't send me back. He pointed out the kiote tracks and the ardiyas. We found quartz and scraps of blackrock. I've used it, since then, as a place to walk when *I* want to brood."

"But from here, where? It's three days to the capital if all goes well."

"Two days, maybe a bit less. There is a shortcut, again, courtesy of my brother. We go through a tunnel in the bluffs."

"In the dark? Your plan is not safe," Ilsanja said, but she didn't sound too worried.

"I told you it's not a plan."

Ilsanja laughed. "Aideen, it is a plan! You had every step arranged before you sent for me! You cannot fail to plan. Now lead the way through this deadly tunnel. I have quartzlight if we need it."

"We may. It's close to an emberbed, though, with a rift, which provides some light."

"Are we at risk?"

"The flames won't harm us unless we threaten them. The thing is, the tunnel comes out on the plateau above Merry Lake. Will that be hard for you?"

Ilsanja's voice was light, but her mount mouthed the bit and tossed its head. "As long as you don't bind me and imprison me in the skeleton of a warehouse, it won't be."

"I promise I'll do none of those things."

"Then let's see how far we can go tonight," Ilsanja said.

4

Sabado, 20 Uno, Year 331

The rift housing the emberbed painted the walls and ceilings of the passage red-orange. The caballos were nervous. Aideen's trail caballo had a mellow disposition, but the mare's ears swiveled, and she danced sideways from time to time. Ilsanja, the better rider, managed her gray gelding far better. Where it was wide enough, they rode side by side, which seemed to calm both mounts.

Aideen's gaze drifted to the rift. How many colonies of flames lived in there? If they claimed this, they would only need to cage one for a day before releasing it, rather than days or even sennights at a time, while it dwindled to blue and lavender. Or perhaps not cage them at all. And if there were a way to store the energy the flames gave off…

"Are you dreaming of the company?" Ilsanja said. She sounded amused.

Aideen flushed. "I am."

Her friend nodded. They rode for a bit in silence. Then Ilsanja said, "I have a theory of why my father wishes to discount the proxy."

"Because I'm someone easily dismissed and ignored."

Ilsanja's laugh echoed off the rocks like music. "No. Your father spent nearly every day in his office or at the cages. He knows his business. My father, now, barely manages one day a sennight. Once his charmed cages earned him wealth, he gave his attention to gaming, hunting, his show caballos, and his tailor. When things between your father and mine faltered, he grew to hate the debates with Don Oswald, because he knew little and Don Oswald knew so much. The only person who knows as much about the company as your father is you."

"I do?"

"Yes. You've learned it. You share your father's vision. You understand the flames, and my father never will. He looks at your uncle and sees a know-nothing who only wants coin, and he thinks a know-nothing will be easier to deal with."

"You flatter me," Aideen said.

"No flattery, not from me. I don't want to say you frighten him, Aideen, but he thinks your uncle is the easier way."

"That's bad thinking for the company."

Ilsanja spread her hands in acknowledgment.

As they rode, the light ahead of them changed from orange to gray and brightened. The passage ended at a ledge, turning sharply east and climbing along the face of the slanted cliff. Far below them spread mudflats and the dregs of Merry Lake. Aideen gripped the horn of her saddle and blinked away vertigo. She shaded her eyes and peered north to the end of the lake where the town had been, or still was, she supposed. The ledge climbed and curved north to cross the broad plateau where once, before she was born, the town of Merrylake Landing had uncovered a huge cache of Ancient.

Ilsanja's gelding snorted and tossed his head again. "I remember the lake being larger," she said. "It was so long we rode a sprite boat from the channel that feeds the canal, over to the town. Did you ever see it, the boat? It had a curving prow, meant to be a dragon or a bird or some such."

"It was a bird, a water bird," Aideen said. "Trevian told me the name once, but I don't remember."

"Nor do I." Ilsanja guided her mount up the incline. Aideen's mare plodded behind, ears forward.

Clouds folded themselves above the cliffs, rain heading their way. They had a few more hours of relatively good light unless the cloud cover swallowed it. She feared the tunnel had not bought them the hours she'd thought it would.

Ilsanja reined in her caballo. Aideen stopped behind her.

"There." Ilsanja pointed down, beyond the lake. "You can barely see the marks now, east of the ruins of the pier, but there, I think, is the skeleton of the warehouse where they held me."

"The stones have all been removed," Aideen said. "And the timbers. Those went first, I'm sure."

"Scavenged. Good."

Beyond the northern curve of the water, a number of buildings still stood. Aideen squinted. No carts, no caballos, no people moved in the wide lanes. No sound carried up to them. The town seemed dead.

"Does this disturb you?" she said.

Ilsanja glanced over her shoulder. "From here? Looking down on it? No." She nudged the gelding forward.

They rode on. Images stormed Aideen's imagination. What if her mount spooked or lost her footing on the ledge? What if they plunged, or slid, down the scree and the bare rock to land in a broken heap in the mudflats? She forced her fears away, relaxed her grip on the reins, and focused on Ilsanja's straight back and the gelding's switching hindquarters.

She lost track of how long they rode, as the clouds unrolled over them like a bolt of cloth, covering the sky, and a fine mist enveloped them. The mist would soon thicken into rain. Ilsanja guided her caballo to one side and stopped. Aideen rode up alongside her.

"Is this our road?"

The ledge broadened and flattened out, a straight line north. Tough, spiny brush grew up along it. "This is the plateau." Beyond it to the east, the plata-gray cliffs stabbed the rain clouds.

Ilsanja started forward and Aideen followed, stroking the mare's neck in gratitude for having delivered her this far safely. They rode side by side, and Ilsanja nudged the caballos into a lope. The rain grew thicker, and Aideen pulled her hood up over her hair. They loped over straight, level ground, a stretch of one of the great Ancient highways, hefted up when the mountains grew, or so a cage worker told her once.

They left the valley and the dying lake behind them, but they were losing light while the rain grew steadily heavier. Aideen peered through the gloom, hoping earth shudders and rockslides hadn't blocked the place she planned to use as a night shelter.

Soon she saw a deeper darkness to their right. She reined in and called to Ilsanja.

Ilsanja rode back to her. "Is it a cave?"

"Of a sort. I came here with my brother once."

"You are full of mysteries," Ilsanja said. "How do we know it's safe? It could be a kiote den, or an oso lair, or an earth elemental's."

"There are no osos this far east, and we've got charms against elementals." Aideen guided her mount toward the shelter she'd been seeking. Even in the near dark, through the gray spears of rain, it was clear this was not a natural structure. The curve of the opening was too even, and a band of lighter stone edged it. As she got closer, she loosened her knife in its sheath and dismounted. The cave was dark. She inhaled deeply. There was no smell of rotting meat or living animal. "It smells clear," she shouted.

"And I trust your nose?" But Ilsanja rode up alongside her. Slipping off her mount, she drew a copper rod tipped with quartz from one of her saddlebags. She woke the quartzlight charm, and the clear stone gleamed golden, casting a cone of light into the cave. "Was this carved by the Ancients?" Her voice echoed.

"I think so. It's large, it's out of the rain. We may have to go a bit for water, but there used to be a stream farther north."

"Not even that far," Ilsanja said. She took the mare's reins from Aideen and went back to the gelding. As Aideen hunched in the threshold of the shelter, Ilsanja led the caballos to a depression near the cliff face. Rain had pooled in it. Both mounts drank their fill.

They brought the caballos inside. The place was high-ceilinged and long, extending back into shadow. Ilsanja searched along the wall until she found a spike of stone—or maybe metal—she could use to tether the mounts, which she said she preferred to hobbling. Following her friend's lead, Aideen unsaddled the mare and rubbed her down with a square of coarse cloth Ilsanja gave her. She checked the hooves as well. Much of what made Ilsanja's saddlebags so bulky was related to the care of their mounts.

Ilsanja pulled out a pair of nosebags. "I'll feed the caballos," she said. "I wish we could have a fire."

"We can." Aideen pulled her hood snugly around her face. "The brush has a resin in its leaves and stalks. Even wet, it will burn."

"But we'd need a starter."

Aideen smiled. It was her turn to be good at something. "Yes, we would," she said. She went out into the rain and sawed branches off the brush. By the time she had hauled in the third armload, Ilsanja had settled the caballos and was rolling out the bedrolls, using the saddle-bags for pillows.

Aideen pulled out her sparker and the small bag of whiterock and paper scraps she'd packed. She set a small cylinder lantern by her bedroll, although with Ilsanja's quartzlight, it might not be needed. The branches released a scent like pepper when she broke them into shorter lengths, stripping the leaves.

"So you and Trevian explored."

She set a chunk of whiterock in a nest of paper scraps, and arranged the branches around it, setting twigs closest to the rock. "Father tried to put a stop to it. He wanted Trevian at the cages, or in the office, and he said it wasn't right for a young woman of my station. But we managed it until Trevian was sent to Sheeplands for a year." With two quick scrapes of the sparker, she coaxed blue sparks onto the paper. Soon the whiterock glowed while the branches hissed and crackled around it.

"Another secret skill," Ilsanja said.

"Anyone can start a fire with whiterock and a sparker," Aideen said. The branches burned strangely yellow, with the blue of the rock at the fire's heart. They spread out their coats to dry. Aideen glanced over at her friend. The light painted Ilsanja's face gold and fired the droplets in her hair into rainbows. Aideen looked away, busying herself with pouring some water from her flask into a long-handled pot.

They sipped sisuree and ate dried pork on flatbread. "If we get an early start, we should reach Lily Bend by midmorning," Aideen said. "I'll send a fast message to the Copper Coalition, and if all goes well, we should reach Duloc by dinner time on Domingo."

"Would it be faster to take a barge upriver from Lily Bend?"

"I think there are rapids north of the Plain of Ancient, but we will ask."

Ilsanja stretched, worked off her boots, and slipped into her bedroll. Aideen pulled off her own boots, added some branches to the fire, and did the same. The ground was hard. "This was more fun when I was a child," she said.

Ilsanja snorted. "I don't doubt it."

They lay side by side, listening to the popping of the fire and the shifting of the caballos. "Swan," Aideen said. "It was a swan boat."

"Yes! Did you ever see one? A live one?"

"No. Have you?"

"Not a swan. Once Mama took me to Evangeline with her for a commission, and I saw more live birds than I could count. Pais Lewelyn is a country of birds. There were herds of them in the sky above the bay. And at the outskirts of the city, some were quite vivid, with bright green wings and yellow heads and red spots on their breasts. But they shrieked like metal being torn."

"I thought they sang sweet songs," Aideen said.

"Not these."

Aideen kept her eyes closed. "I've only seen one live bird. Father planned to buy it from a prospector. He said it was a hunting bird."

"A hunting bird?"

"Supposedly it brought back rabbits and other kills, on command.

He had it in a cage. It was blindfolded with a leather hood, and its feet were tied to the perch with leather strands."

"Your father was going to take up hunting?"

Aideen snickered. "No. He never would have spent time on that. He wanted to display it in the house, because no one else had a bird."

The memory played in her head: nervous prospector, the stillness of the creature in the cage, and how, when he drew it out and removed the hood, the thing studied her with a golden eye lined in bright yellow. "It had a black cap on its head—the color I mean, and black wings. A bright splotch of white on its throat and then streaks of foggy gray down its breast. Its eyes were gold. The man said he would whistle it back and it would bring the rabbit he'd released a few moments before."

A rustling beside her drew her attention. Ilsanja had propped herself on one elbow.

Aideen mirrored the position so they faced each other. "He loosed the tethers and made a tossing gesture with his arm. And the bird took flight, Ilsanja, like an arrow from a longbow. And like an arrow from a longbow, it shot to the west and never came back."

"What do you mean, never?"

"The man whistled and called for two hours, while we stood." *And Father got colder and colder in his anger.* "Then Father struck the prospector and we rode home." She remembered the prospector, on his back, hands raised, a trickle of blood at the corner of his mouth, and how she'd had to run to mount her caballo and hurry after Father, who had already kicked his mount into a gallop down the hill, and how she had stayed out of his sight the next day, not wanting to be the target of his anger. And she remembered that golden eye.

Ilsanja stared. Her own eyes grew wide. She fell backward and laughed, as musically as she had in the tunnel.

"What?" Aideen said.

"Oh! Oh!" Ilsanja pressed her arms across her belly. "Oh, it hurts! Aideen, what a story!"

"*What?*" Aideen said, baffled and insulted.

Ilsanja tried to lift her head, but she was laughing too hard. "Don't you... Don't you see? It's your brother!"

"What? What's my brother? The hunting bird?" And then she saw it. She stared, wanting to be angry, but laughter pressed up from her chest and bubbled into the throat before she could stop. "It is! It *is* like Trevian!"

"He... He..." Ilsanja sat up, still gasping. She tittered, then drew a deep breath and managed to say, "Blindfolded, tethered, playing at docility until the cage door was..." but then she subsided into giggles, rocking back and forth.

Aideen also struggled to speak. "No... It is *nothing...like*," she said. Giggles burst out of her like water from a pipe. "The bird...flew west."

"And Trevian..." Ilsanja gasped for breath and wiped her eyes. "I am mistaken. Nothing like. Trevian flew to the *east*."

Aideen caught her breath. She was spent, as if she had run a fair distance, and yet she felt lighter somehow. She wondered if their merriment stemmed as much from exhaustion as anything, but at this moment she didn't care. "This is how family legends are made," she said. "My brother is now a fleeing bird."

"And I the cage."

"No. My father, or my father's life, that is the cage."

Ilsanja lay back down. "Thank you for the story."

"I like it better too, now," Aideen said.

A pebble dug into her hip, nagging her out of sleep. She woke. Warmth flowed down the right side of her neck and shoulder, and something silken touched her cheek. Fully awake now, she sensed Ilsanja's warmth beside her. Her friend had shifted in her sleep and lay with her head on Aideen's shoulder.

The pebble grew to the size of a cat. She didn't want to move, but she was going to have to. Finally, she lifted her hips and shifted them to one side. Now the rock, the boulder, pressed into her lower back. She could tolerate it, at least.

The caballos moved and snorted. Their heads were shadowed by the dying fire, but both animals peered into the tunnel, ears pricked. Aideen heard what they'd heard. Something growled or panted in the darkness farther in.

She wiggled to one side and sat up. Ilsanja muttered but didn't open her eyes. After adding the few final branches to the glowing fire, she picked up the quartzlight and spoke the word. The charm didn't waken. It was crafted for Ilsanja only. Aideen reached for her lantern cylinder and used a branch to scoop a scrap of glowing whiterock into it. Whiterock was better for heat than for light, but it would do. Holding up the lantern, she got to her feet and drew her knife.

It sounded more like breath now, long heavy exhalations. She eased forward. The gelding whickered nervously, and Aideen's trail-mare nudged him with her nose, calming him. The pallid light only made the cave seem darker, and the sound deepened but grew no closer.

Light gleamed beside her, piercing deeper into the dark. Ilsanja said, "Do you see something?"

"I heard something." The sound hadn't stopped, but it changed to a low-pitched whistle. Aideen took a couple of steps forward. The whistle faded back into the sound like panting. Air brushed Aideen's face and she chuckled.

"It's just the wind. This isn't a cave, it's a passage. The wind is singing through it."

Ilsanja stood next to her, sweeping the quartzlight from side to side. "Shall we explore it tomorrow? It may shave a few hours off our travels."

"Unless it ends in a chasm, or the opening is half a mile above our heads, or the openings are too small for a person, let alone a caballo. Unless it takes us south and adds leagues to our road."

"So, next journey then," Ilsanja said. "You're sure we're alone and safe? No creatures?"

Aideen nodded.

Ilsanja pressed her hand down on Aideen's shoulder. "Then I'm going back where it's still warm, and you should come with me." She put the quartzlight charm to sleep.

They lay back down. In the dark, Aideen said, "Your mother took you to Pais Lewelyn. I'd forgotten."

"I went with her on several commissions. She liked me to see the business end of things, and also just the differences in the way people lived. Probably because she found our ways strange, up 'til the end of her life."

"Did she think you were a charmcaster?"

"No, we knew I wasn't since the time I was small. Mama knew I was keen-witted, and she wanted me to know things. Many things. She wasn't like my father...or Trevian."

Or me, Aideen thought.

"You held my hand," Ilsanja said.

"What?"

"At the funeral. You held my hand while my father lit the flames."

"I couldn't think of anything to say," Aideen said. She remembered her friend, at thirteen, as motionless as a quartz statue by the side of the funeral platform.

"I will always remember that," Ilsanja said. Aideen lay awake, listening to her friend's breathing, for a long time.

The morning dawned clear and green. They set out shortly after sunrise, stopping at the stream to water the caballos and fill their flasks. Sprites darted over the rippling water, glowing like bright beads on a skirt. The flat ground was muddy, and they had slow going until they reached the narrow trail leading through the eastern pass.

The gravelly pass was drier, and the caballos picked up the pace. They climbed steadily and Aideen had to stop glancing over at the steep drop-off beside her. In one spot, the ground curved out above the steep canyon, leading to a stand of rocks arranged like a circle of dancers. "You must have many good memories of your mother," Aideen said.

"Many, and many bad, when her strength failed and the wasting disease took her. Many adventures. And many arguments." Ilsanja glanced over her shoulder and grinned. "She had no eye for fashion."

"Shandren was always dressed fashionably," Aideen said.

"She wore what was fashionable. She didn't create fashion, style. I create."

"I ignore. My own fashion, that is. I'm a mouse when it comes to clothing."

Ilsanja's braid swung as she shook her head. "You wear what is practical, which is a style. Not to say that, guided by me, you couldn't draw all eyes to you."

"No. I won't be your first failure," Aideen said. The thought of all eyes on her made her shudder.

"Do you have many memories of Serafina? I recall only that she always smiled at me."

"Very few," Aideen said. "Impressions, mostly. She smelled like spice. Do you remember?"

Ilsanja nodded.

"And I remember singing and music. She played the guitarra. And she would read me poetry every night. She taught me to read with poetry. She would read a poem, and I would read one. Little more than that."

"Which of us had it worse, I wonder," Ilsanja said.

Aideen didn't answer out loud. Ilsanja had ten full years or more of memories of her mother. She knew which one of them had it worse.

They rode on through a grove of young trees. At an albergue, they stopped to use its latrine, skirting a patch of rumpled ground showing signs of an earth elemental eruption. The shelter's fire circle smelled faintly of blackrock, proof it had been used recently, and its floor was strewn with ash. Aideen wondered at such sloppy travelers.

Soon after they crested the hill. In the distance, the river glowed in the sun, and they could see the prospecting town of Lily Bend. They had made better time than Aideen expected.

In town, she spoke to the barge tender and discovered the boat did turn back only a few leagues beyond the Plain of Ancient, as she had

COPPER ROAD

thought. She withdrew some coin for the road from the small branch of the Banco de Duloc, while Ilsanja replenished their supplies. Her friend met her as she was writing a note to Trevian to be sent by fast messenger.

"Don't tell him I'm with you," Ilsanja said.

Aideen studied the words she had just written. The messenger stood calmly by, but her caballo tossed his head and pawed the ground, eager to be running. "Why not?"

"I'll wager you my dress allowance for a year, if you mention my name he will disappear before we arrive, and all this will have been for nothing."

"A year's dress allowance? You must be serious," Aideen said, smiling.

Ilsanja did not smile back. "I am serious."

Aideen shrugged. She hadn't mentioned Ilsanja's name, yet. She wrote a hurried final sentence and signed the note, "Your Loving Sister." The message to the elmaestro at the Copper Coalition was already in the messenger's saddlebag. She sealed the second note and handed it off with the payment and a tip. "Thank you."

"Yorita." The messenger touched her cap and leaped into the saddle. The dashing movement was weakened by the entrance of a cart onto the road, forcing the messenger to slow to a trot, but moments later, the caballo sprinted up the north road, vanishing from view.

"Very well." Aideen tugged her coat more snuggly into place. "One long day on the road. If all goes well, you may be married by Lunis."

Ilsanja stroked the gelding's nose. "If all goes well."

II

IN THE CAPITAL

5

Erin Dosmanos caught her balance as the narrow ferry boat pulled away from the stone quay. Back on the shoreline, just beyond the farthest building out, two funnels of blue and yellow flame danced. "They're following us," she said. "Why? I freed them."

Trevian said, "They share a bond with you now."

She shuddered. The two fire elementals had killed her family. They had been tortured and trapped by the man who had orchestrated the murders; they were just the weapons, but she didn't have to like the weapons. And she didn't like the thought of them imprinted on her like ducklings. "What if they come into the city?"

"They can't follow us across water," he said, and she hoped that was true.

Her butt and thighs ached after so much riding. So did her neck. She hadn't ridden horseback—caballos, they were caballos here—she hadn't ridden a caballo for this long since she was twelve. The mare Trevian had gotten for her was experienced and trail-hardened, but even so, two days in the saddle were taking their toll.

She stretched and walked to the back of the boat, her curiosity captured by the two cylinders at the stern. They were transparent, as tall as she was, and filled with matching swirls of sprites. The spirals, like whirlwinds, reminded her of the fire elementals. The two cylinders rested on copper plates, and as she watched, the plates shifted up with a clunk, making contact with the quartz tube. At the back of the boat, a paddlewheel rotated slowly.

Trevian had followed her. "They always row the boat out of the quay, to get up some movement, but the copper enhances the sprite power enough to turn the wheel."

"How long do they keep the sprites?" she said.

"One trip over and back. Sprite-takers make a good living in Duloc, with the ferries and the streetlights. And the sprite carts," he added. "Are you tired? There are benches inside."

"I need to stand," she said.

"You can see the capital from there," he said, pointing toward the bow. He led the way and she followed, passing their two caballos who munched a pile of hay, tails swishing.

Last night, in the guesthouse, she fell asleep crying. The sheets were clean, the cot was sturdy, but nothing smelled right. She couldn't tell the shape of the room in the dark. The sounds from outside weren't familiar. Everything was different: smells, tastes, the green of the sky. There was nothing here she could hold on to, nothing that was hers.

If she'd crossed the frontera with the Agustos, back to her own world, though, that would still be true. She would have ended up staying with them, in a different house in a different city in a different state. Nothing of hers was left, not her house, not her family, nothing but the gravestone marking Chip's grave. She'd buried her sobs in her pillow.

The breeze off the lake dropped from cool to cold, pulling at her curls, flapping open the rough coat they'd bought in Lily Bend. Another boat passed them, heading the way they'd come. From their boat, someone shouted a hail, and it was returned. Erin watched the reflection of sprite light on the flat water. Closer to the shore, currents of light undulated, the creatures themselves, swarming over the shallows.

The city had lots of wharves. She counted twelve. Buildings spread out along the shoreline like any town back home. They didn't build much higher than two stories here. The exception formed a kind of backdrop to the town, four floors of a greenish substance that seemed to run the length of the city. "What's the long green building?"

"The Copper Coalition," he said. That's where they were headed.

"What's it made of?"

"Dressed stone from the south, from Pais Lewelyn."

Pais Lewelyn. On the road, she'd asked Trevian lots of questions about this continent and the countries. Pais Lewelyn was a country to the south. Madlyn was to the north. The Crescent had long-standing trade agreements with both, and the caravans moved freely among those three. To the east, beyond something called the Desolation—it sounded like a desert—lay the country of Perlarayna. The Crescent had sent trade delegations there, or Trevian thought they had, but Perlarayna had closer ties to the eastern continent. To the west was Shevastin. His ex-fiancé's mother had come from there, he said, and then didn't say anything more about Shevastin.

"What're those fields?" she said, pointing to the lush green grass carpeting a long stretch west of the town. It seemed like a strange place to grow crops.

"Water drains out of the hills into gravel and sand there. The city runs pipes to drain its waste so it doesn't foul the lake. It's always green there."

Leach fields. She wondered how many people lived in Duloc, but decided she'd wait to ask. The headmaster, or maestro, whatever he was, of the Copper Coalition, needed to know about the parasites. And he'd help them decipher the book and figure out how to read the map that bordered the pages, if it was a map like they thought. Maybe they'd have a map of the whole continent she could study. It would be nice to have a clue what the place she'd landed in looked like.

The most important thing was whether the map pinpointed the

frontera, especially the one the parasites used, so she and Trevian could close it.

The waterfront grew larger. People clambered over the moored boats, bustled along the stone quays, and shouted back and forth as they loaded cargo into caballo-drawn carts. To her right, two boats twice the size of the ferry floated, not tied up to a quay, and smaller flat-bottomed boats made their ways back and forth. She squinted but couldn't see cylinders on either one of the larger vessels. "Those two ships," she said. "No sprites?"

"Those are freight barges. Sprite power would barely move one of them when its hold is full. They use oars."

"What do they haul?"

"Copper, mostly, and other charmed metals when they're coming in. And coin going out. They ride the Copper Road."

"The Copper Road? Is that a figure of speech?"

"I... Yes, it is." He seemed to consider. "There are actual roads, like the North Road to Madlyn, the routes the caravans take to the Coalition offices and the bancos, but the lake and some of the rivers are part of it, too. And they move coin as well."

"I thought the Coalition was a college. A place of scholarship."

He nodded. "Scholarship. And trade."

The ferry veered to starboard. From the stern, another loud clank echoed, and the boat slowed immediately, drifting toward the quay. Erin peered over the side, down into the water. It reflected the greenish sky, but she couldn't see the bottom here.

Wharf workers tossed lines to the sailors who pulled the boat in snug against the stretch of stone and tied it fast. Erin went back and untied her mare. She scratched behind the caballo's ears, and the animal tipped her head into Erin's chest, nearly knocking her over. Erin scratched the other ear and followed Trevian as he led his mount down the shallow ramp. Their mounts' shod hooves rang on the stone.

Trevian led her through a double row of warehouses, interspersed with taverns and guesthouses, onto a street paved with flat stones. Plenty of pedestrians used it, and plenty of caballos and caballo-drawn carts. She noticed the differences in clothing. Many people wore the dark, heavy clothes she and Trevian wore, with a bright hat or a scarf, or sometimes a vest, winking with color. Clusters of people in bright, shiny clothing caught her eye: women in longer skirts and tighter bodices; men in bright suits with embroidered jackets, with tall hats or low-crowned ones with curling brims, like bowlers in her world.

Sprite carts clattered along the street, but they were definitely the minority compared to horses—caballos—and caballo-drawn carts.

They left the warehouse district and started up a slight hill. The green building filled the horizon. The place looked gigantic.

Trevian pointed to the left. "Over there are the offices of the Crescent Council, the courts, and the alder's hall."

She nodded. Most of the buildings were made of brick or stone, and many were moneychangers or bancos. On the next block, more shops appeared, some of these trimmed with wood. She could see houses on the low hills rising on either side. They passed a courtyard with a garden and a dancing spray of water.

The Copper Coalition was not a single building, she saw as they approached it, but a compound. A wall of rusted corrugated metal surrounded several green buildings. At each corner of the wall stood a round, three-story tower. A four-story building sat back from the wall. Trevian rode to a door in the rippled metal, dismounted, and rapped on it.

"Trevian Langtree with urgent news for Elmaestro Tregannon," he shouted.

She nudged her mount up alongside his and slid off. Someone peered over the wall, and the tip of a crossbow quarrel pointed in her direction. She tried to act casual as she approached Trevian. "They're pointing arrows at us," she murmured.

"Of course," he said.

A slot opened in the door. "Who do you bring with you?"

"Erin Dosmanos, an out-of-worlder."

The man on the other side didn't answer. Erin heard the clop of hooves, the rattle and clang of metal, and a steady current of voices. She smelled licorice and burnt hair.

"Langtree. The elmaestro expects you." The door opened and a slim man stepped out, clad in dark clothing and a bright red vest. His gaze was level. "Enter."

Trevian had sent a message to the Coalition from Lily Bend, and a letter to his sister, both by fast messenger. From what Erin could tell, fast messengers were like riders for the Pony Express. Their own trip had taken a day longer than usual because they'd stopped at the ruined Ancient city to let the Agustos go through the frontera and back to Erin's world.

They walked into a wide yard, a combination of grass, bare dirt, and flat rock paving. A young woman in the same dark clothing, with a bright yellow vest, stood just inside the gate.

The gatekeeper said, "Beka will stable your caballos. I've sent for Zachary to take you to the elmaestro."

Erin tightened her grip on the reins. "Is this a good idea?"

"We're safe here, Erin," Trevian said.

She wanted to believe him, but he'd said that before. He'd meant it, and he'd still been wrong.

A double line of people in the red vests sparred with staffs while a woman on the sidelines shouted out instructions. Beyond them, a half-dozen people fired crossbow bolts into targets. Two caballos hauled a long wagon filled with scrap metal. Her nose itched with burnt hair and licorice. There was copper here. A lot of it.

She put the reins into Beka's hands.

Licorice was a spicy candy to her. To Trevian, the word meant boozy or drunk. The language tripped her up just when she thought she was getting it. A lot of it was Spanish, or close enough that she could figure out the meaning, but then there were words like "elmaestro," which they put "the" in front of, like they didn't know what the "el" meant. And some words were like old English words, or something even more different. And the names were mixes of just about everything. Trevian, for instance. There was a name you didn't hear every other minute.

She'd been here five days. Maybe things would start making sense.

She pressed her fingers against the face of her phone through the pocket of her vest. The phone held the only remaining pictures of her family. It had about a fifty percent charge. When it died, and it would, it would just be one more piece of trash for this world to pick over. Maybe she'd go home before that happened.

A dark-skinned boy ran up. "Ready, Gatekeeper," he said. He wore a yellow vest like Beka's. Were they the servant class? And were the red vests security? The boy turned to them. "Yor Langtree, and... yorita, my name is Zachary. I'll take you to Elmaestro Tregannon's office."

She fell in behind Trevian. Yor and Yorita seemed like abbreviations of señor and señorita, but she hadn't heard "yora" yet.

They headed up five steps into a short, wide entryway, curving like a rotunda. The walls were covered with tapestries, but she didn't get a chance to examine them, because Zachary was hurrying them up a flight of stairs. The steps sparkled with veins like frost. Mica?

From the easy way he strode along behind Zachary, Trevian had been here before. Had he gone to school here? It sounded more like he'd had tutors. Maybe prospectors had to register or something.

Zachary took them up another flight and down a long hallway, around a corner, and halfway down another hall, lit with golden sprite lamps, before pausing before a door of chased copper. He tapped lightly. "Elmaestro?"

"Enter."

Zachary opened the door. Erin blinked. The room faced south toward the lake, and its long narrow windows brought in light that was a sharp contrast to the shadowed hallway. The light made a halo around the man who sat behind a polished slab of metal, and it cast his face into shadow. "Langtree?" His voice was deep and smooth.

Trevian tipped his head, not quite a bow. "And with me, Erin Dosmanos, an out-of-worlder. We bring urgent news."

"Come in and sit. Zachary, bring a pot of sisuree and some fruit bread."

"Yes, Elmaestro." Zachary disappeared down the hall, and the door glided closed with a soft click.

Trevian motioned to one of the three chairs in front of the elmaestro's work surface. Erin sat down on a sling of leather held by a sturdy metal frame. Trevian sat beside her.

"I've read your message. You spoke of your uncle and some treachery, and a parasite."

Trevian cleared his throat and told the man across the desk their story: the trapped fire elementals, the death of Erin's family, the lantern, the copper helmets, and the people imprisoned, fed on by the pink parasitic creatures.

Tregannon leaned forward. He had a beaky nose and broad cheekbones. His silvery hair fell onto his shoulders. She couldn't make out the color of his eyes. And, wow, a royal purple vest. Setting up his desk so the light haloed him, she thought. He knew exactly what he was doing.

"And you, yorita, you say you came through a frontera, and are from another world?"

"She did," Trevian said. "I saw her, and I saw her two comrades return through it."

The elmaestro seemed skeptical, and she couldn't blame him. He returned his attention to Trevian. "What is it you think your uncle plans to do?"

"He was in league with these creatures, and he plans to enslave the linked worlds."

"And you found him to be...in his wits? Not turvy? Because this sounds like madness."

"He was obsessed," Trevian said, "but not turvy. And I saw what those things did to the people he imprisoned."

Tregannon leaned back in his seat, folded his hands, and directed his next question to Erin. "What land did you say you were from?"

"I'm from a place called California." She felt like she was at a job interview. One that wasn't going well.

He nodded. "And that is on another elemental world."

Erin mirrored his nod.

"People do come here saying they are from out-of-world. Most often they are from some western kingdom or the eastern continent, and we have simply misunderstood their words. Some hope to dupe folks out of their hard-earned coin."

"I'm from another world. My family studied the frontera. I wouldn't have come here at all if fire elementals hadn't driven me here."

"She has a device from her world," Trevian said. "Show him, Erin. Show him the pictures."

Her chest tightened. Every time she pulled the phone out to feed Trevian's whims, she was closer to losing it. She knew the thought wasn't fair. His request made logical sense. She slipped it out of her pocket and powered it on. When the screen lit up, Tregannon grunted. She put in her code and went to the gallery, swiping to the picture she'd taken of Trevian. Had it only been five days ago? She held it out.

He leaned forward, squinting. "It's..." He reached out to touch. "Where'd it go?"

She retrieved the picture. "Do you recognize him?"

Tregannon nodded. "So...we find those by the basket-full. Is that what they were for? Portraits?"

"No. They were for lots of things." She powered it down and slipped it back into her pocket.

"Show him the...other thing," Trevian said.

She shook her head.

Tregannon sat up. "What other thing? What do you carry?"

Trevian frowned at her. "Erin. This is what we came here for."

She said, "You have the parasite. It's an immediate danger. Show him that first."

The door opened. Zachary trudged in carrying a tray. The room filled with spicy steam.

He poured a dark red liquid into cups and passed them around. Slices of a brown loaf studded with purple berries ringed the center of a plate, but Erin just reached for the cup. The beverage tasted a little like pepper and a little like ripe pear.

Tregannon slurped two quick swallows and set down the cup. A silver ring with a large blue stone covered the third knuckle of his index finger, and his nails were clean and shaped... manicured? Different from Trevian, that was for sure.

"Let's see this creature, Langtree," he said.

Trevian dug the jar out of his pack. The creature lay flat and wrinkled at the bottom, like a deflated rubber ball. When Trevian set the jar on the elmaestro's table, it pulsed, part of its skin rising up like a bubble.

Tregannon hissed in a gasp. "What is it?" He leaned forward again but didn't reach for the jar the way he had for the phone. "Some sort of...fish, or...?"

"No." Trevian lifted his hand off the jar. "It has a stinger. It clings to flesh. It has no mouth, no eyes. It seems to breathe. You can crush them beneath your foot or burn them."

Tregannon rose and went to the corner, where he pulled on an embroidered cord. A moment later Zachary came back into the office.

"Have Profesor Machios come to my office at once," Tregannon said. Erin noticed the emphasis on the last syllable of "profesor."

"Yes, Elmaestro."

"I have more," Trevian said. Erin caught her breath. They had agreed not to mention the gold-and-opal collar, but had Trevian changed his mind? Before she should speak, he pulled out a packet wrapped in soft leather, lay it on the desk, and unwrapped it. It held the six stolen pages they'd taken from Oshane.

Tregannon ran his fingers idly along the spiraled border of the nearest page. "We see these now and then too. Forgeries, or works of decoration inspired by the stories of the four artifacts."

"These are from the original book," Trevian said.

"I know you believe that, Langtree," Tregannon said. "Perhaps your uncle even believed it."

"Could you be any more condescending?" Erin said.

Tregannon straightened up, his eyes wide.

Erin pointed at the jar. "He showed you one of those things, which you've never seen before, but you think the pages of the book with aluminum leaves are forgeries?"

"Yorita, that is a living creature, some form of elemental, most likely, just one we haven't encountered before. But you must understand the book is an item of lost history, or myth, an article of faith—"

"She knows more about the book than you ever will," Trevian said.

The elmaestro frowned and straightened up in his chair. "There is no room for insolence in this office."

Oh, yeah, Erin thought. *Definitely* a headmaster. She leaned forward. "It's not insolence. I'm the guardian of the book. My family has had it for generations. Oshane Langtree killed my parents to get it. He killed the guardians of the collar, and he enslaved the guardians of the lantern." She pointed at the jar again. "He's working with those things to control the five elemental worlds. Are you going to do anything to stop him?"

"These artifacts are miracle tales," Tregannon said. "Where is the book now? The lantern? The collar and compass?"

"The lantern returned to my world," Erin said.

"And the collar is safe."

"The holder of the compass escaped Oshane's attack through her frontera," Erin said. They had no idea where Wing Mei was, even what world she was in, but she sure wasn't going to say that.

When she looked at Trevian, he just raised his eyebrows. Sighing, she opened up her messenger bag. They'd forced her hand, the two of them. She didn't completely trust this Tregannon guy or his arrogance, but the Copper Coalition was supposed to help her. And she couldn't get help without sharing the book, so she pulled it out and set it on the desk next to the loose pages.

Tregannon stared. He took a breath, and another. "May I open it?" It was the first time he'd asked permission.

She nodded.

There was a touch of reverence in his gesture as he opened the book. "I have seen pages before, of course," he said. "I know someone who claims to have two from the original. And I've seen many

89

attempts to create a book, or fragments of it. How long has this been in your world?"

"Over two hundred years."

He frowned at the text. "Can you read it?"

"Most of it."

"It looks strange to me, archaic, I suppose."

Erin said, "It looks a lot like my language, especially farther back. We think they loaded newer pages from the front."

Tregannon stood up as his office door opened.

Zachary said, "Profesor Machios, Elmaestro."

The newcomer wore a blue tunic rather than a vest. His black hedgerow of a mustache grabbed Erin's attention before anything else. She hadn't seen any other mustaches, or beards, so far. The hair hanging in curls to his shoulders matched it. With a tricorn hat with feathers, he could have been in a Musketeers movie.

"What do you have for me, Elmaestro?" he said. His gaze flicked over her and Trevian, and stopped at the jar. His eyes widened.

"A parasite. A dangerous one. And a mystery." Tregannon closed the book. "Zachary, find Profesor Stillwater and have her meet us in the study."

Zachary nodded and hurried off again.

"Join us." Tregannon picked up the jar with care and handed it to Machios.

Trevian said, "Do not touch this with your bare flesh, or let it touch you. It attaches itself, and it's possible it controls thought."

"What *is* it?"

"That's what we must decide," Tregannon said. "Yorita Dosmanos, will you bring your book, please?"

She picked it up and waited while Trevian wrapped up the loose pages.

The few people on the stairs stepped against the wall to let them pass. On the ground floor, Tregannon said, "Machios, I want to know what that creature is by the end of the day."

"I doubt I can solve the mystery so quickly, but I will do what I can." Machios excused himself, holding the jar carefully.

Tregannon had called it a study, but there were no books. Lines of long tables and simple chairs marched down its length. Maybe the place had a library somewhere else.

As they came into the room, a door at the other end opened. A tall dark-skinned woman came in. Like Machios, she wore a dark blue tunic, and a blue band held her black dandelion-fluff hair off her face. "You sent for me, Elmaestro?"

"Yes. We have visitors who have brought us news of a threat. And something of a challenge for you, Ruth, I think." He brought the woman up to speed, capturing all the important points in a couple of minutes. Erin felt a pinch of admiration for him.

"You believe it is truly *the* book?" Stillwater looked at Erin. "We've seen versions before."

"I'm not from your world. It's been in the family a long time, and it's about magic. Charms. So, yes, I think it's the real book."

"Show them the puerta," Trevian said. "That should remove any doubt."

A wavelet of anxiety rippled through Erin's stomach. Trevian was pushing her, and she didn't like it. The book was her responsibility. On the other hand, a demonstration of a puerta should end the skepticism. She put the bag on one of the long tables and pulled out the book again, opening it to a page with a puerta, one of the active blue stones.

Trevian glanced around. "Do you have a scrap of paper or cloth?" he said. "Something you can lose."

Stillwater walked over to the table and opened a drawer. She pulled out a piece of the same bulky paper Trevian's letters were written on and tore a strip off the end. "Will this do?"

Erin nodded. "Thanks." She inhaled, held the paper by the end so the other end waved gently over the stone and spoke the word to activate the puerta. She let go as the paper tugged itself out of her grasp and vanished.

The two scholars and the headmaster gasped.

"You let me *touch* that?" Tregannon said.

"Where'd it go?" Stillwater said.

Erin directed her words to the elmaestro. "It needs a word to activate it. It wouldn't have hurt you." To Stillwater, "I don't know. Another elemental world, probably."

"What did the word mean?" Stillwater said. She tore off another strip. Plainly, she wanted Erin to repeat the trick.

"I don't know. It's the word that opens the puertas. They've been marked with the blue stones." She looked up at each of them. "Do you recognize these stones? We call them opals."

Tregannon and Stillwater both shook their heads.

"There were six once. Three will still open. They're...we think they work like the frontera do, only they're smaller. I mean, you have to activate a frontera, right?"

"Is it the same charm as the one to open a frontera?" Stillwater asked.

Erin shook her head.

"A puerta ate an earth elemental that attacked me," Trevian said. "Erin saved my leg."

Stillwater raised her eyebrows. "Harald Stuart could have used this charm."

Tregannon snorted. "Stuart." He smoothed his purple vest. "Right now, we need to discover the source, and purpose, of these creatures."

Erin said, "And close the frontera they're using."

Tregannon pointed his chin at the book. "The artifact would be better kept in our strong room."

"No." Erin closed up the book and stuffed it back in the bag, stepping away from the table so she had a clear path to the door. She'd seen it coming. Sooner or later, everyone wanted the book.

Trevian shifted also, to stand beside her.

"We can keep it safe," Tregannon said.

"I'm the book's guardian," Erin said. "It stays with me."

Tregannon straightened up again. He was a big man, and Erin decided he was used to using his height and bulk to get what he wanted.

"We hold half the treasury of the Crescent in our strong room," he said. "There's no place safer in the country."

"Erin vanquished an earth elemental and two fire elementals and fought off my murderous uncle," Trevian said. "And she is the book's guardian."

"Perhaps the book needs to stay with its guardian family," Still-water said.

Tregannon gave the rolling-shouldered shrug. "Very well. I think it is a foolish choice, but it's yours to make."

Stillwater faced Erin. "Will you let me study the book with you? It is a great opportunity for us."

"Of course. We came here because I need some help with it, and we haven't had a chance to study the loose pages, or even put them back in the book."

"We should send for Harald," the scholar said.

Tregannon *hmphed*. "Stuart again. Do not bring him here, Ruth."

"I think we must, Elmaestro."

"No. He can send his pages or copies."

Stillwater raised her chin but didn't argue. "Erin, Trevian, let me show you to your rooms and the bathhouse." She led them upstairs.

On the third floor, someone called Stillwater's name, followed by "Yor Langtree!" They stopped as a panting woman in a yellow vest ran up to them.

"A message for you, Yor, by fast messenger." She pushed a square of paper into his hand.

"Thank you." Trevian stared at the paper in his hand. "It's from my sister."

Erin felt cold suddenly. "Is it…Oshane? Did he go to White Bluffs?"

He unfolded the letter. As he read, he bit his lower lip and his body stiffened.

"Trevian? Are you all right? Has something happened to your sister?"

"I… No." He crumpled the paper and shoved it into his trousers pocket. "It's my father."

6

Mircoles, 18 Uno, Year 331

Aideen's letter tugged at him, worse than the healing wound in his shoulder.

Trevian:

I will be careful of our uncle should he appear.

Our father lies gravely ill, unable to move or speak. You know the nature of his will—he has left you as his heir, not me. I fear for the worst and I fear for the future of the Langtree Company should the worst happen. I need you here. I know I have no words that will move you, so I can only write, please come home.

Your sister,

Aideen

I have no words that will move you, as if she thought he had no regard for her. As if she thought he didn't love her. *Did* she think that?

But he could not go home now. The frontera needed to be found and closed, the parasites stopped. There was nothing he could do to heal his father, and Aideen was the more capable Langtree in any case.

"Are you all right?" Erin leaned against the door of her room.

He said, "Composing a reply to my sister in my thoughts."

"Do you need to go home?"

He shook his head. "I cannot. I have to see this through."

"I can deal with the frontera."

"Erin, you are strong and smart, but you do not know us, this land. You need a guide."

"Stillwater could find me one."

"You would go without me," he said.

She sighed. "I don't want to, but if your family needs you, if you need to go back, I understand."

"It is my family, my uncle, who started this. And there is nothing I can do for my father. It is in the hands of the Mother now. Aideen has my proxy, and she will manage the company well. I only need to reassure her." It was time to change the subject. "There is no place safer than the Copper Coalition's strong room."

"No."

"I only think—"

She shook her head. "Everyone wants to get their hands on this book. I'm not letting go of it. That's just not happening."

"You don't trust the elmaestro, and I don't know why. He is a good man."

"Yeah, he might be." Erin gripped the bag and crossed her other arm over it. He wondered if she knew she was doing it. "He might be just like your uncle. Or he just might think he knows better than I do."

"Well, he does. He's the leader of the Copper Coalition. He knows more than either of us."

"He cares about making a profit."

She spoke as if it were shameful. "Yes," he said. "The Coalition cares about profit, about the value of currency, and the price of the charmed metals. That's its purpose."

"So he wouldn't care much about some ancient artifact, unless he could profit from it."

"He is worried about those creatures. He is doing his best to protect the Crescent. He will keep the book safe."

She stared at him. "I'm trying to trust him, Trevian, I am. But don't ask me to give up the book."

"Did I not stay at your side?" he said.

She blinked and nodded. "Yes, you did. Thank you."

"You understand about the sprite lamp?" he said, to change the subject.

She rolled her eyes upward. "You were here when Stillwater explained it and told me where the latrine is. And we're just dropping off our stuff, right? Do I have time to take a bath?"

"Yes. I must write to Aideen."

He entered his room. A whiterock brazier, already filled, sat in the corner, a sparker and a pile of dry leaves beside it. These rooms were all the same, comfortable but simple. A desk and chair sat in the corner, and a sprite danced in the quartz orb on the desk's corner, a black lampcloth folded beside the lamp. Next to the bed, a stand held a metal pitcher and a drinking cup. Trevian set his knapsack on the bench along the wall, pulled out the chair, and sat down at the desk.

Paper and pencil waited in the shallow drawer.

He stared at the page, while the sprite lit on the base of the orb, circled about, lit, and circled again, while the clink of metal and the music of voices reached him through the window as the Coalition went about its work.

Dear Aideen:

I am saddened to hear of our father's illness, but I know the doctors and healers are doing all they can. I cannot return home. The fate of our world—

He crossed that out.

Our world is at risk, and I can provide some small help to save it. You have my proxy, and you are the smarter and more practical of the Langtree children. Everyone in White Bluffs knows this. With your guidance, the company will be safe. I will return as soon as I can.

It did not say what it needed to say. Well, he'd read it later, with a clear head, and write something better.

Aideen thought him selfish, and she was right. Selfishness had driven him to leave Ilsanja Silvestro at the sheriff's house in Merrylake Landing. Selfishness, and a sense of desperation, as if some vital thing he needed to do slipped away from him. And anger, anger at his father and his father's secrets. But he could have broken the marriage pledge quietly and decorously, not abandoned his promised bride in the middle of the night. Not allowing her to be drugged and abducted in the first place, by a man he had called a friend.

He had never been able to express to Aideen the rage he felt toward their father. Aideen glided through her life like a flock of sprites over water, graceful and serene, managing the household after their mother fled, helping with the company ledgers, arranging the necessary social engagements, studying the works at the cages, never hesitating, never doubting. Only stubbornness kept Oswald Langtree from naming his daughter his heir, for she *was* his heir in all the important ways.

Someone tapped at the door. "You ready?" Erin called.

When he opened it, she stood with one hand on her hip, her curls still wet, and his heart lifted a bit.

"Ready," he said.

E rin looked around the large ground floor room. Two walls were lined with shelves filled with books. Finally, books. Along one wall ran a mosaic, a continental map. The Crescent really was a crescent, the horns pointing up. There were *lots* of mountains.

They'd passed many rooms. Erin could have been in a bank, or an office. This room was the closest to a library she'd seen so far.

Stillwater stopped before a long central table with a carved surface. "I thought of this," she said, gesturing. Erin peered down. The table held a detail from the wall mosaic, not just carved but embossed, a three-dimensional topographical map.

"Is this the Crescent?"

Stillwater nodded. "This one's quite old, and with earth shudders and storms, possibly not completely accurate. Still, it's the *most* accurate, and you can see where we've updated things, like the Copper Road, for instance."

"It shows no towns," Trevian said.

"They're marked with the green stone squares or crosses, but there is no detail."

Erin touched a series of inlaid triangles in the map's upper left corner. "And these? Trees?"

"Yes, the northwest. There's Boskay, and that line of silver wire is the Nortay River."

Boskay, Erin thought...like Spanish for forest. Her eye was drawn by a design south of the trees and west of the wire line marking the river. Two lines of wire ran north-south-ish, an inverted V, tantalizingly familiar. At the center of the space between the two branches sat a red triangular stone. "What's this?"

Stillwater leaned closer. "Ah. Pendrelle Delta. That stone marks a place of Ancient. It's not a prospector's site, something different."

Trevian leaned in too. "What?"

"Hard to say. The Ancient records show a fierce battle there, and people have avoided it ever since."

The design teased Erin's memory, dancing just out of her grasp. "I've *seen* this." She walked over to a neighboring table and pulled out the book. Stillwater followed. The woman studied the book with an expression combining awe with desire, and it made Erin a little nervous. Maybe Tregannon wasn't the only one to watch out for. Stillwater was the one who knew about the old languages, though.

Erin turned pages. Stillwater sighed and reached out tentatively, touching the edge of a page with her forefinger. "I envy you this knowledge," she said.

"Um," Erin said.

Trevian joined them. "Erin is an able guardian," he said.

Stillwater nodded.

Erin stopped and tapped a design, four pages in, in the lower right corner, an inverted V with a socket for a stone in the center. "Am I crazy," she said, "or is that the same design?"

"If crazy means turvy, then you are not," Stillwater said. "It's similar, even to the distance from the socket between the two branches. Is it another puerta like the one you showed us?"

"It might have been, but the stone's gone now."

"When did that happen?"

"Before the book came down to me," Erin said. She traced the carvings with her fingers. "Do you have any really sheer paper? Trevian and I made a rubbing of these designs, but the paper is too thick to lay over your map. If you had something we could see through..."

"I know just what would work," Stillwater said.

Trevian cleared his throat. "Before we begin, Erin, we should see where the loose pages fit."

"You're right."

Stillwater looked up from the book. "I've sent for someone I know. He thinks he has two pages from the book. I thought they were forgeries until I saw yours." She walked away and pulled on a braided cord hanging from the ceiling. When a young woman in a yellow vest entered, Stillwater gave directions Erin couldn't hear.

It wasn't easy matching the stolen pages. If a page ended in midsentence, it was possible to make an informed guess about the rest of the text, but one of the pages featured only diagrams. Erin had to read each page to see if the illustrations were referenced.

Two people with orange vests carried in a roll of fabric, and Stillwater directed them to a neighboring table.

"Erin, look at this one," Trevian said. "It's blank. The border, I mean." He held it out to her. It was the first aluminum sheet she had seen without the decorative border. "What does that mean?"

"Maybe the original page was damaged, and they recopied it but left off the border?"

"That doesn't hold much promise for our map."

She took the page. "I'll try to see where it fits." She set it aside, picked up the final loose page, and stopped. Her heart skipped. "Trevian?"

He peered around the page. "By the Mother," he said.

"Yeah." The page held a drawing of a parasite. There were two views. The second one showed one apparently cut open and cross-sectioned. The stamped words in tiny print were hard to read, and she squinted, leaning down until her nose nearly touched the page. "Auditory," she read, following an arrow pointing to a dot within the creature.

"Auditory?" Stillwater cocked her head. "It comes from an Ancient word. It's related to hearing."

"They were studying them," Trevian said. "When the book was created. They were here then?"

Erin nibbled on her lower lip, skeptical. "This page wasn't part of the book when it came to us," she said. "Do you have a way to test the age of metal?"

Trevian snorted. "If it hasn't rusted, or tarnished? No."

"The language might tell us," Stillwater said. She walked back over. Erin pushed the page over to her but kept her hands on it. "Visual," Stillwater said. "That word's the same. It pertains to sight."

"They believed the parasites could see and hear."

The door flew open with a bang, and Tregannon strode in. He was frowning. He shifted his frown and a glare to the profesor. "Did you send for Stuart against my wishes?"

"I did." Stillwater sounded calm. She waved her open hand across the book. "He believes he has two pages of the book. We need them."

"He could send them by messenger."

"Do you think he'd let them out of his sight, Elmaestro?"

"You defied me, Ruth."

"I made a necessary decision, and I notified you immediately." The woman scholar seemed calm, but wasn't giving ground.

"A caravan arrives in one hour, and a large group of prospectors soon after. I don't need Stuart turning my Coalition into a carnival," Tregannon said, but now he just sounded like he was grumbling.

"He won't. He knows our geography better than anyone, Elmaestro. You yourself have said he can be a help when it comes to finding caves and passes, which is most likely what we seek. And he has those pages."

Tregannon huffed. "Perhaps he won't need to be here long." He swept over to one of the desks and sat down.

Stillwater returned to her study of the pages as if nothing had happened. Erin caught Trevian's eye and he grinned.

"What of the book and the map? What are you all doing over there?" Tregannon sounded grumpy.

"Before we can apply the border drawings as an overlay to the map, Elmaestro, we need the book as complete as possible."

"It's good to prepare," Tregannon said, "but you won't start today. I need the scribes."

"What?" Erin spun around to face him. "I thought you knew this was important!"

"It is, but so is the work—the regular work—of the Coalition," Tregannon said.

"You can't spare us a couple of scribes?"

"I have a scheduled caravan and an unscheduled prospector group from a new claim just recently discovered. Even with all the scribes, we'll most likely be working past sunset. If you wanted to leave the book with us, I could have them start as soon as they—"

"No."

Trevian touched her arm. "Erin? We need to shop for provisions anyway. We can go now. Let us start on the book tomorrow, when we can devote all day to it."

Tregannon had acted like he understood the urgency, but here he was putting routine work ahead of this. "We don't know what the parasites might be doing, like, right now," she said.

Trevian nodded. "And if we were tracing the borders of the book at this very moment, we still wouldn't know what the parasites were doing," he said.

She couldn't argue the logic. "Okay, fine. By all means, let's go shopping."

He tapped the cross-sectioned parasite image. "What of this page?"

"Here." Erin slipped it into the book where she thought it fit. She didn't have a way to create a new link, like the copper rings holding the intact pages.

Stillwater opened a drawer under the table and pulled out a skein of copper wire. "Can you make it fast with this?"

"Do you have cutters?"

Stillwater nodded and produced a pair of cutters. Erin made a double ring of wire, holding the pages in place. They didn't turn anywhere near as smoothly as the intact sheets, but it kept the page in place.

They worked for fifteen minutes. Outside, odd footsteps sounded in the hallway, one step clacking like a wooden shoe on tile. "Ruth! Ruth Stillwater!"

Tregannon sighed loudly, stood up, and smoothed his vest.

The door swung open, bouncing off the wall. A man filled the doorway. He was taller than Trevian and broader than Tregannon, most of the bulk in his shoulders. He wore black, with a black and gold vest, a coloring combination Erin didn't remember seeing before. "You promised me mysteries!"

Stillwater advanced on him, holding out both hands. "And I deliver on my promises, Harald."

He squeezed her hands. "I've brought my offering to the table. Do you think you have an authentic artifact? Not another artificer with a clever story?" He scanned the room. "Tregannon, in among the workers?"

Tregannon stiffened up even more. "Stuart."

"Come meet my out-of-worlder friend and see what she brings," Stillwater said.

His eyes gleamed like blue topaz in a face mostly obscured by a reddish beard. He wore a black flat-brimmed hat like Trevian's. Erin had to tilt her head back to make eye contact. He rolled forward, hip first like a sidestep. His footfall snapped down, some hard surface against the floor, and the next step was a quiet scuff. Then she got it; he used a prosthetic. His left leg was carved out of wood or something, crisscrossed with copper wire and medallions.

"Keen eye, yorita. I'm a leg short, a flesh leg anyway, or half of one." He put out his hand. "Harald Stuart. Your name?"

"Erin Dosmanos."

"Dosmanos, related to the sprite-cart inventor?"

"Unlikely."

"What's your story then?" His hand was warm, and she liked his firm grip, but his physical presence was overwhelming, and she stepped back without meaning to. Trevian moved to her side.

"Trevian Langtree," he said, putting out his hand. It looked like a challenge, but if it was, Stuart didn't take the bait.

"Oswald Langtree's copper-hunting son? I thought you were prospecting south of here."

"I—I was," Trevian said. "How did you…? I met Erin, and we uncovered a threat to the Crescent."

"And so you came, not to the Justice Arm of the Crescent Council, which is charged with keeping the country's peace, but to the Copper Coalition."

Tregannon said, "The threat is beyond the reach of the Justice Arm of the Council. It involves the frontera and elemental creatures."

Stuart leaned against the table. He glanced over at the book. Erin had the feeling he had noticed every detail, the loose pages, the stamped writing, everything.

He crossed his arms and smiled at Stillwater. "Very well, a mystery tale for a spring day. Tell me all."

Stillwater hesitated, glancing at Tregannon. The elmaestro waved his hand, obviously exasperated, clearly handing the meeting off to her. Stillwater explained, and Stuart listened without interruption.

A little silence fell when she finished. Stuart looked at Erin, but he aimed his words at Stillwater. "You believe this young woman is from out-of-world."

"I do."

"Not from the eastern continent, or Pais Lewelyn, or even from a small mountain town? She's not a woman with an ear for a story, or a turviness?"

"No," Stillwater said. "We can show you proof. She carries one of the plaques we find in the Ancient."

"Many people carry plaques or pieces of them. They hold a charm well."

"Hers is alive," Stillwater said. "It radiates light and it holds an image of Langtree."

Erin tried to breathe around the tension welling up in her chest. They were going to ask to see the phone again, and since it was the best proof she had, she couldn't refuse to show it.

His gaze fixed on Erin. "You're an artist?"

"Not at all." She pulled out the phone and powered it on. He leaned forward like a striking cat when it chirped and the welcome screen came up. "How?" he said. "Does an elemental power it?"

"Electricity powers it, produced chemically," she said.

He peered down at her and suddenly folded his hands over hers and the phone. "You are reluctant to show me this, why?"

"Not reluctant. Sad."

He continued to stare. After a few seconds, she said, "One thing we used them for was taking images of friends, family, people we love. I have a picture of my family on here. It's all I have left of them."

"So it should be a source of comfort."

"The power is provided by a battery, a storage device. Once it runs out, I will never be able to power it on again. I'll lose them. Again."

She wanted to look away from his stare, but she was afraid she'd start crying if she did.

He squeezed her hands. "Send it to sleep, then."

"But you wanted—"

"I don't need to see any more to know it's the only active plaque I've ever seen."

"Thank you." She powered off the phone.

He swept his hand toward the worktable. "And this is the book with aluminum leaves, one of the four artifacts." He wore a pouch slung across his body, the way Erin carried her messenger bag, and he opened the flap and pulled out a bundle wrapped in gleaming yellow fabric. "I've always wondered if it was imaginary, even with these pages." He unwrapped them.

"Is that silk?"

"It is, and not just tree silk, but a spider silk blend," he said. Erin wondered what "tree silk" was. He set the plates on the table and uncovered them. They had the swirling borders, and Erin felt sure they were genuine.

"Do you know what they say?" she said.

"They're both badly scratched. One talks about frontera and includes some charm. The other shows an image carved into the body with a piece of loomin. A morbid tidbit I've never cared for. I've had enough carving done on my body."

"How did you get these?" Erin said. She studied the page about frontera. Here was the rest of the section on how to close one. This was the page they needed.

Behind him, Tregannon snorted. "A mestengo brawl," he said.

"I was never a mestengo," Stuart said. His voice sounded jovial, but Erin picked up a bit of an edge.

"As good as."

Stuart reached out to touch the border of the book. "I earned my coin with my wit, my knowledge, and my body, not by wearing a purple vest and making rules to drive coin into my strong room rather than into the purses of working people."

"You've never bothered to—"

"Elmaestro. Justice Arm." Stillwater didn't raise her voice, but she definitely put a teacher-edge on it. "Can we confine ourselves to dealing with the threat of this invading parasite?"

A silence fell, broken only by heavy breathing from both men. Her back to them both, Erin rolled her eyes. Alpha males. Some things transcended worlds.

Stuart spoke again, answering Erin's question as if there'd never been an interruption. "I was part of an expedition beyond the Desolation, to visit the eastern continent. A mestengo band attacked us. We fended them off, but I was worried they'd be back, so we followed them to their lair. They'd clearly raided other trading caravans, and among their goods, I found these."

"You could have given them to us," Tregannon said, "where we study such things."

"I could have."

"What happened to the mestengos?" Erin said.

"They found justice."

"Oh." She decided not to ask any more questions.

"We have one of the parasites," Stillwater said. "Machios is studying it."

"An elemental?" Stuart tapped his artificial leg. "A species of earth elemental, maybe?"

"Perhaps." Tregannon cleared his throat. "Oshane Langtree is part of this threat, whatever it is."

"Oshane Langtree," Stuart said thoughtfully. "So, are you close to your uncle, Yor Langtree?"

"He lied to me, tried to imprison me, and then he stabbed me," Trevian said. "He has taken lives. He killed Erin's parents, and he wants to steal the book. He is a villain."

Stuart said quietly, "And are you close?"

Erin tensed, knowing Trevian's temper, but he said simply, "If we ever were, we are no longer."

"How did he escape?"

Erin butted in. "He flew away. Some air elemental thing carried him off."

Stuart nodded. "He is a great collector of charms, Oshane Langtree."

"You know him?"

"By reputation," Stuart said. "When warrants come for trafficking in charms or rare Ancient objects of nearly any type, often the name of Oshane Langtree comes into the story. Langtree won the object he sold them by playing dice. Langtree came across the remains of an unlucky copper-hunter killed by an oso and searched the body. He found a mysterious satchel near the site of an earth elemental feeding, with a charmed artifact inside. He's elusive."

"He has a tethered air elemental," Trevian said. "He trapped two joven flames to do his killing for him."

"And he could cross frontera," Erin said. "He used a charm from the book. He was in my world for a couple of years, we think. He might have gone back and forth; we had no way of knowing."

"Your father has no tender feelings for him," Stuart said.

"My father will not speak Oshane's name. They fought when I was a child, and Oshane never returned to our house. I do not know the reason."

Stuart narrowed his eyes slightly. The faint smile did not slip. "There are rumors about the reason."

Trevian didn't look away. "I've heard them. My mother, of course. She left shortly after he did."

Erin willed herself not to stare. This was the first time she had heard anything about Trevian's mother. And...she'd gone off with Oshane?

"Do you believe them?"

Trevian shrugged. "My mother was a good jefa, a good boss wife to a rising boss, but she was not happy. Her happiness was of no interest to my father. I always assumed she went west, into Shevastin." He drew in a deep breath and squared his shoulders. "Oshane didn't mention her when he was holding me captive, and she was not with him then."

"Do you resent her?"

Stillwater shifted. "Harald, these questions—"

"It's all right. Resent her for leaving, you mean? No, actually, my mother was my icon. I only wish I had followed her example years sooner."

Stuart nodded as if another question had been answered for him. "So. These pages. I understand the desire to assemble the book, but why is it the first thing we are doing instead of hunting down these creatures?"

Erin told him their theory about the borders, and the table map.

"When will you start?" Stuart said.

"Tomorrow morning, I guess."

He rubbed his hands together. "Then I will be here. I wish to see this creature, and perhaps I can help."

Tregannon snorted and started to speak, but Stuart talked over him. "This is a matter of the safety of the Crescent. As a justice arm, I should be here, and I will make a report to the Council."

"We'll make a report together," Tregannon said.

After a moment, Stuart nodded.

Stillwater said, "What of your pages, Harald? Shall we copy them first? Do you want them returned?"

Harald shook his head. "Plainly they are not mine." He made a rolling gesture with his hand. "They have found their home, and here they belong."

7

Mircoles, 18 Uno, Year 331

Caballos, carts, and people jammed the courtyard. Someone had set up three lines of tables in a U, lined with chairs. A row of wagons, covered with thick cloth tarps, snaked across the space and out the gate. The caballos pawed the ground, and apprentices led groups of saddle mounts back and forth to cool them down. Erin counted at least ten people in the red vests among the throng, their gazes scanning the crowd as they walked. Voices and the jangle of tack bounced off the walls. Except for the caballos and all the scrap metal, it could have been opening day of a cannabis festival.

"What is this?" It was the largest gathering of people Erin had seen here so far.

"A caravan." Trevian pointed to the chairs behind the tables. "Those in the lavender vests with the purple piping? They are assayers. The caravan should move quickly because there is already a statement of lading. The wagons' contents must simply match the forms. Caravan leaders draw their pay directly from the Coalition." He swept his arm the other way. "Those in the blue and green are the Crescent Council tax collectors."

There was some commotion at the gate, where a group of men and women in the dark clothing Trevian preferred milled around.

"Now, those are prospectors," he said. "They take more work. The assayers define and value every item the prospector brings up, and each scribe creates a record and notes down the value as set by the assayer. The scribe makes two copies of the record. The Coalition keeps the original, the prospector gets the others."

"It's not usually like this?" she said as they skirted a man and woman who had pushed a wheelbarrow filled with lengths of copper cable through the gate.

Trevian guided her around a knot of people. "It's not strange for two groups to arrive at the same time, but this is a large crowd."

"Did you come all the way here?"

He shook his head, slipping around a man stooped under the burden of a tall pack. "Once or twice only. Lily Bend has an assay office and a banco. I brought my findings there."

The gatekeeper called a sprite cart for them. Trevian helped her in and gave the driver directions. Erin sat back and tried to relax. "Tregannon is putting profit ahead of the safety of his world."

Trevian shook his head without looking at her. "He isn't. He believes he can do both."

She knew the map idea was a long shot, but she hadn't come all this way to go shopping. Tregannon was wrong.

They rolled down a street of tall narrow houses with more wood and less stone, reminding Erin of Victorians back home. The lake rippled ahead of them as they left the houses behind, coming into an area filled with single-story shops and eateries. They weren't near the busy waterfront with its wharves and warehouses. "BOTANICA" read a small sign in steel letters, and Trevian had the driver let them out in front of it.

"What are we getting here?" she said, picturing prayer candles in tall jars.

"Medicine. And tea."

The inside was warm, well-lit, and smelled like tea, or maybe tobacco, or just a lot of herbs. She studied the dark glass jars—and some containers that looked like hard plastic—each precisely labeled.

Trevian lifted down a container labeled *Singeweed Powder* followed by a date.

"What's that do?"

"It slows infection. I know you have your salve, but that won't last forever."

She pointed at a dark glass jar, *Willowbark*. "Is that to ease pain?"

"Yes and bring down a fever." He bought the willowbark and a jar of something called saintswort. After some discussion with the clerk, he added a needle and thread, several folds of cotton or linen, and some tea.

They left the botanica. The street, while still quiet, had filled up with sprite carts and people in clean, simple brown and white garments carrying bulky market baskets.

"That is the promenade," Trevian said, pointing, as they headed toward the lake. A wide sidewalk, paved with white stones, ran close to the shore of the lake. Lampposts of black pipe like PVC stood at regular intervals along the stone balustrade, and banners in gold, green, blue, and silver hung from the posts, rippling slightly in the cool breeze. There were many people strolling along it, dressed in the more colorful and less practical clothing, the fitted skirts and jackets, elaborate hats.

"This is the oldest part of the capital," Trevian said as they wove their way across the street. "The waterfront was originally here, before they crafted the larger freight vessels and built the stone wharves."

Through the window of a storefront they passed, gleaming fabrics in rich colors draped and curved on a stand. "What's this? A dress shop?"

"A tailor's. They're doing well, they've got spider silk as well as tree silk."

"What's tree silk?"

"We import it from Pais Lewelyn. When the tree blossoms, the blooms are picked and pounded. The fibers, fine and very strong, can be woven. Spider silk is much more expensive and comes mostly from the eastern continent."

They went into another store where Trevian bought dried fruit, two kinds of jerky, and some shriveled bluish berries he said was sisuree. "Are you hungry?" he said. "One of the taverns Stillwater mentioned is only a block away."

"I'm not. I'd like to check out the promenade," she said.

He nodded. They made their way back up their street. She stopped and tapped one of the lampposts. It thumped dully, clearly hollow. The substance was smooth and thick. Clearly PVC pipe, and the herb jars were probably made of it too. They must find tons of it here.

The breeze coming off the lake smelled like fresh water, with a touch of something sharp, like fresh oregano. Another scent, salty and savory, teased her nose. "What do I smell?"

"Roasted tree-beans." He pointed to a wheeled cart, like a mall kiosk back home. "There is a mead-seller and a water-seller too."

Trevian bought some roasted tree-beans, served in a cloth pouch, and offered them to her. She'd expected peanuts. The shape was similar, but the taste was more like pistachios. She swallowed and said, "Trevian, tell me what you know about your history."

"You would do better to hear it from Stillwater."

"I'd rather hear it from you. Tell me about the Ancient and when the earth turned. And then what happened."

"Very well."

Erin walked at his side as he told her the story.

In the time of the Ancient, people created wonders. They shared thoughts from leagues and leagues away; they rode the sky in carts made of loomin. They put charmed metal into the bodies of people to make them healthy. And as nations they all shared the same goals of prosperity and peace.

"Okay, I'm pretty sure *that's* not true," Erin said.

"I see now 'sharing their thoughts' might have meant using the plaque—the device you carry." He sat down on the balustrade, and she joined him.

He continued. He had grown up thinking of it as mythology more than history, but Erin could translate some of what he was describing into her own experience. The people from three centuries earlier here sounded just about where her world was now.

Then the earth turned, and the elementals awoke. The great charms of the Ancients stopped working. Many thought somehow the elementals had absorbed the charmed energy, but it was only a theory.

In the next several years of the Interval, people pulled together, rebuilding. Some discovered in themselves the ability to place charms onto certain metals, and the occupation of charmcaster grew.

People found the frontera that had bloomed when the earth had turned. Some people were able to open frontera and pass through them—and return.

At least, Trevian thought this was what had happened.

With the charms and the frontera, and the stories of neighboring worlds, came the rise of the warlords, who terrorized, conquered, and began to gather to themselves all the charms. And then the stories arose of four artifacts created to protect the linked worlds, and four families, each entrusted with one, sent into a sister world to hide the artifacts from the warlords.

Eventually, people banded together in enough force to overthrow them. The Copper Coalition formed, and then nations, and the modern age had begun.

She nodded. "And the elementals awoke at the same time the earth shifted?"

"Yes." He was quiet, and then he undercut the confidence of his answer. "I think so. At least, I've always thought so before now. Was that wrong? Did the elementals cause the earth to turn?"

"I've got no clue. I mean, I don't know." At least she understood the basics better. She wasn't sure it helped.

From the time the Crescent and its neighboring countries were formed, things got more organized. He explained the Crescent Council and what a justice arm was, kind of like an FBI agent. Or a US Marshall, she wasn't sure.

After a while, he stopped speaking. They sat in comfortable silence, listening to the whisper of the water on the shore.

"Now I'm getting hungry," she said.

He hopped off the balustrade and offered her his arm. She grinned and took it.

The trees and shrubs that decorated the mercantile street were starting to bud out. "What month is this?" she said.

"Uno."

"Uno? Is this winter? I thought it was spring."

"It is." He glanced sideways at her. "The new year starts the first day of spring, which we calculate because of the way the sun seems to move along the horizon..."

"Yeah, I know. You named your months after numbers?"

He shrugged. "It was practical."

"One through twelve?"

"One through thirteen."

"Thirteen months?" She got distracted by the smell of grilling meat.

"This is the place," Trevian said. He led her through. Inside it was dark, but the server pointed out the back, and they entered a walled garden filled with lush plants in tubs. Over the short wall, Erin could see the lake. They found a table near the wall. When they had ordered, Erin said again, "Thirteen months?"

"Of course. Thirteen months, four sennights each, with a Long Year every other year."

"A long year."

"Apparently, our world takes more than a year to travel around the sun, so we add two days every other year. It's a time for festivals, games for children—treasure hunts are common." He nodded his thanks to the server and sipped from a metal tankard. "Good ale."

Long Year was a super leap year. She sipped her ale.

A server brought their food. They'd ordered lamb. Beef seemed non-existent, and she hadn't heard anyone mention milk, either, even though they did have a soft, tangy cheese. Her chop came with vegetables in a peppery sauce. As she ate, she tried to put the pieces together in her mind. It was all still strange.

Trevian was surprised to see the caravan had left. A few remaining prospectors milled around in the courtyard, but apprentices had hauled off the chairs and folded up all but two of the tables. "There may be a scribe available now," he said.

"Let's go, then," said Erin.

Stillwater and Justice Arm Stuart waited for them, along with two scribes. Stuart had seen the parasite and he seemed thoughtful, quieter. Erin immediately pulled out the book and started to work with Stillwater. Trevian stood at the end of the table, feeling useless. Erin's book drew her attention like a piece of lover's iron drew a nail, and through it, she went somewhere he could not follow. Stillwater moved at her side, silent and intent, and so did one of the scribes. The elmaestro had left to take care of Coalition business, somewhat reluctantly, Trevian thought.

He heard Stuart's distinctive footfalls. The justice arm stood in front of him, holding a small cloth-bound notebook and a pencil.

"Do you think she will answer questions about her world? The yorita," he said, sounding as eager as a boy getting to ride a caballo by himself for the first time.

"She answers mine. I don't always understand the answers, though."

Stuart nodded. "Did you have any idea about those plaques? What they looked like alive?"

"I didn't. My goal was to scoop up as many as I could and sell them to pickers," Trevian said.

Stuart's grin split his beard. "Oh, yes, just a humble prospector scrabbling to gather coin. As if you aren't curious about *everything*."

"You don't know me, Yor Stuart."

"Don't I? You come from a line of copper-hunters and fabrickers, and you're a copper-hunter yourself." Stuart settled himself against the table and shifted his weight off his artificial leg. "Your uncle is a villain, but also one who asks questions."

"The wrong questions."

"There we agree."

Stuart's gaze shifted past Trevian. Erin's footsteps sounded behind him. "I think we have the book re-assembled," she said, "but it looks like a couple of pages are still missing."

Trevian wondered how this affected their scheme, and the map, but he nodded.

"Stillwater wants the scribes to start work."

"I'll stay with you," Trevian said.

Stuart said, "Tregannon has failed to drive me off. I wonder if I could ask about your world, Yorita Dosmanos."

"Sure. Did you grow up with Tregannon, or something?"

Stuart paused. "Why do you ask?"

"The way you two act. It's like you've known each other a long time."

After a moment, Stuart smiled. He gave Erin a shallow bow. "Again, well-spotted. We grew up in the same village. We shared a tutor."

"And you were smarter than he was," Erin said. "The star student."

"Now there you've missed the mark. I was the *rebellious* student. I asked too many questions. Tregannon's father was a member of the Copper Coalition, and it was clear he would follow his father's path. He and the tutor tried to persuade me to join, but I was skeptical. My mother prospected, not for metals, but for books and artifacts. From her, I learned curiosity."

"You followed her path instead," Trevian said.

"I had little talent for prospecting, but I had a nose for tracking and a small gift for strategy, so I started hiring out as a guard on expeditions. I've seen a great portion of our continent, and it's left me with questions."

"But you *were* part of the Coalition?" Erin said.

"Briefly. Tregannon wanted access to my books...and I wanted access to theirs. It was a short partnership, not a happy one."

"So you went into law enforcement."

Stuart's forehead crinkled. "Law enforce...? Well. We do enforce the Crescent's laws."

At the table, the scribes rolled out an arm's-length of translucent fabric from the roll, and one of them cut it with quick strokes of shears.

"Let's sit over here, yorita," Stuart said. "I'll answer your questions if you'll answer mine."

Trevian sat by the door. Everyone, it seemed, had an occupation but him.

8

He didn't have to sit by the door for too long. After an hour, Erin frowned at the scribe, who was yawning and rubbing his eyes. She walked over to whisper something to Stillwater, who called a halt to the work. The scribe reluctantly made a notation on a strip of the cloth, laid it in the book, and closed the covers. Erin packed the book away.

"We'll start in the morning at seven," Stillwater said.

"I'll come," Harald said.

"I welcome you," Stillwater said, and it was clear Stuart took her meaning because he snorted.

"Whether Tregannon welcomes me or not, I'll come."

The staircase was empty, and sunlight, gleaming through the long, narrow windows, cast bars of deep gold across the steps. At her door, Erin said, "Goodnight, Trevian." He watched as her door swung shut.

In his room, alone with his thoughts, he stared down at the letter to Aideen. The words needed to be stronger, or smoother, but he couldn't shape them. All his sister needed was confidence in her abilities, but he didn't know another way to say it.

He undressed, picked up the folded square of cloth, and tossed it over the sprite lamp. The room darkened, and he pulled back the covers.

Sleep would elude him, he was sure, but soon he lay on a boat of copper floating on a still lake, surrounded by sprites, while the white face of a sheer cliff rose above him—the plateau above Merry Lake. The images faded, and he twisted, stirring awake. He lay on his back, his eyes closed. Prospectors learned to sleep lightly, and even in a place of comfort and safety, he often woke.

Footfalls, a stealthy scuff, whispered from the hallway. He came fully awake and held his breath, to hear more clearly.

It might be Erin, seeking the latrine, or another guest who slept on this floor.

The steps stopped outside his room.

Trevian opened his eyes.

Perhaps Erin had pulled the cord to summon an apprentice or a chica. It was no business of his.

A scuffle and a thump from across the hall. He sat up, bolted out of the bed, and pulled on his trousers. The club Erin called rebar dangled from his belt, and he jerked it loose, gripping it firmly.

"Trevian!"

Another thud and then a crash. He threw open his door. Erin's door was ajar. Legs cartwheeled past the opening, and Erin grunted as she hit the floor. A figure with the red vest of a Copper Coalition guard stood over her, blocking most of Trevian's view. Trevian ran inside.

The assailant tugged on the messenger bag. Erin had laced her arms through the straps.

The attacker dragged her along the floor. "The book," the guard said. "The book."

Erin's gaze glanced off Trevian's face as she slid, and she pulled her legs up against her chest, bumping the man's arms. As he pulled her past the bed, she swung herself sideways, bracing her back. She kicked out and her attacker staggered backward. Trevian dropped the iron bar over the assailant's head, caught the other end in his hand, and pulled it tight against the man's neck.

"Somebody help us!" Erin shouted.

Somehow, Trevian was staggering as the attacker ran backward, using Trevian's own momentum against him. The edge of the door crashed into his spine, making him grunt. Before he could move, the guard drove his head back. Trevian flinched away, saving his nose, but his head slammed into the edge of the door. Then again. His left hand went numb, and the bar twisted free of his grip. The attacker shoved him, and he flailed, falling into the hallway.

The guard wheeled back toward Erin. "The book," he said.

Something bounced off the guard's head with a chime: a sprite lamp. While the creature inside spun, it dropped to the floor, ringing. Trevian got to his hands and knees.

Erin ran at the attacker, flailing with the metal pitcher. The attacker instinctively twisted away, and Erin ducked, leading with her shoulder, jamming into his midsection. Trevian crawled forward and the guard fell over him, sprawling into the hallway. Trevian fished for the bar and found it. The guard was already sitting up, holding a knife. Trevian kicked his hand. The knife spun away, skimming down the hallway.

Erin threw the pitcher. When the attacker feinted, Trevian aimed the bar and struck him across the side of the head, just above the ear. The guard fell over sideways. He started to get up, and Trevian, panting, readied himself for another blow.

Voices echoed from the staircase. The guard flattened his hands on the floor, ready to push up. Trevian put his foot between the man's shoulder blades and stepped hard, holding him down, even though the man struggled. Trevian's shoulder chose this moment to throb with pain. He lost sight of Erin until she reappeared in the edge of his vision, tearing her pillowcase in half lengthwise. "Up here!" she shouted. She knelt and grabbed the man's wrists, pulling them behind him. In a few seconds, she had bound his hands.

"What happened? Yorita! Are you well?" It wasn't Zachary, but another apprentice, and two red-vested guards with him. Trevian stepped between them and Erin, his club ready. If they were confederates of the attacker, he and Erin would have a hard time escaping.

"Langtree!" Tregannon bustled behind them, a plaid robe flapping. "What has happened here?"

Before Trevian could speak, Erin said, "Is this one of your guards?"

"I don't—"

"Is it one of *your guards*?" She pointed at the red vest. Her hand was still, but her eyes were shining, and the edge of her voice was jagged.

The two guards looked at Tregannon, who nodded. The one on the right advanced and rolled the man over. "It's Creighton." He leaned down. "Why did you attack our guest? Who paid you? How much coin did you take to betray your honor?"

The bound man muttered something.

"Bring Captain Montrose now," Tregannon said. The second guard saluted and ran down the stairs.

Erin still held her arms crossed over the bag, and she backed away from the stairwell. "He's one of yours," she said, "the Copper Coalition."

"Yorita, this isn't the Coalition's doing," the remaining guard said. He spread his hands. "This man was bribed or suborned."

The bound man muttered. "I seek a better world."

The guard said, "I'll send you to one," but Erin spoke over him.

"No. I want to hear this." She stepped forward. "What better world?"

The man's eyelids flickered. "There is a new way, a better world."

"I've heard those words before," Trevian said. He rolled the bound man onto his back and pulled his knife, setting it against the edge of the vest.

The standing guard moved, but Tregannon stayed him with a raised hand. Trevian cut through the fabric of the vest and the shirt underneath. The man's chest was bare.

"No parasite," he said.

Boots clacked on the stairs, and a woman came into view. "Elmaestro, Pensker, what has happened here?" She stared down at Creighton. "What is this?"

121

"He attacked our out-of-world guest and tried to steal her posses-sions," Tregannon said.

The woman stepped forward and stood over Creighton. "You betrayed your oath? Why?"

"For a better world," Creighton said, clearly this time.

"What foolishness—"

"He may be under a charm," Tregannon said.

She turned to the guard who had summoned her. "I want Smith, now. He'll have the names of Creighton's squad. Summon them all." She looked at Tregannon. "They just returned from a caravan escort on the Copper Road. If one of them has been charmed or compelled in some way, it's possible more were."

"Send for Machios and have him search them. He'll know what to look for," Tregannon said.

They all stood, silent. The sprite darted frantically from side to side in the lamp, and Trevian reached down and flipped the orb so the opening faced up. The creature flew out.

"Why?" the standing guard said, dodging as the sprite flashed past his nose. Trevian had no answer. The back of his head hurt.

Two more guards came up the stairs. They hauled Creighton to his feet and marched him down the stairs.

"I did not think to add guards to your rooms," Tregannon said, "but I see now that was an oversight."

"What good would a guard do?" Erin said. "*He* was a guard." She jerked her head as if she were shaking back her hair. "He was a *guard*. Could he have gotten into your strong room?"

"He wasn't assigned to strong room duty," Tregannon said.

"That wasn't my question."

At a glance from Tregannon, the woman answered. "He would have had to call in favors, but yes, he could have gotten assigned to it."

Tregannon sighed heavily. "I thought your artifact would be safer in the strong room, but I see I was wrong. We will set a guard, a guard we trust, over your rooms for the rest of the night. I hope we have more clarity in the morning."

"Do you wish me to stay with you, Erin?" Trevian said. Out of the corner of his eye, he saw the guard smirk. After the first flush of anger, he tried to ignore it. Erin's safety, and the book's, were what mattered.

"I ..." Erin thought for a few seconds. "Yes, I do."

"And I will keep watch," the woman said. "My name is Inez Montrose, and I am captain of the night watch. You will be safe under my guard."

"Hokay. Fine." Erin pivoted but stopped with her hand on the doorknob. She nodded to Montrose. "Thank you." She marched into her room. Sheathing his knife, Trevian picked up his club and followed.

W ere either of you injured? Is the book safe? I only just heard." Stillwater brought urgency and a cool draft into the refectory where Trevian and Erin sat, a little past dawn.

"We are well, and the book is safe," Trevian said, watching as Erin rotated her thick-based sisuree cup in her hand. She seemed to recognize the stuff it was crafted from.

"Is there any news?" Erin said.

"There is. Both of you must join us in the laboratory. Machios found one of those creatures in Creighton's armpit."

Erin set down her cup. "That's really *bad* news."

"I thought they put people into a stupor," Trevian said, "but he was fighting. And speaking."

"They were in a stupor so they would feed energy to the lantern," Erin said. "Obviously these things have more control than we realized. Your uncle talked about the world they came from. There are people there, walking around, making decisions."

And preparing to invade, Trevian thought. He pushed away his plate and stood up.

Outside, it was a clear spring morning, still cool but carrying the promise of warmth. Tregannon met them in the courtyard. He'd traded his purple elmaestro vest for a blue work tunic like the technicians wore. They started across the yard. At a set of long tables near the building, a large group of apprentices worked with tweezers and picks, pulling metal out of broken plaques like the one Erin carried. There were hundreds of them, and the yield was rich, but the work was detailed and tedious, and it always fell to apprentices. He walked a few paces before noticing Erin was not beside him. She had stopped. She stared at the table, her eyebrows drawn together, one hand pressed flat over the pocket of her trousers where her own plaque lay.

"Erin?"

"Hm?"

"What's wrong?"

She didn't respond at first. "Nothing," she said after a moment and strode past him, catching up with Stillwater.

They crossed the practice yard. Lights flickered in the windows of the laboratory building. Stillwater pushed the doors and leaned against one to hold it open. Tregannon led them into a long bright room, lined with tables, quartz cages like the ones Trevian's father used, and a few desks. Machios peered into a long rectangular cage. He wore thick leather gloves with drawstrings at the wrist, and sleeves reaching past his elbows. Trevian recognized those as well from his tours of the company cages. They were thick, resistant to earth elemental bites, knives, fire, and maybe even the stinger of the parasites.

"Your attacker wore one of these creatures." He gestured to another cage, one covered with a lampcloth. "We searched the rest of Creighton's squad, those who were here, and none of them wore a creature, but two others have already gone off with other caravans."

"Is he still alive? What does he say?" Trevian said.

"Alive, sobbing mostly, making little sense. He was in a kind of paradise, he said. He pledged himself to a new way. He spoke of belonging. He said he was compelled to find the book." Machios looked at Tregannon. "He said there are others, but the names faded from his mind instantly."

Erin said, "That's convenient."

"He's lying," Trevian said. "David and Miriam, from Merrylake, and the Agustos, they remembered."

"They were connected to the lantern," Erin said. "That might have made a difference."

"It might have." He stepped closer, curious to see what Machios had made of the parasites. He gave a little shudder when he saw the creature.

Machios had cut the parasite open lengthwise and pinned open the edges with long thin shafts of loomin. The edges of the thing flexed and curled.

Beside him, Stillwater gave a long gasp. "Like the page in your book," she said.

As Trevian stared, one pin popped free, landing with a soft tinkle on the wooden surface of the table. The edges of the creature met and melded. No seam or scar showed where the cut had been.

"So far, I've found no organs of digestion, reproduction, or elimination," Machios said. "It heals itself as you can see. And its interior... well, I've never seen such a thing."

The exposed surface glistened, and bits of light winked inside. There were greenish bits and metallic bits, lines and beads of a copper and loominish hue. A memory taunted Trevian, but he couldn't seize it.

"It's like the inside of a phone," Erin said.

"What is a phone?" Machios said.

She waved a hand. "There's a hundred dead ones you're pawing through right outside." She took a breath.

"Like your device?" Tregannon turned to Machios. "She carries a living plaque."

"You think it has similar workings to this creature?" Machios came around the cage, looking eager. "Your device is powered by an elemental?"

"No. By electrical energy."

"It draws energy from the air, or the sun?"

"No, it... Well, some could, probably, from the sun. No, electricity, it's—" Erin sighed sharply and waved her hand. "Lightning is electricity."

"You bridled lightning?"

"Well…yeah. And you can store it, chemically. That means—"

"I know what chemistry is," Machios said.

"Our…devices ran on batteries, or you could get electricity to it other ways. It was generated and shipped down wires."

"Like what your father does in White Bluffs with the flames." Tregannon looked at Trevian. "But yours, yorita, is for storing images."

Erin laughed. "No. It *can* store images, but it's…" She chewed on her lower lip. Trevian had seen her do it before when she was thinking. "They were originally devices for sending and getting messages. You could speak over them to a person far away."

Stillwater said, "Sounds and images. Auditory and visual."

"And you could store information…" Erin glanced from face to face and stopped.

Machios turned back to the cage where the parasite was flexing against the pins. "Sounds. And images." He picked up the large square of lampcloth and threw it over the cage. "Let's discuss this outside." He started for the door before anyone could speak.

In the practice yard, Machios spun around, staring at Erin. "Can you send a message through a frontera?"

"Why are we outside?" Trevian said.

Erin said, "No. Believe me, I tried. I don't have any bars." Trevian stared at her, and so did everyone else. "I need a transmitter, a machine to send the, the signal, the information."

Trevian was only more confused. "Like the lantern?"

"Kind of, I guess. It strengthens the signal. The waves."

"Waves of sound and energy," Stillwater said. "I've read about it. I thought it was a metaphor."

Tregannon said, "*Why* are we outside?"

Machios shook his head. "If these creatures send messages like they control thought, we should assume they are still doing just that."

Trevian felt cold. He saw the shock on Stillwater's face, and Tregannon was frowning.

"To whom? And where?" Tregannon said.

"Where did Creighton get infected?" Trevian said.

Tregannon answered. "He guarded a caravan coming down from Madlyn. They came the usual way through Querida Pass and stopped at the caravan town there, Madalita, as they always do. He drank late in a local tavern that night, the others said, but they noticed nothing strange about him yesterday."

"Is the frontera we seek in Madlyn then?" Machios asked.

Tregannon said, "Possibly."

"Or the caravan stop," Stillwater said.

Tregannon stared at Erin. "*Can* your book locate a frontera?"

"That's what we're trying to find out," Erin said.

"No charms in the book to identify frontera?"

When Erin glanced Trevian's way, he didn't meet her gaze. After a moment, she shook her head. "Not that we've found. The map idea is the best we've got."

Tregannon pursed his lips. "I can't send a company of guards up into the mountains to search every crack and rift. I need to notify the Elmaestro Melendres of the Madlyn Coalition. They need to know the danger." He pursed his lips. "And I can only hope they aren't infected."

"We'll get back to the book," Stillwater said. Erin followed her, and Trevian hurried to keep up.

Erin dropped back several steps behind Stillwater. She kept her voice low. "I thought Oshane said you had a gift for finding frontera."

"He did. I don't know if I can believe him, and I don't want to make promises others rely on, and then fail. And he had a charm, a bracelet of beads. I have no such charm."

"Okay. We'll keep it to ourselves." She paused and touched his arm. "Thanks for staying with me last night. I know you're risking your reputation."

"It's your reputation at risk just as much," he said.

"No big deal." She shrugged.

"Erin, I will always protect you and help you, as long as it is in my power." He sounded like a student mouthing the words of a stage play.

Erin didn't smirk or frown, though. Instead, she nodded. "Thank you. I'm glad you're with me."

"But I think you could use more."

"More, what? Protection?"

He nodded. "There is a charm in the pages Oshane had. It seems to protect the book."

"I saw it. I'm not sure we know how it works. What if it closes it to everyone, including us?"

"You are the book's guardian. Surely it would still open for you."

"Yeah, maybe. It probably would. I don't want to mess with too much magic. Charms, I mean. When I don't know how it all really works."

"We need to protect this artifact," he said.

"I'll think about it."

"Erin, Trevian?"

"Coming," they called in unison and walked after the profesor.

Two scribes were waiting. One had ink and a stylus, while the other held a needle and thread. Stuart stood by the table. "I hear you were attacked."

Trevian told him what had happened, and Stillwater added what Machios had just told them.

Stuart nodded. "And you think they function the way your plaque does," he said, looking at Erin.

"The only thing we know for sure is they control behavior," Erin said.

"How do you think they knew you were here?" he said.

Erin shook her head. "No idea."

Trevian said, "I carried one with us. If it could see and hear, as Erin and Profesor Stillwater think, then…"

Stuart was quiet, staring at Trevian without seeming to see him. "Dangerous," he said. "And insidious."

"Yes," said Erin, drawing out the book.

While they set up and the scribe got started, Trevian said quietly to

Stuart, "Can you recommend a guesthouse? We don't feel safe here after last night's attack."

"I can recommend a place, mine, if you would honor it. I live simply, but I can keep you safe."

"We bring danger," Trevian said.

Stuart's eyes crinkled at the corners. "I have some experience with danger."

"It would be a great help," Trevian said.

He watched them work. When they stopped after two hours for sisuree and fruit, he and Stuart made the offer to Erin. Her eyes had been bleary, and her mouth curved down, but now she grinned. "And it will drive Tregannon turvy, won't it?"

Stuart mirrored her grin. "It will."

For a moment, Trevian felt his heart lift. He snorted a laugh. "Well then, it seems we must do it."

"I'm in," Erin said.

"Excellent," Stuart said.

9

_____

Weyves, 19 Uno, Year 331

E rin's nerves itched. She'd been bored before, but this mixture of anxiety and boredom was new, and she didn't like it. She wanted to help, but only one person could trace at a time, and it was obvious the scribes were good at their jobs. She paced. She sat in a chair, watching. She answered the justice arm's questions, which actually filled up a couple of hours. She paced some more then sat on the table and swung her legs like a six-year-old. Finally, she just rubbed her arms and stared at the worktable while a scribe bent over the book, carefully tracing each swirling stroke.

Stillwater left the room and came back with a wooden crate. "You might enjoy these," she said, setting it down near where Erin had been sitting. "These are not as odd as the books Harald has, but they might be of interest." She opened the lid, releasing the smell of very old leather and the faintly musty odor of paper.

Erin said, "Thanks."

Stillwater lifted out a thick leather-bound volume. "This is a compilation of many different documents. Some are hundreds of years old. I question the scholarship, but there are useful bits."

Erin began paging carefully through *A Collection of Annotated Histories of the Events Before the Earth Turned and the Early Years of the Interval, Presented to Evangeline Lewelyn, Elmaestro of the Copper Coalition, Year 11.* Hell of a title.

There were descriptions of the earth turning. Mountain ranges sprouted out of the ground almost overnight. Erin assumed those were earth shifts as the result of some mega-earthquake. There were even...scientific reports?

She stopped at a page.

Daddy, that's a word for father, said everyone at Aperture One was excited. He said they'd changed the world. Then he didn't come home. No one from that facility came home. He did a couple of vidcalls with us, and he acted like everything was fine, but even I could tell it wasn't and I was only six.

One morning we heard planes. We went outside. A big column of white flame reached clear up into the sky. They told us there was an enforced shelter-in-place order and we all had to stay inside. I forget how many days it was, but then guys in hazmat suits came to the door. They had flame throwers and big guns. They made me take off my clothes, and a man in a suit looked at me all over. They did the same to Mama only she said a woman looked at her. Then we got overalls, and they told us we had six hours to pack. Mama said she was counting on me to be a brave boy, and I could take one box of toys and books. She ran around packing, she was trying not to cry.

We got on a truck. They moved us all to a new town farther east on the Pendrelle River. Oh, that would be north now. I never saw Daddy after that.

"Profesor Stillwater, did you see this?"

Stillwater came and looked over her shoulder. "Oh, yes, the child whose town burned. A warlord attack, I assume. They say right there they have fire elementals."

"No, they say 'flame throwers.'"

"What's that, if not an elemental?"

"A machine, a weapon. And they body-searched everyone. They wore protective coverings. Do you think they could have been searching for parasites?"

Stillwater gave her the kind of look her mother used to. "I think it's a long walk to get to that conclusion, Erin."

Erin shrugged. It didn't seem like *that* long a walk.

She kept reading while the scribes worked until Stillwater called a halt for the day, and Erin saw it was twilight outside.

Stuart said, "I've sent for a sprite cart, if you two are ready. I'm going ahead to let my cook and valet know."

"We need to get our gear," Trevian said.

"I need the book," Erin said.

"A few more minutes, Profesor," the scribe said to Stillwater.

Moments later, he stepped away from the page he had just completed. He marked the place. Erin closed the book and stowed it safely away. She just needed to get her knapsack and she'd be ready to go. That was a relief.

———

This would be the last time he went up this staircase, Trevian thought, as they followed an apprentice who was putting sprites into the lamps along the stairwell. Erin seemed pleased at the thought of sleeping under a different roof.

"I'm glad you found us another place to stay," she said, as if she had followed his thought.

"He seems eager to talk to you. I think he would have offered, if I hadn't asked him about guesthouses."

"Whatever. You have my back. I appreciate it."

"Erin…" He wanted to reach out to her. Instead, he clenched his fists at his sides. "You are the most valiant person I have ever met. I will always be at your side."

"Oh." Her face went blank for a moment. She stepped forward and put her hand on his cheek. "Thank you."

Warmth flushed through his body, and he longed to press her hand in place with his own, but before he could move, she pulled her hand away. Something slid out of the book, trailing a strip of paper. It clicked as it struck the floor.

Trevian stooped down and reached for the tiny object, but Erin grabbed his wrist. "Wait!"

He paused, remembering the earth elemental the book had swallowed. What if the puertas disgorged monsters or weapons? Erin squatted down and peered at the object. Trevian did the same.

"I thought nothing came through the puertas," he said.

"I thought so, too."

The thing was a little over an inch long, shaped like a long letter V. There was an object attached to the wide end, a set of curves and circles made of some white substance. A scrap of pink shaped like a woman's hairbow clung to one side.

Erin reached out, clenched her fist loosely, and nudged it with the back of her hand. It slipped across the floor. "It's a halo kitty hair clip," she said. "With a note."

"What is a halo kitty?"

"It's a, it's, oh, God." She sighed and closed her eyes. "I can't explain —it's a hair ornament, worn by women mostly."

"Like a comb."

"Yes." She picked it up carefully between her thumb and forefinger. A metal leg clasped the paper against the front of the object.

Erin said, "It's something Wing Mei would wear."

Trevian needed a moment to remember the name. Wing Mei was from another of the Four Families, the one who held the compass.

Erin stood up so quickly she nearly hit him in the face. "Let's get inside." Before he got to his feet, she had shoved open the door. He followed her in.

She fiddled with the metal leg, which swung back on a tiny hinge, and lifted out the paper. "It's from Wing Mei. 'If this is a friend, who was your favorite skubikang character?'"

"What's a skubikang?"

"What? Skoo-bee gang. It's an, an entertainment. It's also a trick question." She scribbled, speaking as she wrote. "'Never watched it; I

133

had mandolin lessons.' I can tell her where we are. Maybe she can find a frontera—"

"Are you sure that's wise?"

"Why wouldn't it be?"

He gestured at the halo kitty. "It may be her ornament. Are you sure she sent it, or the note?"

Erin bit her lip. "No, I guess I'm not. Do you think it's a trap?"

"What if she went to the world of the creatures? What if some of Oshane's confederates have her?"

She stepped back and put down the ornament. "You're right, but if it *is* her..." She wrote hurriedly. "There. 'What was your hobby?' At least, we'll know if it's her. If she's being held by someone, she'll give a trick answer."

The woman who held the compass might still be compelled by the parasites. "Do you know the answer to this question?"

"I do."

"How will you know which puerta it came through?"

"I'm hoping there's some residual energy around that particular page. There was when I sent the elemental away, I could feel it." She tucked the paper inside the clip and began turning pages, paging past the first page with a blue stone. At the second she stopped, closing her eyes, letting her fingers hover close to its edge. It might have been Trevian's imagination, but he felt a faint vibration around him. She brought the clip close to the stone and spoke the charm. The clip vanished.

They waited. Steps sounded on the stairs, and Stillwater appeared in the doorway. "The sprite cart is here." She looked from Trevian to Erin. "What are you doing?"

Erin closed the book and slipped it into her bag. "Just getting my things."

"I'll get my knapsack," Trevian said.

Outside, blackrock torches combined with sprite lamps to fill the courtyard with a flickering greenish glow. The gatekeeper directed them to the waiting sprite cart.

Stuart's house had a high fence made of metal slats and poles of the black substance Erin had been interested in on the promenade. The cart driver braked, and they climbed out. The fence was warded, but someone inside the house dropped the wards, and the gate swung open easily. Trevian studied the long, low house as they drew closer. To the north, where the fence curved, sat an exercise yard. The house had a slanting roof rising to a shallow peak above the door, a wing ranging out on either side. It was not the most expensive house in the city, nor in the most expensive neighborhood, but it was not a modest dwelling. Trevian wondered how well a justice arm was paid, or if Stuart had brought back riches from his expeditions.

A fair-haired man opened the door for them. "Yor Langtree."

Trevian nodded.

"And Yorita Dosmanos. Welcome. I am Genaro, the justice arm's valet. The justice arm is in the sala." He stepped back. The entryway was long, and the right wall was lined with books. Erin smiled.

Straight ahead, the walls widened to accommodate a round table. Beyond it was a door, and savory smells drifted from behind it. Genaro guided them to the left, where a wide arch opened up a third of the wall. A hearth faced them, the bluish coals of a whiterock fire twinkling from its bed. Stuart's sala was long, filled with wool weavings in white, brown, red, and blue. The justice arm sat in a sling chair beside a small carved wooden table near the hearth, his shortened left leg propped up on a stool. His hair, clipped short, was more brown than red. To one side, the artificial leg rested in a stand made of the same black pipe as the fence. Stuart's flesh and bone leg ended about four inches below his knee. Trevian's ankle, with its healing elemental bite, gave a faint twinge as if in sympathy.

"Come in, be comfortable." Stuart leaned forward, massaging the flesh above the stump of his leg. "Yorita, does this offend? I don't know your customs."

"It doesn't," Erin said. She truly did not seem discomfited by the scene. She nodded toward the artificial leg and said, "It's made of plastic."

"Plastic? Is that what the substance is called? It's durable, but it doesn't hold a charm well, hence the copper studs and chains. What was it, plastic? Some kind of hardened tree sap?"

"It's a chemical process," Erin said. She sat down, still looking at the leg, and Trevian wondered what intrigued her about it. Was it the wide leather collar at the top with the straps and buckles, or the copper charms themselves? He felt the warmth of the copper from where he stood, and he guessed Erin was sensing it too.

She said, "It comes from a petrochemical substance. I don't know very much about it, about how it's made, but we had a lot of it. My phone, my device, has some. They made flexible tubing, and containers, and things like pipes and ornaments. It was in almost everything. Your cups, the herb jars, your leg, they're made from something called PVC."

Genaro came into the room bearing a tray, which he set down on one of the tables. Trevian sat in a chair next to Erin. Genaro handed around cups and offered dried fruit. He passed Stuart a jar of some cream and a soft cloth. "Shall I help you, yor?" he said.

"No help needed, thanks, Genaro."

"Dinner will be ready in a quarter of an hour."

"Good." Stuart opened the jar and scooped some of the cream onto the cloth. He rubbed it lightly over the stump of his leg. "Langtree, will you answer a few questions for me, while we're waiting, about your uncle?"

The nerves in Trevian's belly thrilled. "Of course, if I can," he said. He stopped his hand from reaching for the knife at his belt. He wanted to trust Stuart, but what if the man were a confederate of the parasites? Had he led Erin once again into a trap?

"You say he has taken lives," Stuart said. He set down the jar and the cloth, settled back into the chair. "He killed a prospector friend of yours. Did you see him do it?"

"The flames killed him. I did not see Oshane order it."

Stuart's lips thinned. "That's too bad. Good journey to your friend," he added quickly. "You said he imprisoned you. Tell me what he did."

"He tied me to a chair," Trevian said.

Stuart relaxed even further into his. "Now *that* I can use."

Trevian discerned the path before him, and he relaxed a bit himself. "He also stabbed me. And I heard him order the flames to kill Erin."

"And you would testify to those things?"

"I would."

Stuart nodded. For barely a second, he was still. Then he leaned forward, picking up a pouch of sheer fabric like a stocking, which he pulled over the end of his leg, smoothing it to be sure there were no wrinkles. "As a justice arm, I am allowed to initiate a certain number of warrants each year." He reached for the artificial leg, slid his flesh leg into its cuff, settled the apparatus, and fastened the buckles. "With your sworn statement, I would have enough for a warrant for your uncle, if I should come across him again. Genaro and my cook Katurah can witness it."

"It would be my pleasure," Trevian said.

Genaro and Katurah joined them for dinner. Through most of it, Stuart asked them questions about the parasites and Oshane. Once or twice, when Trevian glanced Erin's way, he found her gaze on him. He wondered what was in her thoughts.

After the meal, while Genaro served tea, Stuart brought out paper and recorded Trevian's statement. Stuart was a good questioner, and Trevian, who felt like a stammering fool at first, was surprised at how much detail he remembered, like the notes of the flautine before the air elemental had overwhelmed him. He signed, as did Stuart, Genaro, and Katurah.

Stuart rolled the document carefully and slipped it into a smooth cylinder looped around with a braided strap. "I'll register this at the Council offices tomorrow. Yorita Dosmanos, would you like to see some of my books?"

She pushed back her chair. "I'd love to, and please call me Erin."

"Then please call me Harald."

The wide study across the entryway from the sala had two walls covered with shelves. Stuart had many books, and many objects, most of them Ancient. Across the room sat a tall case holding crossbows, a longbow, a short leather-covered club, a compass, several knives, and a set of braided leather riatas, long and short. The tools of a justice arm.

"I can read one word in thirty of this one," Stuart said. "It's one of the Ancient languages. Ruth does better, and she says it's part science and part philosophy." He set the book on the desk in front of the window and opened it. "Can you decipher it?"

"It's Spanish, or really close," she said. "I can read most of it." She sat down. Her head bent over the words. Trevian watched as again Erin went far away from him, into a realm where he could not follow. He couldn't read any Ancient language, and he wondered how she could.

"Okay. This is about something called quantum physics," she said. "The study of very small particles of matter."

"Ah, atomic matter," Stuart said.

"Uh, we pronounce it a-*tom*-ic, but yeah. Most of this is over my head. I mean, beyond my understanding. Quantum physics studied how very tiny particles moved. Oh, and they were interested in the idea of multiple dimensions. It's like different worlds."

"Turn the page and you'll leave the science behind," Stuart said.

She carefully lifted the page and lay it down. "Oh. Pretty."

Trevian peered at it. An illustration filled the page, blue and gold, copper and red. The colors were faded, but he could imagine their luster, long ago. Five figured orbs ringed a sixth in the center. Blue lines ran from each outer circle into the center one, and lines of gold sprang out from the center, touching each of the circling five, like the spokes of a wheel. He leaned closer.

Erin pointed to the caption. "'Mundos elementales.' Elemental worlds. This is a model of linked worlds. Only there are six."

"Ruth was intrigued by the number too."

"Do the lines represent frontera?" Trevian said.

"If they do, they all run through the central world. Notice no lines move between the outer five?" Erin said. She stared out the window. "I've never heard of that. And I've never heard of six worlds."

"Ruth says she has found a few other references, but they are mostly ignored by scholars."

"I'd like to see those," Erin said. She straightened up suddenly, one hand dropping to the pouch holding her book. "I, um, Yor Stuart—"

"Harald."

"Harald, can Trevian and I have a few minutes of privacy?"

"Of course." He stepped back. "Is there anything else you need?"

Erin lifted out her book. "Maybe a pencil?"

"In the drawer." Harald walked out of the room without looking back.

"What happened?"

"I just...the book, it, pinged. I know that's not the word, but..." She leafed through the pages. The halo kitty with a fan-folded sheet lay across one page.

"So soon," Trevian said.

Erin unfolded it. "'Ham radio with my uncle.' That's the right answer. She says she's in a place called Perlarayna. Isn't that in this world?"

"Yes, to the east, across the Desolation."

Erin flipped over the paper and began writing. "I'm telling her who Vianovelle is, and warning her about the parasites."

"*Is* that wise?" he said.

She looked up at him. "I think we have to."

He shrugged. "How does she have a puerta?" he said. "I thought she held the compass."

Erin said, "The compass has the blue stones along the outside, all the way around. We always thought the compass and the book functioned together in some way. I just didn't think it was this way." She stood up. "The puerta stones are the same as the stones in the collar, and none of you have seen them in the Crescent. I wonder where they're from and how you convert them into mini-frontera."

She folded the paper and sent it back. "Let's just keep this to ourselves for now, hokay?"

"Don't you trust the justice arm?"

"I want to, but right now, I really don't trust anyone except you."

"In spite of what I did?"

"You're as much a victim of your uncle as I was. Anyway, I mostly trust Stillwater and this Harald guy, but I don't want to add any more complications right now."

She raised her voice. "Thanks, Yor—Harald."

Harald's limp seemed more pronounced now, as he came back into the room. "Does your book communicate with you?"

"Sort of. Thanks for giving us a moment."

"If I have it, and you need it, Erin, it is yours. We must defeat those creatures."

"Thank you." She picked up the book written in the language called Spanish. "May I look at this some more?"

10

Domingo, 21 Uno, Year 331

Over the next two days, Erin read through the books Stillwater lent her. In between, she consulted with Trevian, who was gathering provisions for their journey, wherever it led them. Trevian, an experienced traveler, prepared for cold weather, wet weather, snow, and injuries, packing their saddle-bags for almost any occasion.

Stillwater ate with them at Harald's Veyernes night and quizzed Erin about her life. At first, it had been fun, but Erin went to bed feeling empty again, a stranger, an outsider. Still.

Footsteps in the hallway woke Erin. For a few seconds, she didn't know where she was. The bed was narrow and hard. The air was cold. Then she remembered. She sat up and reached under her pillow for the book.

The rhythm of the footsteps in the hall was uneven. Genaro muttered something, and Harald gave a one-word response.

She stuffed the book into the messenger bag and reached for her trousers at the end of the bed, pulling out the knife Trevian had given her. She *had* trusted Harald, she really had, but it was the middle of the night. What was he doing whispering in the hallway in front of her door?

The steps receded up the hall toward the front of the house.

She pulled on the trousers, her shoes, the messenger bag, and slipped her jacket over the nightshirt the cook Katurah had loaned her. Outside, a door latch clicked and new steps sounded in the hallway. She opened her door.

"I thought you'd wake." Trevian had dressed in a hurry too. He had his hand on the hilt of his knife. In the other, he held a lamp with a green-glowing rock. His hair was loose around his shoulders. One lock fell across his cheek. Erin felt her cheeks heat up in a blush.

"What's happening?" Erin tried for brisk instead of confused and half-asleep.

"Something tested the wards. Genaro thinks it's an intruder."

They walked up the hall. There was no reason for her to be blushing. She hadn't been thinking about Trevian before she'd fallen asleep, about how smooth his lips looked in the lamplight at dinner. Well, she *had* been, but it shouldn't make her blush.

Genaro and Harald stood in the entryway. Genaro held a crossbow. Harald gave her a quick nod. "We hoped we wouldn't wake you," he said. "Someone tested the ward. There was no breach. We're safe."

"A visitor? A drunk?" When they all stared at Erin, she said, "A... lickerish person?"

"A visitor at this time of night, like a fast messenger, would announce themselves before trying the wards, yorita," Genaro said, "and the nearest tavern is not close."

"There are those who have an argument with me because I've brought family members in to be tried," Harald said. "It's why I invested in the wards."

"Justice Arm?"

Katurah stood in the hallway, her hair neatly braided and a coat over her nightclothes.

"All's well, Katurah," Harald said.

"I heard. There are lights beyond the orchard. Blue and orange. I think you should see them."

"Lights?" Harald limped forward. Erin glanced down. The leg he wore wasn't the bone-white one, but simple black, lacking any copper charms. He moved more awkwardly than before but had no trouble going through the kitchen and outside into the herb garden. Erin squeezed in next to Trevian. She shivered and pulled her jacket tighter. Above her, stars glinted, faintly green. It was too dark to make out Harald's fruit trees, which covered much of the property, but she could see the scraps of whirling blue, yellow, and orange, broken by the invisible trunks. "It's them," she said.

Harald didn't look away from them. "Who?"

"The fire elementals." She turned to Trevian. "You said they wouldn't follow us across water."

He stared at them too. "They must have come along the shore."

"How did they find me?"

"They're attuned to you, Erin."

"Have you tethered them in some way?" Harald said.

"*No.*" Erin drew a breath. "Sorry." Harald didn't deserve that tone of voice. "No, the opposite. I freed them."

"But they seem bonded to Erin," Trevian said.

"Did they set off the wards?" Katurah said.

The flames drifted to one side, where there was a gap in the trees, and she could see them completely now, twirling spirals of fire. *Go be free*, she thought at them. *Leave me alone.*

Harald was speaking, and she'd missed the first bit. "...at the front, and it was done with another charm. That's a human attempt. How did you bind them, Erin?"

Trevian answered before she could protest. "Erin used a charm from the book to *break* the charm used to tethered them. She showed them kindness when she had no reason to."

"They killed my parents."

Trevian said, "They are joven. Somehow, Oshane separated them

143

from their emberbed and the elders. They are lost. Erin is a kind of beacon for them."

"That could prove useful," Harald said.

"No."

Katurah pointed again. "There they go," she said as the flames faded and, finally, vanished.

"Good," Harald said. "I'm no expert with elementals, except I did learn earth elementals hunt in pairs." He stepped back into the kitchen. "I'm a poor host, disturbing your rest this way."

"We're safe," Erin said. She still felt more secure than she had at the Coalition.

"And Katurah, the house is safe now," Harald said.

"I always check the wards in the back, yor," the cook said.

Harald smiled at her. The group separated and went back to their own rooms. Erin slipped the book back under her pillow and lay down on her side. After being outside, even for a short time, she was chilled, but she was reluctant to light the whiterock brazier in her room. She knew everyone used them, but she didn't know how much oxygen the fuel source consumed. Add that to the growing list of things she didn't know about this world.

She pulled out the book. This had been an attack, another one. Trevian's idea to use the book's warding charm suddenly seemed like a good one.

She flipped to the newer page with the charm. Charms were strange. Some were meant to be recited like poems, some you drew, and some just gave directions for actions or thoughts. One ran across the badly scratched page like a line of musical notes. The ward for the book was a set of four lines. She concentrated, thought deeply, and recited them. The book lay in her lap, unchanged. After a few minutes, she decided the charm hadn't worked. That was one more thing to worry about.

She slipped it back under her pillow and lay down.

When she closed her eyes, she saw the light gleam off the lock of Trevian's hair where it lay across his cheek. Would he have been offended if she reached over and brushed it back? Probably. Or maybe not.

She wasn't looking for a relationship or anything. There wasn't time, and she was a complete outsider.

The bedding gradually grew warm, and finally, she slept.

S he didn't sleep well, though, and the jolting ride back up to the compound made her head ache. Genaro rode in front, armed with a crossbow, just like he had since the first night they'd spent with Harald.

"How did Harald lose his leg?" It was a personal question, but Harald was open enough about the prosthetic.

Genaro spoke as he scanned the horizon. "It was in the Desolation. An earth elemental attacked one of the other deputies. It pulled his caballo half-underground before we even saw it."

"You were there?"

"I was there. The justice arm drove his caballo forward and pulled his man free of the creature, but the second one erupted from the earth next to him and got his leg. The deputy pulled *him* free. By then we were close enough, with crossbows, to drive both creatures back a bit and get our people to safety, but the justice arm lost half his leg."

"Sounds frightening."

"It was."

"What's the Desolation? Where's the Desolation?'

"It's east-northeast of here. The landscape gives it its name. It gets little rain; there is almost no vegetation, no shade, lots of Ancient ruins and stranger things even than that. Beyond it to the east is the Spine, and if you follow it far enough, you reach Perlarayna and the gateway to the eastern continent."

"Is the Spine a mountain range?"

"Yes. One of the ones that arose when the earth turned, they tell us."

"Arose, really? What do you mean? Are they volcanic? Fire-mountains?"

Genaro glanced at her. "I know what a volcano is, yorita. The Spine thrust its way up out of the earth in a few days. It tore cities in half and crushed buildings and towns along the way."

It *couldn't* be a mountain range, but the story matched the accounts in Stillwater's book. All these stories sprang from the same source, though, whatever that was. And the stories made no sense. Subduction happened over eons; one tectonic plate didn't slip under another and crumple it in a week or two. Here, though, the poles had shifted about ninety degrees, mountains sprouted up from nowhere, and the elementals awoke all at once. Those things only happened in low-budget science fiction movies, except they seemed to have happened here. But then, no one really knew what *had* happened here.

And the picture in Harald's book showed six worlds. Everything the Four Families had been told was about five. Trevian's people counted five. How could a world vanish?

Stillwater met them in the map room. Zachary was with her, holding the lidded box.

"Great, thanks," Erin said. "I'd really like to look at that big book again."

Stillwater said, "Let me fetch the scribes."

"I tried to put a warding charm on the book last night," Erin said. "But it didn't take."

"Other charms have worked for you," Trevian said, frowning.

"I know." Erin shrugged. "I don't get it either."

Zachary set the box down on one of the worktables. Erin thanked him and set her own book down where they had worked the day before. Trevian once again stood against the door. She opened the box and took out the *Annotated Histories*, leafing through it until she reached the page she'd stopped at.

Stillwater came in with Ilsa, a scribe they'd met earlier. Zachary glanced at the worktable where Erin had set her book and leaned over to push it farther onto the table.

A force lifted Zachary and threw him four feet across the room.

He bounced off the bookcase and fell to the floor. Erin leaped to her feet and ran to him. Stillwater and Trevian rushed over, while Ilsa waited by the door.

"Zachary!"

"What's happened?" Stillwater's voice was sharp.

"I don't know."

Stillwater knelt by the boy's side. He groaned. His head rolled from side to side, and he opened his eyes.

"Are you okay?" Erin checked his pulse. It was fast but slowing to normal as she counted.

"What happened to me?" he said.

"Apparently the charm *did* work," Trevian said.

Zachary tried to sit up. "I'm sorry, yorita."

"No, *I'm* sorry, Zachary. I didn't think it worked."

He put his hand to his head. "It works...well, yorita."

They helped Zachary to his feet. Stillwater sat him down and checked his vision and his pulse, then sent him to the infirmary anyway. She leaned back against the table, her arms crossed, and stared at Erin. "Can any of us touch it now? Even you?"

"Well, I carried it here."

"The rest of us?"

Trevian said, "One of the Copper Coalition Guard tried to steal the book from this building while we slept. Someone tried to breach the justice arm's wards last night. Do not scold Erin for protecting the artifact."

"I am not scolding. I'm asking. Erin wants us to help her with the book." There was a snap in Stillwater's voice. "Can we do that without risking our lives?"

"I'll try it," Trevian said. Erin might have imagined the faint tremor in his voice. He curled his hand into a fist and touched his knuckles to the book. Then he sighed, caught the edge of the cover and flipped it open.

Stillwater sighed too. "Have I your leave?" she said. Erin thought she was being sarcastic, but then realized the profesor was serious. Erin said, "Yes, and your scribe. Anyone *you* designate."

Stillwater chewed on her lower lip for a moment, then copied Trevian's movement and touched the book. She leafed through a few pages. "It's safe, Ilsa," she said.

The scribe didn't move from the doorway.

"Come. Are you an explorer of history or aren't you?" Stillwater said.

"I am a scribe, profesor," the woman said, but finally she came over and tentatively stroked the book with one fingertip.

"Well, now we know your charm works," said Stillwater, "and you direct who has access. This was a bad way to find out."

Trevian said, "How else would we find out?"

Stillwater ignored him. "Let's get to work."

Erin went back over to her table. At least Zachary was okay. And the charm worked. She thought she'd keep her head down for a while, just the same.

Some pages had only a few lines on them.

Episodes 27 and 29 substantiate an alternate dimension each with a different signature, respectively, from the previously identified seven. Episode 28 was inconclusive due to a native error originating in coding. –20130531 T Lewiston

Whatever a native error was. Alternate dimensions, though... something to think about.

She ran across another single page, marked at the top. AAR110814, page 3 of 3. Chip had used that acronym once when he'd been home on leave. It meant After Action Report.

The incursion was contained, with seventy-eight potential vectors neutralized. No security personnel were lost, sustaining minor injuries only. Due to the nature of the vectors, therapeutic support is strongly recommended for affected personnel. Expect post-engagement trauma.

The site is sterilized. No instances of the vector are observed but watchers are posted at the perimeter.

Recommend no further theoretical exploration be attempted near the Aperture One site and further, strongly recommend this report be shared with Orchard Hill soonest.

She didn't remember seeing Orchard Hill before, but there was Aperture One again.

It was clear the documents in the book were in no particular order because the next pages shared more collected stories from survivors during the Interval. The high-tech medical equipment was doorstop-dead, but people worked to provide clean water and follow rules of sanitation. One settlement created limited electrical power through a crude hydro-electric plant. Towns had community gardens. It wasn't perfect. Clearly different cultural groups broke into their own communities, but there wasn't mass warfare or killing.

Without warning, she was back in a land of transcripts, and here was an acronym she definitely recognized.

20130806
> OH Mirrorsite
> 10:40:42
> TLewiston: WTF?????

20130806
> Aperture One
> 10:42:01
> BTalavera: Lost the probe.

20130806
> OH Mirrorsite
> 10:42:56
> TLewiston: Mechfail?

20130806

  Aperture One

  10:43:13

  BTalavera: Totally green board, feed solid, then it's gone like we unplugged it. It won't even come up in Safe Mode.

20130806

  OH Mirrorsite

  10:45:00

  TLewiston: We started getting gonzo readings from the Pit at exact same time. Sending you feed.

20130806

  Aperture One

  10:46:15

  BTalavera: Thanks. Going into conference more later.

The next page picked up in the middle of a different conversation.

20130808

  Aperture One

  13: 05: 03

  BTalavera: 2nd probe is fine. Atmosphere and air pressure nearly earth-normal. Telma, I think it's real. Zup w/your seismic stuff?

20130808

  OH Mirrorsite

  13:09:11

  TLewiston: I don't know. Unusual/unheard of here. I wanted to send the interns home but got overruled. No history of seismic disturbance. Here's some more signal activity from the Pit for you to look at.

20130808

  Aperture One

13: 14: 07

BTalavera: Those signals read almost like music. I know you're concerned, but I don't think you need to send the interns away. It's just a few mild tremors. Besides, what would happen to the great Orchard Hill Mural Gallery if they left?

20130808

OH Mirrorsite

13:20:27

TLewiston: "Just a few mild tremors," says the west coast girl! Yes, my brain wants to make it music too. And OMG, the murals. You should see

On the next page, the text jumped again, starting in the middle of something.

20130811

Aperture One

15:05:05

BTalavera: I swear by the Mother I am NOT bullshitting you. They'll make the formal announcement at 18:00, but it's real. Here are the feeds. Check for yourself.

20130811

OH Mirrorsite

15:15:32

TLewiston: OMFG. Babs, did you guys craft this yourselves? Come on. For real.

20130811

Aperture One

15:19:01

BTalavera: I swear we did not. It attached itself to the probe.

20130811

OH Mirrorsite
15:20:20
TLewiston: LIFE?

20130811
Aperture One
15:23:19
BTalavera: And biomechanical.

The exchange ended there, or at least there were no more pages about it.

Erin leaned back in her chair. "I think we just found where the parasites came through originally. Aperture One."

Ilsa did not look up from where she was tracking ink onto the fabric, but Trevian and Stillwater straightened up.

They both walked over. As Stillwater pulled out her chair, she said, "What did you find?"

Erin rotated the book, pointing out the texts between Talavera and Lewiston. Stillwater said, "That's correspondence?"

"Yeah. What did you think it was?"

"A religious chant or prayer. Constant repetition, words that make no sense..."

Erin looked at the page with a different perspective. "It *does* kind of read that way. This is the kind of thing we do, in my world, on my device. The...plaque?" She tapped the page. "These originated from Aperture One." Seeing their expressions, she said, "Aperture is a hole, an opening. Usually, someone controls the size of the opening."

"I see."

"They sent a device through a hole, and it brought something back. Something like a machine but alive. And then..." She flipped back to the account of the little boy, the explosion, the whole town being moved. "They cleared out a whole town. And this," she rummaged through the pages to find the AAR while they both stared at her, "this mentions both Aperture One and Orchard Hill."

Trevian had been following his own thoughts. "An aperture. You think they opened a frontera and brought one of the parasites through."

"They were doing some kind of experiment with alternate dimensions, and they were excited about it. Maybe this was the first frontera."

"We don't know where either of these sites was," Stillwater said. "If we did, it might direct you on your search, but..."

"It gives us some background. Me, it gives me background. And this scientist, they use the word biomechanical. That's what the parasites are like: living machines."

Stillwater stood up. "I cherish what you are telling me. I'm just not sure there is a practical value to it, as we try to close the frontera."

"I'm not sure there is either," Erin said. She stood up and carefully closed the book. The room was so quiet she heard the tink-tink of Ilsa's pen against the metal inkpot. She stowed the volume carefully in the box. "I don't think I can read any more from this one today."

Another scribe named Einer relieved Ilsa and worked for two hours. Two junior scribes worked diligently, stitching the completed pages together. Erin leafed through some other books, but she couldn't stop thinking, what had they found at Aperture One? Had they really killed all the scientists there? And where was Orchard Hill? Had they blown it up too?

Trevian pulled out his watch. "It is nearly six," he said. Already? She folded up her notes and slipped them into her book. If the notes were even worth anything.

They headed across the courtyard, now thrown into shadow. An apprentice walked a sweat-lathered caballo in a long loop across the courtyard. Someone called Trevian's name. They both stopped for the out-of-breath apprentice who ran up to them.

"A note by fast messenger, Yor Langtree," he said, handing a square of paper to Trevian.

Trevian flinched. "Thank you," he said. He shoved the letter into his pocket and strode off, taking Erin by surprise. She hurried to catch up.

"Are you going to read it?" she said, as they reached their sprite cart. Genaro greeted them, holding his crossbow at his side.

"Yes."

Erin didn't push it. It was probably bad news about his father, or at least he thought it was. She wasn't going to make him probe that wound if he wasn't ready. At the same time, what if he had to go back to White Bluffs after all? What would it mean for finding the frontera and stopping the parasites? She'd acted super-confident in front of him before, but he was right—she couldn't get there herself.

She climbed in next to him.

Once they were settled, Trevian pried the paper out of his pocket and opened it. Erin stared straight ahead so he wouldn't think she was trying to read it. He gave a short gasp. "What turviness?"

"Is it your father?"

"No." He nudged her arm with the note. "Here."

She took it.

Before she could even start reading it, he said, "My sister says she is coming to the capital, this night. And she says 'we.'"

Trevian:

Oshane arrived here and seeks control of the company. He and the partners dispute your proxy. Father continues unchanged. We are riding to the capital and expect to arrive late Domingo night if all goes well.

I hope you will think of all of us and do what must be done.

Your loving sister,

Aideen

Loving? Scolding was more like it. Aideen clearly wasn't her brother's ally in any way. But Oshane was there. "Oshane wants the family business?"

"It provides heat and light to the whole town. My father has power, in many senses of that word, and Oshane seeks power. So do the parasites, I guess."

She held out the letter.

"Who would she bring? And I don't believe the Council would set aside a lawful proxy."

Erin didn't understand the whole proxy thing, but she got the gist of it. "Should we go back to the Coalition to wait for her?"

Genaro spoke from the other seat. "No need, yorita. We'll send a message to Elmaestro Tregannon and a cart for her."

"Maybe she just wants to re-do the proxy," Erin said.

"It was correctly written and duly witnessed two years ago," Trevian said. "If they dispute it, it's for reasons of politics, not lawfulness. And Oshane is there. I worry about what he might have done to her."

Erin grew cold all over. "Do you think that's who she means? Is she bringing Oshane?"

"He wouldn't let her send a message."

"No, probably not." Erin sat back and stared ahead. "If he, and the parasites, want the company, we have to stop them, whatever it takes. Right?"

"Yes," Trevian said. "We do."

155

11

Domingo, 21 Uno, Year 331

Harald had offered Trevian a glass of lick to settle his nerves. Trevian refused it. He wanted a clear head for his meeting with his sister and whatever companion she had enlisted. Now, with ten minutes passed since Harald had gotten a note from the Coalition and left to bring back Aideen and her companion, he was wishing he had something to numb his nerves after all.

Erin said, "Do you think she brought a doctor, maybe? A healer?"

"It's possible."

"What if," she said and fell silent. She looked away, studying the bluish flames in the hearth.

After a moment, he said quietly, "What if what?"

"What if she's got a parasite and the "we" was a slip?"

A shudder racked him. It was all too possible. What would they do if his sister was infected?

"We can remove it," Erin said. "We have before."

He remembered the Copper Coalition guard and the stuporous copper-hunters in Merrylake Landing. He didn't want to think of his vibrant younger sister in such a state. But "we"… It made a sickening kind of sense.

Genaro, who waited by the door to the sala, said, "We will know soon, and we'll take whatever steps we need to."

"I continue to bring ruin to my family," Trevian said.

"You didn't bring the parasites here. You didn't make your uncle bargain with them," Erin said.

"I know that with my reason. In my heart, I feel like I am the person who brings a disease to others yet never falls ill," he said.

"Well, you're not, so get over it. I mean, don't worry about that." Erin launched herself from her chair and began pacing in front of the hearth. "It's your family, and not any of my business," she said. Once again, Trevian struggled a bit to make sense of the words. "We know Oshane thinks you've got a magical—a charmed—ability to find frontera. And you can't let him get hold of you."

"I agree," he said. He glanced around. Genaro had left the doorway. Trevian wished he himself had been that clever.

"I'm pretty sure what Aideen wants, or even needs, is for you to go back with her. So we'll have to come up with a way to help her, and protect your company—"

"My father's company."

"Whatever. And keep you out of Oshane's reach."

"I don't know how we will do that," Trevian said.

"Well, we'll figure something out," she said.

Genaro carried in a mandolin. Erin gasped when she saw it. Without speaking, the valet sat down near the fire. He began to play softly. Erin stopped her pacing and stood, smiling faintly. It was an old song Trevian vaguely recognized. Erin sat back down, leaning forward, hands clasped.

The song ended.

"What do you call that?" Erin said, gesturing to the instrument.

"A mandolin."

She nodded. "Same as us."

"Do you play, yorita?"

"A little."

Genaro held out the mandolin, but Erin shook her head, putting up her hand. "Please, keep playing."

He re-tuned a couple of the strings and launched into a rollicking riding song Trevian had grown up with, following by a mournful folk tune, and something with the strange chords and shifts of a classical piece. Erin relaxed, nodding her head to the rhythm, her gaze never leaving Genaro's fingers.

Erin murmured, "Do you play?"

"My mother taught me the guitarra for a time and how to read the notes. When she left, music left our house with her."

"I'm sorry."

Genaro's fingers stilled. Outside, a cart clunked to a stop, and voices carried to them. Genaro set aside the mandolin and went to the door. Trevian stood up, his chest suddenly hollow, his heart beating fast.

Harald came in and stood to one side. Beside him, a slim figure pushed back the hood of her coat. She was pale, tired, but she smiled when she saw him. Without thinking, Trevian stepped forward and wrapped his arms around his sister. "You look well," he said. "You look well, Aideen."

She hugged him hard. "I *am* well. We must talk." She pulled back gently and edged around him.

Another woman stood just inside the door, her hood also bunched around her face. He didn't recognize her. Even when the long triangular face with its high cheekbones and full mouth registered, his mind refused to believe what his eyes were seeing. Her black hair, usually crafted into curls and rolls around her head, was pulled back from her face. Her dark eyes, the right set at a slight slant, were the same.

"And do *I* look well?" she said.

When he heard the voice, he could no longer deny what he was seeing. "Ilsanja," he said. "Well met."

He was rooted to the spot at first, but some germ of courtesy that wasn't dead within him drove him forward, hand outstretched. She raised hers. Her palm was cold, her grip firm. He was at the end of a gaze he'd seen her give others many, many times, the gaze of Ilsanja Silvestro measuring the item before her.

"Genaro, let's have sisuree, and some bread and cheese," Harald said. "I've spoken to both our visitors about the events in Merrylake Landing, and the parasites."

Trevian released Ilsanja's hand. "Aideen, how is Father?"

"The same, as far as I know."

"I'm glad you are safe, but I don't understand why you've come, why you've both come."

Ilsanja cleared her throat, but Aideen brushed the other woman's arm with her hand. "No, it's my place to tell him. We agreed, remember?"

"Sisuree sounds refreshing, Justice Arm, but I wonder if I may presume upon you for a bath," Ilsanja said, as calmly as if she and Harald were old friends.

"Of course. Katurah!"

The cook came out, holding a plate of sliced bread.

"Assist Yorita Silvestro with her bath, please. Genaro can serve us. Yorita Silvestro, Yorita Langtree, I would like to present Yorita Erin Dosmanos."

Erin, who had been leaning against the arch of the sala with her arms folded, stepped forward. "Hi."

Ilsanja's gaze swept her down and up. "Dosmanos. A familiar name."

"We have Dosmanos cousins," Aideen said. After a moment, she held out her hand and Erin shook it.

"I doubt we're related," Erin said.

"Oh, yes. You're the out-of-worlder," Ilsanja said, shaking hands with Erin.

Trevian said, "How did you know that?"

"Your messenger told us."

He looked at Erin, who shook her head. "I didn't say anything," she said.

"Then...the Agustos."

Aideen said, "Were they the older pair? They said something about returning to their world."

"Yorita?" Katurah said quietly.

"What? Oh, yes. A bath, as my reward if I'm to be scrutinized like a lamb for ticks," Ilsanja said. "Seems like a fair price if the water's hot."

Seeing Trevian's stare, Harald said, "I told them what we expected."

Trevian's face burned. Aideen said, "This infestation sounds serious. Elmaestro Tregannon spoke of it too, and he showed us one of those *things*. If being searched safeguards us and others, it's a small price to pay." She smiled. "Especially if there is a hot bath on the other side of the test."

"I promise you there is," Harald said, giving both women a short bow. Katurah led Ilsanja away, and Harald escorted Aideen into the sala. Trevian stood in the center of the room, not knowing what to do. Erin kept back, standing, and didn't speak as Harald seated Aideen near the fire and Genaro brought her a cup of sisuree.

She spoke of their father's condition and of the journey she and Ilsanja had taken. She had changed in the past two years. The calm, the intelligence, and the capability he had always admired and envied was housed now in a woman grown. He tried to take in this revelation, but it was nearly too much for him.

The room fell quiet as Aideen drained her cup. Trevian wished Erin would say something, but she stood silent and immobile next to the arch, arms still folded.

"I'm glad I had your letter about our uncle," Aideen said. "I might not have been on my guard otherwise. He is quite convincing."

Trevian nodded. He didn't think his sister was under the influence of the parasites, but it might be one was making her speak this way to distract him.

Women's voice rang down the hall. Katurah escorted Ilsanja, dressed in a dark green skirt and blouse, to the sala. Katurah gave Aideen a nod. "Yorita Aideen, would you care to bathe? It will take our tub a moment to refill." To Harald, she said, "No parasite."

Aideen gave Trevian a smile, but it seemed forced. She stood up.

"That tub was clearly stolen from paradise," Ilsanja said. "It's round, made of some white stone inlaid with colored glass squares near the top. And if Katurah here makes the soap, I will have the recipe from her before we leave."

A smile brightened the cook's face.

"The benefits of prospecting," Harald said. "The tub is a piece of Ancient."

Aideen cleared her throat and followed Katurah up the hall. Ilsanja sat down and began pulling her wet hair into a braid.

Trevian thought the room had been quiet before. It was nothing compared to this weighted silence. Ilsanja glanced around, completely at her ease. After a moment or two, she asked Harald about where he had found various items. Trevian joined Erin where she stood.

"I do not know why she is here," he murmured.

Erin said, "You don't? Really?"

"How would I?"

"I think it's pretty obvious, considering the whole proxy thing."

He shook his head, baffled. Ilsanja apparently saw the motion and gazed at him.

He cast around for something to say. "I guess you have married now," he said finally.

"No."

"No?" He felt witless and dry of words. "Pledged, then?"

She stared at him. After a moment, she nodded once. "Yes," she said. "Pledged."

Trevian looked around, feeling as if everyone in the room but him knew something.

Aideen came back, in clean clothes, her hair screwed up on top of her head the way she'd worn it when she was younger. Katurah followed her. "No parasite," she said. "And I will heat up some food for our guests."

Ilsanja stood up, and Harald got slowly to his feet. Erin moved away from the arch. Aideen held her ground. "Trevian, I must speak to you first. It's important. It's why we've come."

Erin cleared her throat. "We can all wait in the study while you two talk, if that's all right, Harald?"

"Of course," he said.

"Shall I serve in the study, yor?"

"No... No. We'll eat at the table." He raised his eyebrows. "Do you think this will take long?"

"One way or another, it will not," Aideen said.

Harald nodded. "Very well." He led the retreat out of the room. Aideen stepped through the archway into the sala and then it was she and Trevian alone.

Y ou want...what?" he said.

"I want you to marry Ilsanja," she repeated, as if it were a reasonable thing she asked.

"Do you remember how I left White Bluffs? How I left *her*? Even if I agreed, why would *she*? I wounded her, Aideen."

His sister nodded. Her face was solemn. Trevian was sure he was the goat in some elaborate joke.

"You did wound her, but she is willing to look beyond that."

"And why?" He shook his head. "Anyway, no. I cannot marry and return to White Bluffs. Didn't you understand what the elmaestro and the justice arm explained to you? Erin needs my help. She and I must—"

"You don't need to come back to White Bluffs." She held up her hands. "Listen to me without interruption, please. You and she will marry here, a duly witnessed marriage, and she and I will return to town with the documents. You and Erin can carry on with your quest. Don't you see, Trevian? This frees you!"

"Until Ilsanja decides she wants a child, perhaps. We will be bound to each other, legally at least. She will be bound to me. Has she thought of that?"

"Well, she said she thinks you will mostly be gone," Aideen said.

It silenced him. It sounded as if his absence was actually a sweetener in the bargain, rather than an obstacle.

"This," he said, stammering, "this is some strange jest, or you have both gone turvy. Did you eat fermented grain or something?"

"We have not. Plainly, Don Leo and our uncle have already decided to overturn your proxy. But Don Leo will not challenge his daughter's share in the company if she is your wife."

"And what's to stop Ilsanja from marrying me, returning with you, and then doing as her father wishes? You will lose the company, and she will have her revenge on me. Have you thought of that?"

"I have," Aideen said.

He did not understand how she could sound so calm.

She said, "Trevian, I love you, and I do not say this to wound you. I do not think revenge against you is a large part of Ilsanja's life. I do not think she has spent the last two years planning for it."

"Perhaps not, but if you offered her this scheme, then she—" The expression on his sister's face stopped him. "Ah. You mean *I* was not a large part of Ilsanja's life. She didn't lack the time to plan revenge. I wasn't worthy of such planning."

Aideen sucked in a long breath and sighed. "Yes."

"Well. That is a perspective." He turned away and stared at the fire.

The scheme was desperate and strange, but in fact, there had never been a case, to his knowledge, where a wife or husband's role as proxy agent had been disputed. Perhaps Harald would know more, but the plan, from that angle of view at least, was sound. The only real question was why Ilsanja would ever agree to such a thing.

As if she had tracked his thoughts, Aideen said, "What Ilsanja wants, what she *always* wanted, is the role of a jefa, her own place in a boss family. This marriage will give her that. And she chafes under the direction of others, especially her shallow father. She wishes to exercise her own interests. She is smart, and observant, and has a gift for strategy."

"This I know."

"She wants that valued."

You do not value me, Ilsanja had said to him, the night he had left her. *You do not value your place in a boss family, and you do not value me.* Was it possible this *was* all she wanted? She had faced the inconve-

163

nience and danger of the journey here, and faced the man who had dented her pride, for a place, a position, of value?

And yet, if some day she wished children, he would be entangled. His heart would not be his to give, when, for the first time in his life, he wished it free to give to someone.

"I will have to speak to Erin about this," he said.

"Have you pledged to her?"

"What? No. No, of course not. We have known each other for days only. But I *have* pledged to help her, to use the book to keep both our worlds safe, and I cannot make a, a whimsical decision—"

"Whimsical?" Aideen said.

"Without at least hearing her counsel."

"Then ask her. Be sure she understands the stakes here. Without this plan, Oshane will surely take a seat in the partnership, and we have no idea what that will mean for the company, or the worlds you guard."

"Do you mock me?"

"I do not. But I am *tired* of fighting, always fighting, to keep the calm and make things right while you quest to fulfill your dreams. Just once, I wish you could reach beyond the sphere of your own thoughts and wishes."

He wheeled around, his face hot. "Do you think my life is *easy?*"

Her eyes widened and she stalked up to him. "I think your life is the one you wanted. You have never since childhood thought about duty because I was there to do it for you. Even now with Father dying and our murderous uncle poised to take everything, you will not do one simple thing to stop it."

"I risked my life to save this world!" he said. The words sounded ridiculous to him, even though they were true. For a moment, he saw himself through Aideen's eyes: indulgent and selfish, all the things he had privately called his father. He had never once thought the things she did might put a strain on her. "I thought working with the company *was* the life you wanted," he said finally.

Her shoulders shook as she turned away. "I am not a great hero like you or Yorita Dosmanos," she said, choking a little. "I'm also trying to save a world, it's just one you ignore because it is tiny, only the size of a town."

He stepped closer and put his arms around her. "Aideen, you are the smartest person I know."

She remained stiff, then relaxed slightly against him.

He judged the timing, and said carefully, "Or you *were*. I think now the justice arm might in fact be the—"

She stiffened again, and pinched his arm the way she had when they were children. "Monster," she said, but she was laughing now.

He hugged her. "I'm sorry about Father."

Wiping her eyes, she half-turned. He studied her profile. "I have lots of questions about how he fell from his office window, especially when the glass was found on the carpet. And he... I discovered something that leaves me distressed and ashamed."

"You learned about the loans," he said, moving around to face her.

"You knew?" Tears still shimmered in her eyes as she stared up at him.

"Father told me. He showed me the ledger sheets, the night before I left. He was *proud*." Some of his anger returned, and he waited until he could speak calmly. "He was proud of being a usurer. We didn't need the coin, but it wouldn't stop him from leeching coin and pride from his neighbors..."

"I've forgiven several of the loans," she said.

He hadn't thought the night could give him any more surprises. "You just forgave them?"

She lifted her head. He didn't remember seeing defiance in her before. "When he is well again, he can chastise me," she said, and Trevian burst into startled laughter before he could stop himself. He hugged her again, hard.

"You *are* brilliant," he said.

"Yes." She stepped back. "I may be, but I need your answer."

And determined. He sighed. "I must speak with Erin. I have promised her my help. I see the logic of your plan, but I will not go forward without her opinion."

There were times when it was more obvious than others that Erin was not a woman from his world, and he could not read her expressions and gestures as he could others'. This was one of those times.

He explained systematically, or tried to, although several times he had to stop and go back to explain again about his father's partnership, or about what had happened with him and Ilsanja. She stood, nodding whenever he stopped for breath. He could not read her face. When finally he finished his tale, she said, "If she says yes to this, I think you have to."

"You're sure? I'll make it clear she has no hold on me. I mean, I'm not returning to White Bluffs with her. She *will* have a hold on me, but—"

"Trevian, I understand. People get married for all kinds of reasons and have all kinds of arrangements."

He guessed "arrangement" was her term for taking a lover.

"If your gorgeous former fiancée says yes to this, then I think your sister's plan is good."

He worked out "fiancée" after a moment. "What does gorgeous mean?"

"Beautiful."

"Oh." He'd thought it meant cold, or angry. "Well, she's always been beautiful. I question her motives, but Aideen does not, and she's a better judge of character than I."

"Yeah, about that." Erin stared past him, gave her head a slight shake. "It sounds like Ilsanja gets what she wants out of it, and if she agrees to what your sister told you, we'll be able to continue our search for this frontera and close it."

"Our mission has been all my focus. This came at me like a mestengo ambush," he said.

Erin nodded. "I understand. It's your decision."

"It means..." He cleared his throat. "This means any connection I might wish to have after this must be an informal one. This marriage, though, it doesn't touch my heart."

Erin said, "Let's not get off-track. Oshane is in White Bluffs. We know he wants to lure you there, it's part of why he's making a move on your father's business. But he also *does* want control of the company for some reason, and we have to stop him. Will this stop it?"

"If we can trust Ilsanja, it will."

"Do you think we can?"

"Apparently, she does not hate me enough to wish revenge, and she desires only the social position being Jefa Langtree brings her. As long as she has that, we can trust her."

"And you and I can get back to finding the frontera and closing it?"

He nodded.

"Well," she said.

He said, "I know what I have to do."

He asked Ilsanja to meet him in the sala for what he hoped was the final ordeal of the night.

"Ilsanja, are you truly willing to do this?"

"With some conditions," she said.

"I have conditions too. I must be sure you will be guided by Aideen's judgment when it comes to decisions about the company," he said. "No one knows its workings better."

"How can you know that? You've been away these last years while she's learned it." Ilsanja sounded mildly interested, as if it were a discussion of whose cook made the best pie.

"She wrote of learning the company."

Ilsanja glanced at him over her shoulder. It struck a pang in his heart, a familiar gesture he had forgotten. "And you trust her, do you?"

"I do."

Ilsanja nodded. "I do too. If you wish for a regular account of money spent, you will be disappointed. You either trust us or you don't."

"I have no need of that." He spoke quickly. "Before we go on, I want to say... I was selfish and my actions hurt you. I regret what I did."

She looked at him, unspeaking. After a moment, she sank down into one of the chairs. "Well, you did hurt me. Fortunately, the boss families of White Bluffs were intelligent enough to put the blame where it belonged, and my reputation suffered only a little. I do wish you had spoken to me. I thought we were friends. We could have arranged things."

The word "arranged" echoed with Erin's comments. He forced himself to ignore that distracting thought, and said, "The night before we went to the fair, I discovered something ugly about my father. Even more ugly than the bitterness I'd grown up with, an ugliness that stretched beyond the walls of our house. I—I was angry, and I could not aim my rage. My choice at the fair was not reasoned, Ilsanja. It was not strategic or measured. It was the flight of a prisoner who sees a cage door opened."

She smiled, as if at a private joke. "I know." She smoothed her skirt. "Back to our conditions. I assume you will return from time to time."

"If I survive our task, I think I will have to."

She gave a brisk nod. "In public, then, we will be the happy boss partnership, but once inside the walls of our house, I will have a private life. We will not share a room or a bed. And if I am to trust Aideen with the company, then so are you. No returning in three years to say you will now take the reins and drive the cart."

"I have no desire to drive the cart, ever."

"I see that. I was surprised to discover how serious your discovery in Merrylake Landing was." She stood up. "Are we in agreement, then?"

"We are."

"Good. The justice arm has sent a note to a magistrate friend, and we can marry tomorrow morning. Aideen and I will head back to White Bluffs, and you can go forward with your quest with your out-of-worlder woman."

12

Lunis, 22 Uno, Year 331

To Aideen's surprise, sleeping arrangements had been easily handled. Trevian slept on a couch in the justice arm's room, and Ilsanja and Aideen shared the bed in the room that had been his. Aideen quietly acknowledged her relief. She had feared she would share a room with the nearly silent out-of-worlder woman.

"This has gone well after all," Ilsanja said as she pulled back the covers and sat down on the bed.

"Did you and Trevian reach a suitable agreement?" It had been too awkward to discuss at their late-night meal, which had been excellent.

"Yes." Ilsanja began to comb out her hair. "Your brother isn't really a fool. He simply cannot move easily in society."

Aideen lined up her boots at the end of the bed. "He seems focused on this task of theirs."

Ilsanja reached over her head, stretching like a cat, one hand loosely holding the comb. "I would have dismissed that as a turvy fancy the two of them had concocted if we hadn't seen that creature in the cage. And she *did* show us the book."

Aideen had been persuaded when she'd seen the pink leather

169

bladder at the Copper Coalition. "I don't see how Oshane fits into this scheme of infection," she said, "But I *do* believe he does." She stood up and looked at her friend. "Tomorrow you'll be married. It's not the marriage celebration you had always planned."

Ilsanja smiled and put her finger to her lips in a gesture for secrets. "I'll share this only with you. This entire trip has been an exhilaration."

"Really? Riding through rain? Crude latrines, sleeping on rocks?"

"An adventure with my friend. And, if I'm honest, the expression on Trevian's face when he first saw me."

Aideen snorted. "I'm glad you haven't lost your touch for malice. If you had, I'd fear you were sick."

"My malice is like the touch of bitterness in kokolatal," Ilsanja said. "It makes the sweetness more interesting." She slid up to the head of the bed and turned half-sideways. "Before we sleep, let me comb out your hair."

Justice Arm Stuart, Genaro, Ilsanja, and Trevian all left one hour past sunrise. An hour later, Aideen sat in the sala with the out-of-worlder Erin. The woman was fingering notes on Genaro's mandolin, which he had lent her. Aideen stared at the pages of a book of poems the justice arm had given her before they left, but she could not concentrate. Her mind led her only to Ilsanja.

Ilsanja had managed to look beautiful in the same dark green blouse and skirt, but her expression had been blank. Trevian fidgeted and spoke little. Well, it was not a joyous occasion, and probably, for her brother, of less interest than registering a claim of Ancient to prospect.

The mournful notes distracted her. "A song from your world?"

The other woman stopped. "Yes. It's called 'Poor Wayfaring Stranger.'"

"It's pretty."

"It's about dying."

"Oh." Aideen turned a page.

The other woman—Erin—said, "You probably don't believe in the frontera." She plucked a series of notes as she spoke.

"Frontera are like sheep. They care little whether I believe in them."

"Really?"

Aideen looked at her. Erin could have been a woman from The Crescent. Her curly dark hair was shorter than many wore it, but women prospectors often cut their hair. "What I never believed were the tales of the Four Families."

Erin smiled. "Try living in one." She strummed a few chords. "I grew up hearing about artifacts and elemental worlds. I never thought I'd end up in one. I trained and everything, but it wasn't real somehow."

"Before you, how many guardians have gone through frontera?"

Erin lay the instrument in her lap. "From my family, as far as I know, none."

"But you knew where frontera were in your world?"

"Oh, yes. The Four Families worked together on finding them. Going through them wasn't what we were supposed to do, except as a last resort. The warnings, the training, was always about people *from* the other worlds and keeping the artifacts safe from them. Which, surprise, turns out to be true."

"Was it frightening, going through one? Coming here?"

"Yes. I thought I'd die, but mainly because of the fire and the hunter-hounds—the flames. Now, it's more strange than anything." Her hand brushed a minor chord from the strings. "And lonely."

"I see."

"Can I ask you a question?"

Aideen nodded, bracing herself for a question about Trevian or Ilsanja.

"What's the difference between a 'yor' and a 'jefe?'"

"Oh! Well, honestly? Coin mostly. Technically, any man is a Yor and any woman is a Yora or Yorita."

Erin raised her eyebrows. "I wasn't sure there was a Yora."

"Yes. People in positions of authority or respect—or wealthy people—are Jefe or Jefa. And housekeepers."

"So Elmaestro Tregannon is a Jefe."

"He is, but he will use his title Elmaestro the rest of his life, even after he steps down from his position."

"And the profesors?"

"Yor and Yora."

"Pecking order. Hokay." Erin nodded. "I think I understand. Thanks for explaining."

"Now will you tell me what it is you and Trevian do at the Copper Coalition with your book?"

Erin lifted the mandolin and tilted it up against a low table. She explained about the borders on the pages and how they might be a secret map. Aideen found herself talking about Yor Oakley, her uncle, and the threat to negate Trevian's proxy. "Oshane seemed eager to draw Trevian back."

"Your uncle thinks Trevian can find frontera. I do too. He found mine. He went right to it; he just didn't realize that was what he was doing. He can't open one, though."

"How can my uncle? Neither he nor my father were copper-hunters, and neither was their father, although he was a prospector."

Erin leaned forward. "I don't know, and that worries me. Trevian said Oshane had a string of metallic-looking stone beads on his wrist, and he mentioned them in passing as a way to open frontera. One thing's clear. Oshane has spent a lot of time searching for charms *and* frontera, and he's found both."

Aideen thought back to the meeting and tried to remember if her uncle had worn a string of beads. "I didn't see it," she said. "Only the golden amulet in the shape of Cheviot the Ram."

"The four-horned sheep? I saw that too. Trevian says it's the amulet that controls the air elemental, along with the flautine thing."

Aideen shuddered.

Erin said, "What are you and Ilsanja going to do next?"

"Go home. The justice arm has a sworn warrant for Oshane, so he plans to accompany us. I guess we will leave shortly after they return."

"I—really? They're not going to... Doesn't the marriage have to be consummated?"

"What is consummated?"

"Um...acted on? Don't they have to have sex or something? Be lovers?"

Aideen frowned, wondering why Erin was pushing Trevian and Ilsanja toward such an unnecessary complication. "From everything you've said, now is not the time for children. Did they discuss it last night? I *hope* that isn't the plan, because it's a delay."

"Oh, hokay. No, that's fine. It's just...different from where I come from. If there's a legal challenge there, someone could say it's not an actual marriage."

"It's an actual marriage. It's a joining of two families." Aideen didn't want to think of her brother and Ilsanja becoming lovers, but they would eventually, of course. There had to be heirs. She snapped the book shut and stood up. "I wish for some sisuree. Would you care for some?"

"Sure, thanks."

Aideen fled to the kitchen.

A ideen skulked in the kitchen as long as she could, and when she returned to the sala with a tray, Erin was no longer there, but in the study, staring at a page in her metal book. She thanked Aideen in the tone of a person who didn't really know who had approached them or what they had done.

"What intrigues you so?"

"This page. It was one Harald had. It seems to show scarification. The page is scratched up, and there's some printing, but it's so tiny I can't read it."

"Self-scarring?" Aideen looked over her shoulder.

"Yes." Erin pointed to an elaborate sigil drawn on a human arm. Two triangles poised on their points with the long sides facing one another. Three lines intersected them. A slanted line pointed up to the left and one down to the right, just outside the triangles. It was something a child might draw.

"That's labeled 'loomin.'" Erin tapped something stamped into the page.

If Aideen squinted, she could see the letters. She was afraid to get too close to the book after what Erin had told them about the charm on it.

"Do the wearers of the creature mark themselves in some way?"

"…Maybe," Erin reached over without looking, pushing with her hand, and Aideen guided the cup into her fingers before she knocked it onto the floor. "Thanks." She sipped. "Or maybe it's the other way around. Maybe it's a vaccination."

"What is that?"

"A way to…strengthen resistance to a disease. A particular disease."

"The way those who survive a serious disease often don't get it again."

"Yes, like that."

"You think this mark protects its wearer from the parasites."

"It could be," Erin said.

"Or it could be a way to invite a parasite."

"It could be that too," Erin said. "I don't know."

"It's a puzzle," Aideen said. If Ilsanja had been here, her eyes would be dancing with the challenge, too.

"I didn't see any marks carved on the victims," Erin said.

"But they were clothed."

Erin shook her head. "Not the first ones I saw."

"Well, that lends strength to your theory then."

Aideen squinted and leaned down closer to the page. "I think there are words under those scratches."

"I wish we could read them," Erin said. She stared at the page. "Do you think Katurah would have a clear glass jar?"

"Why?"

"If I put some water in it sometimes where the water curves, you get magnification. Maybe I could use that to try to read what's written there."

"Ingenious," Aideen said. "Wouldn't a magnifier be simpler, though?"

Erin's head whipped up. "A magnifier?"

"Yes. Harald has dozens of books. I'm sure he has one."

Erin swallowed. "A magnifier. Yeah, that would be *great*."

Aideen searched drawers and soon found a piece of magnifying stone. Erin held it as if she'd never seen such a thing and Aideen had to show her how to orient it lengthwise over the metal, but soon they were taking turns peering down. The scratches stretched like pieces of yarn, and Aideen shut her eyes and reopened them, trying to decipher the figures. "This is a number, but there is a symbol after it I don't recognize it."

"Ninety-four? Ninety-seven?"

"Ninety-seven, I think," Aideen said.

"And it's a percentage symbol. Ninety-seven percent."

"Of what?"

Erin jerked her shoulders upward. "One...hour?"

"Ninety-seven percent of an hour? Why not say fifty-eight minutes?"

"Maybe it's two separate things. An hour of something, and ninety-seven percent."

"Well, this is disappointing," Aideen said. "A lot of effort for more mystery."

Erin's smile startled her. "Welcome to my life," she said, and after a second or two, Aideen understood, and smiled back.

A sprite cart rattled up outside, and the wards dropped. As Genaro opened the door, Aideen and Erin joined the wedding party in the entryway. Trevian's gaze searched out Erin's face, while Ilsanja grinned at Aideen. "Do I see a cup of sisuree in your hand?" she said.

"I'll get you some," Aideen said. Both parties in the marriage seemed more relaxed now. The justice arm herded Erin and Trevian back into his study. Genaro reset the wards, and Ilsanja curled her fingers around Aideen's arm.

"I will go with you. Perhaps there's some cheese. I ate little this morning."

175

"Did all go well?"

"Yes, but longer than we expected. The process of registering and copying the documents was tedious." Ilsanja pushed open the kitchen door. Katurah gave them one glance and nodded at the pot of sisuree on the stove. They filled their cups and went out to the sala.

A few minutes later, Harald joined them. "Erin and Trevian plan to go up to the compound at noon," he said. "I thought we would leave at the same time."

"We will be ready." Ilsanja sipped her sisuree and watched him walk into the study. "Are we heading back the way we came, even to the shortcut?"

"If the justice arm agrees, I thought we would." It was shorter than taking the North Road to Sheeplands and doubling back.

Over lunch, Ilsanja, watching Erin consume sisuree, said, "Do you have this drink in your world?"

"I don't think so. The popular stimulant drink where I'm from is called coffee. For me, anyway. It's more bitter."

Ilsanja said, "Do you like bitter things?"

"Beware," Aideen said. "She'll slip you a nasty brew she calls kokolatal."

"Oh, you spoil all my tricks."

"Kokolatal?" Erin set down her cup. "We might have something like that. We call it chocolate."

"Is it a beverage?"

"It can be. It's used in lots of things. It's made from roasted seeds from a particular plant—"

Ilsanja leaned forward, nodding.

"By itself, it's really bitter, like, uneatable."

Aideen said, "Yes, it is."

"They put some kind of fat in it, like…cream? And they put sweetener. It's used for baking, for candy, and we mix the powder in milk for a drink."

"Milk…" Ilsanja said. Her eyes were shining. "And baking. Is it common where you're from?"

"I'd say yes," Erin said.

"With a sweetener."

"Yes. We use sugar. It's a powdered sweetener, or, crystals, I guess."

"Azucar," Harald said. "They use it in the eastern continent. They also use a syrup of it."

"But you could use honey," Ilsanja said.

Erin gave her jerky up-and-down of her shoulders. "Probably couldn't hurt."

"You've given me a challenge," Ilsanja said. "Thank you."

Erin's brow furrowed. "Um, you're welcome."

They finished their meal and packed their saddlebags. A Coalition apprentice had brought their caballos back from the compound earlier in the morning. The animals were refreshed, and Ilsanja's gelding pranced a few steps and shook his mane.

The justice arm used a mounting block, setting into place with a quick grimace.

"Your valet doesn't ride with us?" Ilsanja said.

"Genaro will stay to help Trevian and Erin." He patted the crossbow slung across his saddle in front of him. "We should be safe enough."

"Good journey," Trevian said.

Ilsanja said, "Do you have something for me?"

He approached her caballo and handed up a square of paper. "As we discussed," he said.

Erin said, "Be careful."

"And you, good luck on your quest," Aideen said. She guided her mare in behind the justice arm's mount, and they rode through the gate at the side of the house, out onto the lakeside road, heading for the ferry landing.

The boat was nearly empty. Aideen shivered as the brisk north wind swept around her, flicking the tops of the lake waves white. They hurried inside. The justice arm moved to the prow of the boat, but Ilsanja and Aideen stayed inside the cabin, sitting on the smooth bench bolted to the bulkhead.

"What did Trevian hand to you?"

"Another proxy statement," Ilsanja said. "Here." She pulled it out of her belt pouch.

Aideen unfolded the stiff paper. It was witnessed by four people, including a magistrate. She read it, then read it again. "Did you agree to this?"

"I would have no other decision."

Trevian divided his proxy vote equally between Ilsanja Silvestro Langtree, wife, and Aideen Langtree, sister.

"They'll dispute this. This solves nothing," she said. "Why did you give up your voting right?"

"I gave up nothing. If the remaining partners dispute it, or even successfully set it aside, then as Trevian's wife I become his agent. And I will vote as you would have voted. There is no risk here."

"There is a risk for you, giving up your voting right. There's a loss."

Ilsanja smiled. "I've lost *nothing*. I know about caballos and fashion, and I intend to know much about kokolatal. I am ignorant about the company, the flames, and how charmed energy moves along copper cords. I would be guided by you in any event. Nothing has changed, except your worth is acknowledged."

"I think you did this for me," Aideen said, smoothing out the paper.

"I did this for *me*. It was lucky Trevian's mind ran along the same trail, but he wouldn't have been hard to persuade. It's what's right."

Aideen refolded the paper and handed it back. "Well. We'll see how *this* is greeted when we return." She gripped the bottom edge of the bench as the ferry bucked in the chop.

The justice arm returned and sat next to Aideen, his artificial leg stretched out in front of him.

"I think we'll have rain again on our journey," Ilsanja said.

The justice arm nodded his agreement.

At the ferry landing, he again used a mounting block to get back onto his caballo. Ilsanja watched with interest. "Can you mount without a block?"

"It's awkward, but I can. I throw myself belly-down across the saddle and swing over my right leg."

Aideen said, "Is riding painful?"

"By the end of the day," he said. "And some days everything is painful. Climbing is...challenging. People expect the stump to hurt, and it does, of course, but it's all the other muscles: the thighs, my backside, my back, even shoulders. That's just the way of it."

"Do you take something for the pain? A tisane or a tincture?"

"Rarely. It's not a habit I want to adopt." He nudged his caballo forward.

The rain held off although the wind grew stronger and colder. Three hours south of Lily Bend, on the North Road, they stopped at a guesthouse. The keeper welcomed them—she knew Justice Arm Stuart by name. The room Aideen would share with Ilsanja was small but clean; the water in the attached bathhouse was warm and the food was good.

"Do you want to get an early start tomorrow?" The justice arm said as he pushed away his empty mug.

Aideen nodded just as Ilsanja said, "Yes."

"An hour past sunrise, then?"

"Yes," Aideen said, as Ilsanja echoed her.

While Ilsanja went to check on the caballos, Aideen lit the white-rock brazier in their room and laid out her linens for the morning. Once again, she and Ilsanja would share a bed. Safely alone, Aideen admitted to herself that it was not their journey, the mission, or the uncertainty at home that was disturbing her sleep. It was lying so close to her friend. She shook her head, unpinned her hair, and sat down on the edge of the bed, pulling the locks into a braid.

"The caballos are well cared for," Ilsanja said, "and we have a warm room two nights in a row." She sat down next to Aideen. The bed was so narrow their arms and hips nearly touched. Ilsanja leaned forward to unlace her boots. "What do you think of the out-of-worlder?"

"I talked with her while you and Trevian were getting married."

Ilsanja cocked her head. "Do you believe the tale of her origins?"

"I do."

"And everything?'

Aideen paused in her braiding. "I do. Do you doubt her?"

179

Ilsanja set her boots aside and reached up to unpin her hair too. Aideen dodged her friend's elbow.

"I find what she and Trevian both are saying to be fantastic, but I don't doubt it. Those pink creatures are terrifying. Do you think your uncle wears one?"

"Trevian thinks not, but I have to say it would explain much. Oshane's plan with the copper-hunters and the lantern, that is strange. And he had so many of those creatures. If he had imprisoned that many copper-hunters, and set the parasites on them...with the lantern, I wonder what he might have been able to do."

Ilsanja fluffed her hair. "For years, I thought copper-hunters only found metals. Even listening to Mama's tales, I never understood how much deeper their gifts ran, and how much like charmcasters they are in many ways. Could they locate frontera, open them? Or even create new ones?"

"That's not possible, is it?"

"We don't know what's possible."

"Maybe that's what Oshane originally planned."

Ilsanja stretched her arms out in front of her. The brazier light played on the fine hairs, making them glint. "If out-of-worlder Erin survives her quest, I hope I have a chance to talk to her more about kokolatal."

"If she survives?"

Ilsanja shrugged. "Their mission is dangerous, after all."

Aideen bit her lip. Of course the quest was deadly dangerous. She said, "Are you jealous of her?"

"No. I'm not ill-wishing her. I'm being realistic. I wish her well, actually, even if she did glare at me like a cat with a vole in its mouth, who sees another cat nearby."

Aideen laughed at the image. "Well, we can't blame her. We did appear in her life with little warning. And you are a woman to be reckoned with."

"Am I?" Ilsanja glanced sideways at Aideen. "She need have no concerns. Shall I send her a letter?"

"What?"

Ilsanja shifted on the bed so she faced Aideen. Her voice grew softer. "I'll compose it now. 'Dear out-of-worlder Erin, if your heart is warmed by Trevian, you need have no worries.'" She stroked Aideen's cheek with one finger. "'He is not the Langtree I desire.'"

Ilsanja flattened her hand against Aideen's cheek. Her heartbeat fluttered like a sprite against Aideen's skin. For an instant of horror, she wondered if Ilsanja meant Father. Then she covered her friend's hand with her own. She could barely speak. "What does that mean?"

Ilsanja's gaze was like a starlit night. "I hope you know what it means. These past three nights, lying by your side, I dared to hope you knew my feelings, Aideen, and shared them."

"If you mean..." She cleared her throat. "If you mean I wish you were by my side every moment, then I do."

Ilsanja's lips were warm against hers. She tasted of sisuree. Aideen moved her head, ending the kiss, and lowered her lips to the place where Ilsanja's neck met her shoulder. Ilsanja tilted back her head and sighed.

"I hoped," she said. "Even when I first pledged to Trevian, you were in my dreams. My secret wish."

"I never dared even to dream," Aideen said.

Ilsanja reached for the buttons on Aideen's blouse and undid them slowly. Aideen copied her gesture. Blouses fell, crumpled, onto the floor. Aideen slipped her fingers into Ilsanja's hair, and they both fell over sideways onto the bed. Aideen was engulfed in her friend's warmth, her scent, the silk of her hair, and her searching, teasing touch.

Later they slept, curled around each other. For Aideen, sunrise came too soon.

III

ON THE COPPER ROAD

1 3

Lunis, 22 Uno, Year 331

As the riders trotted out of sight, a weight lifted from Erin's shoulders. She hadn't really been aware of the tension while the two women had been here, but she recognized it now as it dissipated. She tried to sound on-mission. "Shall we head up to the compound now? Profesor Stillwater thinks they'll finish up today."

Genaro, who stood behind them, said, "The cart is ready."

"I'll get the book and my coat," she said.

When Erin came out with her bag and her jacket, Trevian was standing in the entryway, staring into space. "Are you all right?"

He started. "Yes. I, my father's most likely dying. Somehow that is...material now. I can almost touch it."

"I understand."

"I have no words left to say to him, nor he to me. I don't need to see him, but the thought of him gone—it leaves a hole in my world."

Erin stepped closer, nodding. "I know what it's like." Privately, she thought Trevian was kidding himself about there being nothing left to say to his father, but those words wouldn't comfort him any.

"Aideen was always able to love him without reservation, I think because she was so young when our mother left. I was always torn. Torn and angry."

"I like your sister," Erin said.

Trevian smiled finally. "My sister is as brilliant and calm as a sunny day." The smile broadened slightly. "And Ilsanja? What did you think of her?"

"Hmm. Not the type of person I'm usually friends with."

"To me, she has always been a perfectly crafted dagger. Gleaming and poised, ready to cut you in a moment."

"Well, *there's* a testimonial," Erin said. "So, if we're successful, will you go home to her? Have kids, make a family?"

"Kids? Oh. Children. Erin, right now I cannot think beyond our next step, beyond stopping Oshane and these parasites." He turned toward the door. "I hear the cart."

Genaro escorted them out, reset the wards, and loaded his crossbow. As they rode up toward the Coalition, Erin said, "If chocolate catches on here like it did in my world, Ilsanja's on her way to being rich."

"She has a gift for making money, I think," Trevian said. "Genaro, do you truly fear another attack?"

"Not usually in daylight hours, but I like to be prepared," the valet said.

Trevian peered out from the canopy. "I think all we need to be prepared for now is rain."

***

Erin handed the book to Stillwater and went to page through the volumes that had been brought down, searching for Orchard Hill references. It was a little more than an hour before Stillwater heaved a dramatic sigh and said, "Erin, Trevian, come see!"

Spread out on the worktable, the translucent quilt shimmered like something undersea. The sections were finely stitched together, so well aligned that there was no gap between the edges of the borders. Erin felt queasy. After all this time and work, what if the borders meant nothing? What if none of the opal sockets lined up with anything? What if they'd wasted four days?

Trevian said, "These are not all the pages of the book. Why did you stop?"

"This area will cover our table map, but I told the scribes to stop at the page with no border."

"Logical." Erin was rubbing her hands together. She made herself quit it.

Stillwater, on the other hand, was smiling and her eyes were wide. The profesor gathered up the edges. "Come on, then."

Trevian took one bottom edge, and Erin caught up the other. They carried it over to the carved map. When the profesor shook the fabric out over the map, it reminded Erin of putting sheets on a bed. Stillwater leaned over it. She gestured to the two scribes, who stood at the worktable. They hurried over. Stillwater smoothed the fabric. "Erin, does our symbol match up with the Pendrelle Delta?"

Erin peered at it, then shifted the sheer fabric herself. "There." She was disappointed. The details of the table map were blurry and indistinct.

Stillwater flattened the cloth. "A weight, there," she said. The lead scribe set a round stone the size of her palm on the edge of the table.

"Hold it too, please," Stillwater said. The scribe gripped the unhemmed edge and held it flat.

Stillwater ran her palm along the cloth, flattening it. At the other side of the map, the second scribe set down another stone. Now Erin saw it. With the fabric pulled tightly, the whorls and spirals lined up with the features on the map underneath it.

"Wow," she said.

Trevian shifted his weight from one foot to the other. "Is 'wow' good or bad?"

"Right now, it's good."

Stillwater set the final two weights. They stood back and looked at the design.

Trevian pointed. "That's the vein of Ancient near Lily Bend," he said. "There's a socket there, and that's where your frontera is, Erin."

"It could be a coincidence," Erin said, not wanting to believe, yet, even though her heart was beating faster. "What's this one?"

Trevian leaned down until his nose nearly touched the silk. "It seems to be on the plateau above Merry Lake."

"You never said anything about a frontera there." Erin's optimism nosedived.

"There is *something* there," Trevian said. "Years ago there was a huge cache of Ancient discovered there. And I've sensed something there, but it hasn't been clear."

"If it's buried in a crevice or a narrow canyon, it may still be unknown," Stillwater said.

"Maybe that's why Oshane chose Merrylake Landing," Trevian said.

Stillwater put her hands on her hips. "That socket is over Querida Pass along the border the Crescent shares with Madlyn. It's near the caravan town, Madalita." She leaned down. "I know these sockets are important to you, but there are other repeating symbols. Will you leave our tracing here, so I can study it?"

Erin thought for a second. "Sure." They wouldn't have a need for it. "I think maybe we ought to get started," she said. Her gaze fell on one of the symbols, near the Pendrelle Delta, and she stopped. She'd studied the book for years, and in the past few days, stared at the border designs until her eyes stung, but this... "Is this design from the book? Did one of the scribes add it?"

The lead scribe gasped. "We added nothing!"

"Sorry. I apologize." Erin tapped the symbol, four interlocking circles, like a flower drawn by a child. "I didn't look closely at this one before."

"Why does it interest you?"

"It's probably a coincidence. Profesor, is this close to the area in Pendrelle Delta?"

"Slightly to the southwest of it."

Erin nodded, chewing on her lower lip. Seeing it on the map now, in a different context, the circle with a crablike trefoil over it resembled a biohazard warning. It probably was a coincidence. There was no reason to think, if they'd identified biohazards here, they'd come up with the same exact symbol as her world. But they had cell phones, tablets, PVC pipe, hazmat suits, and WTF. "It's a symbol for danger," she said.

Stillwater said, "A specific sort of danger?"

"People get sick and die," Erin said.

"Then it meant the same here, at least in the Pendrelle Delta."

They'd burned a town there—the kind of thing you might do to control a contagion. A thought for another time, once they'd closed this frontera.

"Well," she said, "I think we should get ready to head out."

Trevian nodded.

Erin made sure to thank the scribes. Profesor Stillwater frowned. "We can send a pair of guards with you," she said.

"We'll be okay. Genaro will travel with us, and he used to be a justice arm deputy."

"Very well then. I have a few things for you." Stillwater beckoned to the scribes and all three of them left the room. Erin stared at the map. Trevian stood at her side.

"Do you think this is right?" she said.

"It is bolstered by the attack on you and the infected guard, who came through Madalita on his way here."

"I guess you'll be able to tell," she said.

"You put too much faith in this conceit of Oshane's, that I can sense frontera."

"You found mine. And you said there's something pulling on you, up above that dried-up lake. I think we can at least consider the possibility."

"I don't want to fail you," he said.

"Trevian, we're both winging it—" She saw the expression on his face, and rethought the expression, "—doing the best we can in the dark here. You won't fail me. We aren't going to fail." She wasn't really that confident, but she needed to start putting a positive attitude out there.

Restless, Erin walked back over to the book. She flipped the pages, stopping at the page with the sigil drawn in the corner. Ninety-seven percent. One hour.

"You have an obsession with that drawing," Trevian said.

"I do, kind of. I think it protects you from infection."

"You have nothing to base that on."

"Well, why did they put it in here? And we haven't seen anyone yet who was infected who had this mark on them."

"We haven't seen anyone with that mark at all," he said. "What if it's a sigil of solidarity? Maybe it's a warning."

"I wish they'd written more clearly. It's like they all knew what it meant, and it didn't occur to them that years later somebody might not know everything they knew."

"Perhaps they thought they'd vanquished the incursion."

Stillwater returned with an apprentice carrying bundles. The apprentice piled objects on the table. "Elmaestro Tregannon provided some of his dried beef for your journey."

"Beef," Trevian said.

"Yes. You should feel honored. And here, he wanted you to have these—" She held out three pins. Erin recognized them. They matched the one the elmaestro wore, and Ruth herself. Two circles, one copper and one aluminum, interlocked. "If you find yourself in trouble, any member of the Copper Coalition will assist you. When I said Genaro would accompany you, Zachary went off to find one for him."

"This is generous, thank you," Trevian said.

"And Erin," Ruth picked up two books, "these are not originals. They are from a set of fair copies. According to our indexes, both volumes mention Orchard Hill. I thought you might like to take them with you."

"Wow." Erin reached out. "Ruth... Thank you. That's amazing."

"I don't know what you will learn."

"I'm sure there will be something."

Erin pinned the Copper Coalition pin inside her messenger bag, and she and Trevian sorted out the other items. They would not add much to the knapsacks or saddlebags.

"Elmaestro Tregannon is not available to bid you farewell, but he left a message. He wishes you well. The Coalition stands with you against these parasites, and we will offer all the help we have."

Trevian nodded. Erin thought he was a bit skeptical. She appreciated the elmaestro's offer, but the Coalition had been infiltrated almost immediately.

Her impulse was to hug Ruth, but she wasn't sure the profesor was a hugger, so Erin settled for taking both her hands. "Thanks, Ruth, for everything. You've been a huge help."

"You've expanded my knowledge in ways I never imagined," Stillwater said and wrapped both arms around Erin. Erin squeezed her back.

They carried the packages out to the cart where Genaro waited. Trevian gave him his pin. They climbed inside, and the driver engaged the copper plate that somehow transmitted the energy of the sprites. Erin still didn't completely understand how it worked.

While they packed up their few remaining clothes back at Harald's, Katurah put *more* food into their saddlebags. The sky glowered graygreen to the north, under a sheet of cloud. Genaro led the caballos around from the stable. Trevian handed Erin a hooded poncho of oiled leather and put one on himself. Erin recognized the type of garments Aideen and Ilsanja had worn when they'd shown up. Out of habit, or obsession, she checked her messenger bag one more time. The book, and the ones Ruth had given her, were tucked in place. She thanked Katurah and mounted up.

Genaro led the way. Soon they were in a neighborhood of simple houses, and then fallow fields. It was another sennight until planting, Trevian said. They rode along pastures where naked sheep, goats, and some large pigs shared space with caballos and even a cow. The city shrank behind them, and silvery mountains rose along their horizon. While the rolling hills they approached were covered with greenery, the mountains beyond were rocky, with slim veins of green running their length. They didn't seem to belong to the rest of the landscape.

The road was flat, paved with smooth stones and well maintained. They passed riders, a few sprite carts, and two long trains of wagons. Riders galloped by, calling warnings and veering in and out of the traffic like motorcyclists back home. Fast messengers, she guessed. She nudged her caballo into a trot to catch up with Trevian. "Are there other cities north of the capital?"

"Cities, no. A market town and a few villages catering to prospectors."

Genaro looked over his shoulder. "In about two leagues, we cross Rio Plata Road. It runs west and east, beyond the Crescent borders. There are towns along it. They've practically grown into a city but nothing like Duloc. We call it Crossroads."

Erin nodded. Over the past few days, Ruth had answered many of her questions. The Crescent's population was about half a million, fewer people than Alaska. Duloc had about two hundred thousand residents. This was a trade road, and they still weren't experiencing anything like gridlock.

Trevian was staring ahead, at the road, when he said, "You question my sister's trust in Ilsanja, I think."

She wondered where *that* had come from. "Not exactly. I'm sure she's a good judge of character. I think maybe her liking for Ilsanja influences her judgment, though."

"They are friends. They have liked each other since they were children."

Erin rode on for a bit while she framed an answer. "Maybe they're closer than just friends."

"Closer in what way?" His caballo tossed his head. "You think they are lovers?"

"Would that be bad?"

"Not good or bad. But you only saw them for a few hours."

"I don't have any evidence." She did, though, thinking back. It was the way they stood next to each other, each hyper-aware, the way Aideen had stroked Ilsanja's arm. The way each woman had watched the other when she thought the other wasn't looking. It was definitely an infatuation, at least. She'd bet on it.

"Well..." Trevian rode on in silence. Just when Erin was reaching for words to say she was probably wrong, Trevian gave a hoot of laughter. A second later, he gave another. "What an awkward household we would have made! Me, pining to leave, Ilsanja, pining for Aideen." He shook his head. "Or perhaps things could have been much simpler. We could have pledged and married, and I could have gone copper-hunting with no pangs of conscience. But no, Father wouldn't have allowed it."

"If they are attracted to each other, are you okay with that?"

"I want my sister to be happy, and I owe Ilsanja a wish for happiness for the way I treated her. The problem, in the future of course, is the one you pointed out."

"Children."

"Yes. I never thought I might repel her."

"Maybe she's not repelled. Maybe you're just not her first choice."

"Maybe." He sat up a little straighter in the saddle. Erin watched him for a while as they rode. Was it possible he was *happier* with her speculation?

The North Road narrowed and began to rise. They left countryside for pastureland, pastures for farms, reversing the landscape they'd seen leaving the capital. A scattering of houses and buildings lined the way, growing denser when they reached Crossroads. It *was* somewhere between a town and a city, Erin decided.

They didn't stop. As the road climbed into the hills, a light rain spattered them. She pulled up her hood. The grass of either side was taller and thicker than she'd seen elsewhere, and small deciduous trees grew in dense groves. The road curved and the hills flattened, creating a meadow studded with stones like teeth. Beyond them rose a kind of wall, a plateau too even to be natural. Erin stared. "What am I looking at?"

Genaro answered. "Farm lots."

"The plateau, it looks artificial. Is it Ancient?"

"Oh, yes."

The symmetrical plateau rose from the rocky meadow like a long stage. The ends were almost perfectly square, covered with a mossy green sod. It was probably about eight feet tall. She couldn't tell how far back it ran. From the road, she could see the neat rows marked out with twine and furrows in the dark brown earth.

Genaro said, "My grandfather told me about this when I was a boy. They meant to plant here, but it's rocky. When they dug farther back, nearly into the hills, they found bales of some plata-colored substance."

"Bales?" Trevian said.

"Yes. Cubes of this shimmering matter, which was compressed and folded and squeezed, and bound with some strange thick straps. They cut one open and some of the material unfolded like a flower and floated away; inside the cubes, they found scraps of vessels as transparent as spring ice, a white substance as fluffy as never-melting snow, and many other wonders. There were more cubes than stars in the sky. So they pulled many of them out, stacked them above the ground. They dug around the rocks to free the soil. See how the earth dips around the rocks? They used a pulley and a sling to carry up basketloads of soil. It took years. And then they planted seeds and waited for the rains. They replenish the soil every Long Year."

"And the cubes?"

"They do not wear down, they do not break, so to my knowledge, Yor Langtree, they don't replace them." Genaro was silent as the caballos trotted along. "A few years ago, riding with the justice arm, I saw the Plain of Ice in the Desolation. I thought, then, *that* sea of shimmering material might be the same thing as the cubes."

"Do you know what it is?" Trevian said, looking at her.

"It sounds like waste plastic."

"You said plastic was firm, like the fence posts and the drinking cups."

"It can be. It can also be transparent and sheer, like fabric, or flexible. They use it for tubing."

"As sheer as spider silk, my grandfather said. And you could hold water in it."

"Yes. And we have a lot. A *lot*. And it doesn't break down. Or rot."

"On your world, you store it in bundles?"

"Sometimes, yes."

Genaro said, "Do you build with it?"

No, we throw it in the ocean. "I don't think so. This is actually a pretty good idea." She decided not to tell them about the Pacific Gyre. "Will we be camping tonight? Sleeping outside?"

"No. There is a guesthouse in another league. It's humble but safe and clean, with a good stable. We should reach it before sunset."

As they rode on, Genaro seemed to be scanning the sides of the road more frequently. Erin called out, "Do you expect an attack?"

"No, yorita, but the drizzle makes it harder to see. I want to be ready."

The road grew steeper and changed from stone pavement to packed earth, but it was still wide and smooth.

"What?" Trevian said.

"Just looking," she said. She didn't want to bring up the fire elementals yet. Maybe they had finally moved on. Maybe they found another herd, flock, colony—whatever—and joined it. She really hoped so.

"Aideen spoke to me about my father's fall," Trevian said. "There are aspects that trouble her. She said he fell from his office window, but she found glass on the office floor."

"So it doesn't sound like he fell out," Erin said. "More like something came in."

"He was speaking, arguing, before he fell. And Oshane, he arrived so quickly, without a caballo or a sprite cart. At least, as far as she knows."

"Could an air elemental break a window?"

"Easily." The only sound for a few paces was Erin's caballo working its bit. He said, "Aideen said there was a waterspout seen in the canal the night before he fell."

"A water elemental?"

"No, but one can be caused when an air elemental flies close over the surface of the water."

"Do you think Oshane planned to kill your father? Maybe they just argued."

"I thought Oshane had no interest in my father's company, but it now seems it is vital to his plans."

"It and you," she said.

He shrugged. "Maybe. I don't know what changed."

"Aideen talked about a plan to expand the company, down mountain, she said. A place called Sheeplands?"

"Interesting. And bold."

"Do you think the parasites see the company as a way to exert control over those two towns? There's also a Copper Coalition man there, and she doesn't trust him at all."

"There's no Copper Coalition office in White Bluffs. They don't like the Coalition much."

"I know, and she said he's cozying up to the City Council. I mean, trying to win them over, saying White Bluffs should make its own currency, and they should have a Coalition office, and Elmaestro Tregannon is old-fashioned."

"He sounds corrupt," Trevian said.

"Or infected."

"*Could* he be? Did I send my sister right back into danger? And my, my wife?"

"They both know what's going on. And they've got Harald. I think they'll be safe."

The rain let up slightly, and the light turned pearly. The trees drifted into ghostly shapes as mist twirled up from the rocky ground. They stopped at a well by the side of the road to rest the caballos and stretch. Erin scratched the neck of her mount thoughtfully, imagining what her mother would have said if she'd told her she was crushing on a married man. Of course, it wasn't the usual marriage. And now was not the time to imagine what a relationship with him would be like. She needed to focus.

They reached the guesthouse before dark, a small building made of rock and rough timber. A woman came to the door. "Welcome," she said. "Food's just soup tonight, but the water's hot and I have fresh bread."

A teenage boy brought grain and water for the caballos. Erin helped Genaro with the tack and checked her mare's hooves for stones. The place didn't have a bathhouse, but there was a huge vat of hot water on the stove, and she washed up thoroughly before meeting

Trevian and Genaro in a large common area with irregular tables and a whiterock fire burning in the hearth. The owner brought out a tray of turnip-like vegetables, with a dish of green sauce. "Husband's down at Crossroads getting supplies," she said.

"Do you own the place?" Erin said.

The woman grinned, creating a net of fine wrinkles across her face. "That we do. Built it ourselves, with a borrowed longsaw and a set of axes." She headed back into the narrow kitchen.

Erin watched as Genaro split one of the vegetables in half lengthwise and spread sauce on it. She did the same and nibbled the side. The root had the prickle of a radish, and the sauce's sweet tang balanced it. It was good. The woman carried out a tureen of soup, three bowls, and a loaf of warm bread. She offered them ale or spring water. Erin opted for water.

The soup was a bit bland, but the bread was delicious and so were the radish-things. They ate without speaking. Finally, Erin pushed back in her chair. "How much farther?" she said.

"We should reach Madalita tomorrow afternoon," Genaro said.

"That's not its name anymore. Sisuree?" The guesthouse woman had come to the table with a pitcher.

"No, thank you," Erin said.

Genaro inclined his head. "With pleasure. What did you mean, yora?"

"Madalita. They changed its name. A year or two ago."

"Why? To what?"

The woman shrugged, then poured steaming sisuree into a cup for Genaro. "I don't remember, something with no meaning. Nobody uses it." She set the cup in front of him. "No respect for history, those villagers. Madalita de la Joya was a prospector in my grandmother's day. She opened Querida Pass and shaved two days off the caravan trek from Madlyn to the capital. It's disrespectful, taking her name away from a village that only exists because of her."

"I wonder why we didn't hear of it," Trevian said.

"I told you. No one uses the new name except them." The woman looked at the window. "You'll have a wet ride tomorrow from the look of it, but the yor here is correct. You should arrive by midafternoon if all goes well."

"Mestengos on this road?"

She shrugged again. "There's one band in the hills, but they target caravans. You're safe enough."

"Thank you for your help," Trevian said.

"And the meal," Erin added.

Erin waited until the woman went back to the kitchen. "What's our plan?" she said.

"I supposed we would pose as travelers to Madlyn, stay in a guest-house, and speak to the townspeople," Trevian said. "If I truly have a gift for finding frontera, perhaps I will lead us to it."

"Townsfolk enjoy gossip," Genaro said. "And I have the name of the tavern where the Coalition guard was drinking, a good starting place."

"What if the town folks are intimidated? Or infected?"

"They can't all be, can they?" Trevian said.

"Your uncle had nearly a hundred parasites," she said.

Trevian rested his chin on his hand. "That's true. We'll be cautious."

Erin wasn't convinced, but she didn't have any better ideas. If they were going to get an early start in the morning, she might as well get some sleep now. She went back to the small room the owner had shown her. The bed reminded her of a summer camp cot. Over a plat-form of woven leather straps lay a thin mat covered with sheets and a blanket. The bench along the wall held a pitcher of water, a cup, and a bowl. A sprite lamp sat on the floor, the insect-like elemental making circles and figure-eights. Outside, a breezeway covered the short path to the latrine. The place wasn't fancy, but it would do.

She put her bag under the bed, changed her clothes, and slipped under the blanket. Her body stayed tense. After about ten minutes, she rolled onto her side, but it didn't help. When she closed her eyes, she saw the design from the book. She tried to distract herself by thinking about Trevian's sister. Aideen had lighter hair, with more of a wave, honey-colored eyes instead of dark ones, but the Langtree family resemblance was still strong. It had been the same with her and Chip.

Chip got Mom's reddish-brown hair instead of Dad's black curls, and Erin had always envied him his cheekbones, but anyone meeting them knew they were siblings.

Her throat ached. Thinking of Chip meant thinking of Mom and Dad. She didn't want to do that anymore.

She rolled onto her back again.

Why did the book specify "loomin" next to the design? Did it have to be carved on the skin with aluminum? Aluminum—loomin—controlled magic, while gold and copper stored and transmitted it, according to Trevian anyway. There was a verse in the book saying pretty much the same thing.

A soft clink sounded from the book. Erin sat up. She pulled up the messenger bag and took out the book. When she opened it, a piece of paper slipped out.

She unfolded it. It was thinner than the paper she'd seen here, almost like tracing paper.

Mei thought Perlarayna was east of where Erin was. The people there were familiar with frontera, elemental worlds, and the artifacts. They had heard nothing about parasites, but Mei thought the Desolation area acted as a buffer.

With the book and the compass together, Mei thought, they could identify more frontera, perhaps even all of them, at once. She didn't know anything about how to stop the parasites.

Mei provided a gem of information. The people she was talking to in Perlarayna thought the frontera from all the elemental worlds opened somewhere in this one. Like the drawing in Harald's book, this world was the center, tying all the linked worlds together.

It was even more imperative to stop the parasites from colonizing it.

Erin rummaged for a pencil and wrote on the back of Mei's letter, summarizing as much as she could—the map, the infected Copper Coalition guards, Oshane's maneuvering in White Bluffs, the mention of Aperture One and Orchard Hill. Fan-folding the paper, she spoke the words to activate the puerta, and slipped the paper through.

Too much was going on in her head to let her sleep—she was

wired and itchy. Idly, she shifted the pages until she came to the page with the blank border. If a corner of it were missing, would it damage anything? It didn't seem like it.

She reached into her bag for her phone. Five minutes a day she was allowing herself now, photos only. Powering it on, she swiped up the Fourth of July photo. Chip would tell her she was right to take the initiative. You have to take risks to succeed, he'd say.

After another minute, she slipped the phone back into the bag.

They had to stop the parasites, and to do it, they had to protect themselves. She rubbed her finger lightly against the corner of the page and yanked it back with a hiss. Yes, sharp enough to cut skin, she thought as she sucked her finger.

Normally, she would talk to Trevian about something like this, but she didn't want to wake him. Besides, she wasn't some sidekick, always running to him just because he was from around here. His world, his Copper Coalition, his family and their issues, his magic, his wife. Well, it was *her* book. Maybe she did know better than him about some things.

With her knife, she sawed at the edge of the page until she held a triangle of aluminum about the size of a guitar pick. The scratched page with the design wobbled because it was tied in with wire, and she found it easily. She studied it, wishing she could draw it on her arm first rather than carve freehand, but all she had was a pencil. A pencil, no rubbing alcohol, just water and some anti-microbial cream. It would have to do.

She went into the kitchen and poured a cup of hot water from the large pot. Back in her room, she rubbed the inside of her upper arm briskly with a bandage dipped in the water. After a few deep breaths, she picked up the scrap of loomin. Sprite light flashed off its edge like Morse code, fed by the shaking in her fingers. She made herself breathe steadily a few moments more, then guided the metal up to her flesh. She'd read about hesitation marks, and she was sure she mustn't leave any if the charm was going to work. Holding her breath, she pressed the tip of the metal into her skin and dragged it down in one long line. It stung and she stopped involuntarily. Unclenching her teeth, she made herself relax, and dragged the tip along the skin from where she'd stopped. Her skin gave, followed by a burning like a bee sting.

And she'd been afraid to even get a tattoo.

Red filled in each line. She cut the second long line, then each of the shorter legs of the two isosceles triangles. The first line intersecting them, the long one, welled with blood. Then the top line. Then the bottom. The design gleamed red, dripping onto her jeans. She lost track of time. Using the same cloth bandage, she blotted the cuts. Her hands shook. Now she needed only the two outside lines, the arrows with one-half arrowtips. When she closed her eyes, little sparks of light danced in her vision.

The final lines done, she blotted away the blood again and smeared antiseptic ointment onto the cuts. She pressed two of her remaining adhesive bandages over them.

Her arm burned with each heartbeat.

She hoped she hadn't just done the stupidest thing ever.

When she stood, black dots swirled in her vision and she staggered. She waited until everything cleared, then rinsed the metal in water and dropped it into her bag. The book went back inside. Except for the flare of pain with every move and the shakiness, she didn't feel any different. Tired, maybe. She'd tell Trevian what she'd done in the morning. She climbed under the blanket and closed her eyes.

The last image in her mind before she fell asleep was the design, glowing in a white light.

14

Martes, 23 Uno, Year 331

It was an hour past sunrise, and Aideen floated in a ball of happiness even the light, steady rain couldn't dampen. They rode at a lope for a while, until Ilsanja slowed her gelding, and the justice arm followed her example, to let the caballos rest. The North Road grew busier. They passed a group of Crescent Council guards in blue and green riding in a chevron, a tax collector in the protected space behind, heading for the capital, and a mail caravan. Fast messengers galloped by in both directions. Some red-vested Coalition guards rode next to wagons, and there were plenty of market carts, riders on caballos, people on foot, and even the occasional sprite cart.

Ilsanja said little, and after a few hours, Aideen began to worry. Did her friend regret last night's declaration? Did she regret last night? Ilsanja glanced her way, caught her gaze, and smiled, and Aideen's worry faded.

The North Road curved away east, and Aideen drew her mare to a halt near the narrower hill trail they had taken on their way to the capital. Justice Arm Stuart turned back. "Is this the place?" At her nod, he said, "This trail used to be part of a trade road to Boskay. I remember it. We should make good time." He nudged his caballo forward, Ilsanja followed, and Aideen brought up the rear.

They rode at an easy pace for nearly an hour. Behind them, thunder rumbled, growing louder. The storm was moving their way. After a bit longer, the justice arm reined in his mount. "The storm will overtake us. Shall we find a guesthouse and wait it out?"

"Honestly, Justice Arm, I fear what my uncle might accomplish in one more day."

"There's a cavern on the plateau above Merry Lake where we can shelter," Ilsanja said. "We're not fresh-dyed spider silk to fade in a little rain."

The man nodded. "Very well. We'll push on then. And call me Harald, please, both of you."

He lowered his reins, and his caballo started off at a trot. Too late, Aideen wondered if he was experiencing pain and needed to stop. She silently cursed her selfishness.

They rode for another two hours, down a steep grade through a grove of white-barked trees. They stopped at the small albergue to water the caballos and let them graze. The justice arm limped noticeably as he headed for the latrine, and Aideen's guilt deepened. When he came back to his caballo to open a saddlebag, she followed him. "I've put my convenience ahead of your comfort," she said. "I am sorry."

"What? The limp? That's the time of day as much as anything, yorita. And this is work. I have a sworn warrant against your uncle. But your concern is appreciated."

"Please call me Aideen."

He smiled. "Aideen." He handed her a packet of flatbread and dried fruit.

While they ate in the albergue, the rain lightened to a drizzle. Aideen rose and stretched and led the way to the caballos. Back the way they had come, the sky was gray, streaked with black lines of rain.

Harald threw himself belly-down across his mount's back and

wiggled his flesh leg over. The animal stood, one ear swiveled back. The maneuver did not look as awkward as Aideen had expected.

They started down the trail. Even with the rain and the stop, they were making good headway, and she dared to hope they would arrive in time to forestall whatever plan Oshane Langtree had set in motion. She dared to hope Father was alive.

She lost track of the landscape, aware only that the trail was steep, and the trees vanished, replaced by reddish crags. Her thoughts drifted from Father and Oshane, to the tale Trevian and Erin had told two nights ago, to the scent of Ilsanja's skin, the touch of her lips, her tongue. Too soon, though, her reverie drifted to questions. Had last night been only a few hours of comfort on the road for Ilsanja? Would she want Aideen at her side when they returned home? How could Aideen, with her unkempt hair and plain clothes, fit into her elegant friend's life? Perhaps by even thinking about it, she had ruined it, poisoning last night's joy with her doubts.

Ilsanja's gray whickered, rousing her out of her thoughts. The gray peered, ears pricked, toward the shallow defile on their left, the one that led to the ring of stones. Here, Ilsanja had shared memories of her mother. They had made good headway today. Ilsanja drew the caballo's attention back to the trail. It narrowed here, and Aideen remembered the long plunge on the downhill side. An echo of the fear she had felt on the cliff face on their previous journey filled her, making her breathing shallow. She shivered, resolving to pay more attention to her surroundings.

In the fading light, the dots of quartz in the red cliff face sparkled like sprites. The caballos' hooves made the most noise, louder even than the occasional roll of thunder behind them.

Harald now held a loaded crossbow across the pommel of his saddle. She hadn't seen him take it out. His head moved from side to side, scanning the red crags. A few paces on, he and Ilsanja pulled their mounts to a halt.

Aideen did too, the mare's nose brushing the gelding's flank. "Is something wrong?" she whispered to Ilsanja.

Harald heard her. "This is a good place for an ambush," he said.

"Those crags are not sheer; there are footholds and hide-holes throughout them."

"This is a little-used trail," Ilsanja said. "Aideen and I, on our way to the capital, were probably the last to use it. Who would know we had come this way?"

"Mmm." Harald continued to scan, lifting the crossbow. "True." He let his caballo take a step or two forward. Aideen listened hard but heard nothing that hinted of mestengos, elementals, or even kiotes.

The soft drizzle grew stronger and colder. A stone, worked free by the rain, tumbled down the crag and skittered across the trail in front of them.

Harald reined in and lifted the crossbow. "Turn back!" he said. "Now!" He loosed a bolt. A scream echoed from the rocks above them.

Ilsanja's mount wheeled, and the mare mimicked the motion before Aideen could even shift the reins. Stones bounced down beyond Harald. Before her mount finished turning, Harald's squealed and reared, a crossbow bolt quivering from its chest. Rock face flashed in front of Aideen's eyes, and she grabbed for her saddle horn as shouts erupted from the rocks above them. She risked a glance back as the mare plunged into a lope; Harald and his mount had vanished.

Rocks rained down onto their path, and the gelding skidded to a stop, shaking his head. Ilsanja tried to drive him forward. A huge rock —no, a shadow—hurtled toward Aideen. It struck her before she could draw a breath, knocking her off the caballo's back, flattening her on the rock trail. She couldn't fill her lungs. When she did, it was with the stench of stale lick, mutton, and the odor of someone who hadn't bathed in many days. Fingers grasped her hair, lifted, and slammed her head down onto the rocks. Lights burst in her vision. Someone rolled her over and pulled her wrists behind her. Rough rope looped around them. "Ilsanja!" she shouted. Cloth, black and coarse, went over her head, and something tightened at her neck.

"Find the justice arm," a man said, somewhere near her. "Make sure he's dead. And Orland, hold that damned caballo."

"My arm—I'm shot."

"You spooked him. You deserve it."

The voice tantalized her, like a phrase of music in a song she couldn't place. Before she could think, the rough hands dragged her to her feet and shoved her against something warm, soft. She smelled caballo.

"Ilsanja!"

The man holding her struck her shoulder. "Quiet, you."

"Here, Aideen," Ilsanja said. She gasped.

"Quiet! Get them on the mounts."

The man holding her said, "Orland needs to ride."

"Get them up, I said."

He took hold of her and threw her across the withers of a caballo, then mounted behind her. She guessed it was the mare.

The familiar voice said, "Dieter, are you still here? Go find the justice arm."

"We saw him fall."

"I don't care. Go find him."

For a moment, Aideen knew the voice, but then the knowledge fled.

The man behind her said, "I'll walk, let Orland ride."

"That's enough from you."

They started forward. She tried to count hoofbeats and could make out only two. Harald's caballo had fallen down the cliffside, taking Harald with it. Was there any way Harald could have survived?

"Pick it up!"

The caballo broke into a trot, jolting Aideen and sending waves of pain through her shoulders and head.

How many men were there? The leader, the man behind her, Orland the injured one, and Dieter. Was the leader expecting the injured man to run behind them?

She should be doing something, trying to measure the distance, she thought, but she could do nothing. There were four men, three with them now if Dieter was tracking Harald. She had met one of them somewhere.

She and Ilsanja were still alive, which was good.

Ilsanja had suffered this before. How was she doing now? Aideen drove her attention away from that track of thought.

She slid onto the mount's neck as the way curved and descended. The good-hearted mare stumbled, overcome by the weight of two riders. A hand grasped the waistband of Aideen's trousers and pulled her back. The way leveled out. They splashed through water. Ahead of them, a horse neighed and the gray answered. They stopped. The rider behind her pulled her down and yanked off her belt, taking her purse and her knife. More hoofbeats sounded, and caballos whickered and snorted. The mestengos had left their own mounts here. If she had to guess, she would say they were at the ring of stones. Ilsanja's gray had scented the mestengo band's caballos and alerted Harald to the ambush.

The man pushed her onto the caballo again, and they started forward. Somewhere a person moaned with each breath, and the leader shouted, "Quit your whining!"

The rain fell harder, soaking her coat and her trousers. They crossed water again, deep enough that the splashes from the mare's hooves soaked the front of her hood, and Aideen had to turn her face to one side to breathe. Then they climbed. She tried to hold an image of the mountains in her mind, to plot where they were or might be, but it was no use. She was shivering. Who would have known they would take this trail? Her heart sank. The only person she had told was Dolores. The housekeeper must have betrayed her, but why?

Finally, they stopped. Someone dragged her off the mount. Her legs were bloodless and she staggered, nearly falling. The man who reeked of lick and mutton shoved her forward.

The voices of the mestengos echoed, and the rain stopped its drive. Another voice greeted them.

"What's happened to Orland? Where's Dieter?"

"I sent him to finish the task Orland bungled."

"You left a man out there?"

The leader shouted, "Do you want your share of the copper, Garth? Don't question me."

Knowledge struck Aideen, and she stumbled. The man holding her cursed under his breath. She counted again. The leader, then Orland, who was injured, Garth, and the one who held her. Four mestengos, five if Dieter returned. As if it mattered how many there were.

"Set down the women and bring in those caballos."

The new voice, Garth, said, "It's barely raining. They'll be fine."

"Fine, set the women down."

Her captor pushed her down against a rock wall. There was a rustle of fabric, and Ilsanja said, "Oof!"

"Are you hurt?" Aideen didn't bother to lower her voice.

"I'm very angry."

In front of them, Garth snorted. He shifted about, and a moment later warmth radiated toward them. Aideen waited until his footsteps faded, and she thought they were alone. "Did Harald fall?"

"I couldn't see."

"Why hasn't he killed us?" She didn't bother to say the name. If she recognized the voice, surely Ilsanja had. She twisted her hands and got her fingertips onto the first of the knots in the rope.

"I don't know." Ilsanja stopped speaking as footsteps approached.

"Let's see what the yoritas are carrying," the leader said. Nausea overwhelmed Aideen for a moment. "Not much coin. Oh, letters? Sealed with the mark of the Crescent Council. Legal documents. I wonder what they could be—"

"Oh, by the Mother, take off these ridiculous hoods," Aideen said. "We recognized your voice, and now you're strewing clues about like a jefe planning a Long Year's treasure hunt."

A moment's silence. "Do you, truly? Know who I am?"

Ilsanja said, "Yes, Vallis, we do. Did you think *I* wouldn't recognize your voice?"

"Well, then." Fingers touched Aideen's neck and she flinched.

He tugged at the base of the hood, loosening it, then pulling it off. Aideen had squinted against the light, but the only immediate glare came from the small whiterock fire in front of them. The walls of the curving shallow cave, actually an undercut, were dyed in shadow. She faced out, staring at a hillside marked with trees. The undercut, long and shallow, curled like a balcony overlooking a deep, narrow canyon. The sky had grown darker and a gentle rain still fell.

Vallis removed Ilsanja's hood. His golden hair was greasy and stuck to his head. There were lines around his eyes.

Ilsanja shook her head and studied him. "You don't look well."

He smiled. He had lost a tooth on the side of his mouth close to Aideen. "Better than you do, I think."

Aideen had worked one fingertip up between the strands of the knot. Pain shot up her arm as she tried to loosen the knot. The rope did not give.

Ilsanja made a play of studying the undercut and the men over by a larger whiterock fire. "Yes," she said. "I see how you prosper."

"It must make you angry," Aideen said. "You can't go to any banco or money-changer because of the exile brand. Even a tavern is a risk, because what if a sheriff, or a justice arm, a tax collector, or even a town council member comes in carrying a watcher-disk? I've been told those sing out like a yipping kiote. You are dependent on these others to do every task for you."

He smiled wider, but the muscles around his eyes tensed. "We know how to deal with justice arms. Soon the inconvenience of exile will be lifted, and there will be a new way of doing things."

"By the Mother, I think you believe that," she said, keeping her voice light.

"Clever little Aideen." He looked away from her. "But you, Ilsanja, you've been busy." He picked up the larger of the sealed documents and twisted it, cracking the seal. He unfolded it, read it, and began to laugh. "Oh, Ilsanja! After what he did to you, you really *did* go crawling back to him! What did your father have to offer up?"

"Poor Vallis," Ilsanja cooed. "With your five-year-old hat, your handed-down saddle. You'll always be the second-best man. Does it sting, even now?"

He grinned. With both fists, he twisted the marriage document into a funnel and held it down next to the whiterock. The edges singed, curled, and caught flame. He let it drop. Without opening the proxy letter, he dropped it into the flames too.

He stood. "We won't ask for ransom this time, Ilsanja. No worries. In Madlyn, there is a clan of families who believe it is their mission to reseed the world with people. Each man takes many wives, and they pay nicely for brides." He stalked away.

"Finally, Vallis's appearance matches his heart," Ilsanja said. She drew a deep breath. "I don't believe he means to sell us."

"If he fears Harald lives, he means us to be his shields," Aideen said. She saw Harald's caballo rearing, sliding. Closing her eyes, she twisted her head away from that memory.

After a moment, she said, "He knew about the marriage."

Ilsanja looked at her, eyebrows raised.

"I feared it was Dolores who had betrayed us, but she did not know why I visited the capital. No, someone else who told him of our plan and guessed we would take the shorter way."

"Genaro? Katurah?"

"...Possibly." She thought Harald was a good judge of character and would not harbor a betrayer. Then again, that was why they called it betrayal. "Or someone at the Copper Coalition." Her fingers and wrists ached, and the knot didn't give.

A bellow of pain echoed through the undercut. Garth—she thought it was Garth—stood over the injured Orland and tossed aside a crossbow bolt. "Dak, get me singeweed and willowbark," he said.

"We have neither." Aideen recognized the voice of the man who had thrown her over the mare's withers.

"What?"

Vallis said, "We didn't weigh ourselves down, remember? If Orland hadn't failed—"

"Lick, then!" Garth said, holding out his hand. The other man, Dak, handed him a bottle. Another roar echoed as he poured the liquid into the wound.

Vallis pulled another bottle out of the pile of harness by his side, worked out the cork, and drank from it. He did not glance at Garth or the wounded man.

A few moments later Garth walked to the fire. He stood above Vallis. They talked. At first, Aideen could hear nothing. Her fingers were numb, and finally, she let her hands drop, hoping what blood came past the tight bonds would flow into her fingers.

Vallis got to his feet.

"—too much trouble to sell—" Garth shouted.

"*I* decide—"

The space lit up with white light, and thunder boomed around them, shaking the walls. As if a plug had been pulled, rain hissed down outside, turning the darkness green.

"The caballos! Damn you, I said get those caballos inside!" Vallis shouted. Dak bounded up and hurried out into the rain. Garth stood a moment longer, then ambled in the same direction.

"He means to sell us after all," Ilsanja said.

The thought of being a captive bride filled Aideen with a cold terror deeper than the fear of dying. "His leadership is fragile." She flexed her fingers and went back to work on the knot.

"As morning mist."

"Is that—" Aideen paused as Garth came back into the cavern, struggling to control the gray and a curveting, head-tossing black who pinned its ears and kept reaching out to nip at the gelding. Garth dropped the gelding's reins and led the black away from the other animal. Behind him, Dak led the mare and five other mountain ponies. He tethered them in a corner beyond the fire. Once Garth had secured the black to a picket on the cave floor, he led the gelding over to the other mounts.

"Is that better or worse for us?" Aideen said.

"Worse. He wields no discipline because he's earned no respect. Garth will decide our fate, and Vallis cannot stand against him."

It was as bad as Aideen had feared. She took advantage of the pounding rain to shift her body slightly so her back pressed against Ilsanja's. "Put your hands against mine," she said. "Can you feel the knots?"

She found the knot binding Ilsanja's wrists. From this angle, it was far easier to work her fingers between the loops of rope.

"And then what will we do?" Ilsanja said, her voice blending with the rain.

"We hope they sleep. And then we run."

"Or steal a mount."

Aideen watched as Garth brought food to the wounded man, who refused it. Garth sat cross-legged next to him, his back to Vallis but half-turned so he could watch him. He glanced in their direction now and then. Aideen slumped against the cavern wall and hoped Ilsanja presented as forlorn a picture as she did.

The ropes tight against her skin slackened, and a moment later she looped her finger into the space in the knot that held Ilsanja and pulled the strand of rope loose.

Garth got to his feet, and Aideen froze, but he walked to the edge of the undercut, unfastened his trousers, and urinated a stream out into the rain. He finished without a glance in their direction and sat back down by Orland.

Aideen's belt and purse, and Ilsanja's, gleamed in the circle of light thrown by their small fire. She squinted. Did she see metal shining? Aideen remembered Dak yanking her knife free of her belt, but Vallis hadn't removed Ilsanja's. She let her head loll to the right as if half asleep. The mestengos offered them no food or water. The men stayed by their fire, and soon, except for gurgle of lick bottles, the space was quiet. Had they set a guard?

The rain slackened, and as the storm moved past them, finally stopped. The night quieted except for the distant growl of thunder behind them. Aideen slipped into a waking dream, where she tried to read a ledger, but the figures were not numbers at all but strange signs she could not decipher. Her whole body jerked when Ilsanja said, "Thank you."

"I'm sorry, Ilsanja. I know I led us here—"

"No. For freeing my hands. At least I am not helpless, the way I was before."

"Oh. But I am resp—"

"I came of my own choice to be with the friend of my heart. I'd change nothing. No, that's not true. I'd change the past few hours, and Harald would be with us. But before that? I celebrate everything."

"Ah." Aideen let herself bask in happiness for a few seconds at least.

They waited. The thunder growled, ever nearer, and twice lightning flickered across the sky before the air rattled around them. Garth stretched out alongside Orland, and Vallis, finally, lay on his side, nearly hidden by the fire. Dak was also stretched out. It wasn't hope deluding her. No watch was set.

If anyone was left awake, it would be Garth, but she feared to wait any longer. "Can you stand?" she whispered.

"Yes. Now?"

Aideen nodded. They eased to their feet, watching the cluster of men as they sidestepped on tiptoe toward the pile of belts and purses. Ilsanja moved as silently as a knife for the black caballo, but Aideen stopped and scooped up the belts, fastening both around her waist. At least they would have one weapon. Ilsanja held the caballo's lead and was stroking its neck. Its ears pricked, and it nudged Ilsanja playfully. She led it away from the picket. Its hooves clicked on the rocks, and Aideen held her breath as they moved past the sleeping men.

Ilsanja led the black outside and flung herself over its back. She swung her leg over and reached down for Aideen's hand. Aideen grasped it and floundered awkwardly onto the caballo's back. A memory of Harald clambering onto his mount stabbed her like a needle. She laced her arms around Ilsanja's waist.

The world lit up, followed instantly by the crash of thunder. The caballo shied, squealing, and Ilsanja kicked it into a gallop as rain pelted down around them, as fierce as before. Behind them, someone shouted.

Aideen clung to her friend, pressing her thighs as hard as she could against the caballo's wet sides. She had never ridden without a saddle, and as the beast plunged forward, she slid first one way then the other.

Garth's voice rose above the rain and the shouting. A crossbow bolt sang past her ear.

Lightning turned the world blue again, and the caballo balked suddenly, bouncing sideways. A torrent of roiling water blocked their way. It was the water they had crossed, swollen to a racing churn—a flashflood as the water dropped by the eastern storm rushed downhill, swelling the stream that had flowed there earlier. The caballo pivoted, shaking its head, and as Ilsanja urged it toward the water, it reared. Aideen lost her purchase and slipped down over the caballo's flanks. She let go of Ilsanja as the mount wheeled out from under her. The ground came up fast, and she splashed into mud.

Ilsanja reached down for her as the caballo danced sideways. "Aideen!"

The ground underneath the animal's dancing hooves crumbled away into the water, and the beast floundered sideways into the flood. As Aideen scrambled up, the earth at the edge of the trail gave way. She stepped back and threw herself flat, clinging to the ground. The drop gaped in front of her eyes like the mouth of a yawning oso, pulling her down. She dug her fingers into the earth, clinging. She would fall...

Several feet below her, a stubby tree grew out of the hillside, lit up by the flash overhead.

She lifted her head. "Ilsanja!" she said, just as the caballo reared again, its head snaking up, and both mount and rider fell and were swept over the cascade and down the mountain.

"Ilsanja!" Aideen forced herself to peer over the edge. Her whole body was shaking. Without the lightning, blinded by the afterimages of the last flash, she could see nothing beyond the tree. Mud caved away under the weight of her hands. She froze, her heart pounding. *Her body, tossed and broken on the rocks below, falling, falling endlessly...*

She wouldn't leave Ilsanja. She pulled her knees up underneath her and hurled herself down, toward the tree. Her outstretched hands caught the slender trunk. She slid, her palms burning, up its length toward the crown, and then hung in the rain, bobbing, while curses sounded above her.

"...leave them! Get the caballos and..." Those shouts were probably Garth. Her shoulders throbbed. She hadn't thought they could hurt more. In the next flash of lightning, she saw a sheet of glistening rock below, tilted slightly toward the brown waterfall. *A landing place.*

She swung out over the sheet of rock and let go.

She landed. Her feet went out from under her. Before she could reach for purchase, she slid. She dug her fingers into the rock's surface but not fast enough. Faster she slid, off the edge of the rock, plunging into the muddy stream of water. As she struck, instinct made her wrap her arms around her head. Rocks struck her arms and ribs, and the water closed over her as she hurtled down.

15

Martes, 23 Uno, Year 331

Trevian leaned back in the chair so the landlord could pour sisuree into his cup.

She said, "You're copper-hunters, aren't you? Do you have charms?" Her voice quavered slightly.

He glanced across the table at Erin, but she was staring down into her cup.

Trevian said, "We have some. Do you need wards?"

Genaro said, "Has something happened?"

"We've got wards we wake at night, and they work fine. And earth elemental wards too, of course, but Efram thought he saw fire elementals last night. This place is half wood. If they're hungry..."

Erin straightened up. She flinched and shifted her left arm in an odd way.

The woman freshened Genaro's cup and continued. "We don't have them here usually. There aren't any rifts in the ground or those vents of steam and smoke. Sometimes if there's a wildfire they'll be drawn to it. But these were hovering out between the trees."

Erin said, "Maybe he saw some traveler's campfire."

She shook her head. "They whirled like spindles, and they were orange and blue. That's not a traveler's fire."

Erin swallowed. She was pale; was she sick? "Like Trevian said, we have some protective charms." She looked at him. "Can we set one to discourage flames?"

He nodded, although the house didn't need wards. The flames were following Erin, but she was wise not to say that.

Genaro chewed his bread and pork and said nothing.

"I'll pay," the landlord said.

"No," said Erin.

"No need." Trevian pushed back his chair. "Let me get what we have."

He and Erin had kept a double handful of charms from his uncle's lair, as well as a dozen David and Miriam LaFish had charmed for them, a way of showing their gratitude to Erin for freeing them from the prison of the lantern. He found two fire-wards easily. Erin walked past his door on the way to her room, still holding her left arm a bit away from her body.

While Genaro readied the caballos, Trevian and Efram buried the additional charms. Erin came out to watch them. When Efram went to help with the mounts, she said softly to Trevian, "Will that work, or do we need to use the collar?"

It was the first time she had brought up the charmed collar herself. She resisted compelling the elementals in every situation.

"There's no need," he said. "They're following you."

"It doesn't make sense."

He bent to pick up his knapsack. There was no need to debate; she might deny it, but Erin knew the truth of the matter as well as he did.

They mounted up and headed north. The storm had passed through, and the air seemed to sparkle. Beads of water flashed silver and green in the grass and along the leaves of the trees, and the sky was the crisp green of early spring.

"What do fire elementals eat?" Erin said suddenly.

In the wild, elementals drew sustenance from the emberbeds and the heat vents, but they were attracted to everything. "They will consume wood, anything that burns."

"So the guesthouse could have been at risk."

He nodded.

After about an hour, Erin reined her caballo off the road into a clearing surrounded by trees.

"What are you doing?"

She dismounted. "Feeding them." She tramped into the trees and began pulling fallen branches into the clearing.

"Erin, you don't need to do this."

"I'm responsible for them."

"You are not."

She dropped a branch and glared at him. "They're following me. They're out of their native territory. They're not going to starve or eat someone's house because of me."

Trevian looked at Genaro for help, but the valet just shrugged. Sighing, Trevian dismounted. So did Genaro.

"Will the grass catch fire if they feed off this? Am I starting a wildfire?" Erin stopped, a fallen branch in her hands. She favored her left arm, and he would have wagered a cento that it wasn't stiffness.

"The grass and the earth are soaked," Genaro said. "So are the trees. Fire won't spread."

Trevian dragged over a large branch. "And they consume quickly, leaving a pile of ash."

They built up a cone of branches and leaves as tall as Genaro. As they walked back to where the caballos were cropping grass, he said, "You've hurt your arm. What happened?"

"Nothing serious."

Something had changed. As they mounted up and continued forward, he could think of only one thing that would make her draw away from him. "The marriage was a necessity," he said. "You agreed yourself."

"What? Oh, yeah. So they could legally stand up to Oshane. Of course."

"Yes. She, Ilsanja, she—"

"She seems smart, and your sister does too."

"Aideen is the brilliant one in our family, the only one who can manage our father."

"You clearly don't get along with him."

"He saw—sees—only one road for me. Only in service to his company."

"I don't think he pictured this road. When Harald talked about the Copper Road, is this it?"

"Part of it. The North Road is the main trade route into Madlyn and the northlands beyond. There are tales, have always been tales, of veins of Ancient as vast as seas, if you go far enough north."

"Did you ever imagine going there?"

"Not exactly. My, my restlessness, yearning—if I use a word from a stage play romance—never led me north. Perhaps it will, someday."

"If you went far enough in that direction in my world, you'd come to a bunch of cities. Large cities, bigger than the field of Ancient where my frontera is."

"It sounds like there are many people in your world."

"There are."

"Do you have any idea how many?"

"Eight billion."

For a moment he thought she had said eight million, which seemed likely. Then he grasped the word. It startled him, and he laughed so loud his caballo's ears swiveled. "Hah, brilliant! Do you have an idea how many, really?"

She glanced sideways at him and didn't speak.

"You." He paused, shaping his question carefully. "Do you believe that there are eight billion people in your world?"

"I do."

He didn't doubt that she *believed* it. "How...how could a world support eight billion people?"

"There's a question," she said. "The cities of Ancient were larger than your cities, weren't they? Didn't your world have more people than it does now?"

"Yes. When the earth turned, many died in the cataclysm. And many vanished. During the interval, between disease and the violence of the warlords, hundreds died as well."

"I didn't see anything in Stillwater's books about what they did with the bodies," she said.

"At first they were buried, but the problem with that was obvious. Some say that's how we learned about earth elementals, when they converged on the mass graves. After that, they burned them."

"Is that what you do now?"

"In the Crescent, we do. I have heard that in the west they line their dead in caves and pile rocks over them, but I have never seen it."

"Some bury our dead and some burn them—we call it cremating."

The somber conversation gave her distant mood, and it disturbed him. "Erin, we will survive this."

"I just want to close that frontera. That's all," she said.

The road curved and rose. The slope was nowhere as steep as their road to Merrylake Landing had been, but they climbed steadily upward into the bare hills. Erin grew more interested in the surroundings. "This looks granitic," she said once. Genaro cocked his head, then seemed to realize the remark needed no answer.

Genaro slowed his mount in front of a road marker. Trevian was used to the markers that sat on the ground, carved out of rock. This sign had a shaft of wood like the trunk of a tree, with a narrow wooden slab fastened to the top. He rode up next to Genaro. The word DULOC was carved onto one end, with an arrow pointing back the way they had come, and the number of miles. Satisfaction buoyed him up as he saw the progress they had made. At the other end was another town's name and a 5.

"Where's Madalita? Beyond that?" He began to worry after all.

"I think that *is* Madalita," Genaro said. "The wood's been scratched away, and those letters painted over."

Erin nudged her caballo up alongside them. "Our landlord did say they changed the name, remember?"

Trevian shrugged. "You can name your town what you wish, but you should think about the confusion you cause for travelers."

"The town formerly known as Madalita," Erin said. She looked at both of them, then shook her head. "Never mind. What is it?" She moved the caballo closer. "Wait. Does that say Via Nueva?"

"They spelled Villa wrong," Genaro said.

Erin backed up her caballo. She stared at Trevian and her eyes were wide. "They spelled it right. Trevian, that means 'the new way.'"

"Way, not homestead?"

She pointed to Genaro. "Genaro, how fast can you get back to the Copper Coalition?"

"Two days, but we passed a fast-messenger outpost at Cross-roads, and I can reach that before sunset if I push my mount. Why, yorita?"

She said, "The guard who attacked me at the Coalition mentioned 'the new way.' And Oshane Langtree's alias—made-up name—in my world is based on those same words. It's them. It's like a code word or something."

"Would they change the name of the town? Risk themselves?"

"Well, think about it, Trevian. Who knows except us?"

"I cannot leave the two of you unprotected," Genaro said.

"You're not. You're going to bring back a Copper Coalition army. And we're going to find the frontera before they find us," Erin said. "Genaro, this is important."

"It's not a coincidence, the words," Trevian said. "We must assume that many in the town are infected by the parasites. We need soldiers, Genaro."

"Then return with me."

"We need to close the frontera."

The valet shifted his gaze between them, frowning. Finally, he sighed and reined his caballo around, heading back the way they had come. "Take care of each other, and if all else fails, stay hidden and wait for us. I will bring soldiers." He kicked the mount into a trot and then a brisk lope.

"Do we go forward?" Trevian said.

Erin fidgeted with her reins. "Yes, but I need to tell you something before we do. And I want you to hold the book."

"What? Why? Are you ill? Erin, have you been—"

"I'm fine. I think." Her caballo sidestepped, reacting to her distress, and Trevian's mount tossed his head, the feeling transmitted from the other animal. "I did something that might have been really stupid, and I...if this whole town is infected, I think the book needs to stay with you."

"What did you do?"

She wound her reins around the horn of her saddle and pushed back the sleeve on her left arm. He gasped when he saw the bandage, already knowing, before she peeled it away, what she had done.

"Erin! Why? We said we would discuss this!"

"We did discuss it."

"We didn't agree! You don't know what that mark does! It could have an evil purpose. And we're riding into a legion of those parasites."

"It was my choice."

"This was foolish! You're already doubting that it protects you from the infection."

She glared at him but then nodded. "Yes, I am. Last night it seemed to make sense. Now that we're five miles away from them, I'm not as confident. Anyway." She opened the pouch and drew out the book. "I want you to carry this. If anyone comes after us, they'll follow me, because I'm the known guardian."

"And what do you expect me to do?"

"I expect you to find the frontera and use the charm in there to close it."

Enlightenment touched him, and it was unpleasant. "You plan to play decoy, to draw them away from me."

"Trust me, it's nothing as complete as a plan."

"Erin. We must work together. This is..." He flailed for words. "This is unwise. We will search for the frontera together, and..."

"Sure," she said. "We will. But if we're attacked, I want you to be the one who gets away. With the book."

"And if they capture you? If you're right, and they realize they can't infect you? What's to stop them from killing you?"

"I'm going to hope I can act well enough to fool them for at least a little bit." She pushed closer to his mount and held out the book. Reluctantly, he accepted it. She pressed her hands over his. "We need to close that frontera. No matter what."

"Not if it means your death."

"Yes. Even if." She shook her head. "And besides, maybe it won't. Maybe we'll find the frontera and this won't matter."

"You are turvy," he said.

"Maybe. Let's get going."

Without waiting for a response, she sent her caballo trotting up the road. He cursed under his breath, pushed the book into his knapsack, and followed.

The road, while steeper, was still wide and smooth. People brought cartloads of metal and other goods over this road, so maintaining it was important. Even stopping to rest the caballos, which they did frequently, they made good time.

He wanted to talk to Erin, to persuade her away from this scheme, but he couldn't find the words. He worried that the mark she had scarred herself with was already affecting her in some way, or that her plan was some effect of grief. Once he said, "You are not alone here, you know."

"I know."

As the hills gave way to mountains, something grew in him—a sense of desire, or melancholy, the way he might feel on waking, seeking to recapture a wonderful dream. It was not as strong as the drive that had led him to the vast field of Ancient where he had met Erin, but it was, in some way, more pointed. Always before it had been mixed with the warmth and pleasure that came from proximity to copper. "I sense something," he said.

"Is it close?"

"Not far. It's ahead of us."

"I'm not smelling copper."

"It's different."

"Is it... Will we have to leave the road?"

"I don't know." He thought for a bit. "Yes."

They rode on. Erin's casual glances at the land around them became more frequent. Her hands tightened on the reins.

"Are you all right?" he said.

"Jumpy. Um, like nervous."

"It seems more than that."

She flicked a glance his way. "I keep thinking someone's watching us."

He held himself back from looking around. "Is it a symptom, or do you think we're being tracked? The caballos don't seem alarmed."

"I can't tell yet. Symptom, probably. Are you still getting that feeling?"

"It grows stronger," he said.

"I think Oshane was right."

He wasn't sure. The yearning could be some kind of natural charm appearing in the mountains. "I don't trust anything my uncle said."

"Well, he believes it."

The desire grew more pointed, and he longed to turn off the road and climb up into the mountains. Just as he was about to speak, Erin reined in her mount. "Someone's coming."

"I hear nothing."

"I don't *hear* them yet. Trevian, I want you to go back."

"We don't even know who they are. Why would I leave you?"

She stared at him. "I know who they are."

"We'll face them and—"

"They're looking for me. Go back. Please."

"Erin, this is turvy. This is—"

She held out her left arm. "I swear, I can feel them. There are... more than four. Six, I think, heading this way." Her caballo tossed its head and pawed the ground. "They'll assume I have the book. I'll slow them down."

"I won't let you make this sacrifice. We can face them and—"

"With a club and a pair of knives?"

"Then you take the book back and I'll—"

"They're expecting me. *You* won't be a decoy, Trevian, they'd still come after me. And I don't know where the frontera is."

He shook his head. It was like arguing with his father, only worse, because he could see the logic of her words. "This is wrong."

"It'll work. Trust me. Close that frontera and stop any more of them coming here. Please."

He glared. He wanted to argue, to fight. Now, faintly, he thought he heard the jingle of tack. He wheeled his caballo around and forced it into a gallop. He did not look back. He would not think of Erin, who he was abandoning, the way he'd abandoned Ilsanja. No, Ilsanja had been safe when he had left her. What he was doing now was worse.

After two curves in the road, he reined in his mount. He shouldered his knapsack, leaped down, and sent the caballo on with a slap to its flank. Letting his anger fuel his muscles, he climbed, aiming toward where the longing drew him. He knew he was working his way back to the place where he had left Erin and slowed his pace. The yearning called him, pointing like the arrow of a compass, but the cliff was steep. His anger didn't cool.

He thought he heard voices. As he moved, slowly and with greater care, any doubt vanished. Voices carried up from the road. There was no shouting or screams. He crouched as the climb leveled out and packed earth gave witness to other footsteps before his. The voices came from farther north, and they faded as he listened. He followed the nerve sense that grew stronger now. This feeling, he recognized it. The joy of copper had diluted it those other times, but he had felt this, this *drawing* twice, once in Merrylake Landing, and once when it led him to his claim on the field of Ancient where Erin's frontera lay. For the first time, here, the feeling was unalloyed. He wanted, more than anything, to climb up the steep rocks behind him, where something called him.

He straightened up slowly and peered over the plata-colored rock that blocked him from the road. Six caballos trotted north, toward the town of Madalita. He could see Erin. She wasn't bound, but the others surrounded her. He wished for a longbow, or even a crossbow, though the range made any shot unlikely. A chance, however small, to free her. But to do what she wanted, to do what they set out to do, his instinct and his body drove him up, higher onto the mountain.

No one looked back. The riders rounded a curve and vanished from sight.

He turned and climbed.

16

Martes, 23 Uno, Year 331

The water tumbled her. Her lungs burned. Aideen thrashed upward, or what she thought was upward, until her head broke the surface. A boulder struck the side of her head, dazing her, but she managed to gulp for air. The force of the flood was too great. She kept her face above water, but kicking and moving her arms did nothing to direct her movements. Sooner or later the water would pin her against the rocks, and she would drown.

Almost as soon as she thought it, the flood forced her up against a smooth roundness, holding her in place. She reached up, desperate. Her fingers slipped on the slick wet surface. It wasn't rock. She opened her eyes. With one kick and a wild tug, she pulled herself up enough to rest against the object. The smell, and the touch of the coat, identified it. She rested against the barrel of a dead caballo.

Her stomach churned. The carcass wore no saddle. Fear filled her. This was the black. Shivering, Aideen pushed herself an arm's length away from the body, scanning the frothing brown water. There was no sign of Ilsanja. Right now, the dead beast was giving her shelter. If she moved, the water would sweep her downstream. But if Ilsanja were pinned beneath the carcass...

She drew two deep breaths and submerged, running her hands along the dead animal's belly. There was no sign of a rider. As she surfaced, once again the water shoved her face-first into the dead caballo's coat. She reached out, grabbed its mane, and pulled herself sideways, and then again, her feet flailing, until she found a rock that didn't tip under her weight. She stood up. The loss of buoyancy, combined with her sodden clothes, nearly pulled her down again, but even in the dark, she could see the shore only a few feet away. The dead caballo's head extended toward it, as if in its last moments it strove for land. Her legs shook. Holding onto the creature's neck, she sidestepped slowly, until the water dropped, and a moment later she fell into the sandy mud, panting.

When she had her breath, she shouted, "Ilsanja!" She shouldn't be shouting. While Garth and the mestengos were not coming after them, there was the one Vallis had sent after Harald. Dieter. She didn't care. "Ilsanja!" she shouted again, knowing it was a dream, it was madness, that Ilsanja had probably been carried farther down the mountain by the raging water.

But what if she had done just as Aideen had?

Her knees shook when she stood, and her chest ached with each breath. Both belts pulled at her, impediments, but she didn't care. She had a knife, and a sparker, and a few cinders of whiterock. And Ilsanja might be alive.

A few yards away the sand became gravel and then rocks, slowing her progress. If she remembered correctly, the way flattened out farther up. And there, maybe she would find Ilsanja, or at least follow the water down to Merry Lake, and eventually home. If she weren't killed by mestengos, kiotes, earth elementals, or hunger.

After a few minutes, she stopped to rest. "Ilsanja!" she shouted. The rain was fading and this time she heard her own voice, weak and high-pitched, echoing around her. She climbed up, slipping on the rocks. Two fingers of her left hand stung. She remembered grasping for purchase on the flat rock, finding none. "Ilsanja!"

Something clicked above her head. She stopped and peered up. A boulder loomed over her, but she could see nothing else. Some sound had echoed. Motion at the corner of her vision made her whirl. A figure stood there, one arm raised. Her heart seized, but the figure ran forward, a rock falling from its fingers, and Ilsanja, sodden, reeking of mud, engulfed her. Aideen wrapped her arms around her friend.

"You're alive," she said.

"Aideen."

They held each other.

"How did you survive that fall with that caballo on top of you?"

Ilsanja held her at arm's length. "I threw myself clear, but not before he went over the side. I saw nothing, for...a long time, it seemed, and then I crashed into him. He nearly clipped me with his hoof, he was thrashing so badly. There was nothing I could do for him. I got caught in an eddy, out of the rush of the water, and climbed to safety."

"I think that caballo saved both of us," Aideen said.

"Did they follow us? I don't know where to go. I don't know what to do. I—"

"Garth was leading them away, but there is one still out here. And Vallis may choose to pursue us on his own."

"Vallis the coward!" Ilsanja's shoulders slumped. "We have no shelter, no food, no weapons."

"You were doing well with a rock," Aideen said.

Ilsanja actually smiled.

"And we have one knife," Aideen said. "Let's climb higher and see if we can find shelter, to start with. Then we'll make a plan."

"I have no wits left to make a plan," Ilsanja said.

"The day when *you* are without wit has not yet come."

Ilsanja was quiet for a moment. "Aideen, your faith in me is a beacon." She sounded like herself again.

They began to climb.

Above them, the way leveled out as it skirted a tall hill. The rain stopped. The relative quiet was shocking. Aideen was shivering so badly her teeth ached, and so was Ilsanja.

Aideen saw an undercut in the hill and led the way toward it. She was rewarded not with an overhang, but an opening, a dark tunnel into the mountain. For a few minutes she hesitated, Ilsanja at her side, equally unsure.

Aideen looked at her shivering friend, and that decided her. "It's shelter," she said. "We haven't encountered elementals or kiotes yet."

"W-w-we have wards for el-elementals," Ilsanja said, her teeth chattering. "In m-my purse."

"All right."

They staggered inside. It was no warmer, but it was drier. Taking the knife, Aideen left the cave and stripped as many branches and leaves as she could carry from the resinous shrubs. Ilsanja had pulled off her jacket and was wringing it out when Aideen dragged the lot inside.

"What use is that? We have no way of making fire."

"I have the sparker, remember? It's in my purse."

"You are a genius among women. Those leaves are soaked, though, and even if we had kindling paper, it is soaked as well."

"I have a couple of chunks of whiterock left. We'll hope for the best."

Aideen tore the leaves in half, squeezing out the resin, and Ilsanja joined in. After she smeared some of the sap into the largest cube of whiterock, Aideen clicked the sparker. The first four times the spark failed, but on the fifth, the resin spat and glowed green, then blue. Soon flames leaped up among the leaves. They added branches slowly. It was a small fire, but it gave them warmth. Aideen spread out their wet jackets, belts, and boots as close to the flames as she dared.

Ilsanja reached for her belt. She rummaged in her purse and pulled out a waterlogged slab of something. "Here. It's my finest."

"What is it?" The substance gave slightly between her fingers. It was soaked through, but plainly it had once been a dried peach slice. "Thank you."

"Savor it," Ilsanja said.

The dried fruit tasted of mud, but Aideen didn't care. Her stomach rumbled. The last thing she had eaten was flatbread and fruit when they had stopped at the albergue.

Ilsanja held her hand out over the fire. "I swore I would never be that helpless again," she said.

"You weren't helpless. We're free because of you."

Ilsanja shook her head. "Your plan, your wit. All I did was handle a green caballo badly. I nearly killed both of us. And I...sitting there, bound, once again armed with nothing but words...I swore that would never happen again."

"Your words are fierce weapons. He tried to shame you, and you flipped that back on him like a trained fighter. And I would never have dared to approach that caballo. I'd be some man's third wife by now if not for you."

Ilsanja rubbed her arms. "Honestly, Aideen, as much as I wish to praise your courage and wits, *and* mine, the fact is, we escaped because Vallis Majeur is stupid."

Aideen giggled. The rush of giggles grew into a laugh, and Ilsanja joined her.

When she caught her breath, she said, "Thank the Mother some things can always be counted on."

Ilsanja put her arms around Aideen and nestled her face against her neck. "Yes. And we *were* brave. They should write a stage play about us."

"Yes." Aideen hugged her back. "Do you think it's safe to sleep?"

"Just sleep?" Ilsanja said, with a flirtatious note in her voice. "Yes. I think so, and I think we must."

They arranged the wards and settled for lying down on the hard, smooth floor of the cave, their arms wrapped around each other. They had no food, no mounts, and little chance of safely finding their way home, but a kind of elation filled Aideen as she pulled Ilsanja close to her.

Ilsanja rose once and went out into the darkness. She came back with two or three more branches, and they built up the fading fire. The whiterock glowed dying green now, but the branches crackled merrily. Aideen made room and pillowed her friend's head on her shoulder, then lay awake herself. There was a dull steady rushing that she thought was the flashflood, plunging down the mountain. Beyond it, and the snap of the occasional burning branch, it was quiet. Her muscles began to loosen, and she drifted into a shallow sleep.

When she woke, the cavern was filled with a gray light, and the fire was a circle of ashes. Ilsanja handed her half a slice of peach. "I searched for water outside, but it is fouled. I fear we may do without."

Aideen stretched. She was surprised at how rested she was—and how hungry. She made herself eat the morsel of fruit in nibbles, trying to make it last.

Ilsanja stared past her at the side of the cavern. "This is human made," she said.

Aideen followed the track of Ilsanja's gaze. The opening, seen in daylight, was a smooth rectangle, but that wasn't what had caught Ilsanja's eye. On one side, hidden in the shadows, was a bent sheet of gray metal, pinned at top and bottom by sharp-edged rocks. The bend pointed out toward them. Aideen stood up. As she drew closer, she saw the edge of the sheet was thick as the width of her two open hands side by side.

"What is that?" Ilsanja asked. "Is it steel?"

"I think it is." Aideen crossed the opening to get a closer look at the other side of the cavern. There were marks on the floor and in the smooth wall. "I think there were two. Prospectors have been here. I think someone claimed the other one."

"Why not that one?"

Aideen pointed to the pile of rocks, and the sharp crease in the metal. "It's pinned. It would take many prospectors to pry that loose."

"It *is* steel, though."

"If they were finding copper or gold here, though, or loomin, they may have decided it wasn't worth the labor."

"Huh."

Aideen started into the shadows of the tunnel. Now, with light, and a different awareness of the place, she knew where to look. "There," she said, pointing to the ceiling a few feet beyond where they had slept, where a ridge hung down. "Words."

S LY PORT SOUTH OH701196

"What does that mean? Does port mean entry?" Ilsanja said. "But why does it say south?"

"The world turned," Aideen murmured.

Ilsanja tilted her head. "Somehow I never thought...our east was their *south?*"

"Or it's a joke of some kind." Aideen walked over to the ridge and looked closely at the floor. "Here," she said, pointing to holes. They were round, an even distance apart. Many were filled with dust, but at least two were empty, smooth-sided, and deep. "I think perhaps there was a fence here once, and prospectors carried it away." She straightened up. "I know where we are. You remember where we stayed on the first night of our journey to Duloc?"

"I can draw that recollection from the dim and shadowy recesses of memory," Ilsanja said, "because it was four nights ago." She gasped. "Only four? It feels like my world completely changed since then."

"Or we crossed the boundary of our small world and begin to see the bigger one."

Ilsanja gave her whole body a shake. "Anyway, where is it you think we are?"

"I think this is the other end of that passage. You remember the sound we heard, that spooked the caballos? I think it was the wind blowing through here. I suspect this goes all the way through."

Ilsanja raised an eyebrow. "And what of shafts, or rockslides, or getting crushed between rocks? All those things you feared before? If we have to turn back, we lose time, and matters are no less urgent now."

"I still worry, but if there is a mestengo looking out for us, staying out of sight may be the good choice."

"You are emboldened by our brave escape," Ilsanja said.

"I'm not. I'm being practical—are you joking?"

"Perhaps. A little."

"Ugh, I'm too hungry to grapple with your wit this morning, Ilsanja. If you wish it, we can follow the water down to the plateau—"

"I've been out there this morning," Ilsanja said. "That way is rough, and the water is high and treacherous. We have light, we have a knife, and perhaps we have the makings for fire. If this way remains as smooth as it is here, it will be an easier journey. And perhaps we will find people in Merrylake Landing who will help us."

They might at least find a caballo they could borrow. Aideen scattered the ashes of their fire. She rolled the remaining branches up in her jacket and carried the bundle under one arm. They set off deeper into the passage.

She could tell from the pressure in her thighs that they were heading slightly downhill. The air was sweet. Ilsanja swept the beam of the quartzlight from side to side, but except for a few places where the sharp-edged rocks had broken free of the wall and fallen into the passage floor, the way was clear. Aideen longed for water, but she said nothing, and neither did Ilsanja.

Several passages broke off from the one they walked, cut straight into the mountain, heading south. They didn't stop. West was their direction. Once they came to a long stretch of shallow steps, more than a hundred, and Ilsanja stopped without warning and sat down, twenty or thirty steps from the bottom. Aideen sat next to her.

"Sorry," Ilsanja murmured.

"Rest is good."

Ilsanja idly played the beam of the light over the wall. Aideen caught her hand, guided it back. "What's that?"

"More letters?"

Aideen stood up. "No. Pictures."

"Paintings?" Ilsanja trained the light where Aideen pointed. The images were simple. Two steep simple curves took up the top corner, crowned with a child's drawing of trees, laden with reddish balls. Below the arcs clustered a set of white buildings.

Ilsanja said, "Is it a city?"

"A compound, I think. Like the Copper Coalition." Aideen put her face close to the wall. In a lower corner on the wall of one of the buildings was a set of letters and numbers, but they made no sense to her.

"Is this place some sort of a temple?"

She shrugged.

"Look. There are more."

Aideen went down the steps, following the beam of light. The next image was a human figure, three times life-size.

"Is that...a deity of some sort?" Ilsanja's voice shook slightly and so did the beam of light.

"I don't know."

The figure was female, apparently. Her left hand was upraised, palm up, and above her palm floated a design, a circle filled with ellipses, crossing each other, a ball made of many rings. She wore pale trousers and a pale tunic of some sort. Her skin was black, purple, and white. The white paint seemed to be used to show where light was striking her skin. Her hair, black and purple, stood out around her head like a sunburst. She smiled. Behind her, over her left shoulder, was a circle of light, more interlocking ellipses within. "There are words again," Aideen said. Ilsanja shifted the light.

TELMA LEWISTON. SHE GIVES US THE FUTURE.

"A deity then, definitely," Ilsanja said. "Do you think her skin was truly purple?"

"I think the painter liked purple." Aideen touched the image carefully. Protected from the elements, it could have been painted the day before.

"Is that another?" Telma Lewiston returned to darkness as Ilsanja shifted the quartzlight. "'Reeshard Alvarez. He opens creativity.' That has no meaning. And he is surrounded by... things. What are those?"

Aideen moved closer. "Machines?" The letters spelled out RICHARD ALVAREZ. Richard wore a strange set of spectacles that covered his forehead, his eyes, his nose, and his cheeks, curving around to cover his ears. Like Telma Lewiston, he wore a pale tunic and trousers. He was surrounded by various boxlike apparatus. In his hand, he held a plaque. The same spinning design that floated above Telma Lewiston's palm filled its interior.

"His skin is green." Ilsanja sounded disappointed.

"I think that is an artist being playful."

"I wager they were Walkers," Ilsanja said. "Mama spoke of those. They are half-human, half-deity of some kind, and they walk among humans, sharing gifts. This was a religious place, a temple complex. I'm sure of it."

"Probably," Aideen said.

They moved slowly down the rest of the steps, keeping the light on the walls. Ilsanja gasped and the light quivered. "Sacrifices!"

Six faces, inside squares of color. Aideen laughed. "I think they are portraits, Ilsanja."

"Are you sure?"

Of course, she wasn't sure. She knew nothing about this place and these pictures. Each face had a single name underneath it. Underneath the six boxes ran a legend.

THE EAGER BEAVERS OF ORCHARD HILL

"What is a beaver?" Aideen said.

"A priest-class? An acolyte? Perhaps these were followers of the two Walkers."

"Perhaps they were. This is a mystery, and a fascination."

Ilsanja played her light over the wall ahead of them, but there were no more paintings. She sighed. "A shame. For moments there, I forgot how much I was craving water."

"So did I."

The floor leveled out after the steps, and they continued on their way.

The Mother blessed them an hour later when Aideen heard a soft gurgling sound. Water bubbled up from a corner of the passage. She looked at Ilsanja, and Ilsanja at her—they had no way to boil it, and thirst was raging in them. Aideen scooped up water in her hands.

"It smells sweet," she said, and sipped. Then she gulped down the rest, and Ilsanja dipped her hands into the spring as well.

They drank for several minutes, rested, and drank some more. Aideen didn't say it, but she was reluctant to move on and leave the water behind.

Ilsanja straightened up. "What's that?"

Aideen paused, listening. She heard it now, a low-pitched, regular moaning.

Ilsanja whispered, "Is there someone in here with us?"

Aideen brought a finger to her lips. The sound rose and ebbed, rose and ebbed again, and she recognized it. It was like the wind, only they were deep inside the mountain. Or perhaps they were *not* so deep inside. She whispered. "Not a person, I think. Air." She stood up and pointed. "That way." She was still whispering, although she didn't know exactly why.

The sound emanated from one of the passages that ran at right angles to theirs. Aideen advanced cautiously. Ilsanja, her grip shifting on the quartzlight, kept one hand on her shoulder.

The sound grew steadily louder, but there was no passage of air against their faces. Aideen's heartbeat increased steadily. Ilsanja squeezed her shoulder suddenly and she stopped. There, on the wall, were more letters.

W RNIN OBSERV LL NON INC SION PROTOCOLS

"Protocols?" she whispered.

"Rituals," Ilsanja said.

"Shall we go back?" Aideen murmured.

"Not for every coin in the Banco de Duloc."

Aideen wished that she had a notebook so she could write down what they were seeing, so she could share it, one day, with Trevian. She made herself step forward, and once she started again, it was fine, except that her heart continued to race.

Ilsanja directed the quartzlight along the wall again. "Aideen, what is that? Is that music?"

Along the wall ran five parallel lines, marked at intervals with dots.

Some straddled the lines; some filled the spaces between. It did look exactly like a line of musical notes. "Can you read it?"

"I did better at dancing than music."

Aideen said, "Father found music frivolous. We had none after my mother left us." She stared at the lines. They ran into the darkness. "Why would the Ancients put music on the walls?"

The air grew cooler, sharply, and she felt a breeze on her face. It brought no scent, and no other sound but the two-note moan like the low notes of a flautine, but it brushed her hair back. "We're nearing the end," she whispered.

A light bloomed in the darkness ahead of them, and they both stopped. "It's a reflection," Aideen said. The beam was shining back at them, bouncing off a surface. From the brightness, it didn't seem like the rock walls to either side of them. She slid her foot forward into the dark.

The reflection grew brighter, nearly stinging, and she shaded her eyes with her hand. The passage widened, curving in a semi-circle, and a transparent barrier marked its edge. Ilsanja shifted the light down, and Aideen approached the wall. It was clear, some form of quartz or glass, run through with a square grid of plata-colored wires. It reminded her in a random way of the copper mesh on the tops of the cages, except the grid was wider and no wires extended beyond the glass.

In front of her, the barrier opened, forming a transparent tunnel over a walkway out over—she didn't know what. The moaning notes rang around them, steadily.

"Be careful," Ilsanja said.

"Yes." Pressing one hand against the transparent wall, Aideen reached out one foot and tapped on the walkway. It was rock, probably carved out of the mountain, and it ran into darkness until she could no longer see it.

"Here, take the light." Ilsanja pressed it into her hand. It stayed awake, and Aideen played it out across the walkway. It ended in another plate of the strange glass and wire.

She slid one foot out, and then another. Her nerves hummed, but she wouldn't turn back now. She took two more sliding steps, and two more. Her free hand touched the wall, and she looked down at her feet.

Below them yawned a circular black chasm. The quartzlight didn't penetrate it. It was like night, if night had no stars. Her feet, her legs would not move. The moaning came from the depth of the chasm.

Aideen had always feared heights. Standing at the edge of the mountain staring down into this passage, what filled her was greater than fear. She stood at the edge of a world, a world that did not know her, did not care for her any more than it might care for a single fleck of mica. Her whole body trembled. The beam of light danced wildly.

"Aideen." Ilsanja's voice flattened and faded. They were surrounded by smooth walls, but nothing echoed. "Aideen, come back. Come back to me."

"I can't move."

"I'll come to you then."

"No!" Whatever this was, this awe, this dread, she couldn't face it threatening Ilsanja. She slid her foot back in a mirror-dance of her earlier steps, first one, then the other.

"Reach back your free hand," Ilsanja said.

Her hand trembling, she did so. Ilsanja seized it, warm and strong, and pulled her. She half-spun and staggered off the walkway, dragging Ilsanja several feet from the wall before she collapsed onto the floor.

"What happened? Are you hurt? What is in there?"

"I don't know *what* it is. It isn't a smoke rift or a volcanic gap. It's a, it's a...I don't know."

"A frontera?"

"Maybe. It's terrible."

"What was the moaning? Is there something down there, or it is a trick of rock and air?"

Aideen smoothed down her hair to give herself time to think. "I think...neither."

"You *do* believe it's a frontera," Ilsanja said.

"Something vaster than what we've grown up hearing of." She got to her feet and said briskly, "Let us get back on our track." At least she tried to speak briskly. Her voice sounded childlike and tremulous.

Somehow, the journey back to the east-west passage seemed much shorter. They left the spring behind. As they walked, she stopped shivering.

"I wonder," Ilsanja said, "if the adventure Trevian and Erin are having is in any way the match of ours."

17

Martes, 23 Uno, Year 331

Greetings, traveler," the lead rider said. There were five, not six. Two had crossbows, but they were stowed, and the lead rider had a large smile on her weathered face. Erin smelled copper—burned hair and licorice—from where she sat, but she didn't need her copper-hunter sense, just her eyes. The woman dripped with chains, charms, and disks. Copper cuffs covered both wrists.

Erin wished she had slightly more weapons than just a belt knife and an aluminum stake.

"Greetings," she said.

Two of the riders rode past her, stopping on either side of her. The others spread out across the road, casually blocking her path. The leader advanced a pace or two. "Where do you head?"

"To the Madlyn border," Erin said.

The lead rider nodded. "You're very close. Let us ride with you for a way and show you our town."

"You were heading the other direction," Erin said.

The woman's smile broadened. "We come out from Via Nueva to

greet travelers," she said. "People get confused, seeking the town of Madalita, and we've changed the road."

"Really? I thought this was the Copper Road, and the Crescent Council maintained it."

"They do, but we've improved it for the caravans."

Erin drew on the reins, and her caballo backed up a few steps. She thought of turning and trying to make a run for it, but she didn't know how far Trevian might have gotten, and she didn't want to lead them right to him.

"I shouldn't have any trouble finding my way then, if the road's even better." Her skin was stinging faintly, like a mild sunburn. They were infected. She was sure of it.

"Come. What's the harm in sharing a cup of ale and a meal before continuing on your way? And alone as well, on a road known for its copper thieves. Surely you and your caballo can use a rest."

Erin decided on a shrug. She tried to make it a shoulder-rolling kind. "Why not? I mean, very well."

The woman nodded. Erin rode toward her. Before she could come alongside, the woman turned her caballo, taking the lead. Now Erin was in the center, a rider on each side, two behind her. Well, if they were controlled by the parasites, at least she was immune. She hoped. And if they were just polite thieves, she'd escape somehow and find her way back to Trevian. The least likely alternative was that they really were friendly villagers, who had no training in the hospitality field. She could hope for that anyway.

They rode quietly for a bit. Then the leader said, "Where do you head in Madlyn?"

"To Bois." She picked a name she'd seen from Stillwater's books.

"Ah. A long ride, even once you cross the border. Do you seek work? Or family?"

Erin rode quietly. Any word out of her mouth probably identified her as an out-of-worlder, if they didn't know for sure already. She remembered back to her few hours with Trevian's wife, Ilsanja. How would *she* handle this? She said, "Do you ask these questions of every traveler on the North Road?"

The woman laughed, a one hundred percent bad actress laugh. "It's rare to see a single traveler, you know. Most people prefer to ride in pairs or hire a guide. Were you traveling alone, all this way?"

"What makes you think I've come far?"

"Your caballo seems weary."

Erin didn't answer. The stinging grew stronger.

"You travel lightly for one going into the midlands of Madlyn," the woman said. Erin decided not to answer that either.

They rode along. The rider on her right shifted in the saddle. She could see him out of her peripheral vision but couldn't quite decipher what he was doing. Nothing good, probably.

The leader gave her a glance. "We know who you are, and what you carry."

Still trying to channel Ilsanja, Erin said, "Is that a riddle?"

"Where is your partner, the copper-hunter?"

"Can you be more specific?" Erin said.

The leader moved her hand. Before Erin could turn her head, a loop of braided leather dropped over her head and shoulders, snugged tight, pinching her arms against her side. The cuts on her left arm twinged. Another riata from the left fell over her.

"Seriously?" she said.

The leader wheeled her caballo. Some communication passed between her and the two flanking riders. One of them reached for her messenger bag. Erin dug her heels into the caballo's flanks, and it lunged forward, but the leader reached out and grabbed the reins. Erin hadn't really thought she'd get anywhere, anyway.

Okay, she thought. *I'm officially in trouble.*

The leader's gaze scanned the cliffs on either side. Erin thought they'd take the bag now and open it, but instead, the leader sent her mount loping forward. Erin managed to grab the saddle horn as her caballo followed. She focused on keeping her balance with her arms pinned against her torso, since they rode at a near gallop.

At least they weren't headed after Trevian.

They rode into a pocket valley filled with single-story buildings. A couple of long stables greeted them, then a large building with a wide covered porch, a tavern. The streets weren't jammed with people, but there was traffic, and one look at the way they moved, their lack of eye contact, made Erin decide not to bother yelling for help. No one was reacting to a woman bound by two riatas. The leader guided them down a side road to a long wooden building set back against the hills. Two riders pulled her off her mount more gently than she expected.

"What are you doing?" she said. She didn't have to act scared; she already was. "Are you thieves? Take what you want and let me go. I have, I have very little coin."

Neither of her captors responded as they brought her to a chair and sat her down. Quickly, before she could pull free, they loosened the riatas, yanked them over the chair back, and pulled them tight again, pinioning her to the chair. She twisted and tugged, but the braided leather held. The leader took the messenger bag and the knapsack, which she dropped on the floor without a glance.

"How dare you treat me this way?" Erin said.

"We wish you to know us," the leader said. "We wish to welcome you."

"You've kidnapped—abducted me! I don't *want* to know you!"

The leader stood. "You have set yourself against us with no knowledge of what we are."

Apparently whatever they did to people involved a monolog first. Erin let herself relax. She had a few more minutes before the woman realized she didn't have the book.

"The community you carry is filled with value for us all," the woman said. Erin didn't completely understand the words. The community? What community?

The woman opened the messenger bag. Erin started. She'd expected more lecturing, more time. The woman lifted out the book Erin had wrapped in her shirt the night before and dropped the bag on the floor. Almost reverently, the woman folded back the fabric. She looked up at Erin, and her face twisted into a frown. "This is not the community!" she said, dropping Stillwater's book on the floor. In a flash, the other riders pulled open Erin's knapsack and began emptying it. The leader upended the messenger bag. Her cell phone skidded across the floor and bounced off the wall. The screen glowed. She hadn't powered it down last night.

"Where is it?" the woman said. "The community you carry—what have you done with it?"

"It's safe," Erin said. "It's incredibly valuable. Did you think I'd just carry it around with me?"

"Yes! You are its guardian! Is it—" Her eyelids fluttered. "It is not at the Copper Coalition," she said.

Goosebumps broke out on Erin's skin. It wasn't just that they were in communication with each other that fast. They still had a mole in the Coalition.

The woman said, "Did you give it to the two female chaotics? Or—"

"The what?"

"No. Your partner."

"I'm not sure what you mean," Erin said. "What's a female chaotic?"

"Where is your partner?"

"I don't know what you're asking."

She advanced and leaned down into Erin's face. Erin managed not to lean back. "The copper-hunter! The man you travel with!"

"Oh, him. He got married. We're not together anymore."

"These are nonsense words."

"No, he really did. Get married, I mean."

"He was with you when you left the city."

"Maybe he went after his sister and his wife. Oh, are they the chaotics? Maybe he followed them."

"He did not." The woman did not sound as sure, though. Whatever network the parasites had, it wasn't that strong around Harald and the women…if that was who the "female chaotics" were.

Behind her, a door creaked as it opened. Another woman circled the chair, holding a bundle of cloth across both her palms. She moved like she was holding something sacred. Erin's throat closed up. The leader reached down and unbuttoned the first two buttons of Erin's shirt. "What are you doing?" Erin said.

"This node welcomes you."

The second woman leaned over Erin and opened up the bundle. Erin thought for a second she would puke as the pink thing flexed and curved on the fabric. She made herself take deep breaths. Images cascaded through her mind: the Agustos, the Merrylake Landing copper-hunters, nearly dead, those things on their chests, keeping them in a coma while Oshane sucked their energy out of them.

The second woman said softly, "You have nothing to fear," and held the thing up against Erin's chest just below her collarbone.

Erin clenched her teeth against pain, but the sting wasn't pain. It was sweet, pleasant. Warmth flowed from the site of the stinger out into her body. The world misted into glowing pink and gold.

She sank into warmth. All pain and stiffness left her body. Tension she hadn't known she was carrying flowed out of her muscles.

Alone, isolated, a stranger, she hadn't really known *how* alone she was. She hadn't known she didn't *have* to be. The node welcomed her. She thought, I am in serious troub///

///This node welcomes us. We sink we float/rise on the sea of belonging. We embrace, are embraced by the belonging. Close here designated Collision Outpost we are one and we are beyond the conduit to Home, where connection sparkles in the air, gleams in each drop of water.///

Her left arm burned.

///This host retains chaotic elements but functions within tolerance. We give us water and it flows cool and sweet down our throat but not as sweet as the New Way, not even as sweet as the union here designated Collision Outpost. We loosen the restraints needed when we were a chaotic. We see now. We see the New Way twin triangles intersecting lines burning with white light this host experiences some distress but functions within tolerance. We see the New Way, it welcomes us we welcome us.

Here designated Outpost we know the community we seek is in the possession of a male chaotic who pursues the conduit. We take the necessary steps to protect the community twin triangles intersecting lines white light this host experiences distress distress exceeds tolerance measures taken measures taken.

The community is protected. We pursue the male chaotic. We maintain security on this host.

We give us food, and it is satisfying, filling, warming, not as warming as the belonging to the New Way and the belonging in here designated Outpost. Distant, designated Copper Coalition, we learn chaotics are close to discovering us. We feel fear. We calm us. We are the New Way.

Distant, designated White Bluffs, we learn the long-range project proposed by the unreliable source is failing to perform within parameters. We calm us. We assess. The project can be redirected.

Close designated conduit we lose access. Close designated conduit we identify threat.

Here designated Outpost we welcome much from this host. We learn of Orchard Hill. We learn of a novel threat, in distant undesignated sector. We assess. We identify a novel threat and a novel community. We identify an external incursion similar to when this host was a chaotic and invaded this world. Location of the novel threat is beyond our communication.

Close designated conduit-adjacent we approach the opening. We encounter obstacles. We engage the male chaotic.

This host is reacting within tolerances. Security is reduced on this host.

Home can access conduit and neutralize threat. We reach for Home. Connection impeded.

This host picks up objects carried when it was chaotic. This host places them in carrier bag. We have three bars. This host rests.

We adjust. We reach for Home. Connection impeded. Home must utilize conduit. Connection impeded. We adjust.

Here designated Outpost, designated host habitation, distress registered. Violent rapid oxidation originating from indigenous elemental events not nativized to this region. We suppress violent rapid oxidation. We suppress violent rapid twin triangles white burning light intersecting lines.///

Her toes and fingertips burned with pain, and the pain swept in, up her legs, up her arms.

///This host experiences physical distress in extremities. Distress exceeds tolerances. Physical distress migrates deeper into host physicality where is the belonging where is the belonging this node is in distress violent rapid oxidation violent violent. This node is, this node is, this node///

S mall stones rolled away under Trevian's feet. He had lost track of how long he had been climbing. The sense of yearning led him up, along a rockfall, toward a narrow ridge.

The folded mountains acted like a funnel, bouncing small sounds to him, like the soft clink of metal. Trevian crouched, then peered over the jagged rock that sheltered him. The faint impression of a narrow track was visible in the dust. The frontera was nearby, and he guessed the sound came from someone set to guard it.

As a prospector, Trevian had learned to be wary of ambushes and avoid them. That hadn't extended to actually ambushing someone himself, though. He didn't know who or how many were around the fold of rock. His chest was hollow; the frontera was close.

After a moment, he stood up and climbed up onto the hint of a trail, pressing himself against the cliff face and moving as quietly as he could. He smelled cooked meat. As he stood, someone less than an arm's length from him coughed slightly, and he flinched. A stream of yellow liquid arced into the air, pattering on the rocks below. The man on the other side coughed again.

Trevian gripped the handle of his steel club and bounded around the rock. The man flailed his arms, his eyes wide, and stepped back, reaching for a knife. Trevian thumped him hard on the side of the head. The man staggered sideways. His hand flailed for his knife again, but he had unbuckled his belt and the sheath had slipped just beyond his fingertips. Before the guard could reach it, Trevian gathered his resolve and struck the man again, and once more as the man fell onto his side and rolled. He lay unmoving, one arm draped over the narrow ledge they stood on.

Trevian pounced, rolled him onto his back, and tore open his shirt. The man moaned, and his eyelids flickered, white showing underneath them. A vile parasite throbbed on his chest. Bitter liquid rushed into Trevian's mouth and rage heated his chest. He pulled out his knife, slipped the flat of the blade underneath the thing, and pried it off.

"No," the man muttered.

Trevian threw the parasite into the dirt and swung his club down onto it, and again, until it was only a smear of pinkish jelly against the dust and gravel.

The man groaned. "No." He tried to sit up, but fell back and lay still, holding his head.

Trevian squatted beside him. "How many of them are there?"

"We—I'm alone. I don't."

"How many? And where?"

"No. I don't know. We, I, where are we? I don't know." He rolled onto his side and wept.

Trevian stood up, disgusted with himself. Where the mountain folded, the fold created a narrow passage. He slipped off his knapsack and entered the passage, turning sideways, dragging the pack behind him. A few feet in, the choking-tight space widened out. He stepped into a cavern and pulled his knapsack after him.

He wondered what copper-hunter had discovered this place. Maybe just a prospector seeking storm-shelter. The opening, and the cave, were not obvious, but he could feel the frontera now. Oshane Langtree was right. Somehow, like his ability to sense copper, he could sense the places where the elemental worlds overlapped.

The cavern was domed like a dioso church, with a wide passage that stretched away into shadow and a narrower one going off to his right. He explored that one first. It ended in a rockslide and a curve of mountain. No escape there, but cool air blew around him. He found no gaps in the walls, but at the top of the pile of rubble he saw a hole in the ceiling, no wider than his shoulders. No light shone out of it; it might go nowhere. After a couple of tries, he successfully climbed up the loose rocks and stuck his head inside.

His head poked up from the floor of a horizontal shaft not much wider than the hole itself. To the north, though, a gap showed him sky and a scrap of mountainside. It was far from a perfect way out, but it was one if he needed it.

He half-climbed, half-slid back down and re-entered the domed cave. The frontera was closed, but it was here. He felt it like he felt his own breathing. He had only to use the charm from the book to close it forever and end the parasites.

The book rested on top of his clean linen and his other pair of trousers. He reached down to pull it out.

The ground struck the back of his head and the world vanished. Cold pain radiated out from the center of his forehead, rippling through his body like a flashflood. Nearby, someone was moaning.

The guard, he thought.

Slowly, vision returned to him, and the pain faded. He sat up, nearly screaming as the pain flared in his head. Had the guard shot him? He reached for his iron spar, then chose his knife instead. As best as he could with his blurry vision, he shifted his gaze to the narrow opening, but there was no one there—no guard with a crossbow, no charmcaster, no copper-hunter with a charmed weapon.

He stood carefully, and the pain faded to a dull pulse. No one else was with him. No one had attacked him.

He spun toward the frontera, rewarded with vertigo so strong he nearly fell again. It had not opened. The attack had not come from there either.

Was the cavern warded in some way? It seemed possible. Would the book's charm work through a ward? Or perhaps he could find another charm in the book. That's what Erin had done, facing the flames…checked in the book for a charm that would neutralize them, although it hadn't worked the way she had assumed it would. And now they had additional pages.

He reached for the book and stopped, an inch above the metal surface. Slowly, he curled his fingers into a fist, remembering Zachary.

He'd persuaded her to ward the book.

But she'd handed him the book, and he had touched it with no difficulty.

The book's smooth cover mocked him.

If Erin was under the influence of the parasites now, the charm could have changed, guided by her thoughts, and the book could be closed to him. And that meant he could do nothing to close this passage from the world of the parasites.

He made a fist and slowly reached down. As the knuckle of his middle finger brushed the cove, pain ignited in his head again. He staggered backward, coming to rest against the cave wall before he fell again. His stomach heaved.

Sweat ran down the sides of his face.

If Erin were under their control, she would tell them the plan, and they would be coming here soon. They were probably coming now. Could he block the entrance? There wasn't enough time, and he didn't know how many people were under the influence of the creatures. If he blocked it with rocks, there could be a hundred workers to clear it. He grabbed the corner of his knapsack and upended it. The book fell, his clothing and other items cascading around it. He scooped up the small cloth case that landed on top of his trousers, the one that carried the charms. Heart racing, he tugged it open and counted out the warding disks. He had four already charmcast with wards. He pulled out two blanks, held them in his fist, and recited the warding charm until they warmed in his hand. Six should suffice. He ran into the passage, fell to his knees, and began to dig through the gravelly soil.

He dug a hole as deep as the length of his hand and buried the first charm. Next to it, he buried another, then slid backward, continuing to plant the charms. He seeded the passage with five and held the sixth in his hand. Back under the dome, he spoke the word to waken the wards. A tendril of scent like the air after a lightning strike curled around him.

Those should hold for a while at least.

The book lay on top of his clothes, mocking him. How could he open it if he couldn't touch it?

18

Martes, 23 Uno, Year 331

Aideen's legs ached with each step and she lost all track of time, but the tunnel they walked grew lighter. Finally, Ilsanja spoke the word to rest the quartzlight. Ahead of them, an arch of brightness swelled, and they could smell the tang of wet vegetation.

"Is this where we stayed?" she said, as the tunnel widened out.

Ilsanja pointed. "There's where we tethered the caballos, I'm sure," she said. "And there's ash on the floor here."

"Can we sit down?" Aideen said. "Just for a moment?"

"As soon as we reach the ash circle. That is our landmark," Ilsanja said. Two dozen more steps and they both collapsed. Aideen groaned with relief.

She said, "We'll need to turn north to find drinkable water, but maybe the way to Merrylake Landing is clear, and it's that way."

Ilsanja nodded without speaking and let her chin fall onto her chest.

"Are you well?"

Ilsanja said, "I think I have never been this tired."

Aideen didn't say, "It's hunger," because the word would make her think of food. In fact, the very choice not to speak the word had made her think of food. She lay back flat on the ground, groaning again as the muscles in her back relaxed. Ilsanja lay down beside her.

Sometime later—Aideen didn't think she had slept—her feet stopped throbbing. She stood up slowly. "Are you rested?"

Ilsanja said, "We can call it rested." She got up also, limping slightly for a moment. "Water first."

"Water first," Aideen agreed.

Outside on the plateau, they saw that Merry Lake had, for the moment, returned to an earlier time. Water rippled over what had been mudflats. A stream of brown, opening like a fan, flowed into the lake from the northeast corner.

"The grand canal will turn brown," Ilsanja murmured. Aideen nodded. The channel that brought water from the lake into White Bluffs did not strain or filter it. She imagined the articles in the *Noticias* and the other newssheets, unless the mud settled into the lakebed before it flowed to the town.

They headed north, to the stream where they'd watered the caballos. It ran clear. However, disappointment waited beyond them. What had been a shallow canyon with a trail was now a wide brown river. There was no way to reach Merrylake Landing.

"We walk to White Bluffs," Aideen said.

"We walk."

The storm had torn itself into rags. Silvery puffs of clouds made a contrast to a soft green sky. The air smelled sweet and clean. Sunlight warmed them. In another time, it would have been a pleasant...late morning? Noon? Aideen tried not to sigh too loudly as they started the trek home.

I wonder," Ilsanja said, panting, "how they will address this in our stage play."

Aideen felt a spasm of irritation that combined with her

growling stomach, the steady throb in her temples, and her constant, hot-coals ache in her feet with each step. She put it aside. "They will use a rotating track," she said. "We will saunter along it, and it will loop under our feet, while behind the stage, helpers will roll the scenery past us. If that's not, in fact, what's really happening to us right now."

They had stopped once to empty their bladders, even though the sound had only reminded Aideen of how thirsty she was again. They had traveled for hours. She knew they were progressing, even if it did feel like they *were* on a wheeled track, moving endlessly with no forward motion.

Ilsanja didn't answer at first and Aideen thought she was catching her breath. "Truly?" Her voice sounded weak. "Have you seen that?"

"Once. When I went to a play in the capital, with Father."

"Was it..." A few seconds elapsed. "Was it good?"

Aideen turned. Ilsanja trudged, head down, and her shoulders were hunched. Aideen stopped. "Are you sick?"

"No." Her friend straightened up. "I'm fine. Keep going."

"You need to rest."

"I am *fine!*"

"You need a rest, and so do I."

"Don't condescend to me! I see how briskly you step out. I won't be the one to hold us back."

"Very well." Aideen crossed her ankles and dropped to the ground. "Go on ahead then. I need to rest."

Ilsanja put her hands on her hips. "Don't treat me like I'm sickly. I'm just as strong as you." Her voice broke, and she blinked rapidly.

Aideen drew a breath, ready to point out that they both needed rest and food. She didn't speak. Instead, she held up her hand. Ilsanja tilted her head, ignoring her, then reached out and grasped it, and dropped to her knees beside Aideen.

"I'm sorry," she said. She shielded her face, and Aideen knew she was weeping.

She put her free arm around her friend's shoulders and pulled her close. "You are a strong woman, a bold woman," she whispered. "I'm glad to have you at my side through this ordeal, every step of which is my fault."

Ilsanja choked through her tears. "I can find others to blame. Vallis Majeur, for one."

"Yes. I will share the blame with him."

"I'm sure we can find others. Those pink parasites, for instance."

Aideen kissed Ilsanja's cheek. "Yes. Let's blame them."

"For everything," Ilsanja said.

Aideen feared the walk through the passage that held the emberbed, but it was, in many ways, the easiest. It was level. She knew it was more than the ease of the trail, though. It was an issue of spirit. Beyond the passage was home.

She studied the rift that ran nearly the length of the passage. Ilsanja squeezed her hand. "Still making plans?"

"Yes, and wondering what that chasm was that we found."

Aideen found speech, even thought, trying. There was only so much energy her body could expend. The passage, the paintings, and that strange chasm were puzzles, though, like a ledger page that didn't balance, and her mind returned to it, worrying at it like a sheepdog harrying a stubborn ram.

"I wish to know what a beaver is," said Ilsanja. "When we get home, I will ask our padray. He knows much about the Ancient religions. But I think that place will always be a mystery."

"Prospectors have picked it nearly clean," Aideen said. Even as she spoke, she was speared with doubt. They had passed many passages that they hadn't explored. What more strange Ancient items might be found in that place? In her mind, she began to compose a letter to her brother, telling him of the wonders she had seen.

Aideen swore to herself that she would never, ever again in her life travel on foot. Caballo-back or sprite carts, or even boats, would convey her everywhere. She was done with walking.

She squared her shoulders. The Mother had dispensed them good fortune again; the closest house to the passage they had taken belonged to Mariah Pentos, who worked at the cages. Mariah would probably not be home but her children would. She tried not to even think of how mud-stained and bedraggled they both must appear as she forced her aching feet up the walkway and tapped four times on the door.

After a moment it opened. Rebecca, Mariah's oldest, stood there. Her mouth fell open. "Yorita...Langtree? And, Yorita Silvestro?" Worry sharpened her features. "Has there been an accident? Is Mother—"

"Rebecca, I think all is well, but we need your help, and quickly, please."

Rebecca stepped aside. "Come in. Shall I...draw you a bath?"

"No time. But—"

"Food," Ilsanja said. "Water and food if it is no inconvenience."

"Of course, of course." Rebecca herded them into the kitchen. She brought out a tub of cheese and a loaf of bread. Aideen's hands shook as she reached for it. The girl started a pot of water boiling and spooned dried sisuree berries into a pair of cups. "What has happened? We heard you were home with your father, yorita, but it looks like you fell into the canal."

"We traveled for the capital," Aideen said. She spread cheese across a slice of the loaf. Her stomach rumbled, and water flooded her mouth. She held it out to Ilsanja, who broke it in half and handed her back a piece. "We were set upon by mestengos along the way. Our escape meant a walk back through a flashflood. We bring urgent news for the sheriff. A criminal has defied exile." She took a bite of the bread, and then somehow jammed the rest of it into her mouth before she even realized it. She made herself chew.

Water spit from the edge of the pot as Rebecca poured some into cups, and the smell of sisuree filled the room. Aideen thought she might weep.

"Diego!" the girl shouted.

From deeper in the house, a boy yelled back, "What?"

"Kitchen, now!"

Rebecca set the cups down. The beverage was too hot to drink. Ilsanja cut another slice of bread, smoothed cheese across it, and said, "You have saved us. We nearly drowned in the flood, and we haven't eaten since midafternoon..." Her voice trailed off. "Yesterday?"

Aideen didn't answer. Her abbreviated version of their adventure had made it sound as if they had been abducted on the way to Duloc, not the way back. "Rebecca, does my father still live?"

"Last I heard, yorita. He lives, but there is no change."

A boy with dark curly hair lounged into the doorway. "What? Oh, your pardon. Yorita...Langtree?" His eyes grew wide, and he stared at his sister. "Yoritas?"

"Diegito, go fetch the sheriff, and run. Yorita Langtree and Silvestro were abducted by mestengos."

His eyes widened. "How did you escape?"

Aideen said, "Yorita Silvestro stole a caballo out from under their noses, in a rainstorm. Sadly, it drowned, and we walked from the hills above Merry Lake."

Rebecca gasped, "Dios! Diegito, go! Go! The yoritas need help!"

The boy whirled and ran out of the room. They heard a door slam.

Rebecca said, "Shall I send for a doctor?"

Ilsanja shook her head. Aideen said, "We are not injured, just exhausted, but we must speak to the sheriff and then the company partners, and I do not think I can walk another step."

"We have no caballos, but I'll ask the neighbors for one," the girl said. "And we have some cold lamb, if you—"

"Please," Ilsanja said before Aideen could speak. "Oh, please. Yes."

Rebecca sliced lamb and heated up potatoes. She put dried fruit on the table. Aideen forced herself to eat slowly. "This is the best meal I have ever had," she said.

The girl twisted her hands together. "Would you like mead? I should have offered first, I—"

"No." Aideen sipped from her cup of sisuree. "We need clear wits about us."

"I'll go to the neighbor," Rebecca said, when they heard hoofbeats on the path outside. Rebecca left the kitchen. Curiosity warred with exhaustion and won. Aideen stood up, wincing, and followed. Every step was like a knife blade thrust through the arch of her foot, but she went to the front, where four caballos stood.

"She was on her way!" Diego said, standing by the caballo of the sheriff.

Aideen stepped out onto the walkway. "Sheriff?"

"Yorita Langtree, are you well? Is Yorita Silvestro with you?"

Ilsanja spoke from behind her. "Here. Filthy, but well."

The sheriff closed her eyes for a moment. "Thank the Mother. We were on our way to search for you."

Ilsanja said, "But how could you know?"

Aideen had let her gaze drift over the posse riders and stopped at a stocky man with most of his face hidden by a reddish beard. Shadows circled his sharp blue eyes, but he smiled when he saw her. Aideen opened her mouth, then ran, pain be damned, toward the caballo. "Harald? Harald!"

19

Martes, 23 Uno, Year 331

///Exceeds tolerances this node is not this node is not///

Her organs were boiling. Erin bit her lower lip hard enough to draw blood, to keep from screaming and alerting the New Way that she was no longer under their influence. Who was she kidding? They already knew.

She grabbed the parasite, ripped it off her skin, and threw it against the wall as hard as she could. The pain dropped away as if she'd flicked a switch, but she was so weak that when she tried to stand her knees gave way.

The parasite protection charm *sucked*.

Woodsmoke. Something nearby was burning. The town's buildings were mostly wood.

She tried again to stand up and managed it this time. She heard no screams. That didn't surprise her. This whole town was part of the New Way whatever-it-was, collective, hive mind. No, not quite a hive mind, but close. Network. They were probably working like one entity to fight the flames.

Flames.

Erin surveyed the room. The woman who had brought in the parasite had come from behind her, and sure enough, there was a door. She knew what would be through there. There were some good things that came from being completely possessed by a collective consciousness. They'd gotten a lot of information from her, but information had gone two ways.

She picked up the bag and went to the door. It wasn't locked. Nothing in this town was locked unless a caravan was in town, because nobody needed to lock anything. There were two hundred seventeen people in this town, and one hundred seventy-eight of them were part of the New Way. The remaining were babies and young children.

She pushed open the door, fully aware of what she would find. She was afraid that the knowledge that had flowed into her would fade, but it hadn't so far. The room beyond was built like a greenhouse, the ceiling and top half crudely covered with panes of clouded plastic. It was lined with tables. The ones closest to the outer walls held real seedlings of various kinds, and through the clouded slats she saw neat furrows and bits of green where some had already been planted. Outside, a set of farm tools rested against the plastic windows. The room smelled like vinegar, and in the center, in neat boxes, lay dozens of the parasites, the nodes.

And this wasn't the only stockpile of them.

She closed her eyes and made herself relax, not seeking, but waiting for them to find her. It was difficult to relax when she had to plan for a group of crazed villagers storming the place. There—she felt the fire elementals.

Something had drawn them to her. The smell of smoke was stronger now. Suddenly Erin wasn't standing in a greenhouse on an alien world; she was running through the burned ruins of her own neighborhood. The people here were aiding and abetting an invasion, but they weren't in control.

The fire elementals were free and feeding, but these people were victims. They shouldn't lose everything.

No houses, she thought. She'd sworn she would never control them, but she was giving them orders.

Confusion.

Flames didn't understand "houses."

She decided to make it simpler. *Come to me.*

When she opened her eyes, they were there. She didn't have to point to the rows of parasite nodes. *Do these harm you?*

Neither flame responded with fear. Before she even began her next thought, one of the swirling funnels swooped down over the neat boxes. The heat, and the stench of vinegar, drove Erin back.

She reached for the knowledge that had flooded into her. That tavern, that prosperous tavern they'd ridden by, that was one. At the other end of town, closer to the Madlyn border, stood a guesthouse, and that was another. She pictured those two buildings in her mind, and the stock of parasites maintained in each one.

To the other fire elemental, she sent the images of the two buildings that hid caches of the nodes. *Will you burn these places?*

And now she heard shouting.

They would come to protect the nodes.

She ran outside and around the house, grabbing the closest farm tool. It was a rake. The plastic roof of the greenhouse fell inward and fire gouted up. She ran back. The villagers couldn't save the nodes, but she thought they'd probably kill themselves trying.

Sure enough, a crowd of people ran forward. Several held buckets. The woman who had carried out the parasite was in the lead. Her face was blank and her gaze fixed beyond Erin's shoulder.

"Stop!" Erin shouted, waving the rake.

The woman ignored her. Erin had trained on guns, archery, knife fighting, and hand to hand. Quarterstaffs weren't her thing, but she thought she could improvise. She held both ends of the handle, feinted, and hit the woman in the torso.

The woman gasped and fell backward, but two more people raced past. Heat radiated onto Erin's back. The whole building was on fire. She swung the rake again, yelling, "Stop! You're too late! They're gone!"

Two ran inside. The first woman got to her feet. She stared at Erin. "You set yourself against us!"

Erin backed away. "I don't want to hurt you."

The woman charged her.

Erin dropped the rake. The woman was too close. She crouched and used the woman's own momentum to throw her past, face down into the dirt. Before she could celebrate, weight bore her down. Two others held her. Their expressions mirrored the woman's. One pulled a knife.

The elementals were there, whirling among the people, and fabric ignited.

"Wait!" Erin shrieked. "Stop!"

Trevian prodded the book with his iron spar and got knocked back into the wall yet again. He wrapped the end of the spar with his spare trousers, to see if cloth would insulate against the charm. It didn't.

Holding the ward, he touched the book. At least that time the pressure that shoved him back didn't carry as much pain. He supposed that was progress.

Scuffing and rattling stones drifted in from outside, and he sensed copper. However many there were, they had climbed up the narrow pathway in silence. One was a copper-hunter. He felt a faint ache as they tested the wards.

"How have you denied us home, traveler?" The speaker was a woman. Her voice carried warmth and authority, as he would expect any good town alder or village headwoman to do. He didn't answer. He tried again to slip the edge of the spar between the pages of the book.

"Why do you approach with chaos and violence?"

Clearly, while she talked to him, others were testing the wards.

Too late, he remembered the hole in the ceiling that he hadn't warded. Well, there was nothing he could do now.

"We welcomed your companion. She has protected the community you hold from your chaos. You have no powers you can extend against us."

The community you hold? He almost asked her what she meant. And it wasn't completely true that he had no powers. The wards seemed to be holding.

He breathed deep, knelt down, and prodded the book again with the spar. The force pushed him back on his knees across the floor. The pain was manageable. He was not making any progress, but when everything else failed, Trevian could be stubborn, and he could see nothing else to do now.

Silence from outside.

The first concerted attack against the wards came, as at least four people rushed it. He was prepared. He'd felt worse when the fire elementals had attacked his camp.

The next blow jarred his teeth in his jaw. More than four. It hurt, but there was still no flicker in the warding.

"Even the strongest wards fail eventually," she said. "They will always fall before the might of the New Way."

"That sounds religious," he said before he realized he'd spoken out loud.

She paused. "We are not religious. We are."

He waited for her to explain that contradiction. They were not religious, or were they? And sure enough, they did call themselves the New Way.

"There is room on this continent for many sects of belief," he said. "Why do you impose yours?"

"We are not a sect of belief. We are."

We are. That was their belief. She was not contradicting herself. They were.

"So are we," he said.

They hit the wards again, and this was nearly as painful as the blows of the fire elementals. They hadn't breached the ward, not yet. But the longer he stayed here, with no food and no water, the more weakened he became, the weaker the ward would become. It would last longer than him, but not much longer.

A failure again.

She said, "Chaos is not the way."

He didn't care to debate. Anger kindled in him. He'd failed again. He'd failed his mother, somehow, so badly that she left him; he'd failed to please his father, even if that man could not be pleased; he'd failed to stop his uncle. He had kept silence with Erin instead of speaking to her from his heart, and he had lost her. And now, when the entire Crescent, maybe his entire world needed him, he failed to close the frontera.

He jabbed the spar at the book. The tip caught the edge of the pages. The book shifted.

Trevian nearly dropped the spar. Slowly, he extended the metal again, touching the book. No pain met him, no force. He knelt again and reached out with the back of his hand. His knuckles touched cool metal. He grabbed the book and tugged it toward him. It slid easily over the ground.

The charm, the charm...the pages clattered as he flipped them.

The woman was speaking, her voice stern now. He didn't pay attention to her words.

Another blow shook the ward, and then another. They were hitting it nearly constantly now.

How would he concentrate on the charm, with them hammering the ward, and with each blow, his own bones and muscles? Erin had said how hard it had been to sink into the state of reflection needed to activate the charm that had freed the flames. He flinched again.

Sink, he thought.

Instead of tensing against each anticipated blow, he let his muscles loosen. He moved off to one side, close to the passage with the hole. Even if he were successful, he doubted he would escape this place, but it was nice to pretend to an optimism. He could imagine, for a few moments, that he would see Erin again.

The blows against the wards stopped. That distracted him and worried him as well. He cleared his mind again, and thought, *I am a copper-hunter and a finder of frontera. I have the ability to charm metal and dance between the worlds. I will succeed at this.*

He turned his mind from his fear and turned the pages of the book, searching for the charm.

D on't burn them!" she shouted.

Hands grabbed her, dragged her away from the flaming greenhouse. The elementals danced among the people. They were confused. And Erin knew the controlled villagers who held her planned to kill her.

"You are chaotic," someone said behind her.

"You risk the community. You threaten."

She closed her eyes and imagined the parasites, and the front of a shirt. Blue and orange whirled around her. Hands twisted into her hair and pulled back her head. Heat bathed her face, and someone shrieked. The grip on her hair loosened. More screams. And...hoofbeats?

"Kneel at once!" someone shouted. Hoofbeats, closer. Erin wrapped her hands around her head and curled up into a ball. She forced herself to lay immobile as iron-shod hooves danced around her.

"Yorita Dosmanos! Yorita Dosmanos!" a distant male voice shouted.

"Here! Don't hurt them, they're being controlled!" She lifted her head. The riders around her wore red vests. They carried clubs, crossbows, and swords. Several villagers lay unconscious around her, and some had charred marks on their chests. Some fled, beating out flames.

The elementals had tried to follow her image and burn the nodes. But where had soldiers come from?

A horse skidded to a stop in front of her and the rider bounded down. "Yorita Dosmanos, are you injured? Come with me at once!" He was her age, maybe, but he exuded authority like a men's cologne.

She sat up cautiously, grabbed her messenger bag, and got to her feet.

"How did you get here?"

"Yor Genaro Sandoval stopped us on our way to Madlyn. What must we do? He says you would know."

"Don't hurt the villagers. It's not their fault. Get those things off their bodies—don't let them touch you! And burn them. The pink things. Burn *them*."

She saw that he wore long leather gloves. Plainly the soldiers had some vague idea of what to expect. A lot of the villagers had run, but many were lying on the ground, dazed, and some were curled up in balls sobbing. Some knelt, hands clasped behind their backs, while other people in red moved among them, gloved, wielding broad-bladed knives.

"They're getting away," she said. "They have other caches of those things. One's the tavern—"

"Burning when we got here," he said. He gripped her elbow and guided her through the chaos.

"And at the end of town, there's a guesthouse with another fifty of them in the basement."

"Your tethered elementals went that way after they left you."

"They're not tethered," she snapped. Black and red spots danced in front of her eyes and she stumbled.

"Are you well?"

"I think...so." The shouting, the screams, were dying, and the crackle of fire faded into the background. A half-dozen soldiers stood guard over a group of kneeling, sobbing villagers, while two others carried out a basket of whiterock from one of the standing houses. They piled the rock into a circle. One knelt and fired it, and as the chunks glowed, another pair of soldiers came over, carrying a length of cloth filled with parasites.

The man with Erin said, "Watch those people." His soldiers moved, angling so they stood between the flames and the people. Even so, five or six of them jumped to their feet, rushing toward the fire as the soldiers threw in the parasites. Erin gagged, her eyes stinging from the smell of vinegar. For a nanosecond, she felt what the villagers did, a ripping-open, a gaping wound of loss as the connection vanished forever. She retched, stumbled away from the officer, and retched again, but stopped short of vomiting.

The villagers collapsed, nearly all of them, into a faint as the nodes burned.

"Yorita Erin!" Across the town square, Genaro ran full tilt and threw his arms around her. "You live! And Yor Langtree?"

"With any luck, he's closing the frontera." She clung to the valet. A sense of normality, as normal as anything could be here, was returning to her. That reminded her of her cell phone. She pushed away gently and opened her bag. The phone had migrated to the very bottom as it always did, and the screen flared to life when she picked it up. It had skidded across the floor, but it wasn't broken. She remembered something else too, but it was gone in an instant. Dismay filled her as she noticed the charge had dropped to thirty percent. What had pulled on the battery? She'd known it would drop, but nothing like that.

Again, the memory teased her. Whatever it was, it had something to do with being under the control of the node. It fled again.

She carefully powered down the phone. "Tell your soldiers not to panic and not to attack the fire elementals," she said. "I'm going to call them back."

20

Martes, 23 Uno, Year 331

I t's a miracle that I still live." Harald stretched out his artificial leg and grimaced. "Or more than one miracle perhaps."

Aideen rolled up the sleeves of her borrowed blouse, which otherwise would have reached her fingertips. The sheriff had ordered pots of hot water and a bowl of soap and found clean underlinen and shirts for both Ilsanja and her. Their boots and trousers were stiff with mud, but she felt human, at least.

The sheriff had been setting out with a posse based on Harald's report to seek out the two of them. After Aideen had blurted out, "Vallis Majeur abducted us, he's violated his exile," she sent three deputies at once to Mark Majeur's house. Two others had dismounted to let Ilsanja and Aideen ride. Her joints ached, but it seemed that the worst of the ordeal was over.

Harald said, "The caballo spilled me onto the rocks and fell into the canyon. My leg was damaged in the fall, but I still had the crossbow and a pair of bolts left. Then it was a long game of cat-and-raton with the mestengo left behind." Harald rubbed his knee. "Finally, I seized the advantage of the pounding rain and came up

269

behind him." A look of grim satisfaction flitted over his features. "I planned to backtrack and find my way to you. I knew they would have caballos. I reckoned without the flashflood. The waters swept me off the rocks and carried me away."

Aideen nodded, remembering the tumbling, the rocks crashing into her, the water closing over her head. Ilsanja reached for her hand and squeezed it.

"When I came to, I was nearly in Merry Lake, and my leg was smashed to splinters. I dragged myself to shore, found some tree branches that would hold my weight. I left the leg behind but kept the charms. Your brother had spoken of copper-hunters in the ghost town, so I hobbled down there like the beggar-god in a fireside tale, and I found David and Miriam. When I began to tell them my story, they told *me* one. They were ones that Oshane Langtree has imprisoned."

Someone tapped on the door. "Sheriff? Mark Majeur is with us."

"And his house? The grounds?"

"We're still searching. He had a guest in his stable, he said, but hasn't seen him yet today."

"Let him wait and keep him guarded," the sheriff said.

Harald cocked his head. "Are you sure? I can finish this—"

"Let him wait and wonder what we know."

"Harald, how did you get here? And before us?" Ilsanja said.

"In addition to being a copper-hunter, Miriam is a fabricker. She fashioned me a leg and the charms helped. It's not a perfect fit, but it works well enough. They rowed me across the lake, and David accompanied me through the channel tunnel that feeds your waterfall, and down the Endless Steps that run alongside it. Which truly are endless, or so it seemed.

"My black and gold shone through the blood and filth, and when we reached the canal, we were escorted straight to the sheriff."

The sheriff said, "We spoke to your housekeeper, who told us you had left days before, so we set out, planning to take the shorter way to save a few hours."

Harald grinned. "I should have known you two would free yourselves." He was full of vitality, but two pink spots showed on his cheeks above the beard, and his eyes were shiny. The leg was giving him pain.

"It was Aideen," Ilsanja said. "I simply followed where she directed."

The sheriff stood and tugged down her black vest. "A violation of exile is no small thing. Nor is abduction, or trying to kill a justice arm. If Mark Majeur had any hand in his son's crimes, he may be joining him in exile."

Ilsanja said, "Vallis got messages from someone."

The sheriff nodded. "Yoritas, please come with me. I want to watch his face when he sees you." She led the way to the outer room, where Yor Majeur sat, flanked by deputies. Strands of coarse gray showed in his golden hair, and the skin under his chin was loose. His suit was made of good fabric, but even Aideen could tell that it was of an old style. He glared at the sheriff as if he were still a jefe, though. "Why do you keep me waiting?" he said. "I assume you have news of my son, and I assume it's bad." His gaze slipped over Ilsanja and Aideen. He looked confused, and then, as he considered the condition of their clothes, contemptuous. "Why are they here?"

"Are you surprised to see them?"

"They have no business here, unless you've come to tell me that my son is dead and this one—" he pointed at Ilsanja "—is here to gloat."

"As of a day ago he was alive and sprightly," the sheriff said, "when he tried to murder a justice arm of the Crescent Council and abducted these two yoritas. All within the Crescent, despite his sentence of exile."

Majeur shrugged. He gave them a sideways look, filled with triumph. "That's no doing of mine."

The sheriff put a hand on her hip. "Isn't it? You've sought clemency for him, and he seemed confident he'd get it. Surely you knew where he was."

"Last I heard he was in the Desolation."

"Tell us about your guest."

"Guest? Oshane Langtree stayed in my stables. He'd come to help, he said, with Oswald dying."

"Why would you wish to help the Langtrees? It was Oswald's son who brought Vallis to justice."

Majeur's face flushed, but he shrugged again. "Oshane made a good argument about the wealth the company brings into White Bluffs. It was persuasive."

The sheriff nodded. "Oh, for the good of the town, then."

Standing behind her, Aideen couldn't see her face. At that moment, she really wished she could.

"Where is Oshane Langtree now?" the sheriff said.

"I don't know. I haven't seen him since yesterday."

"What was he doing when you saw him then?"

"Coming back from a meeting with that Copper Coalition man, the one who seems to make his home here."

"I see. Yor Majeur, make a list of items from home that you will need. One of my people will collect them. You will stay here while we continue the search for Vallis Majeur and Oshane Langtree."

Majeur stood up, and both deputies dropped their hands to their clubs.

"How dare you hold me? On what grounds?"

"Your son has tried to kill a justice arm, abducted two women, and violated exile. Oshane Langtree is wanted for abduction, imprisonment, and an attempt to kill. The link between both those men is you."

"You have no proof of your accusations against my son!"

"The statements of Justice Arm Stuart, who he tried to murder, and the two women he abducted," the sheriff said. She didn't raise her voice.

"He's been unjustly treated from the start! He was just a youth, forced into a desperate act by debt, debt to a villainous man who loaned him money at usurious rates!"

"That argument was already made and considered, Yor Majeur. These are new charges." The sheriff gestured to the deputies. "Take Yor Majeur to the cells."

"You cannot hold me! I'm not some half-turvy, lickerish prospector running out on a bill!"

The deputies drew him away. They were respectful, but they did not slacken their grip on his arms.

Harald limped into the doorway. "He *may* not know about his son," he said, "but I'm not convinced of his ignorance of the whereabouts of Langtree."

"If Oshane met with Yor Oakley, then I think he will go to the Company next," Aideen said. For all she knew, Oshane had already swayed the partners and wrested the company away from her.

Harold frowned. "He disappeared conveniently, as if he knew trouble were coming."

"Yes. And Vallis knew we carried important papers. Which are now burned," Aideen said. "I thought Dolores had betrayed us, but she wouldn't have known about the marriage documents."

"I wonder who did know about those," Ilsanja said, keeping a level gaze on Harald.

The justice arm looked thoughtful. "Both Katurah and Genaro were aware, and Genaro was the other witness. I do not see how they could have become infected. Did anyone else know of the plan?"

Aideen said, "Elmaestro Tregannon. We went to the Copper Coalition first. I told him my plan; it was the reason we'd come, after all."

"If they've infected the elmaestro, the country is in graver danger than I knew," Harald said. "It seems like he would have made greater efforts to take the book from Erin, though." He stared into the distance. "Was there anyone with him when you spoke to him? A profesor or...?"

"No," Ilsanja said.

"Yes. There was a young man in a yellow vest who came in and out. He brought us sisuree."

"Oh, yes, the apprentice," Ilsanja said.

"Was Profesor Stillwater present?"

Aideen shook her head.

Harald straightened up from where he leaned against the door jamb. "Then I will send her a message. She is the one I trust." He limped past them. "Let me stop on the way to the Company, and I'll have David join us. I think we *will* find Langtree there."

Her appearance, with Ilsanja, and the condition of their clothing, stirred consternation at the Company offices. She ignored them as best she could as they went up the stairs to the partners' room. David LaFish, the slender young copper-hunter, stayed by Harald's side. He wore rough prospector clothing, but his black hair fell in a neat braid and his hands were clean. Copper-hunters were no unusual sight here. Two bedraggled jefe daughters were.

Ilsanja murmured, "The springs of gossip begin to bubble and flow."

Edmund stared, his mouth open, then hurried to the door and tapped on it.

"Is he here, finally?" Jefe Silvestro shouted.

"No, jefe, but..." Edmund cast a glance at them and pushed open the door.

"Well, what then?" Silvestro stared at them. He didn't rise from behind the table. Montez sat in his usual seat, and Yor Oakley leaned against the wall in the corner.

"What is this? You two look like half-turvy prospectors coming out of the mountains. Ilsanja never had more sense than a yearling when it comes to wandering off, but you, Aideen! You wanted us to believe you would be responsible, but you jaunt off to the capital and back with a word to no one, with your father on his sickbed."

Aideen flushed. She opened her mouth, ready to defend herself, but Ilsanja pressed an open hand against her arm, stopping her. "Father, what makes you think Aideen went to the capital?"

"Yor Oakley told me. You're a tavern-tale for the whole town right now, I suppose."

Aideen stepped farther into the room to give Harald and David space to enter. "Yor Oakley, what makes *you* think I went to the capital?"

Oakley smiled. His eyes gleamed like polished glass. "Well, didn't you?"

Harald spoke up before she could respond. "Answer the yorita's question."

"Who are you?" Silvestro said, as if he couldn't see the black and gold vest.

"Justice Arm Harald Stuart, here to enforce a warrant for the arrest and trial of Oshane Langtree for abduction and imprisonment."

"Well, as you can see, he's not here. He was supposed to be." Silvestro transferred his glare back to Aideen. "We have a company to run and decisions to make."

"Yor Oakley, answer the question, please," Harald said.

"I don't know where Yor Langtree is," Oakley said, spreading his hands.

"Not that question. Who told you that Yorita Langtree had gone to the capital?"

Oakley gave a shrug. "I don't remember. I speak to many people here in White Bluffs. It could have been anyone."

"Not anyone," Aideen said.

Oakley smiled at her. "Oh, yes, it was meant to be a secret, wasn't it?"

Silvestro interrupted. "Langtree isn't here. Without him, there's no need to meet."

"I think we—"

Aideen sucked in a breath, ready to interrupt, but Harald spoke first. "There is information you need to have, and some that I need from you. This young man is David LaFish. He and his wife live in Merrylake Landing. He is one of the people Langtree imprisoned. We believe Langtree is allied with a group from across a frontera, who plan to invade the Crescent."

"What is this? What has this to do with running the company!" Silvestro slammed his palm down on the table.

"Much," Harald said. He drew David forward. The young man told a tale that made Aideen shiver. She had heard about the parasites from Erin and Trevian, but David's description, bound and helpless in a charm woven by Oshane, then forced into a waking dream where his energy was stolen to feed Oshane's other charms...and the seductive languor imposed by the creatures, chilled her blood.

Montez sat up straight, his face solemn, and Silvestro shook his head, as if overwhelmed by noise.

"Surely these leeches were part of the charm, not an invasion force," he said finally, when David had finished.

"I have seen one," Harald said. "They are like nothing I've *ever* seen here."

David spoke softly, but confidently. "At times, we caught glimpses of Langtree's thoughts and desires when we were in that state. Control of this company was always part of it, and for his own gain, not the good of the Crescent."

Oakley straightened up. "Young man, I don't doubt that you and your wife had some bad experience at the wrong end of a charm, but this tale, surely you can see that it lacks all logic. Pink leeches that control behavior and share thoughts? No doubt that was part of the charm Langtree laid on you, powered by the lantern, which is a strong and dangerous artifact."

David reached up to unbutton his shirt. "I can show you the mark where it clung to me," he said.

Harald said, "Yor Oakley, what did you say?"

"What?" Oakley looked around. "I said this vision was probably part of the charm—"

"Before that. 'Pink leeches that control behavior and share thoughts.' What makes you think they share thoughts?"

"I—you said that," Oakley said.

Montez shook his head. "No. Yor LaFish spoke of sensing Langtree's thoughts, and those may have come through the lantern."

"Well, I spoke wrong then—"

"How did you know that Aideen Langtree went to the capital and *back*?" Harald said.

"I told you, many—"

"No one outside the house knew until this morning."

"Well, the posse—"

Aideen said, "Was on its way to find us. No one spoke of whether we were on our way there or back. You told Jefe Silvestro we'd *been* to the capital."

"Don't try to speak for me, yorita!" Oakley edged away from the wall. Silvestro frowned.

Harald's hand dropped to the short club at his side. "Open your shirt, Yor Oakley."

Oakley sighed and shook his head, as if confronting a fractious child. Then he lunged across the space at Harald, drawing his knife as he came.

2 1

Martes, 23 Uno, Year 331

Trevian found the page Erin had shown him. A blue puerta stone glimmered in the lower right corner. Below the words, lines were cut into the metal, not stamped, but scratched deeply, as if they'd been added later. Five parallel lines ran the width of the page, and five dots were scattered along its length.

Before his mother had left, she had helped him place his fingers on the strings of her guitarra and shown him the marks on paper that depicted notes. Unbidden, he was back in the sala at Midwinter, a cup of spiced cider in his hand. Aideen assembled blocks on the rug before the hearth, and close by, his mother played the guitarra while Oshane Langtree stood behind her and accompanied her on the flautine. Across the room, his father glared at them.

He looked down at the lines and dots. He'd assumed that the words stamped above it were meant to be repeated, that they were the charm.

Shift the current of the passage,
To a different key,

Redirect the energy,
Shape the eddy, close the passage.

His ears popped suddenly, and the puerta stone flickered.

In the center of the domed cavern rolled a ripple of violet light.

His hands clenched on the book. The frontera was preparing to open.

He edged back toward the side passage and cleared his throat. He had never been a strong singer, and his father had forbidden music after Serafina left. Still, it was what the charm required.

His voice cracking on the low and high notes, like a green boy's, he sang the scale. The violet light rippled again like a curtain caught by a breeze. He sang it again. The blue stone flickered but nothing else changed.

To a different key.

He shifted a tone higher and sang the scale again, and again. The puerta stone settled into a regular blinking.

He took the chant back up, five notes up, starting on a different note each time.

The frontera flared.

A man appeared in the cavern, a strange white wand in his hand. Two more people appeared in the space behind him, materializing in front of a sheet of purple-white light. One held a crossbow.

The man in the lead faced him, raising the wand. Clutching the book to his chest, Trevian dived, rolling. A line of white light lanced over his head, sizzling, and a black scar appeared on the rock wall.

Trevian wiggled backward, singing the scale as best he could. Why had the frontera opened at this exact moment? He could not fight off three and continue the charm.

He would fail. He'd always known he would fail.

Scrambling to his feet, he sang the notes desperately. The frontera flashed a blinding white, and suddenly the air felt right again. He finished the scale and began again. All three attackers stopped, doubling over. He backed toward the mound of rubble, knowing, deep inside, that the frontera was closed.

The three newcomers straightened up and turned toward him as one.

The soldiers stepped back as both fire elementals appeared. Erin held up her hands. "It's all right," she shouted. The flame on the left winked out and reappeared over the second pile of pink nodes, which hissed and browned as they burned.

Find Trevian, help him, please, Erin thought. She searched for Genaro, found him at the edge of the crowd. "How many villagers got away?"

He came to her side. "A dozen? Two? We don't know yet."

Erin shut her eyes, drawing on what she had shared when linked to the New Way. "Six of them rode up to the frontera. It's to the south, up in the mountains." She could picture the narrow ledge, the tight passageway, and it frustrated her to be unable to describe it. "I can take us there. Trevian's there. Genaro, these people are innocent. They'll need help."

The officer spoke up. "We'll leave some behind to help, but we must ride on to bring the word to Madlyn. Will those villagers who are still in league—"

"They're not in league. They're infected."

"Infected, then, will they attack us?"

"Their original plan was to run and seek out other groups like them. I don't know what they'll do now."

He nodded, wheeled, and strode back to his caballo, shouting orders.

Several villagers had risen to their knees, but one or two were standing, looking around, stepping back from the others as if waking from a bad dream. As Erin watched, the officer sent three soldiers over to pick out those villagers and take them aside. They seemed to be talking. Maybe the people here would be all right.

"We have to find Trevian," she said.

"Come." Genaro guided her through the chaos of the soldiers until he found two mounts. Erin's head ached and her vision blurred unless she concentrated hard on it. She'd left Trevian alone and at risk. It should have been her. But if it had been her, he would have been taken over like one of the villagers. She didn't know yet if her choices had been good or bad.

With Genaro at her side, she set off to find Trevian.

T revian backed up against the pile of rubble. His feet slipped, and rocks bounced down. The newcomer in the lead still held that fearsome light weapon. With one arm pinning the book to his chest, he scrambled up the mound. Light surrounded him, and pain seared through his chest. When he could see again, he was lying on the ground, and the three newcomers stood over him. One reached down and seized the corners of the book.

Trevian held on with all his fading strength. If he released the book, would Erin's ward activate? He didn't dare risk that it might not, that they would make off with it, after everything.

The man with the wand raised it again. Trevian clenched his teeth and tightened his grip. The pain in his ribs radiated through his body, but he didn't relinquish his hold. He would at least make it as hard for them as he—

Heat washed over him again. The book thumped into his chest, and the three stepped back, shielding their faces. Trevian squinted, his face as hot as if he stood in front of a working forge. A spiral of flame undulated between him and the others—one of Erin's elementals.

He sat up, groaning before he could stop himself. "Thank you," he croaked—what foolishness, who believed flames understood human speech?—and crawled as fast as he could up the rubble mound. Black spots danced in front of his eyes, and air rushed in his ears. He pushed the book into the front of his shirt. Every upward reach of his arm sent pain stabbing into his side, and it got worse, so bad he nearly swooned, when he had to reach up, grip the edges of the hole, and climb into the narrow gap. Panting, he lay face down on the tunnel floor, wishing he could rest, but he didn't dare risk it. What other fearsome weapons did the newcomers from beyond the frontera carry? He drew a breath and tried to shout, "Go be safe!" to the flame. His voice came out reedy and ragged. He pulled himself toward the daylight.

When he reached the hole and peered out, despair sucked away his breath. The only way out was a straight fall onto a tiny ledge that seemed very far away. He imagined how much it would hurt. And once there, he wasn't sure there was a way down. Maybe he would just lie here and rest. Maybe the flame would keep the out-of-worlders from him. Maybe Erin had prevailed in the village...

He shut his eyes. No. He would not fail her. Cursing the sheets of pain that billowed through him, he shifted slightly, gritting his teeth, and made sure the book was secure. Then he twisted himself around until his feet pointed out the hole and pushed himself through.

Caballos overtook them as four soldiers joined them. Erin didn't stop to question why. Her brain was swirling. Worry for Trevian and the book filled her thoughts but nudging and crowding for attention were all the things she understood about the New Way—and what they knew from her.

She still didn't know whether Trevian had succeeded. He'd warded the opening to the frontera so that the villagers hadn't been able to enter. She had experienced that with the New Way. Collision Outpost had been blocked, somehow, from reaching back to Home. Then the protection charm had kicked in, and she had no idea what happened after that.

The New Way had shown her why Oshane Langtree, who they called the unreliable source, didn't have a node.

The Copper Coalition needed all this information, and Tregannon needed to know that his apprentice, Zachary, was infected.

Before all of that, she needed to find Trevian and the book.

Genaro reached out, touching her reins, and she slowed her

mount. "There," Genaro said. The soldiers cantered past, slowed, and circled back. Genaro pointed up the mountainside. "Is that your flame?"

A wisp of blue and orange danced on the cliffside.

"Is there a trail? Anything?"

One of the soldiers rode over and peered up. "It can be climbed, but it looks like hard going." She lifted her crossbow. "And harder going armed."

Genaro said, "Cover us." He dismounted, and Erin did too. They climbed.

It *was* hard going. Genaro set a pace that Erin thought was slow. After a few minutes, she was panting, and she realized that his methodical approach was practical. One soldier climbed with them. Soon the climb shifted into an incline, a little bit like a trail. From this angle, she lost sight of the fire elemental.

Genaro held out his hand again. "Down," he said, quietly. Erin flattened herself against the rocks.

"There's someone up here."

Stones shifted and rattled. Erin heard panting, or maybe soft sobbing. She pulled out her belt knife. Legs came into view, then the body of a man, stumbling. He skidded and nearly fell at their feet. His face was swollen and marked with dusty tracks, and he stared. "I'm alone," he said. "I don't know where I am."

Genaro stood up. "Where's the frontera?"

"Gone. It was..." The man flapped a hand behind him.

"There was a man," Erin said. "What happened to him?"

"He went inside. I was alone. Six came up the trail, but they didn't even look at me. I knew them and they didn't even look at me! And then three more ran out of the cavern. They broke the wards, but the conduit is gone. And they left me."

The conduit...the frontera. "He closed it," she said, slumping with relief.

"Where did they go, the others?" Genaro said.

"Into the mountains. I don't know where. I don't know anything now."

Erin straightened up. "Where did the man go?"

He shook his head.

"Wait here. We'll come back for you." She nodded to the soldier who came up alongside Genaro.

They made their way up onto a narrow ledge, empty of people. Erin went inside. Acrid smoke scraped her throat and she coughed. The cavern was empty. Had they taken Trevian? She stepped back out onto the ledge, cupped her hands around her mouth, and yelled his name. She turned ninety degrees and yelled again, turned, and yelled again.

"There," Genaro said.

A faint sound bounced off the mountains.

Erin yelled.

"Here."

She ran to the end of the ledge and peered down. Trevian sat on a narrow stretch of rock, his head tilted back, his arms crossed over his chest.

She threw herself flat on the ground. "Are you all right?"

"Every muscle in my body hurts," he said. He tapped his chest. "But I have your book. And the frontera is closed."

"We're coming to get you," she said.

It wasn't that easy, but finally, they found a way up from the bottom. Trevian stood up as she clambered up onto the ridge. "I hate your book," he said by way of greeting. "It made me sing."

"And that's a bad thing?" He was pale and favoring his right side where his clothes were scorched. "Did the flame do that?"

"No. Your flame saved me. People crossed the frontera before I could close it, and one wielded a weapon that shot light."

"Oh, shit." She touched his arm. "I thought they couldn't communicate with the other side, but they got a message through. Are you all right?"

"I can walk."

Before she thought about it, she put both hands on his cheeks. "Trevian, I screwed up. I made a mistake, I'm so sorry. You could have died."

He slid his finger into her hair. "I closed the frontera. I think I am a hero."

"I thought I understood how things worked, but I didn't and—"

"Shhh." He leaned down. Now was the moment to pull away, she thought, before things got complicated. Keep it professional. Stay on-mission. Eyes on the prize.

She leaned in toward him.

His lips tasted of salt, and they were soft. His fingers stroked her hair. Something with sharp edges pushed against her chest: the book. He had the book under his shirt. They broke apart, and then laughed.

"Let's get you down to the road," she said.

"You compelled the flames to find me and help me?" he said. He moved slowly, gasping now and then, but they made progress.

"I asked them," she said. "There's a difference."

22

Martes, 23 Uno, Year 331

Harald stepped back. Oakley held his knife underhand, point jabbing up toward the justice arm. David LaFish crouched and threw himself forward, tackling Oakley around the knees. The two men fell to the floor. Oakley's knife jarred loose from his hold. Aideen snatched it up. She grabbed Ilsanja's arm and pulled them both back toward the window, holding the knife just as Oakley had.

Two men rolled. Harald stepped around them, his club drawn. When Oakley pushed David over and rolled on top of him, Harald swung his club, a short, firm strike. Oakley grunted and fell sideways. David squirmed out from under him.

"What is this? You're breaking our peace!" Jefe Silvestro shouted.

David rolled Oakley onto his stomach and drew his arms behind him. Ilsanja pulled off her belt and handed it to the copper-hunter, who lashed Oakley's wrists together.

Oakley moaned. "Copper...Coalition will..." His words were barely intelligible.

Harald leaned over him. "Oh, they *will* hear of this. David, turn him over."

They rolled the Copper Coalition man onto his back. Harald traded his club for his belt knife and cut away the buttons on Oakley's shirt.

Silvestro came around the table. "What are you doing now? Stop this."

Harald bent down and pulled open Oakley's shirt. Against his pale chest, just below his collarbone, a leathery sac swelled and collapsed.

Aideen swallowed bile. Seeing one of those things on human skin made her dizzy, her skin suddenly clammy.

Silvestro froze, only for a moment. "Ilsanja," he said. He took two quick steps and pushed her away from the copper-hunter. "Stay away from that thing!"

"I'm fine, Father."

"Have a care what you say," Harald said. "Assume it sees and hears everything and sends that knowledge somewhere."

"You're speaking as if it's part of the charms of the Ancients," Silvestro said.

David squatted down, pulling his knife. "Erin Dosmanos used the flat of a blade to remove them," he said.

Silvestro swallowed. His tan skin looked yellowish. "And did you destroy them?"

"They burn."

He made a wide detour around the prone Copper Coalition man and opened the door. "Edmund!" He lowered his voice. "Get the sheriff and send a message to Yor Olafson that he has a patient. And speak no word to anyone about why."

Harald got to his feet, rubbing his knee above the artificial leg.

Two deputies came in. They stopped in the doorway, staring at the parasite.

"You must not let it touch you," Harald said.

They both nodded.

"Before you remove him," Harald said, "open your shirts and raise your arms, please."

287

Neither deputy argued. Neither was infected. They pulled Oakley to his feet and marched him out of the room, the doctor following.

Silvestro stood in the center of the room. "Was everything he said a lie, then? The Crescent Council recognizing our achievements, the Coalition supporting White Bluffs, and our expansion?"

"Yes, assume everything was a lie," Harald said.

"Well." Silvestro raised his hands and dropped them. "Well, no need to meet, I guess—"

"Father," Ilsanja said. "We went to the capital for a specific purpose."

He frowned. "There's a posse searching for Majeur and he will be brought to justice. You will be safe—"

"No, that's not it." Ilsanja cleared her throat. "Um, the justice arm here was a witness—"

"We all were, Ilsanja."

"Not to—" Ilsanja shut her eyes.

Aideen stepped in. "We found my brother in the capital and explained my father's condition."

"Not the proxy letter again, Aideen."

"Not the proxy letter," she said.

Ilsanja said, "I married Trevian at the capital."

"You. What. What?"

"I married Trevian Langtree. Two days ago. Vallis burned the marriage document, but Justice Arm Stuart was a witness."

Harald said, "We can send for a copy."

David said, "All this is about a *wedding*?"

Silvestro stared at Ilsanja, and then Aideen. At the table, Montez studied both of them too. Aideen thought he hid a smile.

"Is Trevian returning?" Silvestro said.

Aideen hoped her voice was as steady as Ilsanja's had been. "He will not return. He has no interest in the Company. But he is my father's heir, and Ilsanja is his wife."

"I plan to represent the Langtree partnership."

"Represent?" Expressions rolled across Silvestro's face, like the designs in the tube of glass Aideen had played with as a child, the kaleidoscope. "Well. Married? Of course. No one would question that."

Suddenly he looked at Montez.

Now Yor Montez smiled. "*I* see no objection. I hope you will be guided by Yorita Aideen, Jefa Langtree. She's very knowledgeable."

Silvestro coughed. "Yes. She's helpful with the ledgers." He went to the door again. "Edmund! Come in here. We need to do paperwork."

<hr />

I'm glad I can help you with the ledgers," Aideen said, the doorknob solid and reassuring in her hand.

Ilsanja snorted. "He had to save face."

Aideen smiled. A soft hooting sounded nearby. "Do you hear that?"

"I hear nothing."

It was gone. Aideen pushed open the door.

Dolores hurried into the foyer. "Yorita! You're well! You're back." She reached forward, then stopped, hands outstretched.

Aideen gripped the housekeeper's hands in her. "Dolores. I feared I would never see you again. Yorita Silvestro is now Jefa Langtree, and she will be staying with us for a while. This is Justice Arm Stuart."

Dolores gave a short bow. "Welcome, Justice Arm."

"Is Father—?"

"Sleeping. Dimitri is with him."

"Please prepare a bath for Yori—Jefa Ilsanja, and have food and sisuree brought to the sala for us," Aideen said.

Dolores nodded, but her eyes narrowed. "I will bring you singeweed tea, Justice Arm. You've got an inflamed wound."

Aideen froze. Ilsanja stepped away from Harald, and her hand dropped to Oakley's knife, now riding in the waistband of her trousers.

"Why do you need singeweed, Harald?" Aideen said, forcing herself to speak calmly.

"It's nothing serious," he said.

"Take off your shirt, please, and raise your arms."

Dolores gasped. "Why would you make the justice arm take off his shirt? It's his leg that's inflamed."

"What?"

Dolores shook her head. "My abuelo lost his leg below the knee to an earth elemental. He got around quite well but the place where flesh met the artificial leg was prone to infection. I know the signs."

Harald nodded. "You are right, Jefa. And, Aideen, you are right too. Your pardon, Jefa…" He set down the crossbow, unbuttoned his shirt, and removed it. He held his arms out to his sides and rotated to show his bare chest and back.

"I'm sorry, Harald."

"Do not be sorry for being wise. Until we know how far this infestation has spread, it is good to be cautious."

"Are you well?" she asked.

He smiled. She had noted the flush in his cheeks before, and his fatigue was more pronounced. "Singeweed tea and some salve will both help," he said. "The new leg rubs in a different way, and I walked long on it."

"Perhaps this Miriam is not a good fabricker," Ilsanja said.

"Do not blame Miriam. She was working with the material she had. Normally, a leg takes several sennights to craft. And I think the infection set in when I was swept downstream in the flood."

"Let's settle in the sala." Aideen nodded to Dolores, who hurried away.

They left the entryway and moved into the hall. Aideen looked longingly toward the room where her father slept, but she wanted to get her guests settled first. And suddenly, with a little drop in the pit of her stomach, she thought Ilsanja was no longer a guest in *her* house, that it was the reverse.

Above them, muffled, came the sound of breaking glass.

"What?" Ilsanja froze. Harald slipped a bolt into the crossbow.

"Dolores," Aideen said, stopping just short of yelling.

A windstorm yowled through the hallway, driving them back, snatching the breath from their mouths. The tapestries ripped off the walls and flapped across the floor. Aideen blinked, nearly blinded.

Calm descended. A man stood on the staircase above them, smiling. He'd taken off the bandages, and his burns were healing.

"What are you doing here?" Aideen said. She stepped forward. "Get out."

The flautine in its case rested on his hip. Clearly, he had the elemental with him, even though she could see only the detritus from the wind.

"Is that your welcome, Niece?"

"You *aren't* welcome," Aideen said.

Behind her, Harald said, "Is this Oshane Langtree?"

"Yes."

"Oshane Langtree, on behalf of the Crescent Council, I impose the following warrant and—"

The air turned blue. Wind slapped her, and a high-pitched whine sang in Aideen's head. She gasped for breath and found none. Vision faded, and when it returned, she was lying on the floor. Harald was pressed up against the wall and Ilsanja lay beyond him, unmoving.

A boot appeared in the edge of her vision. She tried to raise her head.

"Everything you have—everything *he* has is because of me," Oshane said. "I raised him, not our turvy fool of a father. I brought him everything, and when once, *once*, I asked him for help, he dismissed me, telling me to leave his house because he didn't like the way I eyed his wife. He owes me his life, and I'm going to claim it."

"Stop," she croaked.

He stepped over her. She grabbed his ankle. He dragged her along the floor for two strides. When he stared down at her, his face was transformed by rage. He raised his foot and drove it into her ribs. She clung to his leg and reached up with the other hand.

"Let go!" His voice was a snarl.

Beads, gray and metallic, glinted in a bracelet on his wrist. She grabbed at it. Stones slid cool and slick under her fingers.

He roared. He kicked her again, and everything shivered around her. She slid across the floor into the wall. Gray beads bounced on either side of her, ringing.

"Curse you! You're as bad as he is."

Her vision went blurry.

Dimitri came out of Father's room, a short club in his hand. Oshane said, did, something, and the hall again filled with blue light and screaming wind. It picked up Dimitri and tossed him backward. He struggled to his knees and the wind caught him again, hurling him up against the ceiling, twice. He fell and lay still.

Aideen pushed herself up on her hands. He was going to kill Father. The world swayed and rolled around her, but she got to her knees, and then her feet. She staggered down the hall.

Oshane had reached her father's room. He stood at the window, taking down the plata-and-moonstone charm. Aideen fell against the door jamb. She must have made some sound because he turned. The rage was gone; the charming smile was back in place. She thought it was the most terrible thing she'd ever seen.

"So this is why we had to come in from the second floor. If Oswald had invested in these charms sooner..." He let it fall.

She could barely speak. "Stop this and go. You can escape."

He shook his head. "Debts must be paid. And tell your brother he fights for the wrong side."

Father's eyes were open, white showing all the way around.

She took one step into the room. "You're controlled by a parasite."

Oshane's smile deepened. "No. I am too strong-willed for them, but I can guide them. I will guide the joined elemental worlds."

"Leave Father alone," she said.

The smile faded, and he looked serious for a moment as he drew his knife. "I won't," he said.

She lunged for him.

He called the elemental again, and wind spun around the room. The mattress on Father's bed rose and sailed off the bedframe, dropping him onto the floor. She grabbed for the knife. Blue light pulsed in her vision. Oshane's other hand closed around her neck, squeezing.

She couldn't draw a breath. Her numb fingers, wrapped around Oshane's wrist, weakened. Gold flared around her, light striking the broach he wore, Cheviot the Ram. The golden broach. She let go of his wrist, reaching instead for the broach, but suddenly he thrust her away. She hung in a shrieking cylinder of blue light, suffocating. His knife in hand, he stepped toward the mattress on the floor.

Her heart stuttered. The room faded into gray.

Ilsanja stood before her.

Oshane grunted and staggered. A length of metal stuck out of his shoulder.

Ilsanja reached up, wrapping her in something that shimmered and flashed.

She fell onto the floor with a thump and sucked in as much air as she could hold, and again, and again. The plata chain rattled with each exhalation.

Harald propped himself against the door and loaded a second crossbow quarrel.

Oshane floundered back toward the window. He shouted—said—something, a word or a sound that knifed through Aideen's head, although she couldn't hear it. Harald braced himself against buffeting winds and lifted the bow. The window glass blew outward. Blue light swirled around Oshane and he was gone. Harald started forward, stumbled, and went to one knee, head bowed in pain.

Beyond the window, the figure of a man wreathed in blue shrank until he vanished.

Aideen sobbed for breath. She crawled to where Father lay.

"Oh," Father said on an outbreath. "Oh. Oh. Oh."

Aideen wept and not for air now. "I know, Father. He's gone now. He's gone."

"Yorita!" Dolores called from the front of the house. Suddenly a swarm of people appeared in the doorway, armed with clubs and bows. Yor Olafson pushed his way through.

"Who's hurt in here?" he said.

"Harald is injured and Father." She reached for Ilsanja's hand. "Ilsanja?"

"Shaken, nothing more."

Harald held up a hand. "I'm not injured, just winded. Aideen, will you help me up?"

Olafson knelt at Father's side. Aideen wiped the tears off her face and stood up. She helped Harald to his feet. "Dolores? You have singeweed tea?"

Dolores reached out a hand. "Are you well? And the Jefe?"

"He still lives."

"Damn it. Langtree escaped," Harald grumbled.

"You and Ilsanja saved my life," Aideen said. "Dolores, can you...?"

"This way, Justice Arm. The kitchen for you. It's closer."

Aideen leaned against the wall and closed her eyes. "Dimitri," she called out suddenly. "Yor Olafson, Dimitri is hurt. He's in the hallway."

"I'm on my way."

Ilsanja took her hand. "He came here to kill your father when he could have fled uninjured."

"He is a madman."

Dizziness spun her, and her knees gave way. She slid down the wall. Ilsanja knelt at her side. "Aideen!"

"Fine... Just..." There was so much to do. "We must notify the sheriff. And...board up that window. Get more of those plata chains..." She remembered the gray stone beads bouncing on the hall floor. "Those beads. They were important. We..."

"Hush." Ilsanja stroked her hair. "You have the world's most efficient housekeeper, and I'll help. Right now you need to rest."

She caught hold of Ilsanja's hand. "You'll stay?" It was a foolish question. Ilsanja had as much right to be in the house as she did now. That wasn't what she meant, though.

Ilsanja leaned toward her. Her warm lips pressed against Aideen's forehead. "You can't get rid of me that easily."

23

Mircoles, 24 Uno, Year 331

W*e have three bars.*
Why were those words in her head? Erin tried to concentrate on moving the pencil over the paper to shape legible letters, while her caballo trotted down the road in the dark. It was close to impossible, but the names, the names she'd known when she was joined to the New Way, of the people compelled by the nodes, might start to fade. She needed to write down as many as she could remember.

They were headed back to Crossroads, where they would send another fast messenger to the Copper Coalition. The apprentice Zachary and three other Coalition members were infected, even if they'd probably already fled. Erin had a lot of information to impart, a lot of warnings to give, if she could remember them. And yet, *we have three bars* kept popping into her head.

The soldiers had taken the man they'd found into the village. Their officer split the group, leaving eight behind to help the dazed villagers and taking three with him to ride ahead to Madlyn. The remaining four accompanied her and Trevian. They planned to get fresh caballos at Crossroads and then push on, even if a messenger ran ahead of them.

There were eight hundred infected people on this continent, and more clutches of nodes were hidden. If the New Way managed to save those and infect more innocent people, there would be nearly one thousand, all connected mentally.

"Erin, why do you try to write?" Trevian said.

She explained. He frowned but nodded.

"There's a lot of news, good and bad. The bad is that they know everything I know, or knew. And there two hundred more of those pink things—the nodes—hidden out there. I know where they...I know where they *were*."

She thought she'd wait on the really scary news, that the New Way thought it had discovered the method of opening another frontera, if it could find the right location. And that it came from a world that had higher tech. It *was* higher tech, itself. She didn't even know how to explain it to Trevian and the others. She could barely explain her cell phone to them.

"Oh, shit!" She hauled back on the reins.

Trevian's eyes widened. "What?"

"Can you hold this?" She shoved the book and the sheaf of paper at him. He took them, his caballo dancing sideways a step or two.

Erin pulled out her phone. While she'd been under the influence of the New Way, the charge had dropped twenty percentage points. She didn't want to power it up, but she thought she had to. She held down the button and watched the screen glow. In the upper right corner, the four ascending bars were merely outlined. "I don't have any bars here," she said.

"But I still have mine. And you have your knife."

"Not those kinds of bars. I..." She stared at him. "Oh, God, Trevian, I nearly killed you."

"We've already talked about that," he said gently.

"No, I don't mean giving you the book. *After* that. When the charm kicked in, I remembered that my phone was on. And it had..." She searched for words that would work. "It's a communication machine. It tries to find reception. Um...there are currents, and—"

"Currents. That was mentioned in the charm that closes the frontera."

"Yeah? Okay, yeah." She remembered that. "There are currents in the air and other machines that enhance those currents, the transmitters. Like the way the lantern works. But there are a lot of them and it creates...traffic. Messages...can run into each other. Block each other." It was a terrible description, but it was going to have to do for now.

Genaro trotted up to them. "Yorita?" he said, canting his head toward the soldiers whose caballos swished their tails and pawed the ground.

"Just a minute, this is important. My phone was searching for those currents, and doing that blocked the New Way from communicating with Home."

"Where is Home?"

"Other side of the frontera."

Trevian stared at her phone. "Can it reach there now?"

"No." She powered down the phone. Three minutes a day now, she thought. Maybe not even that. Maybe the phone was going to be important. "When I got out from under their control, I powered it down. Then they could reach Home."

"And they called for help. The people who came through," Trevian said. "I never thought their influence reached that far. If your machine had been off, they would have killed me straight away."

"They're a network," she said. "And we might have a way to impede their communication."

They stopped for food in Crossroads. While the Copper Coalition Guard bargained for fresh mounts, Trevian, Genaro, and Erin found seats in a tavern, which was nearly ready to cover its lamps and close for the night.

"So, you knew what they were thinking?" Trevian chased a chunk of potato around on his plate.

Erin shook her head. "No. I *was* them. All of them. The ones who are here, anyway."

"How is that possible?" He speared the chunk with his fork.

"I don't know. It's hard to describe." Difficult to describe, shockingly easy to remember.

"Is that how it is with my uncle?"

"No, Oshane isn't part of their...community. I thought he must be, but they call him the unreliable source." She pushed her plate away. She hadn't wanted to talk about this so soon. "With a small number of people, the node can't merge with their, their thoughts." Brainwaves was the word she wanted to use.

Genaro leaned forward. "Is it a matter of bloodline?"

"Apparently not. Being a copper-hunter doesn't make a difference either, we know that. It's a tiny number, like two out of a hundred. On their homeworld, they kill the humans they can't merge with, because they're—" She paused to take a breath. "—chaotic. It's what they call us."

Genaro fidgeted and ate a bite of lamb, but Trevian didn't look away from her face. "At what age do they merge?"

"Ten years old. The children in the village, most of them were still too young."

Genaro put down his fork. "Children?"

She nodded.

"And if they cannot merge? The two out of one hundred? They murder children?"

"Yes. Adults too."

"Monsters," he whispered.

"If Oshane is one of those, why didn't they kill him?" Trevian said.

"Strange, isn't it? Because he has an air elemental connected to him. There's something about air elementals specifically, but I don't know what it is. And they don't trust Oshane, but they think they can use him."

"And *he* is using *them*." Trevian nibbled the edge of the potato chunk. He stared over her head. After he swallowed, he said, "Perhaps that's why the charm works as it does."

"It didn't work. It took a damn hour. I gave away everything."

He shook his head. "No. If they had sensed they couldn't merge with you, they would have killed you instantly. You had an hour to learn what they knew, and in that time they thought they could trust you."

"That's... Wow. That's a pretty iffy plan." She had to agree it made sense though. "I have another question. Genaro, you might know this. Harald might have talked about it. New Way thinks of this world as the Collision."

Genaro frowned.

"I know that word," Trevian said. He slapped his hands together in a glancing clap. "Two things crash together. Boats, carriages..."

"How can a world be a collision? It must mean something else to those things," Genaro said.

Erin stabbed a carrot. "Maybe."

W ith fresh mounts under them, they rode through the night. It was no longer possible to write down names. The guards had conjured up light from some copper and quartz tubes. Erin clung to the saddle horn and concentrated on staying awake. Twice she listed to one side, instinct jerking her back to wakefulness before she fell.

She knew more about the New Way than she would ever be able to articulate, and when she tried to prioritize it, her thoughts faded into a buzz of fatigue. What was wrong with her? She had a few bruises, but she wasn't hurt anywhere near as bad as Trevian was.

When they dismounted in the courtyard of the Copper Coalition, she could barely stand.

Trevian slipped his arm around her waist. "You need to rest," he said.

"No. I need to talk to Tregannon."

The elmaestro had a steaming pot of sisuree ready, and five chairs. Stillwater and Machios were already seated. A different apprentice, a woman, stood behind Tregannon. She'd taken the caballos the first time they arrived. Erin couldn't remember her name.

She dug into her bag and pulled out the sheets she'd filled with names. "Here." She thrust them at Tregannon. "Those are the ones I can remember." Her hand shook.

He reached up. "Sit down before you fall down, Erin. Trevian, pour her some sisuree."

Trevian didn't react to the authoritarian tone. He guided Erin to one of the slingback chairs and poured the hot brew into a cup for her.

She gripped it gratefully. "Zachary?" she said.

Stillwater answered. "He lives. He's coming out of that dazed state, faster than the guard did. The other three fled. Machios wants you to see the parasite that controlled Zachary."

Machios reached down for a shrouded object at his feet. He folded back the dark cloth and held up the glass cylinder. The node inside was flat, purplish-gray, unmoving.

Tregannon spoke without looking up from the papers. "We didn't remove it. Zachary collapsed in the kitchen. When the doctor removed his shirt to examine him, that came with it."

"They ended communication with that node." Basically, they shut it off. They'd decided Zachary was too big a risk. "What about the one we brought? Did they shut it off too?"

"Not as of an hour ago," said Machios.

Tregannon shook his head. "Zachary was in my office most of the time. I can't even remember when he was and when he wasn't. Who notices an apprentice?"

Beka, Erin thought. That was the woman's name, Beka. "He may have information for us," she said. "If they...disconnected him after I broke free."

"There are over one hundred names on here," Tregannon said.

"There are more. I'll keep writing them down."

"They're all infected? So many?"

"So many?" Erin's voice cracked. "Elmaestro, there are eight hundred currently connected in the network—"

"The what?"

"Controlled. Possessed. Whatever. It's a network, they're connected."

"Connected how?"

Erin's head ached. She set down her cup, splashing sisuree on the table, and rubbed her forehead.

"Stop. Wait." Trevian held up his hand as Tregannon leaned forward in his chair. "Let Erin explain what she can, and then ask your questions."

Erin said, "The good news. Trevian closed the frontera from this side. They won't be able to reopen it."

"That *is* good news. An army of eight hundred people infected by those things—that is not good."

"Let's hear what Erin has managed to learn," Stillwater said.

Erin picked up the cup again and drained it in a few swallows. "They came here two years ago, through that frontera. They overtook Madalita pretty quickly, and they've been infecting people via the trade caravans ever since. The parasites, they're called nodes. They aren't..." She squeezed her eyes shut, trying to find the words. It has seemed so clear when she was part of the New Way. "They aren't individuals. They're half machine and half, well, animal-life. It's not exactly half," she said to Machios, as he opened his mouth. "And I don't know how they do it. I'm trying to keep it simple."

"I understand."

"They send messages to each other all the time. What one node knows, they all know. Even I did. But that's not *completely* true, because some are able to communicate directly with Home, their world, and not all of us were. There is some kind of hierarchy."

Stillwater nodded.

"'Us?'" Tregannon said, without looking up, but the way he turned the page of names he held made her think that wasn't as casual as it sounded.

"That's what it felt like. It felt like I belonged. There was no *me*. I could even experience Home, although I think now that was more of an echo or a mirage than the actual world."

"But you're free of them now, are you?" Tregannon said. "Or do they know your thoughts even now?"

"I am. I don't know how I can prove that, except to say that if I were still connected, they'd have the book. They *really* want it. It's more important to them than what you know."

"They really do," Trevian said. "When they came through the frontera and attacked me, it was the book they wanted."

He described the way they moved and spoke. He did a better job of explaining the network to his own people than Erin would have. While the attention was on him, she let her eyes close.

At some time she would have to explain how it had come about, the New Way, the blend of organics and mechanics, the idea of a self-aware network. If she ever really understood it herself...

"...Erin?"

"What?"

Stillwater stood over her. "You need sleep. This has been an ordeal for you."

"Not as bad as Trevian. They knocked him out with an energy weapon."

Stillwater shook her head. "Your selfhood was invaded. This charm you chose harms the wearer."

"But it has uses," Tregannon said.

"How useful is it, if the New Way knows everything its wearer knows?" Stillwater sounded exasperated.

"That would depend on what the wearer knows," Tregannon said.

Ruth rolled her eyes. "This is not the night for that conversation." She pointed at Erin's list. "Perhaps finding those people before they do more harm should be our first step."

Tregannon raised his eyebrows.

"Erin, Trevian, come," Stillwater said. "We have rooms readied, and I want Trevian to see a doctor if he was struck by an elemental weapon."

Tregannon said, "Darwin Oakley is on this list."

"Oakley," Erin said. "He was talking to Oshane. And someone else, an outlaw. Vallis?"

Trevian's hand, holding his cup, jerked. "Vallis?"

She nodded.

"In White Bluffs?"

"Oakley was."

Tregannon said, "Oakley is assigned to Sheeplands. We don't have an office in White Bluffs."

"Was *Vallis* in White Bluffs?"

"No. Nearby. In the mountains. It was…secret. Oakley paid his messengers extra for secrecy. The New Way is interested in your father's company. Oh, my God. Aideen!"

Trevian stood up. "What?"

"Oakley sent Vallis to ambush Aideen and the others!"

Trevian whirled. "I must send a message at once."

Stillwater stood up. "I'll find a messenger." She hurried out of the room.

"I think it failed, or something failed. I can't, if I can just—"

"Enough." Machios stood up as well. "You'll drive yourself turvy. Sleep will help this newfound knowledge settle, and you'll be clearer in the morning."

"What if I forget?"

Trevian shook his head. "We can already see that you won't."

Stillwater came back into the room holding a slip of paper. "As I was giving direction to the guard, a fast messenger rode up on a caballo so sweat-lathered it could have come out of the baths. Your wife and sister are well, and Justice Arm Stuart is on his way to arrest Oshane Langtree."

"But we must still send a message about Oakley," Tregannon said.

Stillwater inclined her head. "It's done, Elmaestro."

"Erin? Erin."

She sat up again. This time Trevian stood over her. He took her arm, his grasp gentle. "Come. You need sleep."

She walked alongside him. Had they really kissed, up on the ledge?

Had she imagined that? When they stopped in front of the door, she said, "Are you all right?"

"My side hurts, but my heart is well." He cupped her cheek. "My heart is very well. Do you wish me to stay with you?"

More than anything she wanted that. She saw him smile and realized she'd said that out loud. "But I want you to see the doctor. And rest."

He stared down at her.

She said, "We'll have time, Trevian."

He lowered his head, and his lips met hers again. No book separated them this time, and Erin sank into his warmth.

"If needed," he whispered, "I will carve time out of stone for you."

24

Taste this one," Ilsanja said.

Aideen set down her pen. Her letter to Trevian filled two pages already, and she had only reached the lines of music on the walls of the cavern. She picked up the warm brown square of cake Ilsanja held out to her.

Susannah was as fascinated with kokolatal as Ilsanja. Aideen broke off a corner of this latest venture. Sometimes the flavoring left a powdery texture they all agreed wasn't good, but in this instance all the elements melded: the hearty taste of oat, the mellow honey, and the rich, changeable flavor of kokolatal. "Yes," she said. "This is good. Very good."

"We have a success." Ilsanja broke off a bite and sat on the edge of the desk, her legs swinging. "I must write to Erin Dosmanos and ask her to tell me everything she knows about how they use this powder in her world."

"Don't you think she'll be too busy saving us from those things?"

Ilsanja shrugged. "She'll need a distraction."

Harald came into the room, limping slightly. The fever had broken and the inflammation around the raw spot on his leg was almost fully healed. His spare artificial leg would arrive tomorrow from Duloc, and Yor Lopez up at the cages had assigned a fabricker to reshape the one he wore.

"News from the sheriff," he said, sitting down. "The Crescent Council has issued a warrant for Mark Majeur for copper theft and aiding a criminal in violating exile, based on Oakley's confession." Ilsanja held out the plate, and he took a piece of cake.

"Copper theft? The caravans?"

His mouth full, Harald nodded before swallowing. "Odd. Different, but good. Yes. Things were simpler than we thought. Vallis was raiding the Company's caravans, and Majeur hired a pair of thugs to destroy the quartz cages. He wanted to damage both of your fathers. Revenge. When Oakley found out about the proposed expansion, the New Way wanted the damage stopped, but it was too late by then. And they sent Oshane to take control of the Company. Oshane convinced Majeur that giving the Company to him was the best vengeance against both men."

Aideen rolled her pen back and forth, thinking. The New Way had driven Oakley to speak honeyed words to the town council, to feed their dream of stamping their own coin, of expanding elemental energy...of challenging the capital, although no one on the council ever spoke those words aloud. "Did they plan to own the entire town?" She'd read the brief letter Trevian had sent, about a village completely under the control of those things.

Harald shrugged. "He was unsure, but it seems like it." He reached for another bite of cake. "This is better than good, Yor—Jefa Langtree."

"Ilsanja. If you continue this formality, I will decide I've been insulted," Ilsanja said.

"How was he infected?" Aideen said.

"He met Langtree a year ago, in Boskay. It happened there." He dusted off his fingers. "Tomorrow, when my leg arrives, I will be escorting Majeur back in a locked wagon to face trial. The Copper Coalition has sent a foursome of their guards to assist."

"Will Vallis's band make an attempt to free him?"

Harald didn't answer for a moment. "If Vallis still lives, which I doubt, he is wrapped deeply in nets of his own weaving."

Aideen said, "Will Oshane?"

Ilsanja answered. "Majeur is no longer of use to him."

They had strung every window and chimney in the house with the plata and moonstone charms, and the doors and windows of the company offices. Oshane was wounded, but as far as everyone knew, still alive and still dangerous, and no one knew where he was.

Aideen stood up. "I will check on Father." She came around the desk and paused, leaning down to kiss Ilsanja, who tasted of kokolatal.

Father lived, even though Yor Olafson had been grave when he spoke to Aideen after the attack. "He is much weakened, yorita. There is little my colleague or I can do for him."

Ilsanja prayed for him every day and went to the dioso temple twice a week to light a candle. Aideen did nothing more than see that he was cared for and sit with him, sharing the progress they had made when she could.

There was good news. The posse tracking Vallis had found a mestengo lair filled with copper, nearly half the stock from one of the Company caravans. Repairs could be made, at last. And Aideen had two bids for new cages from fabrickers. Soon they would be able to hold a joven group in one.

When she entered the room, Dimitri stood and gave her the chair where he'd been sitting. He had recovered fully. Aideen sat down and reached for her father's hand. "The company is doing well," she said. "We are back on track. And I've forgiven your loans, all of them. We don't need to profit from other people's desperation."

There was no change in her father's expression.

She'd said to Ilsanja that they had both ventured out into a wider world. It was a world of wonders and horrible dangers, but a world she had a place in now.

She kissed his forehead.

"Rest," she said. She nodded to Dimitri, who stood in the doorway, and went back up the hallway to where Ilsanja waited.

25

Sabado, 27 Uno, Year 331

H e escaped again!" Trevian threw the dispatch from Harald Stuart down on the table.

Stillwater gathered up the pages. "He is wounded, and at least he has lost that bracelet of beads. Aideen took that from him."

The thought of his sister nearly suffocating in her own house, at the hands of his uncle, filled Trevian with a hot rage. He suppressed it, sitting back down. Aideen was well, Ilsanja was well, and Harald had recovered from an inflamed wound in his leg. If things held to the projections in his dispatch, he would arrive back in the capital later today with Mark Majeur a prisoner.

Through brawls, fights, and attempted claim-jumps, Trevian had never killed. Now, though, he would easily kill his uncle and Vallis Majeur, if he encountered either one again. The two of them were as dangerous as a poisonous reptile dropped into one's bed, and he would rid this world of them if he had the chance.

At the far end of the table, Erin and Elmaestro Tregannon leaned over a map. Erin was still marking places where the New Way nodes had been hidden.

Messages were coming in regularly. Pais Lewelyn reported that they had discovered the parasites a sennight earlier. Madlyn had been unaware. Apparently, several odd occurrences in that country were now clear. The elmaestros of both Madlyn and Pais Lewelyn were sending a contingent of profesors and Copper Coalition Guard to meet with Tregannon. It was a council of war.

Erin straightened up and stretched. "That's what I can remember. Those caches of nodes? Those'll already be gone."

All the nodes in Madalita had burned, but there were two hundred more somewhere on the continent. The New Way would protect those caches and use them to infect as many people as possible, as quickly as they could.

"They'll have left a trail," Tregannon said.

"We need the compass. We need Wing Mei," Erin said. "She's in Perlarayna."

Tregannon nodded. "If Harald is well, I will ask leave for him to lead an expedition," he said. "He was quite familiar with the Desolation before he became a justice arm."

"And we need to find Orchard Hill, wherever that is," Erin said.

"What's the importance of Orchard Hill?"

"They were...excited when they found it in my thoughts. They think they can open another frontera there."

Tregannon's head lifted. "Can they?"

"They *think* they can, that's all I know."

Stillwater looked up from where she was reading Harald's report. "You and I must delve back into the old books, Erin," she said.

Erin nodded. "And any idea why they call this world Collision?"

Stillwater frowned and shrugged. "When the world turned? Many things collapsed."

Erin shook her head. She was still deeply distracted.

"At least we have a clearer view of what we face," Trevian said.

What they faced was strange and terrifying, an enemy who could speak to any part of its army at the speed of human thought, whose soldiers hid among the people, who wished to enslave an entire world.

An enemy who murdered children if they could not merge with the nodes.

"Was it terrible?" he murmured to Erin, one quiet moment the afternoon before, while they were waiting for Tregannon to return from questioning Zachary.

Erin's eyes had filled with tears. "Worse."

He thought he understood, but then she said, "It was *wonderful*. I belonged. I felt like I was back with my family, only more cherished, more loved, than I've ever been."

"You know you were cherished," he said, not sure what else to say.

"I know, but...I was *home* somehow. In those moments, I was at home, more at home than I've ever been."

What a terrible weapon. People would be willing, mindless hosts, believing themselves in a paradise.

Tregannon straightened up too and spoke briskly. "We know what we face, and we know some of its weaknesses. We have a way to find its agents, those nodes. And it cannot send more soldiers into our world. To begin, we will search every member of every caravan." He looked at Erin. "We need to capture some nodes alive, and I have some thoughts about the charm you carved onto yourself."

"Brell," Stillwater said.

He didn't look her way. "This is a war, Ruth. We haven't had one in two hundred years, but I can recognize it. And wars call for desperate measures."

Stillwater stood up and shook her head. "Erin, find me in the library when you're ready, and we will begin a search for Orchard Hill." She stalked out of the room.

The elmaestro shook his head. "She doesn't understand."

"She understands," Erin said. "She just doesn't agree." The room grew silent for a moment, and Erin looked toward the door. "I'm going to go for a walk."

"I'll walk with you," Trevian said.

She smiled and held out her hand. Outside, the courtyard bustled with technicians and apprentices, and a steady stream of messengers flowed back and forth through the gates. The sky was pale green, and

COPPER ROAD

the air filled with the smell of fruit blossoms. In the space of two sennights, full spring had arrived, and Trevian's world had completely changed.

"I understand about the flames, now," he said. "They come when you're in distress."

"I thought so too," she said. "But the day we were on our way here, when we caught the ferry, there wasn't any danger."

"Not danger," he said. "Distress. The walls of the guesthouse where we stayed the night before were not thick, Erin. I heard you weeping that night. So did they. When someone tried to breach Harald's wards, they came. And when you carved a charm into your flesh."

"So why not when the guard attacked me here?"

"They may have tried," he said. "This compound contains multiple wards. They might not have been able to enter. But they sense your feelings, and they respond. And one came when you sent it to help me."

"Asked it."

"It means they understand your thoughts in some way."

She nodded. "Not like the New Way does, but they do understand."

"That is a fact I never knew. We cage them, we separate them from their fellows."

"Might be something to talk to Aideen about," Erin said.

"Perhaps."

A fast messenger rode up. An apprentice approached him and they spoke. The apprentice hurried toward them. "Yor Langtree? A letter from your sister."

Trevian accepted the thick packet. Aideen had written nearly a book. Well, if his father had died, it wouldn't require a message this thick. He put it in his pocket for later.

"I wish to speak to you of something," he said. He had thought he would be nervous, but now all nervousness had fled. She would say yes or no, but the world was different now and he wouldn't fail to reach out, wouldn't take refuge in doubt and fear of looking foolish.

"I'm listening."

311

"I'm a married man now, and any connection I make must be an informal one. And you…I know your world is dear to you."

"It is," she said.

Nervousness trickled back. He couldn't make his mouth speak the words he needed.

He reached for her hands. "I am saying this all backward," he said. "There are obstacles between us, but I…I feel alive when I am with you, Erin. I thought copper-hunting filled my heart, but now I see it does not."

She drew a shaky breath. Her fingers tightened on his. She was nervous, too.

"*You* do," he said. "I don't know how you feel, but I—"

She wrapped her arms around his neck and kissed him. He held her, their hearts pounding. The workers in the courtyard were watching, but Trevian didn't care.

She stepped back. "We have a lot to do."

"We do. And we will prevail." He kissed her knuckles. "My uncle, those nodes, cannot stop us."

"We're partners," she said.

"Partners."

THE END

ACKNOWLEDGMENTS

In addition to all the people I thanked in "Aluminum Leaves," I'd like to add a few more.

First of all, thanks to Falstaff Books, especially Erin Penn, Melissa McArthur, and Tuppence Van de Vaarst for their support. Long live the Oxford comma! Separate thanks to John Hartness for taking a chance on me *and* for introducing me to real barbecue.

Thanks to Linda Kane for the plastic, and Bill Capossere for a thoughtful and generous early read. Thanks to Dave for the coffee and the fanfare.

2020 was a weird year, right? More gratitude than I can express goes to our medical and emergency service workers -- and all the people who were pulled into the "essential service" pool. I appreciate our true public health experts, from the federal level all the way down, for their courage and honesty in the face of political intimidation. In my home county, I want to give my home county's interim Public Health Officer, Dr Sundari Maase, a shout-out for her steadfast, methodical approach to the pandemic throughout. It's reassuring to live in a county where the chief medical officer understands science and prioritizes our health.

If you care enough about the people around you to wear a mask and social distance, thank you.

Until everyone has justice, no one does. I'm filled with admiration for all of those who have raised their voices and risked their lives to stand up for justice... and still are. Thanks to phone bank workers and canvassers who are getting out the vote.

Thanks to teachers everywhere.

Through the sociopolitical, economic, environmental and biological catastrophe of 2020, one Twitter account consistently provided moments of thought and comfort. Thanks to writer Nancy Jane Moore for that. Find her at @WriterNancyJane. Her books are available through Book Press Café and Aqueduct Press.

Others who helped me through moments of discouragement without even knowing it: Laura Blackwell, Laura Davy, Garrett Croker and Juliette Wade. There are so many others. Thank you all.

And thanks to everyone who works to tell stories; who uses words to explore ideas, unravel problems, ask and answer the big, tough questions, and the small, intimate ones. Thanks to everyone who loves playing with language, creating images, and offering hope. We always need you. We needed you more than ever in 2020, and you totally came through.

ABOUT THE AUTHOR

Marion Deeds is the author of "Aluminum Leaves," published by Falstaff Books, and *Copper Road*. Her short fiction has appeared in *Strange California* (Falstaff Books), *Podcastle, Daily Science Fiction*, and the following anthologies: *The Wand That Rocks the Cradle, Beyond the Stars, Unimagined Realms* and *The Noyo River Review*. She's a reviewer for www.fantasyliterature.com. Find her on Twitter at @mariond_d and check out her blog at deedsandwords.com

Deeds lives with her husband in northern coastal California, where she goes for walks, feeds crows, watches the backyard squirrels do yoga, and wishes she'd bought stock in Zoom.